Not Your Ordinary Summer

Janeé Thompson

Author Note

This young adult novel explores topics around substance use, death, physical and sexual abuse, mental health, family dynamics, and how to navigate these complexities as a young Black teenager. **Due to content (language and topics explored), this novel strongly recommended for ages fourteen and older.**

Chapter One

"KYLAH!"

The prison guard of our school, a.k.a. Ms. Turner, calls my name with a hard edge in front of everybody, interrupting the dead silence in the room like she's tryna scare me. It doesn't work, but I roll my eyes, nonetheless. Her voice is like feedback in a microphone.

"You ain't supposed to be drawing right now. This is in-school-suspension, not an art class. Start working on those missing assignments your teachers keep asking about. That's the expectation. Put the drawing away."

Ugh. Why is she even talking to me? How she gon' tell me what to do when all she does is babysit kids who are stuck behind cubicles for doing who knows what to get kicked outta class every day? Doesn't sound very productive if you ask me.

I don't give her the luxury of my attention. Instead, I tune her out like I've been doing and zero in on this portrait I'm currently sketching of my older brother Jarell. A past portrait of him when life was good for us. Before things in our family got really bad.

My pencil wisps over the white paper as I outline Jarell's silhouette, drawing the shape of his baggy jeans and, in particular, the bulky hoodie he used to wear every moment of the day. He wouldn't ever take it off either even when the Los Angeles heat blazed in the summer. Any time I'd touch or try to unzip it, he'd slap my hand away or yell at me not to. He doesn't rock it anymore now, so I wonder why he was so attached to the hoodie back then.

Sheesh. Can't believe that was nine years ago. But I remember those days as clear as water.

"Kylah!" Prison Guard bellows. "Didn't I just tell you to put the drawing away?"

I loved nothing more than when Jarell would come home in the evenings just so we could play together, despite our thirteen-year age difference. Upon his arrival, I'd sprint outside to give him a big hug, but each time I did, he'd have this… look. Sunken shoulders. The hood of his oversized hoodie obscured half his face. Downward tilt of his lips. Even his face oozed exhaustion. But that all disappeared when I'd crash into his legs with my arms wrapped around them like tight rubber bands. It's like I'd zap him, and he'd come to life with a smile.

Now that I think about it, Jarell looked like he'd rather die every time he came home from *school*. I didn't understand it back then, but I get it now because I probably look that way coming home too.

Hmm. I think I'm gonna draw his exact expression. It's too clear in my head not to.

"Kylah, I'ma tell you one last time. You know you hear me talking to you!"

Prison Guard now yells like a drill sergeant. Still, she gets no rise out of me, but inside, my time bomb starts ticking. I take two huge inhales through my nose and two exhales out my mouth.

If the rest of my time here is gonna be like this, then we're gonna have serious issues. It's in her best interest to leave me alone because I really don't care about being in ISS the way she wants me to. Especially since I got kicked out of class for something that could've been avoided, but these teachers don't want me in their class anyway.

I start to shade in the tiny little details of Jarell's face once I'm done outlining the body. His sad frown had always nestled deep between his brows, almost forming a unibrow because they're so thick. Man, if Jarell knew how much concentration I'm giving this drawing, he'd start to believe I still love him. But things just aren't the same. Love is the very last word I'd use to describe how I feel about him now.

Before I start detailing any shadows and highlights, a title for this portrait comes to mind. *The Effect of Bad Schools on the Body*. I write it centered above his head.

As if it's going to change anything, Prison Guard gets up from her seat and stomps to my desk to stand over me with her belly hanging over her too-tight pants right in my face. If I didn't know any better, the way she hovers over me, one would think she may hit me. I'll give her about three seconds to get up out my space before I disrespectfully tell her to move.

"This is why you're in ISS every other day, Kylah. You're rude, you don't ever listen to anybody, and then you get mad when people try to steer you to what you're supposed to do. I've told you multiple times to start working on your assignments, and you wanna act like you can't hear. Gimme this notebook. I'm not playin' around with you today!" she roars and yanks my sketchbook right from underneath my pencil. A thick, unintended line swipes across my brother's face when she does.

I freeze, and for a split second, so does she the moment we lock eyes. A little bit of fear rises in her, but she walks away like she's some bad ass. Like she stuck it to me and made me an example to all the other kids so that they don't try to be off task, either.

Oh. *She got me messed up.* With calm and without haste, I push my chair back, stand up, and shoot daggers at her with my glare. That's when all eight pairs of other student eyes watch me. But no one moves.

"Gimme back my fuckin' sketchbook, Ms. Turner."

Prison Guard turns around, looks at me, and then scoffs.

"No. You have some nerve to be cursing at me. And you're supposedly some star athlete. Some nationally recognized softball player. Well guess what? You're not getting away with this kinda behavior in high school next year. You act this way? You won't be playin' for the team. At the rate you're going, you're a lost cause and you will never be anything in your life. Ever. I'm tired of you bad, disrespectful, no morals having kids thinking athletics is your ticket out. Now take a seat and be quiet."

She sits back down and tosses my sketchbook with reckless abandon as it slides across her desk. It falls with momentum and skids on the floor until it slows down and lands on an open page where I've sketched a portrait of Mama.

Mama.

I stare at it for a few seconds before my eyes land on Prison Guard again, and she's just sitting there, back to work on her computer with a smug satisfaction that tries to stamp this issue as over. My heart stops and my body won't move, but inside, my ears ring. Lungs sink to my hips. And most of all, fists tighten to the point of my nails digging into my palms.

That internal ticking time bomb has expired.

"Okay," I conclude.

I nod, walk to the back of my chair, lift it with ease over my head...

And launch it right at her.

The chair crashes against her desk as everything on it, including her cell phone and laptop, flies off it and at that point, I don't even see anyone else. Every empty chair I see, I kick it. Every empty desk I see, I shove it across the room.

"How do you like it when your stuff is trashed, huh?!" I shout. "You think 'cus everybody else in this school likes you that I won't turn up on you, but on my soul, you got me fucked up, Ms. Turner!"

"Everyone, get out!" Prison Guard orders, and all the other ISS kids slowly amble out like this is nothing new nor an emergency while I tear down every poster in the room.

"If that's how you think you're gonna treat me, that's how I'ma treat you! I'm sick of this school!" I shriek and pace back and forth before I pick up my sketchbook off the floor.

The portrait sketch of my mom's face is smeared. The eyes, nose, and mouth are no longer distinct. Immediately, I slide down a wall and bawl in a corner with my knees up. It's quiet for a long while with just my tears until the classroom door groans open again with a few pairs of feet shuffling inside.

"Kylah..." a familiar voice tries to soothe me, but I don't accept.

"Leave me alone," I manage to say through hiccups.

"Can you tell me what happened?" she attempts again. It's my case manager, Ms. Harris.

"I said leave me alone!"

"Okay. I'll give you some space. We're going to step outside in the hall, okay?"

Her knees crack and her clothes shuffle as she stands up and walks away. But when she leaves, the door remains unintentionally open.

"So, what's going on?" I hear the principal's voice this time in the distance as she tries her best to whisper.

"She won't talk," Ms. Harris responds. "I just tried."

"She snapped. That's what happened," Prison Guard says, and the indifference laced all through her voice makes my stomach hurl. Like she didn't throw my sacred book like it was hot garbage. Like she didn't tell me I wouldn't ever be anything in my life. I pull my knees tighter and hold my breath before I get up and rage out again.

"But what happened that led to it?" Principal Evans presses.

"She wasn't doing any work. She literally was sitting in there staring at the cubicle all day before she finally took out a notebook and started drawing. I tried to redirect her to do some schoolwork, but she just ignored me like I don't even exist. So, I took her notebook, threw it on my desk, and then she snapped when I wouldn't give it back. I'm tired of her being here and not doing what she's supposed to do. I'm not a paid babysitter. She's here almost every week. So don't bring her in ISS if y'all don't want accountability."

"Was she causing any trouble? I've never seen her cry like this," Ms. Harris asks.

"No, but ISS ain't for coloring and drawing. Ms. Evans, you're the one who set the expectation that all students must work on academics in ISS, so don't even think about nodding in agreement with Ms. Harris and putting this all on me like I'm not doing my job."

"I understand your frustration, Jackie. But triggering her isn't the way to go about this. She's quiet and not bothering anyone..." Principal Evans says. "You honestly escalated the situation when you had other options."

"Options like what? With kids these days, everything is a trigger! You're gonna make her the exception? What about all the other kids?

You think that her doodling around in a notebook is helping her learn? I can't have high expectations for my students?"

"You couldn't wait until she was at least finished drawing? Maybe you could have talked with her about it and made it into a teaching moment," Ms. Harris suggests. "It was a perfect opportunity to connect with her..."

"Absolutely not. I don't care if she's in special ed. Drawing ain't in her IEP and the expectation is that students do their class assignments in ISS. It's that simple. You both know I have high expectations for these kids, and that's why they respect me."

"Jackie..." Principal Evans tries to interrupt, but Ms. Turner raises her voice above her.

"Y'all just be letting some of them do whatever they want, and this is why y'all barely have control! Kylah is here more often than anyone, and not a single time has she done any academic work, even when I've tried to support her. This is why y'all can't keep teachers in this school! You don't address the constant abuse we endure from these little devils with no home training, and y'all stay coddling these kids!"

"Yes, I've set the expectation that schoolwork needs to be completed during ISS, but at the same time, you're the adult in this situation. She has a severe PTSD and anxiety diagnosis. You have no idea what's in that notebook for her," Principal Evans declares. "That doesn't excuse her response, and I will deal with that directly, but as an adult, you have to make decisions that maintain the relationship with the kid. Saying you don't care about her being in special education is problematic. Calling students little devils with no home training isn't appropriate. She's fourteen, navigating an emotional and behavioral disability."

"I don't even care. At this point, consider this my resignation. I'm outta here."

Prison Guard storms back into the room, gets whatever personal belongings she had left in the class, and leaves again, slamming the door shut. The silence looms loudly before Ms. Evans re-enters and says that she'll deal with her later. And then, more careful footsteps approach me. I don't budge.

"Kylah, are you okay enough to talk? You know when you're in ISS, the expectation is for you to be doing schoolwork, right?"

I don't respond. I can't even think. All I care about right now are my two ruined drawings. Folks are gonna hate me for this one because Prison Guard is so loved by all these bum ass kids. I don't know why. She thinks she can check anybody, and I don't like that.

"She likely won't talk to either of us. I'm gonna go call her brother and have him pick her up," Ms. Harris says.

"That's a good idea. Because Kylah, no matter how frustrated you get, you cannot throw chairs or kick tables around a room or at people. It's dangerous, and your peers could have gotten hurt. So, you have a three-day suspension. You can come back to school on Monday, and we will meet with you and your brother before you return to class. Maybe by then, you'll be in a better place, and I'd like to learn more about your drawings if you're comfortable," Ms. Evans explains. For a while, it's quiet between us before she sighs and continues talking.

"You can't keep doing this, sweetheart. You're gonna end up tying my hands and recommending yourself for expulsion if people can't have a safe environment to work and be a student with you around. I've gotten so much hate over the last three years by a lot of folks for trying to protect you, keep you in this school, and give you the support you need. Many people don't want you here, but I do because deep down, you're a sweet girl, you are so talented, and you have such a bright future with softball."

I latch on to every word, even though my appearance probably suggests otherwise.

When my lack of response goes long enough, Ms. Evans lets out another exhale and rubs my back before standing.

"I'm rooting for you, Kylah. I know you're acting out because of life right now. But things have to be better. Before you leave to come to the office, clean up this classroom you destroyed. That's not a suggestion, either."

Once both of them are gone, I cry into my knees again. Plummeting down into the corner even more than I am, I wrap my arms around my head, and sink to the floor, waiting for Jarell to come and get me once again. I don't even wanna face him. Hell, even if he knew Ms. Turner ruined our mom's portrait, I can just envision him not giving a single fuck. These kinda days give me no hope. I don't think I'll ever be better, as much as I wanna be.

Chapter Two

I'M GETTING REAL antsy. The wait for Jarell to come and pick me up feels like an unrelenting weight of dread and misery on my chest. Images of many different disappointed looks on his face keep flashing through my mind, a one hundred percent chance I'm gonna see at least one of them once he learns what I've done. What will the punishment be this time?

Will he take softball away? Will I be grounded for another few weeks? Get chewed out in an hour-long lecture? Take my phone away... *again*?

He's definitely sick of my shit, but I need him to understand that I'm sick of everyone else's, too, otherwise I wouldn't be here. I'm sick of Principal Evans, too, who's got me waiting to be picked up in front of these big office windows so that everyone can see me from the hallway after I've put Ms. Turner's room back together without a fuss.

It's like I'm always put on display every single time I get suspended. No doubt it causes people to see me as unhinged, but they never understand what leads me to turn up. It's always the reaction that gets the most attention, and I'm tired of it always being my fault. Nothing is *ever* someone else's fault.

The longer I wait for Jarell's arrival, it seems like more of my classmates have caught wind of my actions because everyone starts staring at me as they walk by the office once class is released. I avoid making eye contact with anyone and internally beg for this passing time to hurry up until someone taps on the window right behind me.

It's my softball teammate, Alaysia Simmons, wearing the shortest shorts possible without getting dressed coded and a crop top showing way too much boob. She glares down at me with a mocking little twinkle in her eyes.

Oh, hell no.

I immediately curl my lip and give her the meanest mug that I hope she feels for the rest of her life.

Alaysia's name is always in some boy's mouth, talking about her body like she's some object. Or even worse, they talk a lot among themselves about how they would "smash" her. Sometimes, they even show up to our softball games just to watch her. She hears it, but it's not like she ever gets offended. She wears that badge with honor, looks much older than her age to woo all the boys, gets good grades, teachers love her, and her parents are married with all kinds of money so that she can participate in any activity she wants.

I would like her as a friend if she wasn't such an ass towards me. Ultimately, I know she only acts that way because I took her lead pitcher spot on our traveling softball team last season, which she ain't ever gonna get back. At least not while I'm on the team. I hate giving her ammo when I get in trouble though because one of her favorite hobbies is to rub it in my face.

I smack my lips. I ain't tryna go there with her because if I do, I just might get expelled.

"Look, there goes the psycho in the office again. She got Ms. Turner fired. I wish Coach would kick her unstable ass off the team," she says, and then laughs after she shakes her head with this fake semblance of disappointment. When I flip her off, she smirks before walking away, her butt cheeks nearly hanging out the bottom of her shorts.

Lying bitch. I know she's gonna go around telling everyone that Ms. Turner was fired.

When she's out of the window to create an open view, right behind Alaysia is *him*. Andre Carter.

His deep, dark brown eyes that always send my stomach flying slam into my gray ones. Oh no. Now, I wish I could turn into the air we breathe. My eyes shift away as fast as they can, and my back hits the chair rest with a thud. I don't know if Alaysia was talking to him or not, but I hope he didn't see that interaction. This whole chair throwing situation is already bad enough, so I don't need anything else adding to it.

I'd hate for him to see me like this.

I just know he hears stories about how much trouble I get into here at school. He's never seen me in action at my worst, but I'm confident he thinks I'm crazy.

It takes everything in me to hold off my tears as it seems like it takes hours for Andre to walk on by. The pressure of our mutual, split second gaze felt especially intense. I wish I could read if there was pity, sympathy, hate, or disgust in it. At this point, I just wanna get outta here. Walking home seems like a real option at this point so Jarell needs to hurry up.

It takes about another ten minutes for him to arrive, and the whole time, Ms. Harris stays in the office, working on her computer nearby to keep an eye on me. I've nearly put a paper bag over my face to conceal my identity, except it's with my sweatshirt while slouched as low as I can be in the chair without my head in the seat. I only know Jarell's here because of the recognizable clanky tag that he's put on his service guide dog, Luna, as her paws tap on the glossed office floor.

"Kylah, sit up, you look ridiculous," Ms. Harris bends down with intense eyes and firmly whispers to me. I obey this time before she stands up straight to greet my brother.

"Jarell, you're finally here. Thanks for coming by. I am so sorry that you have to leave work once again to pick up Kylah. I can't imagine how inconvenient this is for you, especially with the challenges you have to get here," Ms. Harris says.

Then don't send me home, idiot, I growl in my head.

"Why were you in ISS again, Kylah?" Jarell doesn't even acknowledge what Ms. Harris said. He just looks in my direction and asks the question with a slow, low tone that makes me gulp. Oof, I might be in deeper trouble than I think. I opt for the complete truth.

"This girl in my ELA class kept doing this annoying chipmunk laugh during work time, and her friends thought it was funny, so I told her to shut the F up. The teacher yelled at me for saying it, so I called her out for yelling at me and not at the other girl. She was the real one distracting the class, so I just said what everybody else was thinking. The teacher tried to argue with me, so I told the teacher to *shut the F up,* too. So she kicked me out."

Jarell doesn't say anything else. He just directs his attention to Ms. Harris.

"And she's being sent home because..." When he asks, he moves his head in a gesture that suggests for her to get to the point so that his time isn't wasted.

Whoa.

Usually he's way more expressive, engaged, and most of all, angry with me while he's in full support of the teacher when I get in trouble. This time, he's mostly expressionless, but his eyes say it all. Similar to the exhaustion I drew on his eighteen-year-old portrait this morning.

Ms. Harris feels his vibe too and gets to stuttering, sweating, and shaking, trying to figure out what to say that doesn't deliver the news of what I've done so bluntly. Jarell's face moves from blank to confused as Ms. Harris tries to share the details, but Principal Evans steps in to save her.

"Hi Jarell. I'm happy you safely made it to pick up your sister. I know Ms. Harris is trying her best to explain what happened. Kylah made a very poor and dangerous decision after her removal from class. She threw a chair at a staff member because she refused to do her schoolwork in ISS and wanted to draw in her sketchbook instead after the staff member tried to redirect her. She also destroyed the ISS room by kicking chairs, desks, and tearing down posters. She cleaned it up, though. I'd like to give you her sketchbook. She needs to keep this at home, since she's drawing more than learning in class. I'm holding it out to you right now," Ms. Evans says, holding the book up, but I snatch it.

"No!" I exclaim. "Don't be giving that to him. It's mine!"

Jarell closes his eyes as if every ounce of patience drains from his body. At this point, I just turn my head and walk a few steps away from them without even bothering to explain my side of the story about the destroyed portrait. I'm now facing the big windows again as more kids slow their gait down the hall to be nosy and catch me in trouble.

"Is the staff member okay?" I hear Jarell ask.

"Yes, she's okay. Kylah will be suspended for the next three days. She can't keep doing this. How is she going to enter the Senior League World Series acting this way? She's very close to the ten-day suspension threshold, too, being that she's been suspended five times this school year, and now, this is the sixth. If she does anything like this again, we will need to have a manifestation determination meeting, since she has an IEP."

"What's a manifestation meeting?" he asks.

I tune out because I don't really care what the meeting is and wait near the door of the office so we can dip outta here once they're done. I ain't gonna take much more of everyone looking at me funny without snapping.

"There goes the special ed family. He can't see, and she's crazy. I feel bad for their momma," one of Alaysia's sidekicks says as they walk by the office.

And that's the last straw.

Gathering my belongings, I storm out of the office and outside to wait on a bench before I end up beating the hell out of 'em. Imaginary smoke billows out of every hole in my face. I know we're catching an Uber, but I, once again, consider walking home. My chest is pounding and my palms are sweaty, so it may even be in Jarell's best interest to not say a word to me right now.

When he comes outside, that's exactly what happens. He doesn't say a word. He and Luna just stand next to me while he T's up the Uber via iOS VoiceOver.

When it arrives, the only speaking Jarell does is to say hello to the driver. Once we're in and settled, all I really have the choice to do is look out the window and try to enjoy the ride, but I can't.

San Diego wasn't always home, and it definitely ain't my choice to be here. I can't stand that about being a kid. You literally have no decision-making power over your own life, so people end up screwing it up, yet they're the ones who don't have to live with the reality of the decisions.

Even the trees here don't feel the same. Back home in Los Angeles, the trees towered over our home like skyscrapers, sashaying in winds that aren't as hot as here. Also, there's so much culture, food, and good vibes in LA. It ain't like that here in San Diego. Everything and everyone seem so fake.

Apparently, San Diego wasn't always home for Jarell either, so I don't even know how he ended up here. I have no idea what his life was like before I was born. He was only around for the first five years of my life where I grew to love him, and then he disappeared until... well... the day I moved in with him against my will two and a half years ago. I don't even wanna think about that day – it's all a blur anyway.

When we get home, I practically run out of the car and into the apartment, not even holding the door for Jarell and the dog. I sit at the kitchen table and just wait for him to say whatever he needs to say to me because I don't want him knocking at my door later to try and talk. Once I'm settled in my room, I don't wanna be bothered.

But he doesn't even look my way.

He just turns on his usual Contemporary Christian playlist on his Bluetooth speaker and begins feeding Luna and washing the dishes. A chore that is normally my duty.

Sweet!

I shrug, after about five minutes of sitting there without him addressing me and leave. I go to my room, plop on my bed stomach first, and take my phone out to see what's poppin' on TikTok.

When I put in my passcode and open the app, after about a

minute, a big white screen pops up with an hourglass picture.

Time Limit. You have reached your limit on TikTok. Ask for more time.

What?! Ask for more time? Since when?! I try to open Instagram, and I get the same notification after about a minute of scrolling. I press my luck with messages, and sure enough, I get the same notification.

Wait.

Jarell shut off my phone without really shutting it off!

I huff and puff before I charge out of bed and stomp to him. He doesn't move, turn around, or even flinch at my angry walk up. He's just completely soothed by this music, and for some reason, that just makes my stomach clench.

"Why did you put time limits on all my apps? I thought I was off punishment since last week," I bark the second he's in my line of sight.

The dishes clink and clang, but no noise comes from him.

"Hello?!"

He shakes his head still not giving me his undivided attention.

"I get you're blind, but you ain't deaf. Why did you shut off my phone?"

"Did you really think you weren't gonna have any consequences after what you did today?" he finally speaks in an even, almost monotone, voice.

"Well, you didn't say anything at all to me at school, in the car, or here, so..."

"You threw a chair at a teacher. I couldn't care less about why, so I don't wanna hear it. *You threw a chair at a teacher, Kylah.* If you're gonna treat another human this way, I ain't about to give you my hard-earned money in the form of a phone." He sticks his hand out and motions for me to hand it over with his back still facing me.

"Really, Jarell? You already had my phone for the last month." I squint. "I just got it back, and you're really gonna put time limits on all my apps?"

"Does it look like I'm joking?" He finally turns to face me. "And you're back on punishment until I say so."

"But Jarell, you don't understand. Both teachers started it this time!" I yell. "But you won't ask me about that, now will you? Because you never believe me about anything!"

"Because you haven't given me a reason to, so I don't care. You get suspended every month, but nothing will ever be that serious to throw a chair at someone. Get that through your head. Keep acting crazy, and your phone won't be the only thing I take away. I swear to God, softball is next, so you better start thinking about how you gon' straighten up."

And he just says that as smoothly as butter. As if he's not peeved at all.

After another huff and a puff, I throw my phone on the table and storm away to my room, slamming the door because I ain't about to fight that softball battle with him; it's one I'm guaranteed to lose. *Ugh.*

That's one thing about Jarell.

He makes anything and everything worse. I cannot survive any more weeks on punishment. I throw myself to the bed and stare at the ceiling, thinking of my long term plan to run away from this apartment forever. I never asked to live with him anyway.

I lie in the same position for hours on end, coming up with no real solution until I simply accept that there's nothing I can do about being in this shithole. Doing my hair is the only option to stay occupied other than drawing and reading. I pull up a chair to my cheap little vanity table, take a comb, and part my hair down the middle so that there's two big chunks of hair on each side. Then, I french braid one side, staring in the mirror at my fingers in action.

My hair is my favorite part of me. It's luscious, extremely long, thick, and has curls for days. Weeks. Years.

The long lusciousness comes from Mama. Her black hair always tumbled over her shoulders when she bent down to talk to me when I was little. I can just hear her voice now. Soft, peaceful, and affirming. I close my eyes. Flashbacks of my tiny fingers combing through her locks that flowed like a cool river on a sunny day brings a kind of calm I need right now. I open my eyes and continue working through my curls and feel as proud of my hair as I was about Mama's.

Its color comes from my dad. His hair was blond, so with a mixture of both my parents, mine is light brown with natural blond streaks that glow like gold in the sun. I close my eyes again, praying I'd get to replay a similar memory of my dad that's as warm and fuzzy. But I get nothing except a flash memory of a big body lying limp on the ground, saturated with blood and a small, bloody bullet wound in the middle of the forehead. And it's Dad glaring back at me with his piercing blue eyes.

I gasp and jump back so hard that my entire world falls back, my stomach drops, the chair flips back… and then ***CRRRBOOOOM!!!!*** The chair crashes against my dresser while my body goes with it.

Now, the air is still. My lungs suspend air flow while my legs stick straight up in the air, butt bent, head stuck, just to see if Jarell will come into my room to see if I'm okay. He had to have heard that. Right?

But he doesn't come.

Why? Why does my brain do this?

He died nine years ago, but he still haunts me like demons. First, it's Mama's portrait being destroyed, and now, I'm hallucinating about Dad. Today just needs to end. I want all this to stop.

Chapter Three

TWENTY-FOUR HOURS LATER, and it feels like I'm already in a hell called boredom. I managed to sleep like a baby last night, which is great because that almost never happens. But with all my friends at school, no phone on me, Jarell at work all day, and me staring at the walls after binge watching one of my favorite shows, it's a complete nightmare. It's unlike me to be so... inactive. Sedentary. Isolated. I hate school, but I do like the social part of it, and losing that is the worst part about being suspended.

It's close to eight at night, and Jarell hasn't even come home yet from work or anything. This is starting to happen more often, too, when he comes home really late on certain days. He says he's with his friends, at church, walking at the beach, or at the gym, but I don't truly know.

On those days, a part of me worries about his safety, especially with him being blind and all, but most of me gets happy as hell to get a taste of living all on my own with no authority to bother me. I've even managed to cook my own junk food dinner tonight. A frozen pizza and homemade cheese fries with bacon bits on top without having to worry about being forced to eat Jarell's health nut bullshit with him always saying, "You eat what I make."

I'm still eating my meal, in seventh heaven, watching the next season of *All American* in the living room with all the lights off when the front door swings open and closed. Immediately, Jarell and a familiar woman's laughter overpowers the sound of the show.

"Ughhh," I grumble.

The last thing I need is hearing her kee kee-ing all night.

Here's one and probably the only thing Jarell could do that would erase all the disdain I have for him: Ditch his new girlfriend and go back to the one he had in high school who he always brought around back in the day. I can't remember her name, but I do remember her being beautiful and kind.

She made it a priority to spend time with me, even if Jarell wanted her all to himself. She would even buy me Christmas presents, play Barbies with me, and love me until one day, she just disappeared and never came back. Not long after, Jarell disappeared too once everything had happened with my dad. That's a whole 'nother story.

His new girl, Brooklyn, is... somethin' about her that I don't like, but it's not like she's done anything wrong. Actually, she's been trying to find ways to get to know me. She comes to all my softball games with Jarell; I don't think she missed a single game last season. And she gets into it, too, watching every pitch I throw and is the loudest one cheering when I strike someone out. Maybe I only feel the way I do about her because she's a current extension of Jarell. I can only imagine the things he says about me to her.

Man. Night ruined. I don't even wanna face them. Especially Jarell, because I don't wanna hear his mouth about the fact that I'm not supposed to be watching TV since I'm on punishment.

So I take my food, turn off the TV, rise from the couch, and walk away to my room before they can see me. Good thing the front door is in the kitchen.

Once I'm long gone, my eyes meet the ceiling while another bout of distant laughter between Jarell and Brooklyn invades my room. That's it. I'm gettin' outta here tonight. But... where am I gonna go? And with whom am I gonna go if I can't communicate with anyone?

I sit still for a little while and fume to myself.

Wait.

My Chromebook.

I beam and clap my hands before rushing to my backpack. Jarell isn't smart enough to know I can email folks on my school Chromebook, and mostly everybody I know has their emails linked to their phones. *Damn, why I ain't think of this earlier? I coulda been making plans...*

Opening my Gmail account, I type in the email of my best friend, Preston Smith-Rodriguez, the very first real friend I made after moving here. I call him Prez though, combining part of his first name and the very end of his last name. Preston just seems too proper, like I'm his grandmama or something. I ain't really with that.

Once Prez's name is in the receiver bar, I type a simple message to him.

Me: hey

When he doesn't respond after a few minutes, I send him another.

Me: wyd? i hope you up. please. sos. on punishment and tryna get up outta here

Preston: Hey, LaLa. Yeah, I'm up. I'm not surprised you're on punishment. I tried to text you cus I heard you got suspended. Got your phone taken again? Is it true that you threw a chair at Ms. Turner?

Me: yea. ms. turner threw my sketchbook and ruined some of my drawings, so I ruined her room

Preston: You threw chairs because of *that*? How long are you out?

Me: 3 days. she shuldnta did that. she can't be treatin my property however she wants.

Preston: You gotta chill, LaLa. It ain't a good look.

Me: where u at?

Preston: At the crib playing Fortnite

Me: come 2 the park. wanna help me bat?

Preston: Yeah, just give me a minute. I'ma slide thru.

Me: Bet

I close my Chromebook and get all my stuff together.

Sneaking out of our houses through our windows to play baseball in the wee hours of the night is a regular thing for me and Prez... especially when I have my phone. Luckily, neither of us have been caught. I can just picture Prez's mom, Miss Juanita, cussing him out from A to Z in Spanish with a launched flip flop right in the middle of the forehead. I smile at the thought. I don't even wanna think about what Jarell would say if I got caught. Probably nothing.

Once my gear is ready, I open my window and duck out of it. I'd be real surprised if Prez actually made it out the house tonight though because A: it's kind of early for us (it's only ten-thirty) when the norm is midnight, so his mom is probably still awake, and B: I'm sure he's on the phone with his girlfriend Gina while gaming. There's no other person on planet Earth that texts and calls another person so much like she does with Prez.

It's a beautiful night; clear skies, the Big Dipper more visible than ever, barely a breeze, and the air is a flat room temperature with that grassy, summer smell. I get to the park before him and begin batting on my own for a little while until I hear subtle crunching in the distance. I turn toward the sound, and Prez walks up to me with long strides.

"Sup LaLa." He greets me with a smile wide enough that his dimples poke through his golden-brown skin. His baseball glove is on, and he punches the inside of it with his bare hand. He even has his cleats on.

"What's good, Prez," I say and look him up and down. "I see you ready to play. I ain't think you'd gear up this late, though."

"Yeah. Once you said you was practicing, I felt how much I miss playing so I had to come prepared."

I give him a side glare. "Prez. You were just here the other day with your team."

His smile widens even more before he laughs. "That's the point. Can't go too long without playing, but I definitely gotta take it seriously if I'm gonna play with you!"

"Man, whatever. You extra." I toss him my softball as he's giving me this strange look with a little twinkle in his eyes. I blush and ignore it. "I'm gonna need your help with batting, too, but I wanna start off with pitching. Anything you wanna work on?"

"Batting, hands down. Last weekend, I had all strikeouts. I was so trash, man. Coach was on my ass after the game, too," he replies, shaking his head as we walk together toward the diamond.

The right side of my mouth lifts. "Well. That's not surprising. You suck."

He shoves my shoulder in play. I shove him back. He tries to swipe me on the head, but I duck, and he misses. Next thing I know, we're chasing each other, play fighting, and laughing. I consider myself a pretty good sprinter, but he's much more agile and fast. He catches me in literally no time and puts me in a joking headlock as my long hair becomes trapped around his arm. I try to wriggle loose, but his knuckles meet the top of my head. I'm laughing so hard, I can't even breathe.

"Okay, okay, I quit!" I squeal. "Stop, *Preston!*"

He sighs and lets me go. "Yeah. I don't suck any more than it sucks that you gettin' in trouble all the time."

Something about his tone makes me pause, so once my locks become free as I adjust myself, I glare at him, and he looks just as grim as he sounded.

"Really, dude?" I raise a brow and catch my breath. "How'd it go from us messin' around to you gettin' all serious on me?"

We start walking back to the pitcher's circle on the diamond again as my question lingers between us for a stretched moment. Then, his eyes cut at me.

"I'm just worried about you."

"Why you worried about me?"

"Because." He jerks his head to move his tight, black curls hanging on his forehead away from his eyes.

"Because?"

"Because I know where you're trying to go. You have the first game for the Senior League Softball World Series in a few months. As the starting pitcher." He shakes his head with a laugh. "Dude, you're literally the ESPN favorite for being the best pitcher in the world in your division. That's huge. And I'm scared you're gonna throw that all away by being reckless. They have rules on the team about being a good student. You wanna be all over the news for the trouble you get into?"

My eyes pivot from his. "I hear you, but you don't understand, Prez," I whisper and put my glove on.

He smacks his lips and shakes his head. "Come on, man. You

always say that and never tell me anything, but I'm your best friend. Why do you think I don't understand?"

"Because you don't. You ready to bat?" I huff, shift my weight to my left leg, and give him an exasperated gaze.

After a while, his eyes go from concerned to defeated before he turns on his heels and walks to home plate with his bat. "I wish you would stop holding back and let me understand what's going on. But yeah," he surrenders, "I'm ready to bat."

Now the air between us gets kinda thick. I'm okay with that – I'd rather have it this way than to explain all the reasons why I got suspended again. I hate Prez even knowing I get in so much trouble all the time. Everyone else, except Andre Carter, I can't care less about. Prez doesn't need to know about my life either, regardless of our status as close friends. I never, ever want him to know what I've done in my past, know about my family, nor do I want him to know what landed me here in San Diego.

"Aye!" he calls out and snaps me out of my brief daze.

"Yeah?"

"Baseball pitches. None of that softball shit," he says and throws the softball I threw to him earlier to the ground.

"I already know that," I reply and pick up the much smaller baseball next to me. "Eventually, I need your help so I can practice softball pitches, too."

"Nah, you don't need to practice that. Softball is weak sauce."

"You talkin' all that mess, you ain't gonna be able to hit this heat I got on the baseball side either, Prezzy. You remember what happened the last time you underestimated me."

He gives me a low gaze and a salty smile.

He damn well remembers because it was how we officially met, right here, on this very diamond two and a half years ago.

Prez plays baseball on the male version of our organization's traveling team while I play softball on the female end, and we share this diamond for practices at different times of the evenings. Back then, when the boys practiced, us softball ladies would hang in the bleachers to watch, check out their skills, and cheer them on with no shame while we waited for our turn.

But whenever we practiced first and the boys had to wait their turn, they would try to make fun of us and act like they weren't checking us out until I called them out for it one day. Some of his teammates started talking shit to me, and Prez played 'follow the leader' about how bad they thought we sucked until I told them to prove themselves with a baseball game against our team.

The result? We crushed them a solid eight-to-one with me pitching baseball style. When we won, I didn't need to talk trash. For what? I just shrugged, knowing I proved a point, and sat in the dugout to chill while watching the boys cry among themselves like babies. When everyone else went home, Prez came and sat very close to me without a word between us for what felt like hours until he finally mumbled a dejected, "Good game." We've been tight and inseparable ever since. Bonded by the hip.

Prez and I stop with all the talk and get right to practicing. I'm throwing fire at him too, no mercy. From curves, to change ups, to ultra-fast, Prez swings, swings, and swings, and connects with none of them.

"Damn, LaLa," he whines and throws his bat with a frustrated sigh. His fingers run through his curls and push them back. As if that's going to change his batting percentage. "You're too good."

"You're not seeing the pitch I'm throwing. You're too eager to hit anything out of the park. It's okay to get a ground hit. Pay attention to the spin of the ball. A spin that looks kinda weird and slower than all other pitches is likely a curveball. A weird spinning pitch that's high in the zone is a hittable curveball. Come on. Try it."

Intentionally, I throw a curveball that's off location and higher than where I usually want my pitches to land in the zone. Prez hits it, but it's a foul ball.

"There you go! Try it again."

I throw another one, and he misses it. He slams his bat on home plate and screams the F-bomb.

"Getting mad will take you out of your game, too, Prez. It's just practice. Focus," I say.

He sighs and bends his head back and forth to crack his neck. "You're right." He shakes his limbs, takes a deep breath, and gets back into his batting stance.

"Okay. You got this!" I encourage him.

I wind up and throw a slower curve as the ball spins clockwise out of my hand. Prez squints, eyeing it before putting his weight on his back leg and swings, blasting the ball out yonder and to the parking lot.

"You did it, Prez!" I squeal.

"Hell yeah!"

We both celebrate for a split second, and then freeze when shattering glass and a car alarm disrupts the celebration.

"Oh shit," I whisper while he covers his gaped mouth with his hand. The car lights flicker on and off to the rhythm of the alarm. "I think you smashed someone's window!"

"Let's get outta here. I think that car belongs to those people over there," he says and rushes to grab his stuff. I do too before we sprint off the diamond while the angry car owner is yelling at us off in the distance. We run, our metal bats clinging against each other, and disappear in the nearby woods where we know they won't dare come to catch our breath before bursting into collective laughter.

"You have the worst luck," I say.

"Man, you telling me?" His brows hike up while taking out his phone and his thumb swipes through whatever he's checking. "Kinda glad that happened though, 'cause I gotta go."

"Why? It's way too early for us to be done, man."

"My girl. Gina just called me four times. I wanna make sure she's good," he replies.

I smack my lips and roll my eyes. I have no clue what he sees in her. She gives me "crazy girlfriend" vibes. What's actually crazy though is that it doesn't bother him that she's so desperately clingy. Always asking where he is, who he's with, always crying about him not physically being with her. I think he embraces it, which is super cringe because any time I bring it up, he defends her. I don't want him getting any ideas about jealousy if I keep mentioning it, so I don't. She doesn't know who I am, but I already know once she finds out, we gon' have a problem. Because one thing I ain't giving up is Prez no matter how she feels.

"Bro, you know she's good! It's one in the morning. Any time she calls this much, it's just her trying to check on you. She's fine."

"You don't know that for sure."

I scoff. "See, you claim you wanna understand why I'm in trouble a lot at school, but I'm just as confused about you and Gina. She's so thirsty."

"Gina's a good girl, LaLa. It's more than just her calling all the time."

"Not saying she isn't. I'm just saying she be doing too much."

"And so do you. I'll hit you later, a'ight?"

I pause and cross my arms.

"Wait, wait, wait. So, you're just gonna leave me to walk home all alone at one in the morning just to talk to *Gina*? You can't at least walk me halfway like you normally do?"

He gives me a low gaze. "You wasn't worried about being all alone when you snuck out your window two hours ago. It ain't much difference between eleven and one."

"Prez. You can talk to her while you walk me, okay? I promise I'm not gonna say anything. Look, I won't even judge," I say and put my hands up in surrender. "I do think it's bogus of my best friend to leave me out to walk home by myself this late."

"I don't believe you about not judging, so no."

"I promise, I won't. I'll think it, but I won't say it. Pinky swear," I offer.

He doesn't take my pinky swear promise. Instead, he just cuts his eyes at me one last time before quickly dialing up his girlfriend's number. It doesn't even give half a ring before she picks up.

"Gina?" Prez calls out.

"Where are you? I've called you like four times! You never ghost me like this late at night. What's going on?" she frantically screams so loud, it's like they're on speaker phone.

"My bad, G. I was at the park practicing baseball."

"With whom at this time of the night?!"

"Nobody. I was just on my own."

"You can't really practice baseball on your own, Preston!" she barks.

"Well, I was."

"...are you lying to me?"

"No, I'm not, Gina."

"Okay... I guess. Where are you? Can you FaceTime me?"

"I'm outside walking home. I'm not gonna FaceTime you until I get home."

"Seriously, Preston?"

The way she said "Preston" makes me gag. I cover my mouth and fake barf while Prez gives me a death glare so hard, I nearly laugh out loud, so I cover my mouth with a hand.

"Yes, G."

"Makes me think you're with someone."

"Why don't you trust me, Gina?"

"I do! I just don't trust these dirty sluts."

"Good thing I'm not with a dirty slut."

"Mmm hmm. Better not be. What do you wanna get into this weekend?" she asks.

"Not sure. I got baseball practice for sure."

"Well, I wanna be with you. Can I come to practice?"

I fake barf again and this time, Prez swiftly and subtly backhands my gut. I open my mouth to yelp out, but no noise comes out and instead, I hold my belly and drop to the floor with quiet giggles.

"Gina, you know Coach don't allow girls at practices."

"I know. Just thought I'd try."

They keep talking and doing this awful mushy flirting as I keep trying to stifle my laughter all the way up until we reach Jarell's apartment.

"Hold on, Gina."

He puts himself on mute and gives me another death glare. I smirk and crawl through the window.

"Bye, Prez."
Prez waves me off once I get inside.
"Later, LaLa."

Chapter Four

IT'S NOT LIKE *Mama to miss my softball games. Ever. But most of all, this ain't no regular game. It's the championship in the eleven-year-old Los Angeles city league. The championship match against the team we kept losing to during the regular season. She's gotta be here to see this. I'm gonna be so locked in in the pitcher's circle that these other girls won't know what to do! I'm aiming for a complete shut out, which means nobody on the other team scores on a pitch I throw. But Mama is my motivator, and she's not even here!*

We just talked yesterday about how excited she was to bring the assorted chip packs and juice for the team as a "good season" gesture. This morning, she even said she was gonna bring cupcakes as a surprise! So how can she not be here? It's one of the biggest games of my life! And I can't wait for the team to try her homemade funfetti cupcakes. They're amazing!

"Hey Kylah, what's your mom bringing after the game? Is she gonna bring Kool-Aid Jammers? Those are the best," my teammate, Vanessa, asks. She's putting on her cleats in the dugout and picking the bat she's gonna use on the plate.

"I think so," I say, as I re-dial Mama's number for the sixth time on my cell.

I tune out whatever other question Vanessa asks about snacks while I wait for Mama's hello in the pocket of silence between each ring.

It never comes.

"Where the heck is she?" I whisper and put my phone away with a huff. The game starts in literally ten minutes.

Vanessa pauses and gives me a slight frown. "What's wrong?"

"Nothing."

I walk away to sit on the bleachers. Despite Mama not being here yet, I lift my chin and close my eyes, allowing the breeze to massage my face and the sun to toast my skin. Even the wind combs my hair as my game time ponytail blows behind my back. I love playing softball when the weather is like this. Even the smell of the bright brown dirt comforts me.

But the feeling is short lived.

More time passes by like it's rushing for the game to start without a care in the world that Mama isn't here. I wish I had a magic wand to freeze the seconds. And now, our team is in the huddle to talk strategy before we hit the field. Once we do our pre-game chant and break, I pull my phone out one more time and call Mama again.

No pickup.

Wait... is everything okay?

I go out on the field with my glove and the ball. First inning. I keep looking, scanning, and checking the bleachers for Mama after each and every pitch I throw, but she never shows. I pitch a great game, but it wasn't the shutout I planned. We win the game seven-two, along with the championship trophy, and that's cool and all. It doesn't matter, though. All I thought about the entire time was how no one showed up for me. Not Mama... nobody. After the game, it feels even worse.

Nobody gets snacks. Or cupcakes. Or Kool-Aid Jammers everyone anticipated to get.

My cheeks burn while having to answer the same question over and over. "What happened to your mom? Where are the snacks?" And then explain why we don't have them. Even someone else's horrible mom has the nerve to say, "Don't worry, honey. You don't need those snacks. We can go out to eat. That's much better than what you would've gotten anyway."

The tears puddle in my eyes, but it takes everything inside not to let them fall. I get these side glares from my teammates the more and more excuses I give, but thankfully we won, so the attention on the snacks doesn't linger the way the trophy captures everyone's attention.

I take that time to hide away from everyone as the trophy poses as my friend in the dirt while my back leans up under a palm tree. I gaze from afar at my teammates and their happy, stupid families with my knees to my chin and arms wrapped around them.

*Really. Why didn't she show up today? Why **wouldn't** she show up today? I hope she's okay...*

My phone buzzes in my pocket. Oooh, oooh, this has got to be her!

I look at the screen, and it's indeed her. Thank God! At the same time, I've never felt such a mix of relief and flat out anger with her. How could she miss my game?!

"Hello?" I say, my breath caught in my throat. "Mama? Where are you?"

"K-Kylah?"

A deep voice calls my name. I think I recognize it, but I'm not sure. It's a voice I hadn't heard in many, many years. Not since I was about five. So I don't think it's who I think it is. I hope it isn't... it better not be... Either way, I'm scared. Why is a man answering Mama's phone?

"Who's this?"

"I know it's been a really long time. But it's me... your brother."

I pause as my eyes shift back and forth, trying my absolute hardest to deny that it could be him. No way. This has got to be someone else. But no other person comes to mind of who it could be.

"J-Jarell?"

"Yeah."

My blood boils so quickly, it spills over to the point where I stand straight up against the tree. One would think I'd be happy to hear my brother's voice, but I'm not. At all. "How are you on Mom's phone? You don't even live here anymore!" I rage.

"Where are you? I need you to come home. Something's not right..."

"What are you talking about?"

"Something's going on with Ma..."

"What's wrong with her? What did you do to her?!" I scream.

"Nothing! I didn't do anything. She called me randomly this morning for the first time in years and said some weird things... I-I just need you to come home and tell me what's going on..."

"Is she okay? What did you do to her, Jarell? You haven't been around in years, so what's going on?"

"I promise I didn't do anything. Please, just come home..."

I don't say anything else. I hang up, sprint to my coach, and beg for a ride home. What the hell is going on with Mama? Please don't tell me she's passed out again from using. She's gotta stop doing this...

~ ~ ~

My eyes peek open, and the world is blurry. My head pounds

harder than what I can imagine an elephants' stampede is like. The blurriness fades once hot tears wet my cheeks, then my neck... then my bed.

I squeeze my pillow so tight that I'm kinda surprised the feathers don't burst out. Lately, this dream keeps popping up, and I always wake up to wonder if Mama would've just come to my game like she said she was going to, maybe she wouldn't have... maybe we wouldn't have found her...

I sigh and let out a whimper into my pillow. Oh, what I would give to hold her. Smell her. Touch her. Talk to her. Anything. I will give anything. I hate it here with Jarell.

I wipe my eyes and somehow find the energy to lug myself up just like the sun struggles to break through the heavy clouds today, but I'm still half asleep. I reach out to my nightstand and pat it several times, searching for my phone. When I don't find it, I pat the bed around me, trying to see where I put it.

Oh yeah.

Bozo's got it.

"Damn, man." I'm frustrated with myself for allowing sleepiness to make me forget that as my body plops into the blankets again. I'm almost at a point of dozing off into a deep sleep, but a fist pounding on my door jolts me awake.

"Kylah, get up," Jarell orders through the door.

"No," I respond with a groggy voice.

"Get up, now. I've called off work for the first half of the day, so I'm taking you to therapy this morning."

My brows fold in. Therapy? I mean, I know I have a therapist and all since I've been diagnosed with PTSD since moving out here, but I usually only go twice a month. I'm not due again for another few weeks.

"Jarell, go away. It's too early for that," I contest. "Plus I already went last week. Why are you trying to force me to go again?"

"Kylah, I'm not playing. You'd be getting up for school at this time anyway. Since you're throwing chairs at teachers now, I ain't allowing you to be mindlessly violent no matter how much she made you upset. You ain't finna just sit around here and enjoy a suspension by sleeping in or kicking it and doing whatever you want like you did yesterday. You're gonna take this time to repair any harm done to that teacher and be accountable for your behavior. Dr. Anderson was able to get you in due to a cancelation, so get your butt up and get dressed. Your appointment is at eight o'clock."

I turn my face into my pillow and groan in it again. I hate to acknowledge this because therapy is always the last place I wanna be, but quietly admitting that Jarell is right hurts my stomach. I really haven't thought about Ms. Turner or what I've done at all since Jarell picked me up from school to start my suspension.

I lie here for a few more moments, allowing Prez's, Ms. Evans's, and even Jarell's words to me over the last couple of days to sink in. Sheesh. What I did at school was a *really* big deal. I made her quit her job, I could've seriously hurt her, and I could be expelled from school right now. Yet, this is the first time I'm even *thinking* about it.

That's scary, and it ain't the only thing that is.

The anger, the turn up, the crying after I demolished Ms. Turner's room... My entire reaction to my sketchbook being thrown is terrifying because it... it felt like I had zero control over my mouth or body.

I've never felt this way before. This... blind rage.

Being suspended ain't a new thing to me, but I've never done anything *this* bad. I really didn't mean to hurt her. At the same time, what am I supposed to do when people disregard very important things to me like my sketchbook with everything I've ever cared about in it? *And* she told me I would never be anything in my life.

How do I even go back to school without people wanting to keep a ten-foot pole's distance from me? I'm surprised Prez even still wants to talk to me after hearing about what happened. Maybe he'd think differently if he'd been in the room to watch it all go down.

Man. There's so much to talk to my therapist about. It's so overwhelming that the idea of hiding in my blankets for the rest of my life seems like the much better option.

"If you don't get up in the next two minutes, I'm taking the door off the hinges." Jarell interrupts my thinking with a threat that's got some serious bass and authority to it.

"Okay Jarell, damn! I'm getting up!"

I yank the covers away from my body and rise out of bed, moping around my room to find the clothes I want to wear. Once I find everything, I snatch my room door open and go to the bathroom to get ready. Jarell's already standing near the door as if he was waiting for me to come out. As if he was clock watching. I walk right by him, rolling my eyes.

We both finish up our morning hygiene routine and head off in an Uber to the private clinic where my therapist, Dr. Anderson, is located. Because it's so early, we're the only ones here. Jarell, Luna, and I wait in the lobby for her to call my name. Once she comes out of the back and does, Jarell and Dr. Anderson greet each other like they're best friends. She gives me sympathetic eyes before escorting me to her office.

I won't lie. Even though I don't like coming here, this room always gives me a meditative vibe. With natural plants all over the room, soft ambient lighting, and the aroma of essential oils shooting from the scent dispenser, I wish I could sleep here. I'm sure it'd be the most peaceful sleep I'd ever get.

"Good morning, Kylah. This appointment will be a very short one today because I have an eight-thirty coming up, and you and I already met last week. Sounds like this was more of an urgent meeting than anything, so I agreed to fit you in. Does that sound okay?"

"Yeah." I shrug.

"Perfect. I spoke with Jarell last evening. Sounds like you had a rough day at school on Tuesday," she states, sitting next to me in a rolling chair with her legs crossed while I slump in a more comfy, fluffy one.

"Yeah. I'm suspended."

"I'm sorry to hear that. Would you like to discuss what happened? I'd be happy to understand your perspective."

"There ain't much to talk about." I fidget and look away from her penetrating glare. Quiet looms, but she makes sure the only one who will break this pause is me. "I threw a chair at a teacher."

"Why?"

"Because she threw my sketchbook across the room. So I threw the chair and ruined her room."

"I see." Dr. Anderson nods. "Tell me what you were thinking about before you threw the chair and destroyed her room."

"Well... I was thinking about how much I wanted to treat her like how she treated me."

"Say more about how she treated you."

"She said I would never be anything in my life. Then, she threw my book," I reply.

Her eyes expand and stay that way. "Ahh, we're getting somewhere. Let's unpack this a bit more. Let's talk about the sketchbook first. Why such a big reaction over your book being thrown? Do you believe throwing a chair at your teacher is a response that matched her action?"

My chest stirs, replaying Ms. Turner's apathy in my mind all over again. It takes everything in me not to ball up my fists.

"To me, at the moment, I felt like it was deserved. I don't feel like that now, but I've got many different sketches that mean a lot to me in there. My mom. My dad. My old friends from Los Angeles... a lot! So when she threw it, it slid across her desk and the floor, and it smeared the one portrait I drew that means the world to me. It's of Mama, so I reacted that way because it's the *only* picture I have left of her."

I sniff as the tears immediately well and glide down my cheeks.

"All of her belongings and pictures got thrown out when we cleared out her apartment we used to live in after she died. So, I drew her from my own memory. It took me weeks to get that right, and Ms. Turner ruined it."

Dr. Anderson simply sits and continues to let me pour out with tears. It takes a while for her to speak, giving me the time I need to cry.

"First, I want to acknowledge how you feel. Something so meaningful to you was treated with such disregard. Especially because of the history of your parents. I'm sorry your teacher triggered you that way. Let's unpack her comments about you not being anything in your life, too. How did you feel when she said that to you?" she questions.

"I don't know... like I failed."

"And then you destroyed her room?"

"Yeah. If she's going to destroy something I really care about, then I'll destroy hers."

"It was shared with me that you threw the chair directly at the teacher. Were you trying to hurt her? Or were you trying to destroy something she cared about?"

I pause to reflect.

"I don't really know. I just blacked out. All I cared about was making her feel like how I felt." I dip my head.

"So Kylah, do you think you achieved what you set out to do? Did your actions make you feel any better?"

Gotdamnit, why would she ask me this? A question she already knows the answer to? My eyes remain fixed toward the ground, and the tears continue to slip.

"No," I admit.

"In your mind, did you achieve *anything*?"

"I achieved the fact that she quit her job."

She raises a brow. "You're proud of that?"

"No. I'm just saying she quit. I didn't want her to. I honestly didn't mean to hurt her."

"So, what I am hearing you say is that you intended to make your teacher feel how you felt in the moment, but what you did led to a bigger impact you weren't proud of. Am I correct in my summary of that?"

Ugh. Dr. Anderson can read me so well sometimes.

I nod. "I guess so."

"Alright. Now that we've come to a collective understanding about what happened and your feelings about the aftermath, let me give you a mini lesson on intent versus impact, okay? Sometimes, when we get our feelings hurt, our first thought is revenge. We want that person to feel pain. And we'll participate in actions that try to do what we intend, but the outcome is way bigger than we want it to be. So we constantly have to reflect on how our actions affect the other person or the community around us. And in that reflection, you need to circle back around and figure out how to repair any unintended harm. We can get more into how to repair with others later. But, I want to spend the rest of our time talking about strategies you can use to avoid the level of rage that you ultimately found yourself reaching to begin with."

My head drops back. She's gonna tell me the same shit she's been telling me for the last few months about ways to manage my anger that I've yet to use consistently. I already know where this is going. She stares at me for a moment, sensing my irritation. But it doesn't deter her.

"How did your body feel before you threw that chair?" she questions.

"I honestly felt calm. In my head, I already knew what I was gonna do," I respond.

"How did it feel afterward?"

"Hot. Felt like I had exploded. My head hurt."

"Okay, but you said you felt really angry the minute she told you that you would never be anything in your life. That was the trigger. First, I want to acknowledge how wrong your teacher is. That's not something an adult educator should ever tell a child. You are capable, talented, and you will be whatever you want to be in your life. Based on your grit and your personality, I'm sure of it.

"I also want to recognize the importance of your sketchbook. Many of us don't know the book is so sacred to you. You're grieving, and your heart is in there. I completely understand and want to validate that. She was also wrong for mistreating your belongings.

"However, two things can be true. Kylah, you are old and equipped enough to be able to recognize your triggers. And that's when you have to utilize the strategies that we've worked on. The moment you felt your body tense up and those thoughts filled your brain about hurting your teacher, what's the first thing you should've done? If you could do it all over again?"

I pout.

"Take deep breaths, close my eyes and count to ten, squeeze a fidget, journal, or ask the person to repeat themselves."

"And in this case, if you could do it again, which one would you have chosen?"

"Probably the one where she had to repeat herself," I answer. "And if she would've repeated it for real, it would've told me she truly believed it."

"Good choice, and I agree. And then, you need to tell a trusted adult about what she did so *she's* the one who has the consequences. So, how are you feeling about everything right now, then? Since yesterday?" she asks.

I wriggle in my seat a little bit at that question. One thing I can say I don't like more than anything is feeling or being vulnerable. Having to admit how I truly feel right now sucks, but I also don't want to be dishonest. I've been with Dr. Anderson long enough to know she'd detect a lie through my teeth.

"Um... ashamed, I guess."

"I'm glad you feel that way."

"Why?"

"Because, number one, it's normal. Two, it's encouraging because that means you're more likely to fix your behavior moving forward. You're at the point of your development and learning of these strategies where you should be taking better ownership of your anger and your actions. And you haven't been doing that for the past six months. At all. Over the next couple of days, I want you to think about being accountable for your behaviors. I will talk with Jarell about helping you write an apology letter."

I smack my lips and cross my arms, sliding down even more in the chair. Dr. Anderson continues.

"I know I am your therapist, and I am supposed to show empathy, understanding, softness, and sympathy. I will still show those things. But I will also challenge you. Getting suspended from school as much as you have while you also have the necessary tools to manage your behaviors and anger doesn't add up, Kylah. There's no way you should've gotten to the point of throwing a chair. It's really unacceptable. You need to take the necessary steps to do better because I know that's what you want for yourself. You've shared that with me. So why do you keep acting this way?"

"I don't know." I shrug. But I do know. I just don't want to answer if she's just going to blame and shame me. So instead, I just sit in silence, kinda stunned. Dr. Anderson has never been this direct.

She's fed up.

It's wild when your own *therapist* gets frustrated with you.

But it's cool, though.

Because I'm frustrated with everyone else too, yet nobody acknowledges that part at all. It's always my fault, it's always about how I act, and I always have to think of everyone else's feelings. Nobody considers mine. And I'm tired of it.

Chapter Five

THE ONE DAY *Mama lets me go outside to play, it's not only way too hot, but I'm so bored playing on the same equipment of this playground. The same ol' lame slides. The same raggedy monkey bars. The same worn down climbing equipment. I wanna do something new. Plus, we kinda have a similar playground at school for recess.*

I hate that Mama likes to stay inside the house all the time. I should have begged to play outside on a different day because nobody wants to come out when the heat is this hot.

After going down one of the slides for a fifth time by myself, I sludge over with a soaked forehead and back to Mama who's sitting in the shade.

"Mama, can we go to a different park?" I whine.

She looks up at me from under her big ol' sun hat, her long curly hair flowing down her shoulders with a small little notebook in her hands and a pen. She stops writing and tilts her sunglasses down to see me better.

"What's that again, baby?" she asks.

"Can we leave and go to a different park?" I ask. "Can we go to the splash park with the water and pool?"

"No. If we leave, then we're going home," she replies. "It's hot as

hell out here anyway."

"But I'm bored! This playground sucks. Plus, there's no one to play with."

"Kylah, you're bored with any and everything all the time. Going to the pool ain't gon' be any different. If you're not running a hundred miles an hour, then it's boring to you," she shoots back.

"Well, if we can't go to the splash park, can we go to a different park with different slides?"

She closes her little notebook and gives me a long look.

"No. You and I agreed to a couple of hours out here, so that's what I'ma give you. Besides, like I said, you're just gonna get bored with another park. I'd rather have you participate in a game with other kids or something."

"What am I gonna play?"

Mama takes her sunglasses off this time and starts to look around the area to see if other kids and their parents are around. I look around, too, and there's nobody my age at all out here with the exception of another little girl, but she looks just as boring to play with. She's drawing with her finger in the sand. I'm not gonna do that. I wanna climb, jump, swing, flip, and run!

"Hey, what about those kids over there on the baseball diamond?" Mama points across the fields.

I follow her finger and see a bunch of kids together in two separate teams. One team is in a line, and the other team is in the field. One person is in the middle of a circle and rolls the ball to the other team. The first person in the line kicks the ball that was rolled, and then runs.

"They're playing kickball! That would be perfect for you! You want to play with them?" Mama asks with a huge smile on her face.

"They look like big kids." I look up at her with hesitation.

"Yeah and so?"

"But I'm too little. They won't let me play," I pout.

"But can you try? You never know what'll happen if you don't try."

"They're going to make fun of me for being too little." I look at Mama with a frown.

"What if they don't?"

"Mama..." I jump up and down and whine some more. "Can we just go to the water park?"

"And you're too old to be throwing a tantrum, so stop it. Let's go over there before you get popped," she threatens. "Or we can go home."

"Fine!"

Mama grabs me by the hand in addition to all of our stuff, and we march over to the baseball diamond.

"Hey, kids!" Mama waves her hand like a wild person.

All of them stop playing and look at us.

"Hey, will you let my little girl play? I think this would be a great experience for her. Would you be willing to teach her how it's done?"

Everybody looks at each other, seeming to share thoughts from their brains without speaking. Mostly the boys scrunch their face, basically about to say no. But a brave girl steps in. A girl with two long, black, braided pigtails.

"Sure! She can be on our team!" she exclaims. Then she walks over to me with a grin, showing all teeth. "What's your name?"

"K-Kylah."

"Nice to meet you! I'm Selina. How old are you?"

"Seven."

"Cool, that's around the same age I learned to play kickball, too. I'm fourteen now. These are my siblings and our friends!"

Selina introduces me to her brothers, sisters, and friends. Some are a little younger than her, and some are older. They have a big family! She has three brothers and three sisters. I wish I had more brothers and sisters, too. I only have one, and he's gone. I pout. I miss Relly so much.

After I meet them all, Selina starts to teach me how to play kickball. I turn and look at Mama, and she's also smiling just as bright as Selina, nodding and encouraging me to go on and play. I gulp and return my divided attention to the tutorial.

"And when he rolls the ball, you kick it! And run as fast as you can to first base. You have to hurry though, because if they get the ball, they can tag you. They can't tag you once you're on the base."

"Okay. I'm ready to try!" I say. I don't want to hear her talk anymore. I just wanna do it. "When will it be my turn to kick?"

"You can try now! Come to home plate."

Selina brings me to home plate, and I'm right in front of the boy in the circle with the ball. He looks so cool! Like he has a lot of power, and everyone's watching him. I want to try rolling the ball next after I kick it!

The boy stares at me for a second, like he's not going to take it easy on me just because I'm little and rolls the ball really fast to home plate.

"Orlando, not so fast! It's her first time!" Selina shouts at him.

But I don't care. It rushes to me, and I swing my leg back and kick it. The ball goes flying past the guy in the middle and the person at the second base. I leap up to celebrate.

"Yay!!! Go Kylah!" my teammates scream at me. "Run!"

Oh yeah! I gotta run! I sprint to the base Selina told me to. They try to throw the ball to the base, but I get there first. They can't tag me.

"Yeeaaahh!!! Good job, Kylah!" my team claps and cheers for me.

Mama really is cheering for me on the side much harder than my team. She's jumping up and down and telling me good job, too.

We continue playing for the rest of the afternoon. I even got to be the person in the middle of the circle to roll the ball to the other team. I wish I could play this game every day! After a couple more rounds, the big kids seem a little tired, so they stop the game to go home. Selina and her siblings thank me for playing and say that they want to play with me next time. Mama also thanks them and tells them that they are really nice kids. Once the area clears out, I rush over to our stuff to get water and to go home, too.

"Mama, that was so much fun! Can you bring me back tomorrow?" I ask.

"You did amazing today, baby! I'm so proud of you, honey. Now as far as coming back tomorrow? I'm not sure because we don't know if they will be out here again tomorrow. But what I can do is look into signing you up for a softball team so that you can practice and play regularly."

"What's softball? Is it that I kick or roll a softer ball?"

Mama laughs and runs her fingers through my curls, untangling them. I swipe at her hand because I don't want her trying to fix me.

"No, sweetie. It's actually just like baseball, except the ball is a little bigger. I used to play when I was a little girl, too, but my family never had enough money to let me continue playing. Anyway. What do you think?"

"Yeah!" I exclaim, pumping my fist. "If it's like kickball, I wanna play!"

Mama smirks with a light little chuckle. "Oh, my baby." She wipes the sweat off my forehead. "I think we've finally found something that will keep you active and keep your attention. I think you'll be amazing.

I didn't realize how athletic you were until I saw you playing today. I think this will be an amazing outlet for you!"

"What does athletic mean?"

"The ability to jump, run, throw, sprint. Skills that many good people who play sports have. I have some pretty talented kids! Jarell was athletic like that, too."

"You mean, Relly?" I look up at Mama with sad eyes. I notice hers are, too.

"Yes. Your brother. He absolutely loved to play sports." A slow and gloomy smile spreads across her face.

"I miss him, Mama," I whisper and hug her legs.

"I miss him, too, baby. You ready to go home?"

"Mmm hmm!"

Mama takes my hand, and we walk toward our apartment in silence, but let the joy of today settle in our hearts.

~ ~ ~

This suspension feels like a lifetime. It's finally the weekend, but I've been holed up in my room, reading Black teen lit, emailing Prez, staring at the ceiling, thinking about Ms. Turner, sleeping, and having a mix of dreams and nightmares since my therapy appointment. That's it, that's all. I've had no inspiration to draw like I normally do. I only come out if I have to pee or eat. I even tried my luck to escape boredom with Prez to sneak out to play on the diamond again, but his silly excuse was that he's gotta lay low because his girlfriend was too suspicious about the last time we were out.

But all of the boredom ends today, this Sunday, with the first practice of the softball season in a few minutes. And it's a hundred and twenty days away from the first pitch of the Senior League

Softball World Series tournament in Delaware! I promise to make it all the way to the top and win the trophy, just for Mama, since she's the one to introduce me to the sport. I wish I had dreams about those moments more often like I did last night than dreaming about the darkness of losing her.

I've *gotta* make her proud.

Once I'm ready to go, I move with a purpose to the front door with all my stuff. I try to duck my way out of Jarell or Brooklyn saying anything to me because it'll be one of the rare times they see me outside the confines of my room. But my plan ends once I see what they're doing.

They're in the living room, sitting on the floor with a crazy number of blank pieces of colorful paper scattered everywhere around them. Jarell's holding some sort of folded version, showing Brooklyn whatever he made while she awes and coos like a baby seeing candy.

Ugh.

Jarell makes origami sometimes, and it's really fascinating and cool when he finishes them. It's one thing I'll reluctantly admit is a dope talent he has, but the process is super messy. I hate when he decides to do it because I'm the one cleaning up the paper from the floor that he misses picking up. Hopefully this time, Brooklyn's the one to clean up after him. That is her boyfriend after all.

Pausing and rolling my eyes at the prospect of me picking up the sheets later, that gives just enough time for Jarell to hear me start to walk away.

"Kylah," Jarell calls out. "Wait."

I roll my eyes and slow down. Brooklyn's eyes are on me, too.

"What?" I mumble.

"You alright?" he asks, looking in my direction. This time, his voice actually holds some sort of genuine concern, but I don't take the bait.

"Why wouldn't I be?"

"Just... I don't... you never come out of your room," he struggles to say.

"There's a real good reason for that."

"What's that?"

"Because I don't wanna see or talk to *you*."

I don't give him a chance to respond. I pace out of the front door of the complex and quickly walk to the diamond.

~ ~ ~

"Alright, girls. Today is the first of April, which means, today starts the official regular season, but we are exactly four months away from the Senior League World Series on ESPN. We will be doing some intense training to prepare for the season because elite players like you need to stay in shape. We're going to be doing lots of sprints, batting practice, practice scenarios and situational innings, and finally, a short scrimmage. Practice ends at seven today, so we have three hours together. After practice, I want to meet with each of you individually to talk about..."

Coach goes on and on in our huddle, explaining what'll happen tonight. I'm focused and tuned in to the rambling this time, but I can't help but feel a crawling, creepy sensation anyone gets when they feel like they're being watched. I finally look away from Coach, and I'm proved right. She's looking right at me with a raised eyebrow and a slight smirk as if she can't wait to bother me tonight.

Alaysia Simmons.

Can't she just leave me alone?

She's seriously an attention seeking bitch, but I give her attention alright by crushing her on the field every chance I get. When our eyes lock and she's persistent about mugging me, I look away. I got better things to focus on.

After five more minutes of Coach running his mouth, the huddle finally breaks, and we run to do the tasks we're mandated to do.

Coach wasn't lying when he said he was gonna work us out. With the sun beaming relentlessly on the field, it's to the point where the team is nearly on the ground gasping for air. Once he has this grand epiphany that should've been obvious twenty minutes ago that we're too exhausted to do the drills anymore, he finally gives us a water break to end the cruelty. I'm hella tired, but I'm not completely spent like the rest. I just go by my stuff and take a swig of water from my Gatorade bottle and chill while everyone else still has their hands on their knees.

I'm all by myself during this time, so I'm ripe to be approached by Alaysia. It doesn't take long for the vulture to pounce with her almond skin glistening with sweat.

"So, you got suspended again." She talks the second she walks over after spraying a mouth full of water from her Gatorade bottle. I'm not looking at her, but I know she's sporting that sarcastic, magnet attracting smile.

My lips twist. "What's it to you?"

"Nothing." She shifts her weight. "You get suspended so much that you're out of school more than you're in. You're gonna be a jail bird when you grow up."

"Why do you care? My life ain't got nothin' to do with you. Get you some business somewhere else," I retort. When she doesn't budge, I smack my lips. "Leave me alone, Alaysia. I wasn't even bothering you so don't come bothering me."

"Here's why I really care. For someone who's just fucking off in school and getting suspended every week, you're making it real hard for the people on this team who take being a student athlete seriously. You're wasting an important spot on the field when you're not even gonna be eligible to play in high school. Then you got the nerve to be in the huddle all cocky and shit, thinking you're gonna be the lead pitcher at the Senior Leagues or whatever, but you're too much of a hothead to take that throne. And guess what? This season? I'm comin' hard for your little starting pitcher spot. You gon' fumble it right over to me by doing something stupid, just watch."

This time, my eyes meet hers. She's glaring me down like prey with her arms crossed. Daring me with those long ass lashes that I don't even know how she can see through. I raise an eyebrow and stand square to her so that she doesn't think she's got some authoritative dominance over me. She can forget about it. All people would have to lose the ability to blink before she's ever in that pitcher circle over me.

"Girl. Maybe in your wildest dreams, and even that ain't possible." I scoff. "Move around."

I start to walk away from the situation and slightly shove her out of the way with my forearm, but she doesn't let this go so easily.

"Mmm hmm. And never in your wildest dreams will you ever be with Preston, but that don't stop you from being all up in his face every day. He doesn't want you, so give it up."

I turn my head and freeze, but it's like someone lights my skin on fire. Alaysia thinks a reminder that Prez isn't my boyfriend just because I'm around him a lot is a dig at my soul or something, but it ain't the flex she thinks it is. After I nearly murder her with my gaze and she gives me a smug look back, I walk up to her with measured steps until we're nearly nose to nose.

"First of all, Prez ain't got nothing to do with softball or us, so you can keep his name out your mouth. Second, I told you to go mind your business, but you're still talking to me. Catch a hint because beating your ass won't be in my wildest dreams. It'll be in real time so stop playing with me," I threaten.

"Hit me. I want you to," Alaysia whispers. "I been waiting for this 'cause I ain't scared like how you've got everyone else."

"Hey!" a familiar voice bellows nearby.

Alaysia and I both turn our heads, and it's Coach. He walks up to us, stands in between our bodies, and slightly pushes us both away to create some distance.

"All that arguing gotta stop. Whatever anger you got, take it out on each other on the field. You know we're having a scrimmage tonight, so if you're really mad? Channel it there. I hate you kids always trying to fight. Grow up."

Alaysia and I exchange dirty looks before we head to separate dugouts to prepare for tonight's scrimmage. Our water break is over, and Coach splits the team in half with me being the pitcher on one team and Alaysia being the pitcher on the other. Once that's settled, we go out to play.

I don't pitch too horribly, but tonight, Alaysia does out pitch me to the point of my team losing by 3 points, including striking me out twice. Whatever, the shit is just a scrimmage, and I know for a fact that my less-than-optimal performance is because of all the stuff that's on my mind about my mom. But before we go home, she makes sure she gives me one last laugh as if she's mocking me and the fact that her team won. *Oh, how excited I'd feel to see my fist meet her metallic mouth...*

"Kylah, come here," Coach interrupts my thoughts before I can zip up all my equipment to head home.

"Sup, Coach?"

"What's going on? You don't look like yourself. Especially out on that field."

I shrug. "It was just a bad game, that's all. I ain't worried about it." I zip up my bat bag and lift it to my shoulder.

"Nah. Not buying it. Wanna know why?"

"Why?"

"I got a phone call from Jarell the other day, asking me for help. He wants me to be at your meeting tomorrow with your teachers because this is the sixth time this school year you've been suspended. Really Kylah? Six times? And throwing a chair at a teacher? I had no idea you were acting this way!"

My shoulders sink to the grass. See, Jarell already called my fuckin' therapist, so why the heck would he call and tell Coach, too? What does he have to do with anything related to school? Coach is like the very last person I want to know about the trouble I get into. It's like he finds any and every new way possible to make my life miserable.

"Well, are you gonna say anything?" he questions.

"Don't have anything to say," I slowly draw out. I won't dare give him eye contact.

"Okay. I hope you have more to say tomorrow. I'll handle you then."

Coach walks away after staring me down. Hard. Once he's gone, my head tilts so far that I think it touches the top of my back. Coach being at my school meeting is the last thing I would've thought I'd be dealing with tomorrow. It already feels like everyone's piling up on me about this situation. I know I'm wrong, but I don't need all these reminders from all these people that I am! I've got a strong feeling that I ain't gonna ever live this one down.

Chapter Six

♥ MY APOLOGY ♥

DEAR MS. TURNER

THERE'S SO MUCH I WANNA SAY ABOUT WHAT HAPPENED LAST WEEK. MY THERAPIST AND MY BROTHER ARE FORCING ME TO WRYTE THIS APOLOGY, BUT I SERIOUSLY WANNA DO IT ANYWAY, REGARDLESS OF WHAT THEY TOLD ME.

FIRST, I WANNA SAY THAT I'M SORRY. I'M SORRY FOR DESTROYING UR ROOM, AND I'M SORRY FOR THROWING THE CHAIR AT U. MOST OF ALL, I'M SORRY FOR MAKIN U QUIT UR JOB. I FEEL TERRIBLE ABOUT THAT. A LOT OF KIDS AT SKOOL REALLY LIKED U, AND IT'S MY FAULT THAT UR GONE NOW. U'VE BEEN TRYING HARD TO GET ME TO DO THE RITE THING AT SKOOL, AND I'VE BEEN ACTIN LIKE I DON'T CARE. THERE'S LOTS OF REASONS WHY I'M ACTIN THE WAY I'M ACTIN, BUT THAT'S NOT AN EXCUSE TO DO WHAT I'VE DONE TO U. I'M SORRY. I PROMISE I'M NOT THE KINDA GIRL U THINK I AM. I WANT TO BE SOMETHING ONE DAY. I GOT REALLY SAD AND MAD WHEN U TOLD ME I WOULD NEVER BE ANYTHING BECUZ U DON'T UNDERSTAND THE KINDA LIFE I'VE HAD. I WATCHED BOTH OF MY PARENTS DIE IN FRONT OF ME AND THERE ARE PICTURES I DREW OF THEM IN THE BOOK U THREW. STILL, THAT'S NOT AN EXCUSE FOR TRYING TO HARM U. I WAS WRONG, AND I OWN MY MISTAKE.

I HOPE UR OK. I HOPE U FIND ANOTHER JOB WHERE THERE'S NO ONE LIKE ME THERE. AT THIS POINT, I'M SURE THERE'S MANY PEOPLE WHO WISH THEY NEVER MET ME, AND I KNO UR ONE OF THEM. I GUESS I'M JUST MISUNDERSTOOD. ACTUALLY, I'M HEARTBROKEN AND DAMAGED, BUT NO ONE KNOWS OR REALLY CARES. I'M NOT HELPING MYSELF BY DOING WHAT I DID TO U. ANYWAY. THIS ISN'T SUPPOSED TO BE ABOUT ME. THIS IS SUPPOSED TO BE ABOUT ME APOLOGIZING TO U. ONCE AGAIN, I'M SO SORRY FOR EVERYTHING. THANKS FOR READING. PLEASE FORGIVE ME.

FROM,
KYLAH

Chapter Seven

THERE'S NOTHING WORSE than going to a meeting in the principal's office after a suspension from school. So, with Coach Harper being here, it feels like literal trauma. We're all crowded in this little conference room with a big table, but there are so many people here. Jarell, Luna, Coach, Principal Evans, Ms. Harris, some of my other teachers...

And my apology letter to Ms. Turner in a sealed white envelope with her name on it that no one but me has read. It wasn't hard to write because I meant every single word after reflecting in therapy, but it will be hard to turn it in. For some reason, other people knowing I've apologized is embarrassing. Especially since I feel like I'm owed one, too.

Everyone in the room starts to do these friendly introductions and with small talk before the adults discuss the main subject — me. I wish they'd hurry up because being in this room longer than I have to be is gonna make me check out. Thankfully, Principal Evans gets the hint, so she gets things moving.

"Thank you all for being here today. The purpose of this meeting is to support Kylah and figure out next steps of how we can help create a safe environment for not only her, but also for other students. As you all know, Kylah has been struggling to regulate her emotions and continues to harm others when things don't go her way..."

The more and more she talks, the more and more I slouch in my chair until my head is barely above the table as I fidget with a random pen, twirling it and mindlessly trying to balance it on my thumb. I kinda like Principal Evans, but every time we have one of these meetings, she says the same ol' negative things about me to Jarell, but she never says those things to me one-on-one. It's all positive with me. I don't understand the fakeness.

"I'm sorry, Principal Evans, but I gotta interrupt. Kylah! Sit your butt up!" bellows Coach Harper who's sitting right across from me and glaring like I've committed murder. I reluctantly obey. "And you better sit up straight for the rest of this meeting." He points.

I keep my gaze settled on my lap while Ms. Evans continues to talk.

"As I was saying, we are unsure at this point of how to support Kylah here at school beyond the several IEP meetings where we've adjusted her academic and behavioral support. We really do not want Kylah to be in an alternative school, but if this continues, that's how she will spend the last quarter of her eighth-grade year. Is there anything at home that seems to be helpful that we can replicate at school?"

Jarell shakes his head and sighs, swiping a hand down his face.

"I'm so sorry about all of this. I'm trying everything I can at home she will respond to. I try my best to get her to the therapist she actually tolerates as much as possible. I've gotten her on a traveling softball team, which you already know, and a lot of my money goes to paying that. She loves softball, and she's a superstar. She's got a promising opportunity to play on an international stage, and that seems to be the only outlet she has. The only thing she cares about. I've tried taking her phone, but that doesn't help either."

"All of that ain't working because the real issue is that I don't wanna live with you, Jarell!" I shout at him. "I don't like you. It's that simple."

His face contorts with confusion as his hands shoot out with curiosity.

"Kylah..." Coach Harper warns, but Jarell keeps talking.

"Look, I get that you're upset about a lot of things, but I refuse to let you use that as an excuse for how you're acting. Living with me has nothing to do with your behavior at school. You're not even turning in all your assignments. You need to talk to someone about whatever you're feeling inside because I know from experience it'll make you feel better. The way you treat me and everyone else here at this school ain't cool," Jarell says.

"Yeah, a'ight. You're trying to force me to talk to a therapist and have me share my business with her outside of school, but you completely take away my social life with people I actually care about and wanna talk to. I'm always on some sort of punishment with you. Ma never did that! Besides, I didn't even ask to be here. You forced me to San Diego and made me leave all my friends and the life I loved in LA by taking custody of me!"

"Is that what this really is about? You moving here from LA? Because it's almost been three years now so that can't be the only reason you're acting up like *this*."

"Figure it out." I cross my arms and shrug.

He closes his eyes and shakes his head before shifting his attention to everyone else in the room.

"You see how she talks to me? I don't give it energy. At the same time, she needs accountability, so no, I don't let things slide and she gets consequences. I don't even understand how she and I got to this point, but—"

"If you don't get it by now, Jarell, you never fucking will!" I screech, and Coach Harper slams his hand down on the table so hard, it rattles the whole room. Even Luna sits up.

"Kylah! That is enough!" He leans over and screams directly in my face. My eyes swell like balloons.

"You don't treat family that way. Ever. That man is feeding you, giving you stability, putting clothes on your back, raising you, and financially investing in your dream all while he has complete vision loss."

"I don't care." I shrug, giving him a dead glare.

"See. Your piss poor attitude is the real issue, so let's cut to the chase here. You have two months of school left before your eighth-grade promotion. It seems like academically, you're failing, and behaviorally, you can't get it together. I don't like having athletes on my team who can't show responsibility and human kindness. So, here's the deal. You have one strike, and that's it. By the next progress report, if you have anything less than a C, and you get kicked out of any class to be in ISS just *once*, you will not be playing for the international team this summer. I will replace you with Alaysia Simmons for pitching so fast, you'll forget you play softball."

I gasp as my jaw falls to my chest. Oh, hell no! Anyone but Alaysia Simmons!

"Coach! Why would you do that? Alaysia, though?" I whine.

"Hush! You're treating people like crap, yet you have an expectation that people should treat you with kindness while you keep all the good things in your life. That ain't how the world works, and that's not how I mentor athletes. Understand this Kylah – mean and irresponsible people don't get privileges. Understand this too – you are always replaceable. And with the way you act, people would rather replace you with less talent and a better attitude than to keep a very talented ingrate with a bad attitude. So, the choices are yours. You can keep acting a fool, or you can straighten up. I will let Alaysia know she's on deck to take your starting pitching spot at practice tonight. I want you there when I tell her, too. I ain't playing."

It's like a vacuum sucks the air from my lungs away. Am I really hearing what I'm hearing? Coach replacing me with Alaysia Simmons? He's gotta be outta his mind. Like, super far gone. I can't even form the words to argue. All I see is red now with Jarell being the darkest form of red.

It's not worth it to say anything else at this point, as bad as I wanna make my case. I just sink into my chair and let the adults talk. I don't even hear what they're saying. All I know is that I have some progress report sheet that I must get signed by every single teacher every single day that shares how I did in the class in order to keep playing softball. Principal Evans gives me the progress report sheet before everyone stands up to leave. That's when I slip her the apology letter in exchange. She gives me grateful eyes once she realizes what it is, and I just roll mine.

"Kylah, I want you at practice today at 3:30 sharp. A minute late, and you're running sprints the entire time."

"Alright, Coach. I got it," I mumble and walk out of the principal's office.

It's like a wind of fresh air hits my face once I'm out, but it also brings tears to my eyes. I'm never one to be crying in front of everybody, but that meeting's got me so fuckin' heated that this time, the tears do fall.

Luckily, the first person to see me crying as I step foot in the hall is Prez as he happens to be walking by with his happy-go-lucky look he always has when walking around this trash ass school. His smile disappears when we lock eyes, and without hesitation, he pulls me close for a hug.

That makes me cry harder.

"What's wrong, LaLa?" he questions.

"Can we just get away from this office? Let's go to the cafeteria or something," I weep, and he turns me away from the office so fast, I could thank him for the rest of my days. I just hope I don't see Andre on the way there. If I do, I may not come back to school ever again.

When we get to the lunchroom, we find a spot in the corner somewhere and he wipes the tears from my eyes.

"What's going on?" Prez asks.

"Coach was at my meeting just now with Ms. Evans. He said that he's gonna replace me with Alaysia on our team as the head pitcher and for the Senior Leagues if I mess up one more time. Even if it's something little. He's telling her today, and he said I have to be there when he tells her."

Prez gasps. "What? Damn. Not Alaysia..."

"Yes."

"Why?"

"Because I got suspended."

"But this ain't the first time you've been suspended."

"I know. He's not trying to give me any chances."

"You had to have done something more. I don't think he would try and replace you with your enemy while also having you there while he tells her. That's kinda cruel, don't you think?" Prez asks.

"It is! I'm so mad, Prez. I don't know what to even do right now."

"Well, we gotta go to math, that's what we do next." He smiles.

"I know that, but you know what I mean, Prez." I roll my eyes. I don't have time for his stupid corny jokes right now.

"I hear you. I'm just playing," he responds.

I wipe more of my tears away and am about to get up to head to class, but Prez's eyes lift as if he's giving someone his attention. I follow his gaze, and Jarell's standing there. Ugh!!! I wish he would just get lost, my GOD!

"Hi..." Prez greets him cautiously.

"Hey, how you doin'? I'm sorry to interrupt. I heard my little sister talking on my way out, and just want to talk to her real quick." Jarell nods. Luna settles in front of us and stares ahead, getting accustomed to the new environment.

"Oh, it's no problem. I didn't know you were her brother. It's finally nice to meet you since she never really talks about her family. I like your dog, too. Can I pet it?"

Jarell smiles. "Unfortunately, no because she's working. She's my service dog since I'm blind."

"Oh, my bad." His head dips. "I didn't know. Well, I'm Preston. She calls me Prez, though. I'm the one who tries to keep LaLa out of trouble." He slaps his chest with bravado.

"Oh, cool. LaLa, huh?" Jarell chuckles. "That's the first time I've ever heard anyone call her that."

"You know... nicknames are reserved for best friends." Prez smirks and shrugs in jest.

Jarell laughs again. "Well, it's nice to meet you. I'm Jarell, Kylah's older brother. It's nice that you're looking out for her. She needs good, positive friends," he says, and then shifts his attention to me.

"What do you want?" I mumble. Whatever upbeat energy they got going on between each other, I refuse to engage.

Before he speaks, Jarell sucks in a breath. "Kylah, I don't wanna say much in front of your friend, but you gotta stop acting like this. I'm trying really hard..." he whispers the last sentence as his eyes move to the ceiling as if he's holding something in.

I explode.

"Get away from me, Jarell! Who cares that you're supposedly trying hard? It's your fault I'm even in this situation. You brought Coach here to this stupid meeting, and now, I only have one chance to be perfect to play in the biggest tournament of my life. Fuck you."

"Kylah!" Prez exclaims, giving me wild eyes. "Yo, that ain't cool at all. What's your problem?"

"I don't care, Prez."

Imaginary smoke seems like it releases from my nose again as Jarell gives me an intense look I've never seen before. It's one hundred percent loaded with a whole lot of feelings I can't decipher.

Deep down, I'm mad at myself for saying it, and the look on his face makes me want to instantly take it right back, yet there's this ugly part of me that rises and prevents the apology from forming. Instead, I dig my heels further in.

"I said get outta my face."

Jarell doesn't say anything else. He just wraps Luna's leash around his hand and tells her to find the exit. And he walks away. When they're out of earshot, Prez snaps his head to me.

"Yo, what the fuck, LaLa? What's *wrong* with you, man? Why are you so angry and mean all the time?"

"You don't understand, Prez. He's literally made my life so much worse in ways you have no clue," I say.

"Well, can you tell me?" he questions. "What did he do so bad that you'd say something like that? Are you overexaggerating?"

"No, I'm actually not. Come on. Are we going to math class or not?" I rise from the lunch table and put a hand on my hip.

"Nah." His eyes relax, and he gives me an unwavering gaze. "I'm tired of you pushing me away when I ask you what's going on. You wanna be close with me and all, calling me your 'best friend,' but you never let me in. Plus, what you said to him was mad rude. I ain't cool with that LaLa."

"Because, Prez! It's not your business!"

"Fine," he utters and starts walking away. "You know what? I hope Alaysia gets the pitching spot over you. Because your attitude is trash."

Without another word, Prez continues on his way without me.

"Wait, Prez!" I call out, but he doesn't stop. He just keeps it moving as if I said nothing at all.

"Fuck," I whisper and put my head in my hands.

Because the last person I need to lose is Prez, since everyone else is ganging up on me.

Chapter Eight

I WOULD HAVE never bet in a bajillion years that something like today would happen. A day Prez is so mad with me that he won't even acknowledge me. Much less, *look* at me. After he left the cafeteria following my outburst at Jarell, I tried talking to him multiple times throughout the day to apologize, but he kept ordering me to get away from him. By the end of the day and after many failed attempts, I gave him his space.

School is out, and I sprint out the building so fast to get on the bus that I'm sure I run a few kids over to get there, especially since Prez and I aren't leaving together like normal. All I want to do is go home and draw. Draw Prez's face the moment I yelled at Jarell.

Can't describe it. Can only draw it.

I move like a slug after getting dropped off. Facing Jarell after everything that happened today is like being forced to enter a cage with the calmest lion on Earth. You never know what he's thinking, if he's in the mood to snap, or if he just doesn't care enough to.

When I walk inside the apartment, my instant view is PDA with a taller Jarell hugging Brooklyn's chunky curves from behind with his chin on her shoulder as she cooks their late lunch at the stove. Flowy Christian R&B music plays in the background, setting the ambience for their affection as she sings along to the lyrics while they rock in gentle fashion from side to side.

She sounds like an angel. I picture myself sitting at the table with a hand on my chin, watching her get into her singing bag with dreamy eyes, but... we live in reality and not in dreams.

Just as I close the front door, Jarell smiles and kisses her jaw multiple times.

"Sing it, baby," he whispers, and kisses her again. "You always sound amazing."

She giggles and elbows him in the stomach in a joking way. He stops with a smirk. Neither of them pays me any attention, and that's if they even realized I've walked through the door. In the small pause of her singing, Jarell opens his mouth and begins picking up where she left off, singing the worship song.

Oh God. He sounds like a dying cat.

Brooklyn turns around and looks him upside the head and bursts with uncontrollable giggles, attempting to stop him by shushing. He just laughs right along with her with no shame.

It seems like she forced this whole religion idea on him too because when I first moved here, Jarell wasn't as open about God, Jesus, and the Bible. At least not while I was around. I mean, he was into it because of his music playlist that he always looped, which drove me nuts, but he definitely wasn't as forward about it until she came into the picture.

Sometimes I'd come home from school or softball practice and overhear them praying in his room, mostly about peace of mind, praying for those less fortunate and poor, the city of San Diego, and... even me, my future, and my plans. But I know prayer doesn't really work. It's like asking the wind to make moves on your life because I mean, who really listens to prayer? It can't be God. If there is a God. I can pray for my parents back all I want, but that's not happening, so why would any other prayer work?

Once I muster up the energy to move after closing the front door as quietly as possible, I try to sneak by unseen like I always do to go to my room, but Brooklyn's eyes meet mine, and a huge smile on her face results from it.

Fuck.

"Hey, Kylah!" she calls and shifts her body so that Jarell can't hold her anymore. He rolls his eyes and steps back. He thinks he talks shit quietly under his breath, but I hear it. Don't know exactly what he says, but it's not positive. Brooklyn continues. "I know I don't normally do this, but can I talk to you?"

"What is it?" I mutter and turn to her.

"Jarell, the food is just about done. Can you do one last taste test, baby? I wanna talk to Kylah," she says and gives him a peck on the lips after she hands him a food filled stirring spoon. Yuck.

"Of course. Good luck," he whispers and gives her another kiss.

Again. Yuck. When they're done doing their sappy crap, Brooklyn gives her attention to me and grins before she takes a few steps forward.

"Are you sure it's okay that we talk? Why don't we go to your room?"

"I guess," I say and head there without another word.

I'm so tired of being mad at everybody that I've surprised myself when I invite her to such a special place as my room. It's so sacred – where I feel the safest. I dream here. Cry here. Draw here. Goal set here. Find remorse here. And anything else that I don't show to the world.

When we enter, I move some fluffy pillows on my bed away to allow more space to sit. Once there's enough, I crawl to my favorite corner and snuggle with my oversized teddy bear.

What does she want with me?

"How was your day at school?" Brooklyn questions in a ditzy way, looking square at me with all teeth. Damn, don't her cheeks hurt? Either way though, I can't help but admire her for a second.

One thing about Brooklyn – she's stunning. I'm shocked every day that she isn't an Instagram influencer or in fashion blogs. Her mocha brown skin, similar to Jarell's, has golden undertones like royal, smoky quartz without a single imperfection in sight with a spirally afro. I don't know how, where, or what Jarell does to pull such beautiful girls, but at least he's got that going for himself.

My eyes shift away before this becomes too uncomfortable and answer her. "You already know how my day went. I'm sure Jarell talked to you."

"Touché." Her voice shakes while rubbing her hands together. When she struggles to get out the next thing she's thinking, I don't hesitate to break the discomfort.

"Brooklyn, what do you want from me? Whatever it is, just say it."

It's silent for a little while as I watch her, still, hesitate to say what she means.

"I'll just be honest with you because it's what you deserve. I want you to know that I care about your brother. A lot. I see a long term future with him, God willing. And I know if he's in my future, you are, too. I just want to develop a positive relationship moving forward, Kylah. I'd love to get to know you more."

She pauses for a second to gauge my emotion, but I don't give her much. In response, she fidgets with the bottom of her shirt and bites her lip before continuing.

"I enjoy getting to see a side of you on the softball field that I don't get to see at home. You are such a talented and dedicated athlete who loves what she does. But I hardly know you outside of that. To be honest, I hear or see a lot of the bad. I also know that's not who you are though. I want to be able to bond with you and do other things outside of softball that you may like."

I blink with raised brows and nod, tilting my head from side to side to weigh the pros and cons. *Hmph.* Nice of her. At least she cares enough to try. It's more than I can say about a lot of people. I can give her that.

"Thanks, Brooklyn, but I don't think you should force a relationship with me because of Jarell."

"It's not that at all," she counters. "I just think it's important to develop genuine relationships with those your brother loves, too."

I scoff. "Jarell doesn't love me. He might put up this front for you and share all the things he says he's doing to support me, but he doesn't *love* me. That ship sailed years ago."

I squeeze my teddy bear tighter. Her body shifts awkwardly. The way her eyes wrinkle, she wants to challenge that, but holds back.

"Well... I can't speak for Jarell, and you and him are going to have to figure that out on your own together. But what I can do is speak for myself. I know you don't really like me either, just based on the way you react when I'm here. But I just want you to know I'm willing to start fresh, earn your trust and connect with you. You can decide what and how that looks. Maybe after a while, you'll start to think differently about who I am. I know I'm willing to think differently about who you are."

I shrug, but my belly warms. It means a lot to hear that. Especially since no one ever wants to know the true me. And especially since today was so bad. I need a win … and some love.

"Cool. I'm down, as long as you're not trying to be my mom. Don't think that the start of you getting to know me is putting you on a path to parent me because you're with Jarell and he takes care of me. If that's your intent, then you can call this whole thing off right now."

She looks at me with a twinkle in her eyes that also holds some humor.

"Jesus, girl, you're so smart. But that's not my intention. My only motive is to love Jarell and his family. That's all. From what I know and understand, you are the only family he has, so that makes it even more important for me to do my job to love you, too."

"That's fine. Thanks for being honest, but you also gotta show me you mean what you're saying," I reply. "Or else this won't work, either."

"That's no problem. So, let's start with this. What do you like to do other than softball? I'd love to start being invested in the things you care about, too."

I put a finger on my chin. "I love to draw and do art stuff. I have a good imagination."

"Oh word? I didn't know that about you. Do you have drawings or artwork that I can see?"

"I do have a lot of drawings, but I'm not showing them to you. They're very private. No one has seen them."

"Okay, that's fair. Maybe one day I can take you to a paint and sip. Without the sip. And we can create something more public or make something together." She smiles and then laughs.

"That would be dope," I say.

"Perfect! What else do you like to do?"

"Shopping and roller skating are cool, too. That's about it."

"Okay, same. If I could shop every day of my life with unlimited money, I would. We can do those things one day, too. I need more clothes anyway. Are you interested in church at all?" she questions.

Is she crazy? She knows better than to ask me that. "Hell no. That's the one thing I don't like that you did. You turned Jarell into some religious freak. I'm not about to be turned into that."

Brooklyn chuckles again.

"Girl, Jarell was already well on his way to being all about Jesus before we started dating. He made *me* more unapologetic and less embarrassed by it. Said he wasn't always like that, either."

"He wasn't..."

"Yeah. He shared that he's had a hard life. I don't know all the details, but he said God was the last resort for him and admitted He should've been the first to begin with. Becoming a believer has changed his life."

As she's saying all this, I pause and squint. The very soft spot I have deep inside for Jarell activates, wanting to know more. What hard life has Jarell had? He left his family, me and Mama, for years by choice. From my understanding, if life was hard, it was because he *chose for it to be hard.* So what happened beyond that?

"That's... interesting... and maybe a lie, but whatever. Why are you telling me all this anyway?" I question, shaking my head. "Jarell being a religious freak is not my problem."

"Just a conversation. I think you'd benefit from a relationship with God though, Kylah. It's better than you think."

"I'm not doing it, Brooklyn. So just drop it. Besides, if God was even a little bit of a decent God, he wouldn't have let what happened to my parents happen."

"Hey, you never know. The situation you're in might be the very thing God was trying to place in your life for things to get better and for you to live up to everything you want to be. Because God still loves you. Jesus loves you."

I roll my eyes.

"Mmm, yeah. Right. Time's up. I gotta go to practice," I say and rise from the bed toward my gym bag. "Can't even be ten seconds late today."

"Okay. Well. It was good talking with you, Kylah. I'm so glad you took the time to. Let's go shopping soon," Brooklyn says and stands to her feet.

"Just let me know when," I reply and walk out of my room with all of my gear toward the front door.

Brooklyn follows shortly behind, and I make my way past the kitchen where Jarell is already sitting at the table eating, with two other plates made. Brooklyn sits at one of them, and the other remains untouched. Man, I can really go for that right now – I haven't eaten at all today. But the way accountability from Coach is set up ...

I have to skip out.

And I would rather go hungry than to sit next to the man who caused all the unnecessary stress to happen today. Period.

~ ~ ~

When I make it to the diamond, very few of my teammates are here. Maybe like one or two other girls, and Coach is near the dugout looking at his playbook without any awareness of who is or isn't arriving to practice. *Hmph.* I don't even know why he made a big deal about me being here early. He wouldn't have known if I had come early or late anyway. I take another route to the dugout just so I don't pass by him. If he says anything I'll listen to, it needs to be him apologizing for humiliating me in front of my teachers and Jarell.

I sit in my favorite spot in the corner and get my gear prepared before I take one of the bats and practice my swing just outside the dugout. I get into a groove and almost forget anyone exists until Coach, from afar, starts to walk in my direction. I roll my eyes and go back to the dugout to sit and maybe avoid him. But unfortunately, he follows.

"Kylah." Coach greets me with a nod. I stare straight ahead. "Thanks for being here on time." I nod back, but that's as far as acknowledging him goes. I don't know why he thinks that's an invitation for him to sit next to me, but he does. "How did the rest of your school day go? Got that progress report for me?"

I shrug while digging in my bag for my cleats to change into and come across the progress report I'm supposed to complete each day. I forgot about that thing, so I'm glad I remembered to mindlessly stuff it in my bag earlier. I pass it to him, and he scans it with meticulous eyes, carefully taking note to see if something went wrong after our meeting.

"Looks like the rest of your day was decent... according to your teachers," he says. "I knew you could do it."

I take off my everyday shoes and pick up my batting gloves. In the pocket of growing silence, Coach sighs and places an unwanted hand on my back.

"Kylah. I'm doing this because I want you to succeed. You will not be able to succeed if you're throwing your life away at school with bad choices."

Still, he gets no attention from me, but he keeps going...

"You can't operate in the real-world treating people like the way you have. My God, Kylah, you have such a bright future in softball ahead of you. You're so good, I see you going pro in the Olympics one day. But the other part of being an incredible athlete is being a great human being. You have to start working on that now because you've got a long way to go."

As he talks, the tears well. I keep my eyes away. Why do people talk about me as if I'm the worst girl on the planet without considering how other people and their choices have, at times, determined how I respond? I can't understand how or why I'm always the problem.

"Are you hearing me, Kylah?"

It's just enough time for the waterworks to clear at the bottom of my eyes before they fall down my cheeks. Once I'm confident the tears are gone, I give him laser eyes that I know burn his face. He dishes an unreadable look in return, shaking his head like there's no hope for me.

As more of my teammates arrive and slice into the tension between Coach and me, his face lights up at one of their arrivals. I follow his gaze, and it lands on Alaysia. Ugh! This conversation ain't over – by far!

"Alaysia!" Coach calls out.

"Yeah, Coach?"

"Come here for a second."

There's no way for me to maintain the silent treatment after that. With a swift jerk, I growl, cross my arms, and slam my back against the concrete wall.

Alaysia's stupid ass comes sauntering over, and I'm immediately disgusted. When she's close enough, her eyes ping pong between me and Coach with confusion as to why she's there, and the second our eyes meet, I intentionally roll mine and look away.

"Have a seat, Alaysia. Next to me over here."

Alaysia sits on the other side of me so that Coach is in the middle of us.

"Let's talk for a minute. I think both of you girls are great on the field at what you do, and you certainly have strengths no other team comes close to being blessed enough to have. But! Alaysia, I brought you over here specifically to discuss an opportunity for you to be a leader again. I don't want to get too much into your teammate's business, but regardless of all her strengths and talents, Kylah has a lot to work on to keep the lead pitcher position that she earned away from you last season."

If she wasn't sitting here, I'd be bawling right now... and maybe pounding Coach in the face. This bench we're sitting on just needs to go ahead and swallow me whole...

"In case things fall apart where she's not leading the team in the circle, I need you to be prepared to take the starting pitching spot. That means, during practice, no more gossiping and getting in the middle of drama the way you do sometimes. You need to be locked in because that starting spot is on the horizon for you."

On the horizon? Does Coach really think I can't rise to the expectation of staying out of trouble? Does he not believe in me? I sink further into the bench. My skin pebbles to the point where I can hardly breathe. *Count to ten in your head, Kylah. So that you won't knock his head off.* I can't see her, but it's like Alaysia's voice has been lit by the sun.

"Coach, that's amazing! I've been waiting for this moment, so you know I'll be locked in," she squeals.

"I know you have. My only suggestion is to be ready. That's all."

"You got my word. Thanks, Coach. You're the best," she says

sweetly, and stands to her feet. When I look up, she's already gifting me a devious smirk and walks away. I blink, while my fists become tight balls underneath my armpits.

When Alaysia is clear out of the dugout, Coach says, "Now that's that. Hopefully this is motivation for you to keep it together."

Without another word, he walks away to get practice started now that the whole team is here. When he's gone, I release what's been building up inside and the tears come thick and heavy. Another one of my teammates, who is a real friend, Tina, notices me right away and comes over to sit next to me before flipping her brunette hair to her back.

"Hey. What happened? What's wrong? I saw you and Alaysia talking to Coach as I was walking up..." she says.

"It's nothing." I sniff.

"I know it's something," she objects and gives me a side eye, shaking her head. "You don't have to tell me, but I'll say this. Coach has got to stop bringing you around Alaysia. Doesn't he know you hate her?"

"He don't care," I mumble.

"I just think it's wrong. She's so annoying, too. But I know why she's gunning for you though."

"Why?"

"Well, my parents talked to her parents at one of our games last year, and I overheard them one day. They said you're standing right in her path of a full ride scholarship to a private high school for softball next year so that she can get into the college she wants. She's trying to be the starting pitcher there, but she doesn't get much playing time in the circle because of you, which takes away the scouts seeing her play the position. So, she's doing anything she can to dethrone you to prove herself."

I sigh and stand up, this time, with such a resolve that I can feel my chest flexing while I start to channel my tears of anger into a whole 'nother set of thoughts. "Thanks for the info. Let's go. I'm ready to practice."

Tina gives me a look of sympathy, but I don't care about it. We walk together toward the diamond to meet up with everyone else.

Forget all this sad shit.

Alaysia is my target, and I'm not letting my foot off her neck when it comes to destroying her on the field tonight. From the sprints to the drills, to the scrimmage, I pledge to beat her in everything. After tonight, she's gonna wanna quit. She's never gonna even think she'd be able to take my spot again. She's gonna need to go to another team, especially if she wants that scholarship because she ain't gonna get it playing on this team. And same with Coach. I'ma make him eat those words. Make him wish he never had a thought to replace me.

And that's exactly what I do.

Any running we do, I come in first place... by a large stretch. Any at bat we practice, I hit the ball further than she and anybody else does. Coach doesn't acknowledge it like he normally would. He's trying to act like he's not bothered, but I'ma show him where it really matters.

The scrimmage.

Coach divides us into our normal evenly matched squads with me as the pitcher on team one and Alaysia the pitcher on team two. The scrimmage is a tight game with us going back and forth up to the final inning, and my team is down four to three. I'm up to bat with two outs and two on base – one in scoring position and one on first.

When I walk up to home plate, I don't even give Alaysia my gaze.

I keep the focus on my routine. I lift the bat up at eye level, stare at it for a second, and get into my stance.

I'm a lefty, and most pitchers hate pitching to us. That includes Alaysia. She's had a few times where she's struck me out, but today? I'm on a whole 'nother level of locked in that I feel out of body at the moment. Too in the zone. And my foot remains on her neck.

Alaysia throws the first pitch. Let's see what she's got.

It's kinda in the zone. Wait... I think it's a little too wide. Woah. I can't decide. I squint and don't swing.

"Strrriiikkeeeee!"

Dang it. Alright. I'll secretly admit that was a good ass pitch. *Focus, Kay Kay. Focus. You cannot let her strike you out. You've got two outs, and if you strike out, it's over.*

I close my eyes, take a deep breath, and I get in my stance again. Alaysia's got a smug. It just makes me madder. I grip the base of the bat tighter.

I wait for what seems like forever. She's taking longer than usual, trying real hard to give me some heat. Another pitch slips from her hands. I squint to analyze it as it comes barreling toward me. It spins a little strange. My brain clicks. Ooh yeah. I know what this is. Curveball.

With my back leg grounded and keeping my eye on the ball, I swing at the hips and send the bat all the way through.

CRACK!

It connects. Hard. When my bat finally stops its momentum, I just stare Alaysia down. I don't even watch the ball because I know I sent it into the woods. Gone.

"That's game, bitch," I say to her. We win. Six to four.

"YEAAAAHHHHH!!!!!!"

My team comes rushing out of the dugout to meet the homecoming at the plate. My enemy won't dare look me in the face. She just turns her back to the celebration. I run all my bases, make it to home plate, and my team cheers and pats me on top of the head.

"Kylah, you're like the best player I've ever seen in my life!" Tina exclaims. "I can't wait for the Senior Leagues to play with you!"

As the dust settles and practice is over, I gather all my belongings before I walk home. I'm usually the last one out of the park because I'm either stretching or still working on my game, but this time, I leave in the middle of the pack. Coach is at the edge of the parking lot, giving each of my teammates a farewell until I reach him. He looks like he's going to say goodbye with a smile like he did to everyone else, but as soon as he realizes that it's me, an uncomfortable look washes over him. I shake my head. *How pathetic.*

"You might wanna think twice about her taking my spot. You'll get embarrassed just like how she got embarrassed tonight." I stare him down dead in the eyes before looking him up and down and walking away.

When I make it home, Jarell and Brooklyn have their worship music on at kind of a loud volume, which I'm thankful for this time because then they won't hear me come in the house. I tiptoe ahead and toward the living room. They both are on their hands and knees, holding each other's hands and praying. I don't bother to lean in and listen to their prayers this time. I take that opportunity and advantage to go unseen, like I've always been trying to do and failing miserably. I go to my room, shut the door, and head straight to bed. It doesn't take long for me to fall into a deep slumber.

Chapter Nine

MY BRAIN IS *scattered. I attempt to type a full sentence for my essay that's due tomorrow, but end up typing the sentence halfway, only to finish the rest of the sentence with the last pieces of lyrics I hear from the loudspeakers booming against the walls.*

"Ughh!" I rumble and pound my fist on the desk.

Slamming my school Chromebook lid closed, I yank my room door open with so much force that the doorknob barrels into the wall. I storm out and head directly to the commotion. It's like the bass of the song is attached to my organs because it rattles my entire insides.

"Yo, can y'all get out of our house? It's a school night and I'm trying to get my homework done!" I yell at Mama and the four guys in the house after turning off the blaring music. If we get another noise complaint, I'm sure we'll get kicked out. The police have already been here one time too many.

"That's yo' baby girl, 'Diya?" One of the guys slurs to my mom while ogling my shape like he's trying to teleport the clothes off my body. "How old is she?"

I squirm as if a hundred centipedes crawl all over me.

"Don't be looking at her like that. Fuck is wrong with you?" Mama thunders with red eyes.

Shame rises in his expression, but he reluctantly tears his eyes from my body.

"Baby girl, go back to your room. You don't need to be around all these men. I don't want them looking at you all perverted like that," Mama orders, and she's got a slight slur to her words, too. I look at the coffee table in front of her, and she's got a few cans of what says Four Loko. The two guys who sit on either sides of her have their cans in their hand or on their lips with the bottom up.

"But Mama, I can't even concentrate on my homework with all the music, the laughing, and the partying. When are they going to leave?" I complain.

"They'll be gone in a minute," she answers.

"A minute? Why can't they go now?"

"Aye, get this little girl up outta here, man we tryna have a good time," a third guy, who walks in from the kitchen, says to Mama with a scornful look before turning to me. "Aye little bitch, go to your room."

"Woah, you better watch your mouth talking to my daughter like that," Mama stands up and yells at the guy, but he steps to her and raises a fist. Mama instantly cowers and sits down.

"That's what I thought," the guy says with a satisfied nod.

The contents of my stomach bubble, and it almost comes up. I don't know whether to run to protect Mama or run to my room. My legs are like cinder blocks after that. I've never seen Mama this way. I shake my head. Can't believe what I'm seeing... man I wish Jarell was here to protect her. Protect us. These guys wouldn't dare do all this if he was here.

"Man, y'all doing too much," one of the guys with the Four Loko cans says. "Let's give her her shit so we can go," says the same guy who was looking at me.

"What shit?" I ask. "What shit is he talking about, Mama?"

Mama points. "Girl, I done told your butt about being in grown folks business. You're eleven. Go to your room like that man said. You don't need to worry about what's going on out here."

"Well, yeah I do because whatever he's talking about, you're just gonna take it and act all crazy. I don't wanna see you like that anymore, Mama," I say, the tears welling up in my eyes. "I love you."

"I love you, too, baby, but Mommy is fine, okay? I'm just having a good time. Can you go to your room? I'll have them out of here soon. I promise," she says with soft eyes.

I want to believe Mama. I really do, but I look up to see the man pulling a few orange pill bottles out of his bag. It makes my stomach jump, and the contents of my dinner from this evening fills my mouth, but I swallow it back down.

I guess the orange bottles are the "shit" he's talking about...

I go to my room, but I leave the door open, watching the shadows on the wall to keep track of what they're doing. Eventually, Mama takes the pills from the guy, knocking a few back and swallowing them with her Four Loko can. But she doesn't just take a sip. I watch her throat against the wall... gulp... gulp... gulp... The sound of an empty can slamming on the coffee table echoes to my room. I squeeze my eyes shut, and tears release from their corners.

And after about five minutes, I watch her fall into a passed out slump on the couch as the guys around her laugh... and then surround her.

I shut my door, lock it, and move my desk against the door to barricade it.

I don't want to see what will happen next.

I refuse to.

~ ~ ~

"Arrrgggghhhh!!" I yell at the edge of my dream.

With my face buried in my pillow, tears begin to soak it. Jarell can probably hear it this time, but somehow, I don't care. My stomach is in knots. Knots of longing and a deep desire to hug Mama. Especially after today. Especially after the encounters with Coach Harper.

I cry and cry and cry until my head starts pounding. Maybe I'm not so loud. Because Jarell doesn't come to my door. Not to check on me, not to comfort me, or anything. Deep down, I wish Jarell would. I'm at a point of breaking. Maybe we can talk. Maybe he can tell me why he'd leave me and Mama to suffer the way we did. There's gotta be a reason... right? It would mean the world to me to hear the truth because I really, really need it. I'm tired of feeling so alone and lost in the whirlwind of guessing. That's the real torture.

Chapter Ten

I **BARELY SLEPT** through the rest of the night after I finally stopped crying. I don't care. I've got to take care of business with Prez before I go to school today. I can't take his silent treatment for too much longer. My other friends at school are okay, but they don't mean anything close to what he means to me.

Since I've known Prez, I've never known him to be petty or hold grudges against anyone, so it's confusing. He won't even answer my emails. I keep thinking back to what I said to Jarell that might've set Prez off, but I can't think of anything that grave to the point where he'd drop me like a hot potato and leave me there.

So, I leave Jarell's apartment super early to the point where the sun barely peeks over the horizon. He's in the living room doing pushups with headphones on, oblivious to my exit, and I walk to Prez's house. When I walk up to his porch, I just stand there for a second before knocking.

I hadn't even thought about what the hell I'm even gonna say to him. Ask why he's so mad? Apologize? What would I be apologizing for?

Plus, this is unfamiliar territory. It ain't like I come over here often. Prez and I are close, but I've been here maybe three times tops, and in all those three visits, the porch was the furthest I've made it to his world because it was always for us to go to the park and play. Any interaction with his mom had been at the park itself.

Swallowing and building courage, I knock on the door. After a long pause, it swings open, and there he is, standing behind the threshold.

"Hey, Prez." I meet his gaze for a short second before shifting my eyes back to the ground. My skin warms faster than a space heater.

"Hey."

At least his voice is soft and inviting. I look back up to see if his face matches his tone, and it does. My lips curl up a little bit. At least I got that going. I stuff my sweaty hands in my jogger pockets.

"Prez, I'm sorry for whatever I said or did. I didn't think you'd be so mad with me," I say.

He shrugs. "I'm still kinda mad, no cap."

Back to the ground my eyes go.

"Oh... well... can I make it right? Somehow?" I look up, and his soft expression has already shifted to unconcerned. I continue, desperately. "Please. This is so weird."

He sighs. "Come in."

He steps aside and allows me to enter his home for the very first time. After he shuts the door and steps out of my way, I take in my surroundings with a full and slow spin. The house isn't flashy, fancy, or mansion-like, but it's cozy with a lot of charm. There's a ton of photos on the walls of different people of all colors, shapes, ages, and sizes. Are they Prez's family?

When my attention leaves the photos, a cool fireplace with multiple colors is built into the wall with a TV mounted above it, but the couch and chairs are vintage. The lighting gives a soft ambience, giving the whole room a sort of heavenly glow. It's modern with a traditional twist. The vibe fits though! Super unique and a place you'd wanna return to.

When I was growing up, back when Jarell lived with Mama and me, I remember our home being very dark, regardless of the time of the day. I'd just be flipping the light switches on and off, on and off, believing they were broken. I just knew, on a magic flip with one of my magic hands, light would appear. It never came.

Jarell's place isn't much better. It's not like things don't work or the lights don't come on. It's just... such a dude's place. The living room has standard charcoal gray furniture, all the same design with basic black end tables and a TV on some cheap plastic stand. No wall decor, no nothing. He only has the necessities with no fun or character. Or anything that makes it feel like home. Wished I lived here instead with all their memories and people. *We have no happy memories we can just put up on display.* And any we do have had been drowned with so much misery that the memories might as well not even exist.

My stomach turns at the thought.

I walk deeper into Prez's living room and approach a small wooden end table with a picture on it that catches my eye. Before I can pick it up and look, thumping footsteps bounce down the carpeted stairs. When new faces appear, it's Prez's mom Miss Juanita and, I think, his dad. I don't know his name though. Never met him.

My immediate thought is that I'm completely wrong about who Prez looks like. I've always thought Prez looks a lot like Miss Juanita. But now, seeing his dad? It's like he cloned himself. He's got the same golden-brown skin and a killer smile just like Prez. Only difference is that he's got a beard, and his hair is not a curly fro'.

His tiny mom looks like what most people think a stereotypical Puerto Rican looks like. Her smile isn't as perfect, but man is it warm! Kinda reminds me of Mama sometimes.

"Kylah!" Miss Juanita greets me and moves quicker down the steps. She pulls me in for a light hug. I easily accept. "I haven't seen you in a while. How are you, mamacita? Softball superstar?"

"I'm okay," I reply.

"It's good to see you. Is everything okay?" she asks.

"Mmm hmm." I nod, though my body is kinda quaking inside. I've never had Prez so upset with me nor giving me the silent treatment like this, so I'm unsure what to really expect. I am glad, though, that they interrupted us so I wouldn't have to talk to him right away. I still haven't quite found the words to say.

"Kylah, huh?" Prez's dad's voice booms once he's down the stairs. He leans against the wall with a curious look at me – eyes squinted, head tilted and all. "I've heard a lot about you."

I clear my throat. "Really?"

"Yep. But the thing is – Preston – I thought you had a girlfriend already? You have a new one? Or... now do you have two?"

Miss Juanita rolls her eyes and waves him off.

My heart tanks to my toes, so I just know the color in my face does, too. Oh my gosh. I don't know what it is with everyone thinking I'm Prez's girlfriend. Let alone, enough for me to be sloppy seconds. My hand clutches my temples. Oh geez. I don't think Prez's dad and I will be off to a good start.

"Dad!" Prez exclaims, giving him a wild gaze. Even though Prez's skin is brown, he's still light enough to turn visibly red, which he does. "That's not my girlfriend!"

"What? Why you yelling at me?" his dad objects with innocence and a joking twinkle in his eyes. He winks at me in jest while Prez rolls his like his mom and doesn't see the wink at all. My chest calms down a bit enough for me to laugh. *Whew.* I thought he was serious.

"I only have one girlfriend, and that's Gina," he counters.

"I know, son. I was just messing with you. Looks like you still can't take a joke." He shakes his head, still grinning before he chuckles once more. "It's very nice to meet you, Kylah. I was serious about hearing a lot about you. I'm glad Prez has a good friend in you that also plays baseball."

"Thanks, Mr."

"Robert. Robert Smith, but just call me Rob. Mr. Rob works just fine."

"Okay. I'll call you Mr. Rob."

"Cool."

"Okay, hijos. I am heading out to work with my husband. You two have a great day at school today, okay?"

"Thanks, Miss Juanita," I say and bow my head in respect. She smiles and rubs my back lovingly.

"Oh, and Preston Michael, antes irte a la escuela, necesitas lavar los platos. Deberías haberlos lavado ayer." Miss Juanita talks a thousand miles an hour. It almost sounds like jumble, so my head spins.

Prez gripes under his breath. He understands every word. "Ugh. Sí, Mamí. Sí."

I forget Prez also speaks Spanish. He never really uses it around me, so it throws me off guard to hear him respond.

From whatever she said and how Prez responds, Miss Juanita huffs like she doesn't believe Prez at all. Mr. Rob doesn't either as they give him a look like he's gonna be in trouble later, and then tells us to have a good day at school again. They go out of the front door together, leaving me and Prez alone.

I sigh. *Now what?* I redirect my attention to the picture on the end table that caught my eye just a few minutes ago to use as my scapegoat. I pick it up and stare.

It's a picture of Prez, Miss Juanita, Mr. Rob, and another small boy I've never seen before. At first, I wanna put the picture down because I can't stand seeing the perfect little family. But something else draws me close. A feeling of love and connection blooms like a rose in my chest.

"Prez, who's this?" I ask.

Prez leans in over my shoulder with curiosity. His eyes meet the photo and scans it before he gives me a very small wince like he's in pain and takes a step back.

"What's wrong?" I question with a frown.

"Nothing."

"So, who is it?"

"My little brother," he says with an off-putting attitude and moves toward the kitchen. I follow him, curling my fingers around the picture on my lap, taking it with me.

"Really? I... I didn't know you had a brother. Thought you were the only child," I say.

"I understand why you'd think that." He heads to the cupboard and reaches up high to take out a large bowl.

"How come I've never met him? I feel like he would've been at the park playing ball with you or something by now."

Silence has been the name of the game between us all morning long, so I shouldn't feel so awkward by it but for some reason, the stillness between us right now feels a lot different. It's... loaded.

"I mean…" He pauses. "Isn't it obvious?"

He says this with his back to me, so I don't even get a chance to take his expression all the way in. But what I do have is his tone. An imaginary blow pummels my gut when I connect the dots.

Prez grabs Cap'N Crunch from the top of the refrigerator. He pulls Lactase, which is lactose free milk for the people who get the bubble guts after drinking dairy, out of the fridge and sits at the island counter. The bowl tinkles with little yellow squares before the milk swallows them up. I sit next to him while he slurps and slurps his meal. I kind of want a bowl now, too, but after that stomach punch, the hunger went away.

"Um…" I squawk out and clear my throat once more. "What happened to your brother?"

Prez puts his spoon down and leans back in the chair. He gives me a solemn look with his curls covering his eyes before a sad, but fond smile crawls across his face.

"We were visiting my abuela's house in Puerto Rico for the summer. She has a pool we always swam in, so we couldn't wait to see her. Right before we went to her house, we were at my aunt's house to bring her to Abuela's, too. While we were there, I was really mad because my little brother stepped on my favorite video game. He broke it, so I started yelling at him. We got in a fight. Mamí broke it up and told me it's just a game and that she'd buy me a new one, but I was just so mad, LaLa. I said I hated him because he never gets in trouble for anything. So, we went to Abuela's house without talking to each other, and we got ready to swim. Abuela always tells us to wait for her to get outside before we jump in the pool so she can watch us. But Rico didn't listen and got in the pool. Abuela wouldn't let me out yet and kept me in for a few minutes, telling me to get over my attitude with Rico and make up with him because I was the oldest. When I got out there to apologize to him, I found him. He was... he was..."

"Don't say the rest," I interrupt firmly with a hand up. "I get it..."

He bites his lip and stops talking, but the hurt in his eyes slaps me so hard that mine water. We stay quiet, sitting in the stillness. When I give him eye contact, he doesn't look at me, but when he looks at me, I won't look at him. It's like this for a while until we're almost comfortable with it, but I don't wanna be.

"I'm so sorry, Prez."

He doesn't reply, so I just stare at their family picture again. Dressed in various shades of brown and cream, they all smile brightly in the middle of a colorful forest with leaves surrounding them. Prez has his arm around his little brother, Rico, and their cheeks press together. My goodness. I had no idea Prez feels the same kinda pain I feel of losing someone so close.

"How long ago was this?" I ask.

"The picture or the accident?"

"Both."

"He died two years ago. Around the time you started going to school here. That picture was about a year before it all happened."

"Wow. Well... even though he's gone, you still seem so... happy. Like his death never affected you."

He squints, causing his curls to lie even closer to his eyes. He swipes them away. "What? Why would you even say something like that?" he asks with a hard edge.

I shake my head and put my hands up. "Don't take it the wrong way. I mean it as a good thing. It just... it seems like you're handling this whole... grief thing... better than I ever have. That's all I'm trying to say. I'm sorry if it came off as offensive. I've lost important people, too."

His face relaxes. "Really?"

"Yeah. Both my parents aren't around. That's why I moved out here to stay with Jarell. Well, he forced me here against my will by taking custody of me."

He gives a large head nod with a slightly open mouth with realization.

"What happened to your parents?"

My shoulders drop as I inhale through my nose, hoping he wouldn't ask. I'm sure he felt like since I asked him about his brother and he shared that I'd probably tell the truth about my parents in exchange.

But I won't.

"I-I should go," I stutter. "I gotta get to my bus stop. I just wanted to say that whatever I said to make you mad, I'm sorry Prez. I just want us to be cool again. I hate this whole not speaking thing."

He nods but doesn't say anything, however, his body language screams forgiveness and a desire for us to return to normal. Now that I have my answer of how he really feels about our friendship, I walk away. He doesn't say anything to stop me. I keep moving toward the door with my bag in tow and twist the knob to leave.

"LaLa," Prez calls. A gentle one.

I pause and whirl around to give him my attention.

"It's fine you won't tell me about your parents. I understand how much it probably hurts. But what's going on with you and your brother?" he questions. "Why do you act like that toward him?"

I allow another quiet pause to grow between us. Dropping my bag, I look toward the ceiling. When our eyes meet again, he's still gazing at me, persistent to know more. I cross my arms and lean against the wall nearby.

"It wasn't always this way." Surprisingly, the waterworks start again. I blink to make them go away, and they do.

"We used to be real tight. He was like a dad to me when I was little because we're so far apart in age. Thirteen years. Loved him like I loved no one else. I still lowkey do, and you're the only person I'll ever admit that to. But he just... he did some things that made me lose a lot of trust and respect for him. Things I can't forgive him for."

"Is what he did really that bad to the point where you can't forgive him? Or is it that you *won't* forgive him?"

"I don't know." I take a beat. "Somewhere in between."

"Did he... you know... hurt you?"

I shake my head. "Not in the way you're thinking."

"So then, what?"

"It doesn't matter, Prez. Maybe I'll tell you another time. We should get ready to catch the bus," I say and pull my backpack from the floor. Once it's on my back, Prez keeps watching me, but it's not mean or malicious. Or the annoyed look he'd always give me when I'd cut a conversation short. This time, it's like he wants to give me a hug or something. It's strange. An uneasiness settles in my tummy.

"Why you lookin' at me like that?"

He shrugs. His skin turns slightly red again as if he was wrong for thinking whatever he was thinking.

"I just..." he starts to say, "I just feel sorry for you, LaLa. Whatever it is about your brother, it's got you so messed up that you won't let it go. I guess I felt like that too after Rico died, but then I started to hate feeling so mad and sad all the time. So, I had to... accept it. That it happened, you know?" He walks toward the door and grabs his bag, too. His school bag is much larger than mine. "Maybe if you accept what happened, you won't be so angry."

"I'm not ready to accept what Jarell did," I reply.

"You're gonna have to, someday."

I huff and roll my eyes, opening the front door. "You sound like my therapist." As I step out, Prez pulls a light jacket from a coat hook next to the door and pulls his keys from his pocket to lock the house.

"Maybe you should listen to 'em."

"Hmm. Okay. With your wise, Zen ass. Anyway, I guess I'll take the bus from your stop today."

He smirks and wraps an arm around my neck and over my shoulder as we walk side by side to the bus stop in silence. I don't know what I'm gonna do about Jarell right now. All I wanna do is capture that sweet moment of Prez and his brother. In portrait form.

When we get to school, it's back to business as usual with Prez and I walking the halls side by side. It feels amazing. We stop at my locker to get all my belongings first and greet some of our mutual friends before we head to his to link up with a couple of his baseball friends and some others who don't play ball.

They're cool people, but I don't really talk to them that much. They always seem a little reserved when I come around. I'm not sure if it's because I'm a girl and they secretly crush on me, or if they think I'm crazy because I get in trouble at school a lot, so they don't want to be bothered with me. I haven't asked Prez about it because I'm afraid of the answer, but it doesn't stop the thought from crossing my mind every day. No matter what the answer is, it's always cool to be around them though because they're some pretty decent guys. They're not sleazy assholes a lot of people would expect athletes to be.

Especially Andre.

He's laid back, stays out of drama, and is so unproblematic just like Prez is. But there's a major difference. Prez is cute.

Andre is *fine*.

Tall with skin the color of soil, fluffy lips, his fade neatly tapered, and the straightest white teeth I've ever seen, I never understood why everyone else always made fun of his dark skin, particularly when we first met in the sixth-grade through Prez. He'd never clap back at anyone who talked about him either. Didn't have to. He was so confident in himself in such a humble way that eventually, everyone stopped making fun of him and did whatever they could to be his friend. He was always so nice to the people who talked about him, too. I see why he's the student council president.

Crazy part about this all? Andre and Prez are best friends and have been long before I moved here. Also not surprising since they are cut from the same kindness cloth. I've considered myself lucky to have the opportunity to take in the beauty that is Andre while spending time with Prez without it being all awkward. Neither of them knows my feelings for him though. I'd like to say I've been real slick about it. I'm not that brave to reveal all that yet.

I just don't know if Andre is attracted to mixed girls like me. Sometimes, he doesn't even look my way, but then there are other times where I've caught him taking interest in me when Prez and I are talking. When I'd make eye contact with him because I'd get that feeling someone's watching me, he'd hurry up and look away. But I don't want to jump to conclusions and say that he might be into me. That's a huge stretch.

Prez's locker is open, and he's choppin' it up with his baseball teammate Eleazar in Spanish, so I go to the other side of his locker where Andre's is about two lockers down. He's switching out his shoes for another pair for whatever reason. Now that Prez and I are back on good terms, I'm feeling a little brave today. So, I lean up against the locker near Andre's, but not too close. I need to make it seem like I'm still with Prez and not seeking him out.

"Hey, Andre." I greet him with a sheepish grin.

He briefly gives me his eyes before minding them back on the shoes. "Sup, Kylah?"

"Nothing much." I hug my sketchbook to my chest. I don't know what else to say, so I look ahead and pretend to act normal.

"So…" I start when the silence lingers too long. "When are you gonna come to the diamond and practice with me and Prez? Don't you think you need to sharpen up that swing?"

"How would you know that I need 'sharpening'?" he asks with a slight frown.

Shit. Okay, maybe that wasn't the right thing to say. I clear my throat to say what I mean.

"Everyone who plays does. I'm not saying that you suck or anything…" I shrug.

"Yeah, I mean I could always use practice. But don't y'all be going super late at night? Ma Dukes definitely ain't finna let me out that late. I don't know what y'all parents be doing," he says with a laugh.

"Well… we don't necessarily ask…"

He smiles. "I shoulda guessed that."

"What's that supposed to mean?"

He continues to smirk and shake his head. "Nothing. Besides. Baseball ain't really my thing. That's Preston's thing."

"What's your thing, then?"

"The drums."

I blink. "Really?"

He nods. "Snare drums, to be exact."

"I didn't know that! Where do you play?"

"I play for this junior marching band on the drumline. Our drumline plays a lot for the holidays, like Juneteenth, Fourth of July, and sometimes, we travel and visit HBCUs."

"What's an HBCU?"

His body halts, and he gives me a glare like I should know this. My cheeks burn. "Uh... Historically Black Colleges and Universities..." he answers.

I scratch my head. I guess that's what happens when you come from a family that never went to college, much less graduate from high school. The world of college is incredibly distant, like on another planet. It has never crossed my mind, nor have I even desired to go there.

"Oh..." I mumble.

He chuckles. "You lose points off your Black card for not knowing that."

"I get a pass for being mixed. Mom's Black. Dad's white."

"Yeah, whatever. You're raised Black though. Ain't no way you aren't, just by the way you talk and move." He shuts his locker with a sparkle in his eyes and walks away. I find myself following him with my gaze, still smiling. "See you later, Kylah."

I don't say anything back as Prez wraps up his conversation, and he and I are just about to head off to homeroom when, from a distance, a light voice calls out toward us.

"Preston! Wait!"

I can't tell who it is at first, but it registers when Alaysia comes moseying up, switching her hips back and forth a little harder than usual with her lips puckered. I gag for real. She sees it and flips me off. I lean up against the locker, looking her up and down from head to toe. She speaks back with her eyes, and they tell me to get lost because she's got some private things to talk about with Prez. I shift my weight and plant myself there with no intention to disappear. She huffs at me before giving the prize her attention, flipping the half of her hair that isn't in a ponytail to her back.

"Hey Preston." She greets him with this corny, high-pitched voice. *Ugh.* Where did she learn that talking like this was cute? "Can we talk for a second?"

"Sup, Alaysia," he greets her with a bright tone. "What's good?"

"Nothing much. Just wanted to see what you were doing this weekend."

"Uh…" he stammers, and then blinks. It ain't like Alaysia asks him what he's doing over the weekend often, if at all, ever. That's my job. Or, I guess, Gina's. "I got baseball practice in the morning, but that's it. Why, wassup?"

"It's my birthday on Saturday, and I'm having a party from five to ten at the bowling alley. I'd love for you and some of your crew to come through."

My lip curls before I interject. "You know we have a tournament this Saturday and game at seven at night if we win our first game at three, right?"

Alaysia rolls her eyes and her head toward me.

"Excuse me. No one was talking to you, so mind your business." She pops her pink bubble gum and licks the excess from her overly shiny lips. "Second, I ain't skipping my fourteenth birthday for some game. We will have plenty of other tournaments that'll be way more important than this one. Besides. You should be tryna focus on keeping your position because you know you can't handle yourself enough to keep it."

I don't even say anything. What's the point?

"Nothing to say?" She leans her head toward me and leads with her ear. "That's what I thought, little bitch. Anyway," she says and turns back to Prez.

"Alaysia, you gotta chill. I'll be at your party, though. Thanks for inviting me," Prez says.

"Good. Make sure you bring some of your baseball friends, but honestly, you're the main one I want there. Just don't invite Kylah." She snarls.

I gag harder this time. She gives me a disgusted look.

"I wasn't coming anyway." I shrug. "Trust me."

"Good. I'll see you this weekend, Preston."

When she gives me one last mean mug and a flirty smile to Prez, she walks away, catching up with a few of her girlfriends down the hall. They smile and giggle, whispering unknowns to each other, but they look back and eye Prez with a kind of gross desire while paying no mind to me. He's grinning back at them like an idiot. I smack my lips.

"What?" he asks with his arms out. "What's wrong now?"

"Are you seriously about to go to her party?"

"Yeah, it's bowling. Why not?"

"First, it's Alaysia. You see how she treats me?" I point at my chest. "She just called me a bitch."

"That doesn't have anything to do with bowling."

"Plus, Gina will kill you!"

"I'm not worried about Gina. I'm just going with my crew to have fun, and that's it. Why you so worried about Gina, anyway? You don't even like her, remember?" he says and gives me a side eye.

"No, let me ask you this. Why are you so comfortable with Alaysia talking to me any kinda way? Ain't you supposed to be my best friend?"

He chuckles. "Man, y'all little softball beef ain't got nothing to do with me. That's y'all problem. Plus, she's a girl. My dad taught me to never get into girl drama."

"You know she's flirting with you just to get at me, right? Because she thinks I like you."

He looks me up and down. Slowly. "Does it bother you?"

I squirm a bit, cross my arms, and look away. "Kinda."

"Why? Got something you wanna tell me, LaLa?" Prez says with a smirk, making his deep dimples appear. He steps closer to my face with a lustful look at my lips that makes my stomach nearly flutter to the moon. A kind of look that's got me gasping. In a good way.

I play it off and scoff. "No." I step back while pushing him away. "I don't like you like that with your fat head. You're cute. I'll admit that only because you're my bestie, so don't get no ideas. But Gina can have you. I can do better than you, anyway."

Prez's head tilts back as he bursts with lots of laughs.

"With who? Dang, you ain't have to do me like that."

"Don't worry about with who. I'm just saying. At the end of the day, Alaysia's stupid. She's doing all this with you to make me jealous and to get me to fight with her. She doesn't actually care about being with you, and she doesn't actually like you."

"You're overthinking it. You know I don't care to be with her, either."

"Yeah right. You like that bullshit by flirting back," I say and start to walk to class. He follows. "I'm telling Gina."

"Man. You know Gina will be more mad at you for telling her than she's mad at Alaysia," Prez says.

"I don't care. Give me her number," I say with my hand out and a smile.

"No." He slaps my hand like a high five.

Both of us head to our mutual class without another word about Alaysia and her antics and sit next to one another with an unspoken disagreement about how that whole exchange was handled.

Sometimes, Prez is just way too nice. Or maybe, he's kinda taking this newfound attention he's getting from all these girls to his head because it wasn't always like this. Girls weren't checking for Prez like that last year or our sixth-grade year. I just hope he knows what he's doing to not get caught by his girlfriend with these mindless games he's playing. He shouldn't even be at that party. I just wish it wasn't her to be the one he's toying around with.

Chapter Eleven

INSTEAD OF GETTING on the school bus this afternoon, Brooklyn waits for me outside in her new navy-blue and tinted windowed BMW with the rest of the parents who pick up their kids. That car catches almost everyone's eye as Prez and I walk out of the school with his arm around my shoulder again. He thinks I'm going to the bus with him, but I stop to tell him I'm getting picked up today. Nodding like it's no big deal, he lets me go. I wave to him, and he goes the opposite direction.

As I walk toward the car, Brooklyn is beaming at me in the window with a frantic wave. I can't help but give her a small smile that leads to a snicker. She can be so dorky. It's borderline secondhand embarrassment. But if I was her, I'd be cheesing hard, too, considering I've been hiding from her for the last two years.

Getting in the front seat, I marvel at the interior. Beautiful and sleek tan leather seats with a huge navigation screen. It smells fresh off the lot. Geez, this car is sharp! How'd she get such a luxurious car like this?! I'ma need to find out because if she's been hanging out at our house, and the whole time, she's famous or whatever, I'm gonna have to reevaluate some things.

"Hi Kylah!" she greets me once I'm settled. "How was your day today?"

I lean the seat back to lounge and give my legs some room. "It was cool. Nothing special. Nothing to be giddy like you about."

Her face contorts as she bites her bottom lip. "Well, I hope our time together is special today. I'm so glad you decided to come."

I smirk and give her a side eye. "Yeah. I think everybody standing outside knows you're glad, too."

This time, her head dips while one of her hands fidgets with the front of her shirt as she pulls off. I giggle to myself. It's so easy to throw her off. Let me stop messin' with her.

"Where we going?" I inquire to alleviate her discomfort.

"Hmm, I was thinking of going shopping. Don't think I didn't notice your Jordan shoe collection when you invited me into your room. I think I'm okay with adding to your collection. How does that sound?"

My eyes balloon. Free J's that I don't buy with my allowance? Hell yeah! "That sounds great! Thank you. I haven't bought a pair in a while."

"Cool. I might get a pair myself, depending on what the selection is."

Who just has money laying around to buy TWO pairs of Jordan's in one day? Here I am, thinking she's jobless, yet she's got all this money to blow.

"Can I ask you something?" I question with a slight, pondering frown.

"Of course. Ask away."

"What do you do for a living? I don't really see you working, since you're always at the apartment," I reply.

"I do a few things. I have a couple of cookbooks published that make me a lot of pocket change, and I run a food truck at the beach on the weekends. That's why me and your brother are always cooking. During the week, I work in IT, but I work from home, and I'm off on Monday's."

I nod big. "Oh! That explains why you're always at the house on Monday's."

"Yep!"

"Well, since all those things pay you well, you should buy some decorations and remodel Jarell's apartment," I suggest with snark. "It's so cold living there. It needs a woman's touch."

"You know? I thought the same thing! That I should offer to decorate the house. I need to get permission from him first. If I get the okay, would you help me?" she asks.

"Definitely." My body gestures in agreement. "I've been wanting to do something for the apartment since I moved in."

"Cool. I'll make note of that for the next time we spend time together."

The car ride remains silent except for R&B Christian playing and Brooklyn singing along. She really does have a beautiful voice. What can't this woman do? What the heck does she see in my brother? There are so many other men out there that she could've chosen. Whatever.

The ride isn't long before we reach the mall. Once we're here, we head straight to the shoe stores, starting with Champs. I don't know why, but they always seem to have way more variety than Foot Locker or Finish Line. Everyone seems to be stingy on the selection these days. The in-person stores and their options tend to be super lame. It's like you gotta go online or go to the hole in the wall shoe stores who are not a part of the chains.

Brooklyn and I start browsing, making comments to one another about what's cute, what's not, what's different, and what's trendsetting until we start analyzing what we truly want. Of course, the Retro Jordan selection is scarce with all these knock offs that if I wore 'em, I'd probably get ribbed for days. I give up on the J's in the women's section and move to the men's. I grab a pair of orange and black Air Max and ponder whether I like them.

"So, who's the guy you waved at today before getting in my car? Is that your boyfriend?" Brooklyn suddenly asks as she picks up a women's Timb and examines the boot.

"Oh, Prez?" My smile twists. "That's not my boyfriend. He's my best friend."

She pauses and gives me a long look in disbelief.

"What?!" I ask with my arms out.

She blinks several times, her false lashes fluttering like feathers. "That's not your boyfriend? I find that hard to believe."

"Why? You can believe what you want. I actually hate when people ask me that. It is possible for girls and guys to be friends, you know."

"Okay." She sighs. "It's just that I've experienced too many girls saying that a certain guy is their best friend when they're lowkey dating. Especially with the chemistry between y'all like I just saw."

"Well, that ain't me. And I don't know what chemistry you're talking about, either."

"I guess it's how you both interacted while walking. He had his arm wrapped around your shoulder, and you looked so at ease in a way I'm not used to seeing you. And he's a handsome young fella. You don't find him attractive?"

"That's what homies do when you're cool with each other. And yeah, he's definitely cute, which I've admitted to him, but I've also made it clear that I don't like him like that."

"Do you think Prez likes you? I think he does. It's obvious, and I've only seen y'all interact for ten seconds."

"Maybe. I notice all the times he's tried to flirt with me." I roll my eyes. I put the orange and black AirMax back on the display stand. "I think he just likes to joke around to see how far he can get. But for real, he probably likes the *possibility* of being with me more than the reality. He'd have a hard time with me anyway because I'm a hot head. And he has a girlfriend, too. Her name's Gina, and he's obsessed with her just like she's insanely obsessed with him. She's got him wrapped up."

She raises both brows. "Wrapped up, huh? You think she would approve of him having his arm around you like that?"

I scoff. "Hell no. She doesn't even approve of anyone *looking* at him. Good thing we don't go to the same school. She would murder me."

"Hmm. Interesting," she says as she picks up another shoe, this time, some Crocs. "I'll let it go. Are you interested in dating other boys if it's not Prez?"

"Ugh. No. Boys are a distraction, and 90 percent of them are annoying."

It's true. All of them are super immature. Except for Andre. She don't need to know all my feelings for Andre though, so instead, I say, "I'm too focused on softball right now. I'm tryna to play in the Senior League Tournament."

"Well, that's good that you have a productive focus. Boys can be a headache."

I turn to face her squarely, glaring at her like she's full of it. "If that's the case, then why are you with my brother? How'd you even meet, and what do you see in him?"

I shudder in disgust. I don't know if she picked up on it or not because when I bring it up, she simply grins as if she's been waiting for months for someone to ask her that.

"That is one beautiful man," she mumbles in lust.

I smack my lips and give her a look.

"Alright, sorry. To be serious, you probably already know this, but I met Jarell at church. It was my first time there, trying to find a new church home, so I was shy. When I got there, praise and worship were going, and your brother was just so into it. Singing, praising, and worshipping unapologetically. Something you rarely see in men at church, and it was really attractive to me. I approached him after church just to tell him that I liked how uninhibited he was and realized he was also blind with his dog! That intrigued me even more. We had a nice conversation, exchanged contact info, and then it was history. After about two or three months of talking daily and meeting each other at church, we started dating."

Mmm. I should have known this was the story. Predictable ass story at that. I cross my arms and continue listening.

"Kylah, your brother is a very special kinda guy. Unlike anyone I've ever met. He's super reserved, but so gentle, kind, selfless, a deep thinker, a great listener, and authentic. I love what he does for a living too, teaching little kids to learn Braille since he's fluent. It's so cool to see him have such a positive outlook on life while blind, and he lives like a normal guy. I've never seen him try to be someone he's not. He doesn't pressure romance, he's abstinent until marriage, which I appreciate, and he loves my curves! But most of all? He truly loves the Lord and has a relationship with Him. I'm very lucky to have met someone like him."

I don't say anything. I just huff where she can't hear and pick up some low top Retro Eleven's that catch my eye. When one of the shoe workers walks by, I ask her to fetch me a size eight in men's if they have one available. I move ahead just a little bit to check out other shoes I may want to try. As if feeling the energy between us shift, Brooklyn sighs and stands next to me.

"I understand you and Jarell have a rocky relationship, and I don't know why. That's up to the both of you to repair any damage done, and it seems like things are getting worse between you two. But I don't want to make it seem like I'm saying all these great things about him when you've obviously experienced something different. Just know that if you want to ever talk about it, I'm willing to listen. And I promise I won't go back and tell him. I'm just sharing how I've experienced your brother in the time that I've known him. I'm fully aware my experience is different from yours."

"He's not perfect," I mumble.

"No one is. When you're ready, let me know how I can help. Since my plan is to be with him long term, as I've shared with you before, I'm committed to developing my own relationship with you regardless of how you feel about each other. Whether we work out or not, which I pray that we do, I hope you and I still have a bond. You may not see it, but you are very important to Jarell."

"Well, thank you for genuinely wanting to know me and not just because he's your boyfriend."

Right after I say that, the worker brings out the shoe I want to try on. I sit and take my personal pair off and prepare to try them both instead of just one. Brooklyn sits next to me as she helps take all the paper stuffing out. Once they're ready, I put them on and walk around. When I come back to the bench, Brooklyn's got an orange pill bottle in her hands as she stuffs one of the pills in her mouth. I frown when I see the big letters OXY on the side, but her hand covers the rest.

"What are you doing?" I nearly yell at her, then another breath rises to my throat and lodges there like my airways clam up and close.

"Me?" She frowns, but my attention is mostly on the pill bottle in her hand.

"Yeah... why are you taking those?"

"Oh! I feel the onset of a migraine coming. I get them bad, so they help me out."

"They're opioids..."

"Yeah." She looks at me crazy. "They're meds that help with severe pain."

"Can't you just take Tylenol?"

She pauses. "Uh... I don't think that's any of your business, Kylah. With all due respect."

I press my lips tight and nod, sitting down next to her to take off the shoes. She pulls out a bottle of water from her purse and takes a swig, swallowing the pill.

A growing, intense uneasiness settles in my stomach when I hear the water gulp down her throat. I blink several times to get it out of my head, but for some reason, I can't, and it rattles me to the core.

"Brooklyn, can we go?" I ask, my skin becoming clammy and cold. Oh my God. An impending panic attack is here, and I feel myself heading to a downward spiral. Fast.

"What's wrong?"

"Please." I beg, and tear up, still watching her hold the orange bottle in her hands. My stomach turns, and I look away.

"Kylah, is everything okay?" She stands up, her gaze now holding a significant level of concern. "You're going pale on me..."

"I just want to leave this store. Please. Can you put the pills away so we can go?" I cry as a flashback of Mama passed out on the couch and an empty pill bottle next to her takes over my psyche.

"Okay, okay. What about the shoes?" Brooklyn tosses her medication in her purse.

"I like them. So, let's get them and get out of here."

"Kylah, are you okay? Seriously, you're scaring me..."

"I'd be fine if we could take care of buying these and leave!" I yell to the point where others stop what they're doing to look at me.

"Okay..." she nods frantically. "Okay."

She accepts the shoes without even looking at the price and snags the pair of Timbs she'd been eyeing. After purchasing, we rush out of the store and head into the much cooler hallway and begin to walk with no sense of direction or destination. Brooklyn and I don't exchange words for a little while and let this awkward moment marinate in the pockets of silence as we stroll.

I wipe the remaining tears and sweat from my forehead and take deep breaths to allow the fresh air to penetrate my lungs and the bad memories of Mama fade away. Once they do, I begin to wonder who else saw me freaking out. I put my hand on my forehead. *Nobody I know was there... right?*

"Are you okay? Do you want to go home?" Brooklyn finally breaks the tension between us, still gazing at me with wrinkled brows and scanning me from head to toe.

"I think I'm good now."

"What happened? You didn't start panicking until I took my medication..."

"It's… it's nothing. I'm okay now, Brooklyn. We don't have to go home," I assure her, but my cheeks still bake with embarrassment.

"You sure?"

"Yes. I promise. The last place I wanna go is home. I just… I just needed some fresh air. That's all. Just… please don't tell Jarell, alright?"

Brooklyn doesn't say anything. She just studies my face, searching for the lie I think she's already found. I don't and won't meet her eyes. Thankfully, her gaze retreats and she simply nods with a semi-tight mouth. She almost seems offended that I won't talk, but she doesn't mention it.

I'm eternally grateful.

The rest of the time we spend is her modeling different plus size outfits for me and me giving my honest opinion on how they fit on her chubby body. I have such an athlete's build with strong arms, slender, but muscular legs, and a defined, full six pack with a belly ring I wasn't supposed to get but snuck and got last year with a teammate. Yet the more and more I observe her, I find myself longing for some of the softness she has. I'd love for her to give me more curves, boobs, and femininity. Even a roll or two. I'm way flatter chested than I would like to be.

When she selects the pieces she likes, we head to the register. I don't feel comfortable buying anything else from her since those J's were $230, but she ends up secretly buying me some new joggers I had been staring at to add to my tomboy collection. I had tried them on but put them back on the rack because I didn't want to seem greedy. I don't say anything but give her a grateful look when she hands me the bag after she buys her items.

On our way out of the mall, we stop and look at a few more things in the windows that catch our eye, but we're not serious about buying before heading to the car. We stuff all our bags in the backseat, and she takes me home with a silent ride, except again, for the Christian music playing that I tune out because it all starts to sound the same. When she pulls up to the front of Jarell's apartment, she takes a deep breath and smiles at me.

"Thanks, Brooklyn. I appreciate the clothes," I confess with a small little grin I'm sure she can hardly see.

"I'm glad you did, and I'm glad I got to know you a little better today. I hope we can do these kinds of things more often," she replies without the spunk from earlier.

"I'd like that. Depends on what we do, though."

"We can go shopping for decorations for Jarell's apartment next time. Until then, take care of yourself," she says.

"Will do."

I slide out of the car and take my shopping bags along with me. I'm just about to close the car door, but Brooklyn calls out my name.

"Yeah?" I say.

"When you come home from school from now on, if I'm there, will you please say hi?" she pleads with puppy dog eyes.

This makes me actually laugh out loud. I sigh, tilt my head back and forth before, at last, saying, "Fine."

"Okay. I'll see you soon, Kylah. Take care."

With that, I shut Brooklyn's car door, go inside Jarell's apartment, and walk right past him, heading to my room and isolation for the night. I internally beg for Brooklyn not to be texting Jarell about what happened today.

When I get settled, I immediately grab my sketchbook to calm my mind and nerves, opening it up to a fresh, crisp white page.

There's nothing like the woody smell of a new page. And there's nothing like the ambiguity of its blankness with the power to bring it all to life with color, personality, and vibrance.

I begin outlining Prez's facial and bone structure and the ringlets of his black curls that always grace his forehead. I smile. At times, I'd watch him grow annoyed with his hair as he'd try to move them from his brows with his hands, or he would shake his head to reposition them. Yet, he's never grown any bravery to get a haircut no matter how his body language suggests that he can do without them. No lie: it'd make me sad if he ever did. His hair is such a staple and signature of who he is and how everyone sees him, since all the girls can't seem to stop cooing about it.

When I'm finished with that, I begin his eyes, lips, and nose until I have a full draft sketch of his face. But then, I start another face.

Prez's brother.

I think I remember his name to be Rico. I close my eyes, allowing my mind to resurface what I viewed in their photo the other day that permanently etched itself in my head. The adoration. The pure love they had for one another. The joy.

Once the photo has morphed into a clear image in my mind, I outline Rico's little face, cheeks, chin, and the tiny fro' he sported. As I bring him to life with the facial features I remember from the picture, I tear up.

This just reminds me so much of what Jarell and I used to have.

His hugs. Care. Protection. My tiny hand in his when he'd walk me to school. The times when he'd bathe or feed me when Mama wasn't around, and I'd always be fascinated with how well he'd do without sight.

I miss Jarell. Back in the old days. I hope one day, things can go back to the way they used to be, but... it doesn't look like they ever will.

I keep drawing into the night until my eyes get a little heavy. I try pushing through to get a full draft with Prez's arm draped over his little brother and their cheeks pressed together just like their family portrait, but my eyes get heavier and heavier, and my head nods... nods... nods... until I sink into my sheets with my sketchbook opened.

Chapter Twelve

WE'VE BEEN ON *the road for a long time now. I wanna get out of the car to play, but it's like we're never gonna stop driving.*

"Daddy! Where we going?" I whine.

My head rests on his big chest in this truck we're in as I sit on his lap with an iPad to play games. I've always wanted an iPad! I'm so happy he gives it to me. I wish Daddy was around more often. I might get more Barbies!

"We're gonna go to my house, baby girl," he says.

"Really? It's my first time coming to your house! You live so far away. Can I stay?"

I look up at him after I ask. He looks down, smiling at me with his eyes. They're so blue that they look like the blue from my crayons when I color in the eyes of people on my coloring sheets.

"That's the plan."

"Yay! Is Mommy coming?"

"That's the plan, too," he says.

"Yay!"

He chuckles and hugs me. I relax in it, feeling comfortable and safe.

"What are we gonna do when we get home?"

"*Well, I was thinking we'd settle in for a little bit before I take you to go get some ice cream,*" *he replies.*

"*Yay!*"

"*Then, I don't know. There are so many things to do. I'd love to take you to Disneyland one day.*"

"*Really?!*"

"*Yeah! It's not super far from my house. Just a few hours away.*"

"*Can we go today? Please, please, please?*" *I beg.*

"*Not today, sweetheart. A day in Disneyland has to be planned.*"

"*When can we go?*"

"*I don't know. I'll let you know soon.*"

"*Okay, Daddy.*"

The drive seems to last for a long time before we finally stop. I think we're here!

"*Okay, my sweet baby girl,*" *Daddy gently says.* "*We're home. I know that was a long ride, but you did such a good job. We're gonna go inside and you can take a nap, okay? Then we'll go out for ice cream.*"

"*Yay!*"

"*Alright. Let's go.*"

"*Will Mommy and Relly be coming with us? Relly told me not to talk to you. So will he come, too?*"

"*He told you not to talk to me?*" *he asks.*

"*Well...*" *I dip my head low. Whoops. I wasn't supposed to say that.*

"*Don't listen to your stupid brother. I am your father. I proved that to you. Weren't you happy to see your mother and I together when we picked you up from school?*"

My face lights up. "*Yeah!*"

"*I knew you would. Let's go on in, okay? I'll get you tucked in Daddy's big plush bed, and by the time you get up, we'll head out.*"

What's your favorite ice cream?" Daddy asks.

"Chocolate! With sprinkles."

He chuckles, and I place my hand in his as we walk toward his house together.

"Chocolate with sprinkles it is."

We get inside the house. It's very big. Much bigger than Mommy's house.

"There's so much space!" I exclaim.

I start to run around, but Daddy grabs me gently by the arm and pulls me to him.

"No running in the house. You're five, you should know that. Come on, let's go upstairs to Daddy's room where you can take a nap in my bed. I know you're probably tired, and I have some things I need to take care of," he says.

"Aww man!" I pout.

"I'll even let you jump on it for a while. I know that'll tire you out."

"Ooh, yay!"

Once we get inside his room, Daddy is right. The bed is so large that it almost takes over the whole room. Without wasting a second, I climb on top of it and jump up and down as high as I can, giggling the higher I go. Daddy watches me with a smile and a warm look in his eyes.

"Look Daddy!"

I try to do a flip, but I can't do it. I have to practice more.

"I see!" he awes. "Come on. Let's lay down now."

The last jump I take is me landing on my back and onto a pillow. Daddy comes and tucks me into his thick, warm blankets.

"Okay, sweet girl. I will be back to wake you up to get ice cream, okay?" he says and kisses my forehead.

"Okay, Daddy. Goodnight."

"Goodnight, baby."

He walks out of the room and shuts the door. I try to go to sleep, but I can't. I can't stop thinking about the ice cream, and it's a place I never went to sleep before. So, my eyes just ping pong from one end of the room to the other. What else is in this room? Does he have toys I can play with?

I get out of the bed and search. I pull out the drawers, dig in the closet, and peek under the bed. No toys. Aww man. Where is the iPad? I look around the room for that, too, but I can't find it. Where's Daddy? He knows where it is. And I'm ready for ice cream now.

I am about to leave the room, and I hear a loud scream. Uh oh... what was that? I look at the open window. It came from there. I climb to the window and look outside. There's a little building right there. Hmm... is Daddy in there?

I climb to the ledge of the window and jump out of it, falling to the ground and scraping my arm.

"Ahh!" I stay on the ground, crying and holding the wound that starts to bleed, but no one hears me. I walk to the little building where another scream comes from it. I stop crying and move toward it.

The door is shut, and the knob is a little high. I stand on my tip toes and try to reach it, and I do! I turn it, and the door easily opens. Walking inside, there's Mommy! She's sitting in a chair crying, tied up with rope. But then, in front of me, there are two people wrestling and fighting on the floor.

"Daddy? Relly?" I call out.

They don't hear me. Not even Mommy hears. But someone does. It's a tall, dark-skinned man I've never seen before. He rushes to me with a big black gun in his hand. I stare at the gun, and then at him.

"Are you gonna hurt me?" I whisper, shivering.

"No, but you're gonna hurt him with the brown hair. I'll even help you do it."

"But that's my daddy..." I cry.

"Yeah, and that's your brother who needs to be saved. Come here," he orders and yanks me painfully by the arm toward him. He places the gun in my hands and stands behind me with his hands over mine, forcing me to aim as my back rests against his belly.

"No... I don't wanna!" I cry.

"Shut up!" he growls. "Alright. You're gonna take this finger and press it, okay?"

"No..."

"Do it! Do it now!"

I just cry and cry, staring at Daddy hovering over Relly with his own gun.

"Come on, shoot it! Hurry up!" The voice pressures me to press it.

"No!" I cry.

"Come on! Your brother's gonna get hurt! Look, your dad's about to shoot him. Press it!"

My eyes squeeze shut and quiver before my pointer finger presses down and...

POW!!!!

Mommy's scream shatters my ears, but I don't open my eyes. I don't wanna open my eyes. When I finally do, I stare at the floor first. A slow stream of red, thick water moves toward my feet before it wraps around the front of my toes. When I look up, Daddy's laying on the ground staring at me...

"MOMMY!!!!" I yelp before she demands me to her side...

~ ~ ~

I shriek, jerking awake as my sketchbook flies from my bed to the floor.

My chest heaves up and down at least ten times as I struggle to receive the air that my lungs, at this point, plead for. I gulp once I think I'm okay and frantically glare down at my sheets and the surrounding bedding to ensure my safety, only to realize that they're soaked. So are my shirt, panties, and skin.

"Oh my God!" I scream, slapping at my face and tugging at my clothes, anxious that I might be doused in Dad's blood. I glance at my hands; the fluid is transparent.

It's just sweat Kylah. Just sweat.

"Fuck," I squeak out and punch my pillows several times as my tears add to the sweat.

Grabbing my favorite teddy bear, I cuddle and squeeze it tight before burying my face in its belly and audibly cry my heart out. I don't care who hears it. And it lasts through the entire night, and into the morning when I start school.

I rest through much of the school day because I'm paralyzed with anxiety to the point of me putting on my sweatshirt, pulling my hood up, and laying my head down each class period. My body feels so sluggish that a significant part of me wants to sleep, and the other part of me is so afraid that if I close my eyes, I will have another nightmare in front of everyone. Each time the teachers or Ms. Harris say something to me in an effort to make me pay attention, I barely respond. After a while, they think to send me home, but I refuse. I don't want Jarell coming to get me at all.

I know I've got Prez worried, too.

We've got three classes together, and each time our gaze connects, his brows wrinkle with unease, but he holds back from saying anything to me. Until lunch.

"LaLa, what's going on? Are you okay? You seriously look sick," he asks, walking alongside me as we head to the lunch line for burgers and fries today. "Why won't you go home?"

"Because I don't want to, Prez. I'm fine. I just need sleep, that's all," I reply. My voice cracks with exhaustion and a tinge of tears as my feet drag on the ground.

He detects the teary part.

He picks up a lunch tray for the both of us and even grabs my food for me. I give him my gratitude once we're seated, this time, in a secluded area of the lunchroom where no one else sits, which is unusual for us. Most times, we're surrounded by our mutual friends, laughing and joking among each other. Especially him, since he's so animated with his friends. But the fact that he's opted to stay with me makes me feel cared for.

"Kylah, this is more than you not getting enough sleep last night. Tell me. What's going on?" he presses.

"I'm telling the truth, Prez. I only had an hour of sleep," I mumble, and put my head down near my tray. I can't even eat. I don't even want to eat.

The image of my father's blood seeping toward me after shooting him has got my stomach in a grinder.

I can just feel Prez staring at me, but I don't raise my head. I keep it down and close my eyes. Even in the midst of all the noise around me, I'm about halfway asleep. Prez rises up from across the table, sits adjacent to me, and rubs my back with the flat of his hand gently, comforting me until, this time, I actually doze off for the rest of the lunch period.

~ ~ ~

I'm due for more time with Dr. Anderson after school. I swear, even though I meet with her twice a month, the weeks in between feels like it goes faster than the speed of light. Like the universe knows I hate going to therapy and speeds up the days just so I can go.

When I enter today, it's less rushed than the last time. Dr. Anderson sits in her usual spot in her favorite chair, and I lounge in the low comfy chair with my legs spread out and my knees up high. Once we're settled, Dr. Anderson looks at me with a smile like she always does to start our sessions. I don't smile back, but I also don't look mean either. At least I don't think I do.

"Kylah, how are you since the last time we talked about your school suspension? You look exhausted. Did you sleep?"

I shake my head and rub my eyes.

"Okay. We will get to that in a second. I just wanted to address our last meeting. I know I was a bit hard on you. Sometimes I will be that way when I believe that you can do better," she says with a tinge of remorse. I just shrug.

"It's no big deal, Dr. Anderson. I'm used to people being hard on me. I'm an athlete." I yawn.

"I understand." She nods. "Speaking of being an athlete, Jarell shared with me that you have progress reports for grades and behavior you're submitting to your coach each practice. How is that going?"

I smack my lips. "I don't have much of a choice."

"Is that a good thing?" she asks with low eyes and this sort of smugness that's very subtle, but I detect it anyway.

"You seem to already have your mind made up, so I'm not sure why this is a question."

"Structure and accountability isn't a bad thing, Kylah," she says, fixing her tone.

"Who said it was?"

She pauses, realizing that arguing with me is a losing game, so she just plasters some fake joy on her face instead. "So, what's got you so tired today?" she interrogates.

"Nightmares," I admit.

"Interesting. With PTSD, I know you've struggled with them since we met, but they haven't come up in a while. Would you say they're happening more frequently, or less frequently since we've last talked about them?"

"More."

"Hmm. I'm listening."

"I keep dreaming about my parents. With my mom, they're all about what happened on or around the day she died. It's... it's like I'm there on that day all over again. And then with my dad..." I swallow. "I keep dreaming about his dead body and the gun in my hand after I shot him."

"I'd love to take some time to unpack these dreams and connect them to coping with loss and grief, but I want to keep this a bit high-level for now. Do you detect a pattern where the nightmares happen more times than others?"

I take a few moments to truly think.

"They seem to pop up when I have something big coming or going on. Like the World Series tournament coming up. It's like my dreams won't let me be great," I explain.

"I see. How are you coping with your dreams? What strategies do you use to get your mind off them?"

"Softball. Or drawing. But sometimes, I'm so tired after the nightmare that I can't even concentrate on drawing. It's so frustrating," I complain. "Most of the time, I don't know what to do. Well, sometimes I do know, but I'm so tired that I can't get myself to do it."

"What do you know you should do?"

"Meditate before bed. Journal. But I don't like writing. So I guess I just need to meditate. Also, nightmares don't come as often if I sleep with my windows open to bring air in."

"What else do you believe is stopping you from coping or getting past your nightmares?" Dr. Anderson asks above a whisper.

"Um... I don't know."

"Have you talked to another trusted adult about your dreams? You only see me twice a month, so just talking to me about them won't do you justice to get the support you need. What about your brother?"

"Hell naw. I'm not talking to him."

"He's your caregiver, Kylah. Tell me more about why you won't trust him with this."

"Because he's the main reason why this is happening to me." Immediately, I start crying, and I hate it. I hate this for me.

"Why would that be the case?"

"I don't want to talk about that."

She gives me a closed look. I smack my lips.

"Your brother really cares about you. What would it take for you to be ready to talk to him? He's shared with me how badly you treat him, Kylah. What did he do that's got you treating him this way? As your therapist, please help me to understand this. For someone like Jarell who cares about you this way, there's got to be a misunderstanding..."

Now, I'm full-blown bawling.

"I see that you're distressed now. Talk to me..." she whispers. "I'm here to listen."

It takes me a few moments to get my breath together so that when I do talk, I'm not a blubbering mess.

"To tell the truth... I had to choose between him and my dad," I weep. "When we lived in LA, it had always been me, Mama, and Jarell, but I never had a chance to meet my dad. Jarell always told me not to talk to him because he was dangerous, but he never told me why. Strike one. So when I met Dad outside my school one day, he wasn't like Jarell said he was. He seemed like he wanted to get to know me more and to love me. It felt like Jarell was lying.

"Long story short, the day I killed my pops, I walked into a shed outside and saw him and Jarell fighting on the ground. Dad had a gun and was going to shoot him. Some guy, who I still don't know to this day, was there to see it all go down and told me I had to kill Dad because I needed to save Jarell. He forced me to aim, and I pulled the trigger. But here's my thing. Why did I have to be the one make that choice? Plus, Jarell still hasn't told me why they were fighting or anything. I feel like he had to have done something for Dad to even want to kill him. From what I knew about Dad, he wouldn't just do that for no reason. So that's already got me side eyeing Jarell. He's too secretive about it to not have played some role in this. Strike two."

Pulling my shirt up to my eyes, I soak it for a few seconds before I continue.

"What makes all this worse is after all of that, Jarell left me and Mama behind, disappearing and moving away without even saying anything for almost ten years. Strike three. So now, just because Mama is dead, I'm supposed to accept Jarell back into my life and live with him? That shit ain't fair. It's not fair to me at all!"

Dr. Anderson doesn't say anything. She just lets me continue.

"Deep down, I love Jarell, Dr. Anderson. He used to be everything to me, and he's literally all I've got left in my life other than softball. And he's doing so much for me. I get all of that. But ever since I've been with him, he hasn't once brought up any of what has happened in our past, acting like I'm supposed to just forget about everything and move on. I feel like it's his fault that Dad is gone. If he's not going to tell me the truth about what happened that day or really, the truth about anything, then I will continue making his life hell until he does."

Dr. Anderson shifts in her seat and gives me a look I can't really read. At first, when she opens her mouth to speak, nothing comes out as if she retracted her original thought to opt for something that might land softer. She takes a second to think about what she's about to say before slowly starting.

"First of all, thank you for sharing this, Kylah. I appreciate you opening up. It's been a while since we've been together with me as your therapist, and this is the first time where I've felt like you've shared more than you normally do. It helps us make some progress. If you don't mind, I just have a few questions for you."

"What?" I mumble, slouching in my chair.

"Have you thought about asking Jarell what happened?"

"The first time I asked him, around the time I moved in with him, he said that I'm too young to know. He truly thinks therapy after being diagnosed with PTSD is the cure to everything when really, I just want him to tell me the truth. I want him to tell me about my dad. I want him to tell me why he left me and Mama for so many years!"

"But why do you have to make his life hard just for you to get answers? Remember, we talked about revenge, intent, and impact the other day, and you see how this is going for you. Not well. Were you this upset with your mother for not telling you about your dad? Or did you ask your mom about why Jarell left? If not, why not? Could it be that Jarell was trying to protect you from something?" Dr. Anderson reasons. "Could it be that Jarell is really not the bad person you think he is?"

"First of all, Ma wasn't the one fighting my dad when I walked into that shed, okay? And I did ask Mama. She told me he left because he wanted to do his own thing and that he refused to talk to either of us anymore. So I don't care what you're trying to make Jarell out to be. He needs to start talking or else I'm going to assume there's something he's hiding. There's literally no excuse that nobody... fucking *nobody* has told me the truth! Jarell is the one that holds it!"

"I hear you, and I want you to know your feelings are valid, Kylah. I can't imagine killing a parent, and we've talked about that. But... please understand that if your brother is the only one that holds the truth, then it would serve you well to think about developing a healthy relationship with him. I really would like to explore forgiveness with you. And talk through how to show that forgiveness to your brother."

"I'm not forgiving him, Dr. Anderson. There's nothing you, therapy, Jarell, my best friend Prez, or anyone can do to make me feel any different. I don't want a lecture about how I need to accept him back into my life while covering it up as forgiveness!" I snap.

Dr. Anderson just nods the entire time I speak, looking at me with this stupid glare of pity that I just want to slap out of her eyes. To avoid getting angry, I close my eyes, take a few deep breaths, and count backward from ten.

"I appreciate that you've identified your trigger and are using your strategies to calm down. We will talk more about your brother in another session, Kylah. I don't think you're ready right now, and you may not be ready for a while. Just know that I do support you in making things right with him. It's only going to help you heal," she expresses.

I stand up and grab my bag, not even caring that we've got forty-five minutes left of this fucking session. I don't even say anything to her. I storm out of her room and out to the lobby, rushing past Jarell without saying a word. I'm not getting in an Uber with him.

So I walk to the nearest bus stop and look up when the next one comes so I can ride that home since I have a pass. It's going to take at least an hour to get home versus fifteen or twenty minutes, but I don't care.

I'd much rather deal with the stench of the bus and weird people than to even be around him right now. Dr. Anderson can shove all that forgiveness crap for all I care.

Chapter Thirteen

I STAY HOME from school "sick" the next day. Jarell doesn't give me lip about it either before going to work because... well... if I were him, I wouldn't even think about attempting to utter a peep to me. Even though we haven't even communicated since I left the therapy office, it seems as though he senses my energy because he's largely stayed out of my way. I don't know if Dr. Anderson said anything, but it ain't like it matters.

I spend much of my day drawing in my sketchbook in a deep focus, trying to create a new portrait of Mama to replace the damaged one and eating snacks. The amount of times I've torn out a page, crumpled it up, and threw it to the ground to start over should be criminal. I almost give up, but I refuse to let Ms. Turner win and take away the only tangible memory I have of her. It's just that, if I'm gonna create it again, it has to be perfect.

Jarell comes home from work teaching little kids at his usual time in the early afternoon with Luna. Instead of him spending a lot of time in the kitchen, he comes straight to the land mine living room, running into several decor pillows I've thrown to the floor in order to make more room for me to lounge on the couch. After directly stepping on one and then attempting to step over another with Luna's help, he ends up crushing a couple of balled pieces of paper on his way to find a seat.

"Kylah, why is all this stuff on the ground?" Jarell questions, instantly irate. "You know it's a trip hazard. Got me stepping on clean stuff with my shoes on."

"Well, you shoulda took your shoes off when you came in the house, and then you wouldn't have that problem, would you?" I shoot back.

He gives me a long look in return, grappling with if he wants to argue with me, or to be the bigger person. He chooses the latter by shaking his head and picking up the pillow he stepped on, tossing it toward where I'm sitting. It doesn't make it to the couch and falls to the floor again where it's going to stay until I feel like getting it.

He finds a seat on the accent chair across from me as Luna jumps into his lap and cuddles with him. With one hand, Jarell rubs her back and with the other, he listens to his text messages. One of them is from Brooklyn, telling him that she's on her way to the house.

"A'ight, you heard Brooklyn. She's on her way, so clean up this living room," he orders.

"She can go somewhere else in the house. Kitchen or your room. I was here first. I'm always the one having to move," I say as I begin to shade in Mama's dark hair. *Ugh. I don't like it.* I tear out the sheet, ball it up, and throw it to the floor with the others.

"Because you don't pay the bills. Simple. So it don't matter where you want my guests." Jarell tilts his head to the side. "Plus, I never asked you to move. I said to clean up."

I smack my lips and toss my sketchbook on the table to get up. That "bills" argument is such bullshit. Of course I don't pay them, but if I had it my way, I would. So, at times, I should be considered for my preferred spaces to relax without it having to be completely neat.

"Yeah, you pay the bills, but you also took me in, so you should be thinking about how unfair it is to always make me have to clean up for somebody. Brooklyn and her pills can stay home for once. Or you can go over to her place," I declare and restore the couch the way it was with the decorative pillows.

Jarell pauses with a scowl.

"Huh? Pills? What are you even talking about?" Jarell asks.

"Oh you didn't know?" I whirl around to face him squarely. "Brooklyn takes whole ass oxy's for migraines."

Jarell doesn't respond but blinks several times as if each one generates a question in his mind.

"Crazy how that's supposed to be your girlfriend, but you don't even know she takes pills," I mumble. It's just in time since the apartment buzzer sounds off.

Jarell's openly confused expression morphs into a closed one as Luna barks and heads to the door to greet her. Jarell follows. I don't budge from the living room and continue working on my portrait. I'll only move if Brooklyn asks me to, which I already know she won't.

I open another page in my book to try and draw this portrait for probably the twelfth time now, but this time, I start with more careful planning through measurements and a design plan. This one has to be the charm.

"How was your day at work, babe?" Brooklyn asks Jarell once she's settled inside and had her time with Luna.

"It was decent. It went fast. Had a breakthrough with one of the kids today. You know the little boy I've been telling you about that's been struggling to work with me because he has separation anxiety with his parents?"

"Oh yeah! Little Max?"

Jarell laughs. "Yeah, him. He finally allowed me to work with him on his Braille alphabet today. It was a good feeling."

"That's awesome, Jarell! I know how hard you've been trying to get him to warm up to you."

"Yeah, it was cool. Highlight of the day. How about you? Anything eventful?"

"Nope. You know IT is as boring as it comes sometimes. Highlight of my day? Seeing you..."

Their conversation comes to a lull, but suddenly, I hear smacking and their juices mixing together. Oh God! I roll my eyes with a heave. I'm close to telling both of them to get a room, but it stops when Jarell starts talking.

"Aye, you gotta chill out." He chuckles. "You're gonna get us both in trouble."

"Sorry."

It goes quiet again for just a second before the cupboard opens and a bunch of pots and pans loudly rattle the apartment.

"How's Kylah doing?" she asks. "Is she here?"

"She's alright. She's in the living room, I think. I didn't hear her go to the room."

"Okay. Well, I'm gonna go down to the beach and set up my food cart later tonight. They've got Zumba on the Beach, beach volleyball, and other events that I think will be good for business. You want to come? And do you think Kylah would want to come? Is she still on punishment?"

"She should be, but at this point, I don't know how effective it is to keep her on it," Jarell replies.

"Okay. I'll be sure to ask her. Do you wanna come down to the beach tonight?"

"Mmm, nah not tonight. Got some things I gotta do for work to prepare for."

"Okay. Well before I head out, I want to cook y'all dinner. Any ideas? What do you have a taste for? I kinda want something unhealthy. Like... baked mac and fried chicken."

"Now you know I ain't gon' eat all that." He laughs. "Tryna stay fit, you know."

"So? What's one meal gonna do?"

"Make me wanna eat it all the time because it's so good. Last time you fed me that, I wanted to eat it for the next few days," Jarell says before a light snicker in his throat.

"Well, let me treat you."

"Nope. See, you cooking that is why you got all them curves on you now," he says with a load of lust in his voice. I roll my eyes again and shake my head.

"But you like it, though..." she teases back.

"Mmm hmm. I love it." He kisses her somewhere on her body.

"Alright, fine. I'll cook something else. Jarell, what was your favorite food as a kid? Anything your family passed down for recipes?" Brooklyn asks him.

"Mmm... when I was a kid, my favorite food was always chicken nuggets. I think that's every kid's favorite food, though."

I slap my forehead. What a dumb answer. Shaking my head, I begin to outline the shape of Mama's eyes.

"Come on, Jarell. Don't be silly. I mean, something passed down, babe. Not some common answer like nuggets." She giggles. "What's a food your mom or grandparents passed down to you that you enjoyed? I'd love to recreate it for you. Bring that sense of home since I know you're not from here." I can hear the smile in her voice.

"Oh, my bad. Uh..." he ponders, "nah. I've never met any of my grandparents, so I wouldn't have had anything passed down that I know about."

"Really? None of them?" Brooklyn doubles down.

"Nope."

"Well dang. Who were you raised by, then?"

"Just my mom. You know this, Brook."

"Yeah, but what about the rest of your village? No aunties? Uncles? Dad's side?"

"No. My dad died before I was born. I don't know any of my extended family. Mom or dad's side," he replies with a tinge of shame, sadness, and longing in his voice. "And I don't have a favorite food that was passed down. My mom never cooked because she was always working."

"Oh... I'm sorry to hear that." The disappointment rings through her voice, too. "I'll just make your favorite tonight, then. Seared salmon, homemade potatoes, and broccoli. Sound good?"

"That sounds perfect," he says warmly. "Let me know what I can help you with."

The moments ahead are nothing but the cupboards slamming closed, drawers opening and closing, silverware clinking, the fridge and freezer lights illuminating against the wall from it being opened and closed, and water from the sink running. I'm excited for what Brooklyn is about to make. When she cooks, no lie, her food is always good, especially in comparison to Jarell's. For a while, it was the only time I'd be happy for her to come over because Jarell has absolutely no soul when it comes to food options. That fool would eat pine nuts for dinner and be completely content. And would look at me crazy if

I said I ain't wanna eat it.

"Hey, so uh, I got a random question for you, B. Been thinking about it since you got here. Are you... taking pills?" Jarell suddenly asks with a thick tone.

"What do you mean? Are you tryna say I'm abusing drugs?" Brooklyn responds, clearly insulted by the question.

"No, I'm not saying that. My fault. I should've worded that better." Jarell sighs before pausing for a long moment and then continues on. "Kylah mentioned something about you taking pills when I was trying to get her to clean up before you got here. Oxy, to be specific. She... never normally says things like that, so... it must've been heavy on her mind for her to bring it up."

"Oh. I see," Brooklyn says, leaving the silence that follows full of ambiguity.

"What's *that* supposed to mean? Do you take them?" Jarell hesitates.

"Your sister is what I mean. You hardly even speak to her, and this is what you ask me? After, probably, an offhand comment she made?" she seethes.

"Woah. Relax, B. Why you comin' at me so hostile? I'm not sure why you're getting upset..."

My heart starts racing. *Please don't mention my panic attack. Please don't mention my panic attack at the mall, Brooklyn...*

She takes a breath before speaking. "Yes, I take oxy to treat migraines. You already know I get them, so I'm not sure why me taking pills is such a surprise," she shoots back.

"Yeah, of course I know that, but I never knew how you treated them beyond sleeping or me comforting you. I didn't realize you also took medication."

"Okay. Well now you know."

"And that's fine. I just... wanna request that you not take them around Kylah," he says pointedly.

Oh damn.

I ain't think he'd go there head on like that. My stomach flutters, but my brain swirls with a whole lot of mixed feelings. I'm oddly thankful that Jarell just flat out said it because... yeah, I would rather not ever see another oxy bottle again in my life. But another part of me knows this can go left real quick...

Brooklyn, whatever you do, just don't mention the panic attack, I think inside.

I don't need her giving Jarell another reason to schedule an impromptu appointment with Dr. Anderson, whom I don't plan to go back to any time soon after what happened yesterday.

"And why wouldn't you want me to take my own medication when she's around? You think she's going to take them?" she questions.

"No. It's just..." he falters.

"It's just what?"

"You don't need to worry or think too deep about it," he says in a softer tone. "I'm just asking that, if you can and are able, to please not take the pills with her around."

She sets a spoon down on the counter. "Okay, I'm not letting this go that easy." I hear the top of the pot she's cooking with close. "Why would you tell me I can't take my own medication for pain around your sister and think I won't ask why?"

"Because it's a story she has to tell on her own time," Jarell answers.

Damn, good response.

"Well, her story also is your story in some ways, but you won't even open up to me about any of it," she counters. "At what point do you start letting me in a little bit, Jarell? I'd like to know you and your sister better, but it has to start with you, too. It's becoming not enough for us to be on this surface level wave after two years. I'm at a point where I'd like to start learning more about your family."

Jarell remains silent for a stretched moment.

"There really isn't much to discuss about our family, Brook," he confesses.

"Jarell, how am I supposed to get closer to you when you've got walls up? When you won't share anything? Don't you see a future together?" Brooklyn asks.

"You know I do, baby."

"Then, you gotta open up to me. As your long term girlfriend, I should know more about your family and background. If we're thinking of engagement, then I've definitely gotta know. I should have an idea about your mom and the woman she was. She brought in and raised an amazing man in this world."

"I hear you, B. I just... listen. I don't wanna open old wounds that I've worked really hard to sew," Jarell discloses.

"But these are the kind of things that will bring us closer together. Allow me to be there for you to close those wounds again," she pleads. "It's about building trust."

"B... please. Just let it go. My question to you had nothing to do with my family's past. All I'm asking is that you not take those pills around Kylah. Can you commit to that? It's all I'm asking," Jarell replies.

"No. I refuse to let you end this conversation. How the hell are we supposed to progress in our relationship when you keep being dismissive? I've 'let it go' on topics like this so many times and just brushed things under the rug when you want me to. I've been nice and understanding, but now enough is enough! You've got to start facing these conversations head on. The only thing I know is that your parents have passed away and that you took in your sister. Yet, you know my whole entire family. My sisters, my mom, my dad, granny, aunties... and they *love* everything about you. But I'm feeling like it's not being reciprocated, and that's not acceptable. I really care about you, babe. But you're making a lot of this hard."

"Look. I'll tell you when I'm ready, but right now, I just want to help you finish this food. Is that too much to ask?"

A long halt...

"Actually? Yes, it is too much. I'm getting impatient with you acting this way with me, Jarell."

"Brook..."

"Don't 'Brook' me. I'm going to let it go right now but understand that this is a conversation we will revisit. You can't keep operating in secrecy like this, especially if you say you care about me."

"Okay," Jarell says with a concluding tone, signaling that their discussion is over. On his terms.

The previously warm energy between the two becomes icy; even I can feel it from a distance. *Yikes.* I didn't think that me telling Jarell about her pills would lead to all of that. Causing an argument wasn't my intention at all, but... it is what it is. I'm thankful that he finally stepped up for once in my defense and told her to keep the pills away from me without telling her why. A small part of me wonders if it's an attempt to get on my good side, but... I don't know.

It's gonna take a lot more from him to even come close to my good side. Telling Brooklyn not to take pills around me will *never* be enough. And to be honest? I'm kinda with Brooklyn on this. Jarell won't tell anyone anything, including me, and...

It's a serious fuckin' problem.

The food cooks silently for a while with them in the kitchen, and I've given up on my portrait for now. Instead, I decide to lounge on the couch and watch The Powerpuff Girls on Netflix until it's interrupted by both Brooklyn and Jarell coming into the space.

"Oh, hey Kylah. I thought you'd be in your room. What happened here? What's with all the paper on the floor?" Brooklyn starts with a smile, but then looks around the living room with a scowl.

"Tryna draw a new portrait, but it wasn't working, so I tore 'em out to start over."

Jarell smacks his lips and shakes his head.

"Kylah, I told you to clean this living room up before B got here. You had plenty of time to do it. Please do what I'm telling you to do," Jarell demands.

"Jarell, leave me alone," I retort and shift my attention back to the TV.

When the silence between all of us lingers for a little too long, I look at them both with an attitude to understand why they're still standing there, and the frustration is all over Jarell's face. His shoulders sink before he ultimately walks around to pick up the crumples of paper he can feel from the floor himself. Brooklyn exchanges surprised glances between me and him, struggling to decide whether she wants to stick up for Jarell, yell at him for being docile, address me for being rude, or to not say anything at all.

She settles for the latter.

"Kylah, your food is ready at the table," Brooklyn says just above a whisper, a little hesitant. "Salmon, potatoes, broccoli, and I made some garlic bread, too."

"Thank you. I appreciate you making it," I say and sit up on the couch. "It all smells good." I sigh and swipe a hand down my face. "Sorry. I promise, my attitude isn't with you."

She gives me a long look that I can't read. I'm not sure if she believes me. "Well, I hope you enjoy it."

"I'm sure I will. Thanks again," I respond with a smile.

She gives me a half smile before addressing Jarell. "Jarell, I'm gonna head out to the beach to get everything set up for the food. I'll see you later, okay?"

"Alright, cool. I'll call you tonight."

With that, Brooklyn turns on her heels to leave, and Jarell is done picking up the paper balls he could run into. Several others still remain on the floor, but he doesn't say another word to me. He just goes into his room and leaves the apartment with Luna shortly after Brooklyn does without even announcing where he's going.

Good.

Now I can eat my warm meal in peace.

Chapter Fourteen

IT'S FINALLY THE weekend and at last, it's officially the first tournament of the softball season. The last summer of my middle school career on the San Diego Sluggers before things get super serious in high school. Well, it's serious in middle school too, which is why the Senior League World Series is on ESPN. I'm just excited to treat these little local tournaments in San Diego as my personal warm up before hitting the big stage in a few months in Delaware.

With the Senior League World Series, the age bracket is thirteen to sixteen. There are ten major regions who play: Europe-Africa, Asia-Pacific, Latin America, Canada, and then all the regions in the USA. I'll be representing USA West, obviously, being from California. I can't wait to wipe the absolute floor with these international players. I just have to stay focused and stay out of trouble… I'm ready to put Cali on the map, considering that USA West hasn't won the tournament in years!

Just as I'm thinking of all of this, I gotta start getting ready for our first game this afternoon. Setting down the start of a self-portrait in my sketchbook in my sheetless bed that I've scrapped to be washed after all the sweating my dreams cause, I rise to start gathering my stuff to head out to the softball field. As soon as I do, a rapid knock at my door startles me.

"Who is it?" I yell out.

"Hey, it's me. Can we talk before we leave to the diamond?" Jarell's voice travels through the hollow door.

I grumble under my breath. "What do you want, Jarell?"

"I just want to talk. Please. Will you let me in?"

Seriously? What could possibly be important enough to discuss right before my first game of the season that couldn't be discussed any other day? A part of me actually hopes he comes in here to piss me off. Just so I can take my anger out on the ball and the pitchers' circle to set the tone. There's nothing I love more than any small reason to go off on my opponents and play the best games of my life.

I unlock the door and swiftly snatch it open before moving away to continue packing my duffle bag for the tournament. He takes my cold invitation and enters in, but not too deep. He looks in my direction, waiting for some sort of guidance about where it's appropriate for him to sit or stand, but I don't give it to him. Instead, I search for a certain pair of shoes I want to wear when I'm done playing tonight.

My blue and black snakeskin Retro three's might be the move, but I think maybe I should rock these new Retro Cool Gray's Brooklyn got me. I might go hang out with some of my softball friends somewhere after our seven o'clock game if we win this three o'clock one. I know I'll turn some heads in these shoes.

"Hey um... so..." he starts. I've never seen anyone look so awkward in my life the way Jarell does right now, standing like a lost small puppy. I shake my head and put my new J's in the bag.

"I'm sorry to bother you, but this tension between us is really starting to get to me, Kylah. It's either you're extremely defiant and rude, or it's like I don't even exist to you."

Now what should I wear with the shoes? There are so many things you can do with Cool Gray's. I think my ripped, acid wash light blue jeans would work, especially for hanging out. I just don't know if they're clean or not. I shift to my closet to search for them.

"Kylah…"

After sifting back and forth through several hangers, my eyes are on the prize. Found them. I pull them up to examine if they're dirty. Looks good to me. Then, you know, the infamous nose test. I wrap the denim around my face to smell any sign of them needing to be washed. They smell like nothing. Check. They go in the bag.

"Kylah, please listen to me, okay? I'm sorry. I know you stormed out of therapy the other day, and I know you're upset with me for telling Coach Harper about what you did at school. Is that why you're so angry with me?"

I ruffle through my clean laundry basket for clean undergarments – socks, bra, and panties. They go in the bag.

"Kylah, it may have been the wrong decision, or it may have been the right one. I just don't know what else to do beyond what I've been trying to do to help you stay out of trouble. You've been suspended over the last two years for cussing out staff, skipping class, fighting, and now you're throwing chairs at teachers and endangering their safety. What was I supposed to do? I can't keep leaving my job to get you from school. Those little kids need me to teach them how to read and write Braille. You're lucky that teacher didn't press charges."

Got the jeans and other stuff, and now I need a shirt. Should I do a bralette? Crop top? Or a graphic tee? I'm not sure if I'm feeling girly or tomboyish. I guess it depends if Andre is gonna be around. If Prez comes to watch me play, then Andre might be there. It's very rare, but I've seen him at maybe two of my games since moving here, so it's possible.

I forgot that it's Alaysia's birthday today, and Prez plans to go to her party. Which means that Andre might go there with him. Never mind. Guess I'll go "stud-ish" today. Lowkey, I really wanted to show off my six pack and belly button ring with a crop top or bralette.

"What can I do to fix this? By this, I mean our relationship. I hate that we're at this point, Kylah. I might not always show it, but the way you talk to me and treat me hurts."

My jaw clenches and I briefly close my eyes to stay regulated before I walk over to my dresser right behind him and pull out the drawer where I have all my graphic tees folded. I grab my favorite Boondocks one. I close my drawer and slightly push him out of the way with my shoulder since he's too close and throw the shirt in my bag.

He sighs. "I'm willing to give you a break from therapy for a little while if that's what it takes because I really want to make things work. You're my little sister, Kylah, and I love you. I want to see you succeed, but I can't help if you aren't willing to come to the table. I want you to love being here, and I want you to feel like someone loves and cares about you. Unconditionally. Because I do. So what do you need from me?"

Half of my heart really softens after hearing that. Surprisingly, to the point of tears burning the corners of my eyes. But... I actively fight the urge to hug him or acknowledge it and continue to focus on getting ready. Now I just need to pack up my bats, helmet, batting gloves, cleats, mitt, water bottle, sunscreen, socks, and my uniform in my athletic bag. Oh, and my hat. I move all around my room between the closet, under my bed, and my dresser for all these things and find most of them. I shouldn't forget my sunglasses either.

"Kylah, please," he begs before he whispers, "say something."

I think I have everything. I go to my vanity table and gather my waist-length hair into a high ponytail before braiding it in one big braid. I'm about halfway down after about thirty seconds of silence when he huffs in frustration.

"If you're not going to talk, I have something to give you, then. Something I want us to do together."

Jarell places a small book on my dresser with a subtle *thunk*. I look at it in the mirror, frowning with curiosity.

"That's Ma's journal. Diary. Whatever you wanna call it. I packed it up after we cleaned out her apartment. I know how much you've been struggling lately with her being gone so this might bring you some comfort. Maybe it won't. I don't know. But all I know is how you're treating me ain't working, and you need something that will give you comfort. Maybe it's in there."

Once I'm done with my braid, I lift one packed bag and secure it to my back, and then put the other one on my shoulder. I stare at the book for a second. It's worn, the edges of the pages look like they've been folded over and over, and it's secured by a small latch.

Hmm. I appreciate this and all, but what Jarell doesn't understand is that I want and need answers from *him*. Not Mama.

I walk out of my room without a word to Jarell, leaving him standing there, and go to the living room to see Brooklyn sitting on the couch. Oh! I didn't even know she was here. She's so quiet...

"Hey, Kylah! You ready for your game today?" She greets me with a warm smile. I'm surprised she even wants to be here, considering the argument she and Jarell had the other day, but ... I don't know. Maybe she thought about it. Maybe they talked on the phone and made up last night or earlier. Who knows? I wasn't there. But I can't help but smile back, even if it's small. Her enthusiasm is so contagious, especially during the times when I don't want it to be.

"I never have to get ready because I stay ready," I reply.

She chuckles. "I love it. You're gonna do great like you always do."

I move to the refrigerator to grab extra water. "Thanks. By the way, I'm wearing my new shoes later tonight. I think I'm gonna kick it with some of my friends after the games. Thanks again for buying them for me."

"Not a problem. It was my pleasure. Are y'all ready to go? The game starts at three, right? It's a quarter after two, so we should start to load up the car."

"Oh, you're coming?"

"Of course, I am. I love coming to your games."

"Cool. I was just gonna ride my bike to the park since it isn't that far, but I guess I'll ride with you. Less gear to carry."

"Awesome."

Just as she says that, Jarell walks out from my room with a look that makes Brooklyn go still. I wouldn't have cared at all about it, but my stomach jolts something fierce when I notice his whole demeanor.

Shit. I *did not* expect him to be *this* defeated. I blink and turn away before I start feeling like the worst human and head to the couch to sit and tie my shoes.

"Babe, are you okay? What's wrong?" Brooklyn slightly panics.

"Hey. It's nothing," he says, and connects Luna's harness to the leash with his head hung low. "Let's go."

Without another word, Luna walks Jarell past me and out of the front door. It's like the strain between him and I instantly flared the second we were inches of each other. It throws me way off guard.

Moments go by in silence with a stunned Brooklyn staring at the door he just walked out of before she turns to me.

"Is everything okay?" She frowns.

I shrug. "I don't know about him, but I'm cool."

"Did something happen before I came?"

"Not that I'm aware of," I say.

"Okay." She gives me a look like she doesn't believe me at all. "Well... let's go. I'll talk to him later."

The car ride is mostly silent, which is fine because the park was literally only a three-minute drive from the apartment. When we're here, I get out and walk toward the diamonds with all my bags. A few feet back, Luna, Jarell, and Brooklyn follow.

As the grass and dirt chomp beneath my feet, Jarell and Brooklyn's voices float in the mix of the noise.

"I don't understand why you keep putting up with this, Jarell. You keep letting her treat you like crap without any consequence, so that's what she's gonna continue to do," she says. "You're allowing this to happen."

"I know but..."

"But what? Why won't you say anything back to her? What is going on between you two that she would even act like this? What is it that you're not telling me, Jarell? What *really* happened between y'all?"

"I don't say anything because I know if I do, it won't be pretty. I've been praying and trying to figure out my approach with her. If I come off too hot, it'll drive her away even more, and deep down, I know how I can get. I have to constantly be the bigger person, even when it's hard to be. With Kylah, I have to take some L's to get a W. Maybe you can ask her what her problem is. She seems to be responding to you better than she is to me."

"But I'm asking you. What do *you* think it is?"

"I don't know for sure…" he answers in a flat tone.

"Really? I don't believe that you know nothing. You had to have done something for her to continuously act this way toward you. When I meet and talk to her, she doesn't act like how she does to you the way I thought she would've. So what's up? Did you hurt her?"

"Brook, chill out with these questions, a'ight? You're making assumptions about me that ain't even cool and is outside of my character."

"Well, you don't ever tell me anything about anything, so all I can use are my assumptions based on what I see," she responds.

"Yeah, but you know that's ridiculous. I wouldn't be doing all the things I do for her if I was hurting her. You don't even see me hurting her, so what are you talking about?"

"I don't know anything beyond what you tell me."

"Whatever, B."

"Well m-maybe…" she stutters, "like I said the other day. Maybe you should start opening up and telling me some things about you, your past, and your family so I can understand y'all's dynamic a little better. I already shared this with you before, but I feel so connected with you, yet so distant at the same time. I've never felt like this with anyone before. I just can't imagine that Kylah's acting this way for no reason."

"I know it's for a reason, but I don't have all the specifics. I don't know what to do with her anymore," Jarell says lowly. "Hell, I never did know what to do. I've already asked her what I need to do to fix things with her, and she won't tell me."

"Well… I guess you just have to keep showing up, Jarell. Show her you care, and just pray that eventually, she'll come around. That's all you can really do. Other than that, I just need you to stop being mute about things when I ask you. I'm supposed to trust you, and we're supposed to be going long term with this thing we got going on. Telling me the truth about you and your sister is a start."

"I hear you," Jarell says. "But I'm not gonna get into this with you again. Not here."

Neither of them exchange any words after that. I shrug and keep it pushing to the dugout where the rest of the team is. I think I'm the last one to arrive today. In the dugout, Alaysia's already talking about her party at the bowling alley tonight, what she's going to wear, who's invited, how happy she is that she's now fourteen, etc. A portion of our team is annoyed with her bragging, another portion ignores her altogether, and the final portion entertains her antics by kissing her ass and telling her that they wished they could go and for her to have a live stream. I join the crew who completely ignores her, and our group starts to talk about how excited we are for this season.

During the multiple side conversations, Coach Harper and his assistants enter the premises.

"Alright ladies! Let's huddle," he says. "It's almost game time."

Everyone stops what they're doing at once and comes together. Coach stands at the center of the circle with his clipboard and notes to go over everyone's field assignments and batting orders for the tournament.

"Welcome to the first game of the season! It's been a hard few weeks of practice, and now it's time to show how hard we've worked to prepare and get some in-game experiences before the World Series. So here's the lineup for the field today. Kylah," Coach calls me out.

"Yeah?"

"Your progress reports have been looking really good since your meeting at school. So, you will be the starting pitcher. Tina, you're shortstop, Macie, you're first base, Sarah, you're second base, Katie, you're obviously the catcher. Keisha, you're third base. Alaysia, you're back up pitcher." He goes on to give everyone else their assignments. "Now for the batting order. Alaysia, you're first this year! You've improved so much over the off season and now is your time to shine. Let's see what you're made of. Libby, you're second. Natasha, you're third, and Kylah, you're fourth."

I grin. There's nothing better than being the fourth batter. A chance to load the bases and be the one to bring everyone home. I sneak a gaze at Alaysia, and she can't help but sneer. I bite my lip to stifle a giggle. Then, Coach spends the next five minutes discussing strategy, gives us reminders about the signals and cues to steal bases, importance of double plays, and all the other small stuff that makes our team successful.

Everybody does our team chant before we grace the field.

This one's a breeze of a game. I pitched decent innings – gave up a couple of ground hits and double, but we won six-one. Meaning, we have a game at seven tonight. If we win that one, we play two more games tomorrow. I anticipate that we'll win this tournament pretty easily.

Many of my teammates decide to leave after our game to come back later for the next game since we have three hours in between, including Jarell and Brooklyn. Thankfully, Alaysia's gone and not coming back.

I choose to stay at the park to watch some of the other teams and what my competition will be. I'm mostly there to check out the other pitchers. Some are trash and truly amateurs, and others have a decent shot next year at the high school level. What's crazy is the buzz about our team and how afraid they are to come up against us. And mainly, me. We're not even on the field playing right now, yet I overhear many conversations about us and how they will know they're a good team if they can hang with us. I ignore them and mind my own business. I don't care if these teams aren't really competitive. I see every opponent as a threat.

As I'm deep into scouting a really close game between two of the teams who are in our bracket, my teammate Tina comes and sits next to me, glued to her phone and shaking her head.

"What?" I question, trying to figure out what's up with her. "I ain't even think you were staying."

"I wasn't. I already left and just came back. Come look at this," she says.

Motioning her phone my way, I turn my attention from the game and to her phone. It's a live video of Alaysia at her birthday party.

"Now Tina, you know I don't care about this," I say, giving her a side glare.

"No but look. Look who she's talking to. Isn't that one of your best friends? And doesn't he have a girlfriend?" she asks.

Taking a closer look, I realize that it's someone else on Alaysia's page recording the party live. But Alaysia's got Prez in a corner. Their body language definitely suggests they're talking about something not appropriate for our age. Well, at least she is as her breasts graze his chest. His body language is kind of stiff and guarded. Either way, it's complete bullshit 'cause it ain't like he's pushing her away, either.

What the hell. I can't even believe Prez is messing around with her ass. My fists ball and my lips tighten. I can't wait to absolutely rip into him at school. He should know better, man. That's literally my enemy.

"Yes, and yes," I answer Tina and look away.

"Wow. She's so... ugh." She shudders and closes out of the live stream.

"Yeah, I'm over her. Anyway, what are you doing tonight? You wanna go to the movies? Maybe me, you, and Keisha?" I ask. "I wanna see that new scary movie that came out."

"Yeah, I'm down. I'm not doing anything else. You want me to ask Keisha?"

"Yeah, ask her."

"Sounds good. I'll ask my mom, too. Maybe she can drop us off. What time you want to go?"

"The latest showing," I say.

"Cool. Are you not grounded anymore?"

"Jarell ain't my daddy," I snort.

She presses her lips awkwardly. "Right. I'll be back."

Tina moves away and I close my eyes and try to tune back into the game I was watching until six thirty, when most of our team has arrived to prepare for the next game. Tina and Keisha are down for the movies tonight, which makes me happy. Just as we solidify our plans together, Coach gathers us together to talk strategy again.

"You all did very well last time, so let's do it again. These are games we should win, so don't mess around. This is great preparation for our next tournament in Los Angeles in a couple of weeks. So be locked in and stay locked in."

My mouth drops instantly; I don't even realize that I reacted so quickly. Los Angeles?!

"Wait, Coach, we're going to LA?" My eyes expand.

"Yes. May sixth through the tenth."

"Yo, that's dope! Can't wait!" I exclaim, beaming. I really get to go home. Yo... May can't come fast enough!

"Don't look too far ahead. You can be excited, and you should be. But we gotta win this tournament first. Stay locked in and focused."

Everyone nods, and then do our pre-game chants and rituals before we head out to the field. This game is also another walk in the park. We win seven to zero; I pitch a shutout. My teammates hyped me up the whole time in the stands. Every last one of them. It's just a whole different feel and vibe when Alaysia's not around. We're so much more cohesive.

After the game, I link up with Brooklyn and Jarell before Tina's mom takes me to her house. Immediately, she tells me how great of a game I pitched. With pride, I say thank you. I can't care less about the game at this point, though. I think this is a good time to tell her about our first traveling tournament of the season before the movies.

"Hey Brooklyn, guess what?"

"What's up?"

"We're going to Los Angeles for our first traveling tournament of the season."

"Oh? Really?"

"Yeah! I get to go back home!" I smile.

"That's awesome! Congratulations!"

When I sneak a look at Jarell, he looks shocked and uneasy at the same time.

"Did you hear that, Jarell?" Brooklyn asks. "The team is going to LA. It'll be exciting for you both to visit home, right? It'll give you some time to bond. I'd love to take you both there. You guys will have to show me around and take me to the best food spots."

"I mean... yeah. Well... I guess we're going home, then," Jarell says, rubbing the back of his head and shrugging.

Without a word, I smile. I just pray I get to see some of my old friends. I have to make sure I hit them up on social media before we drive there. But... I gotta get my phone back, somehow, since Jarell still has it. *Ugh.*

Chapter Fifteen

"MAMA?" MY VOICE *bounces off the walls. "Mama, are you here?"*

My feet shuffle across the old, wooden floor of our apartment as I search for her in the living room area first. No sign – the area is a complete mess with beer bottles lying everywhere on the coffee table with some having tumbled to the ground. The room smells like foreign bodies had been in the space not too long ago as a couple of ash trays with fresh cigarette butts also sit among the bottles. Empty candy wrappers and other trash also decorate the table.

I squeeze my eyes shut and move toward the kitchen. No lights are on in there either, but at least the kitchen looks pristine compared to the living room space.

"Mama..."

With another dreadful step, I turn toward the hallway where the bedrooms are. The hall light is also off, seeming like the road to eternal darkness.

One of the room doors creaks open, and I freeze.

A tall, male body exits Mama's room. For a second, I think it's another one of the dudes who constantly come in and out of the house like it's a revolving door, but that face looks so familiar that I nearly stumble. The face I'm used to being barer than it is now, but it was the eyes that I recognized before anything.

"J-Jarell?" I whisper.

"Kylah? Is that you?" he asks with a frown, yet his tone screams surprise and shock.

"What are you doing here?" I bark.

"Wow, your voice is so different now," he says in a breathy way, but his tone is also loaded with something else that I can't understand.

"I said, what are you doing here? Where's Mama?" I order.

"Uh..." his voice quivers before he swallows and gives me a look that makes my stomach hurl. His eyes are wet, but I watch him struggle to keep his composure.

What the heck is going on?!

"Where is Mama?!" I yell this time.

"The ambulance is on the way..." he squeaks out.

"What do you mean the ambulance is on the way? What's wrong with her? Is she okay?" I bellow and storm toward her bedroom, but Jarell catches me across the chest mid stride.

"No," he dissents firmly. "You are not going in there."

"She's my mom! You can't tell me what to do! Besides... why are you even here anyway? You haven't been around for years. Don't be coming up in here tryna run stuff."

"I'm not trying to run anything..."

I swiftly interrupt. "How'd you even find out where we live? Leave us alone!"

"She's the one who texted me... and then called me. Out of the blue, so I came to check in on her and..."

"I need to know what's going on with her. Move!" I demand and push him hard enough in the chest to make him stumble and lose his *grip of me.*

"Kylah no..."

He's right on my heels, trying to stop me from getting to her room, but it's too late. I burst right in and instantly wish I would've just listened the moment I encounter no one other than Mama.

Lying limp on the bed with a bottle of opened pills right next to her. I pick up the pill bottle and it reads:

200mg OXYCODONE

Her eyes are halfway open and nearly crossed with no sign of awareness, and her mouth hangs open as her tongue also hangs out.

"Mama!! Mama, come on and get up! Do not do this whole 'passed out' shit to me again! You were awake when I left. You were supposed to be at my game! What happened?! Where are the snacks and the cupcakes? What happened!!!" I scream to the top of my lungs. I shake her body violently, but her limbs flop like a fish out of water.

"Kylah, I said stop! Let's go."

On his second sentence, Jarell's voice cracks like he's about to weep, and that makes me lose it.

"What did you do to her?!" I rage and start punching Jarell over and over as hard as I can. He puts his arms up to block me as best as he can before he catches two of my punches and puts my arms in a hold where I can't swing and carries me out of the room.

"Kylah, I didn't do anything to her! I promise I didn't!"

"I don't believe you!"

"If you would just listen to me for a second, and calm down..." he shouts, but I realize my legs are free and knee him right in the groin as hard as I can so that he can let me go. He jerks forward and winces, dropping to the floor, and fulfills my wish. I run back into her room, and she's still laying in the same position, not having moved a muscle.

"Come on, Mama. You usually get up. What's wrong now? Do you need some water?" I cry. "You gotta stop doing this, Mama."

I curl up against her and wrap my arm around her cold body. It's like she just walked out of a freezer.

"Come on, it's me. Get up! I said, get up! Mama! Get up!" I scream louder and louder so that I can't hear the sirens that wail in the near distance.

~ ~ ~

"Mama! Mama, get up! Mama, please! MAMA, don't leave me like this!"

"Kylah... Kylah! Wake up!"

A deep voice screams at me, and my body violently shakes back and forth before I open my eyes. Jarell hovers above the bed, his brows deeply creased between his eyes with his hands on my body.

I huff and puff, attempting to adjust to my surroundings before I finally realize I'm in my bedroom. Once again, my sheets are drenched. So is my tank top, my boy shorts, and my face.

Damn, what the hell? I was just at the movies!

I blink several times, trying to remember how I even got home last night, but once reality sets in, a barrier somewhere behind my eyes collapses and starts flooding my face and chest.

"I can't take this shit." I sit up and weep in my hands, feeling more humiliated than anything. A few moments pass, and the bed dips a little bit beside me, indicating Jarell's presence. With skepticism, he rubs my soaked back.

"It's just a nightmare. It's okay," Jarell says. "I'm here with you as long as you need me to be..."

At first, my body immediately goes cold at his touch. At the edge of my lips are a few insults in addition to the urge in my limbs to hurt him by hitting or kicking the same way I did on the day Mama lost her life. But the look in his eyes makes my heart sink to my knees. His orbs almost never show emotion because of his blindness, but for whatever reason, the load of sorrow and regret living in them right now breaks me.

I don't know how to even describe it; the look is so intense that it steals my breath. For the first time since I've lived here, a small seed in my mind believes Jarell really does feel some kind of way about how things in our family ended up. Because on any other given day, he acts like he never cared due to his lack of even attempting to bring me to the table to talk about any of this.

WHY?!

Why did all of this happen to me? To us? *What happened to our family?*

I don't care that I'm mad at Jarell. I don't care that he's sitting next to me while I'm at my absolute worst right now; hair all over the place, the bed sheets damp with sweat, and snot running down my nose. No amount of therapy will help this. When will these dreams stop? How am I supposed to make it through the rest of my life this way?

Jarell doesn't say anything, but his arm tightens around my shoulder as he pulls me close to him. The level of warmth that little move provides breaks every fiber of tension in my veins, and I just surrender for a moment to grieve, audibly laying my pain bare to him.

"Jarell... please." I hiccup. "I'm just gonna keep dreaming about Mama the longer I have no answers. Why did she turn to drugs? Why *would* she, huh? Didn't she know she still had me to take care of? How could she not care about what would happen if she died? I mean… didn't she know I loved her?"

Jarell's head dips, removing any access I had to his expression. His eyes settle on his lap, but he blinks several times to let me know he's grappling with how to reply.

"What do you know, Jarell? Did you know she was taking drugs? Please… tell me…"

"No, I didn't know, Kylah," he interrupts my begging with a firm dissent.

"So then why would she use them? Was life really that bad for her? Is it my fault? Is it because I killed Dad? Did she hate me because of what I did?" I weep some more. Jarell remains stone silent. "Jarell, why did I have to be the one to kill him? Maybe she felt sad that she had to live with me because I'm the one who took him away…"

"It's not because of anything other than her own choices," he responds with confidence. "You shouldn't blame yourself."

I shake my head fervently. "Hell no. I know it's bigger than that. She wasn't taking drugs when you were around, was she?"

"No."

"If it's not me, did she start taking them because you left us? Because that's what I'm thinking, too. Any time I'd ask her about you, she always got sad. We were both sad. And she told me that you wouldn't talk to her anymore. So there's gotta be something you're not telling me…"

"Kylah, I truly don't know why she chose to abuse drugs, alright? Other than that, I'll be honest and say I haven't told you the answer to many of your questions in order to protect you," he says, and then he whispers, "I don't want to see you hurt…"

"So what you're telling me is that you **do** know why all this shit ended up the way it did with our family? Why I killed Dad? Why

Mama died?"

"Some of it, but not all of it."

"Okay, so what is there to protect, Jarell?! She's dead! He's dead! They're not alive to be able to hurt me! In what way is not telling me this information in order to protect me? I swear to God..." I mumble, clenching my fists.

"Because I don't want you to see either of your parents as villains, baby sis," he confesses, his voice cracking. "I want you to hold happy memories of them and have a good life without any of that negative baggage because it will just weigh you down. I will carry it if you just focus on softball, doing well in school, therapy, and graduate from high school like I never did, and –"

"That's not going to help me!" I scream. His eyes squeeze shut at my abrupt explosion. "And what do you mean by 'seeing them as villains'? What did they do that was so wrong?"

"Kylah, please just listen to what I'm trying to say..." he says with his eyes averted.

"No! You just need to stop playing in my face. You know? Are *you* the real reason why the both of them are gone? You act like you are, and if that's the case, I hope the worst for you."

He gives me a bewildered look.

"What?" he roars, whatever restraint he uses finally snaps. "Look. I know you don't like how things ended up with Ma and your dad, but the way you come at me is not something I'm gonna keep putting up with. I've tried to be patient, understanding, and empathetic, but the disrespect from you is too much."

"Then you shouldn't have taken me in, Jarell. At this point, I'd rather be homeless if you won't tell me the truth!" I screech.

Jarell pauses and gives me another long glare. The heat rising in his eyes starts to cool, and it seems like he taps into another time period for a second before he snaps out of it and the heat rises again.

"You don't know a thing about being homeless, Kylah. You better be careful about what you say."

"It don't matter. I've figured out how to survive up to now, and I'll figure it out again when I'm on my own. That's all I know, and that's all I need to know."

He shakes his head and moves away from me to stand up. "I just don't understand how you can be so ungrateful. Pretty much everything you could want, I've worked my complete butt off to try and give to you! What more do you want?"

"Oh, you want a cookie, Jarell? What you did by taking me in was what you were *supposed* to do. And to be honest, you probably didn't even want to. You took me in because you felt guilty," I say, my tears continuing to flow full throttle.

Jarell's frown deepens.

"Felt guilty? Let's be clear. I wasn't supposed to do anything, so your misplaced anger is wrong. I'm tired of being treated like crap by you, and it ends today. I've done nothing to deserve how you talk to me, Kylah. Showed nothing but love to you, and I get crumbs in return."

I roll my eyes, growl, and throw my hands up. "You wanna know why? I treat you like that because you abandoned me after I killed Dad, and you left me with Mama for seven years without saying anything. No bye, no check ins, no nothing. I didn't love anyone else the way I loved you. You were everything to me, and you just disappeared. You know how that made me feel?! It made me feel like everything was my fault and that you hated me. You hated Mama, too. Of course, you feel guilty, and that's why you took me in," I weep and hiccup before

I continue.

"You never called to see how I was doing. You didn't leave your number. Not even as an emergency contact. It was like you didn't think of me at all. I love Mama, but you left me with someone who smoked and drank, and after a while, she was always high. Then she started bringing these random dudes over to get drugs to take pills or shoot up her arm, and all I wanted was for you to come and get me and keep me safe. But you never came. So, I just locked myself in the room so they wouldn't come near me."

Jarell's brows crumple.

"Kylah, how was I supposed to know all of that was going on? I didn't know she had gotten herself into hardship like that…"

Now I want to punch him in the face.

"You would've known if you didn't leave me! But you found the courage to call me and show up when she's laid on the bed and dead, right? I don't even know how you found out. It was too late for you to be showing up. And now you won't even tell me the truth about anything!" I cry. "You did nothing for me when it counted, and now you're trying to make up for all of it and playing the victim. I hate you so much that it makes my stomach hurt."

"Kylah…" The growing frustration is now in his body language more than his face.

"If you wouldn'ta left, Mama wouldn't have started drinking and taking drugs, and deep down, you know it. You probably knew she had a problem, and you let me grow up in that. You could have gotten her some help, and you just let the problem go on…"

Jarell explodes, his eyes now bloodshot red.

"I'm not Ma's parent, alright?!" he screams. "I wasn't responsible for her. She was responsible for herself. I had my own life to live and

I needed to get away from her to do that! A whole lot of bad things happened to me, too, almost to the point of no salvage, and guess what? I didn't have an older sibling to come save me the way you're crying about me not doing. The reason why I left our family is not for you to understand because that's between me and her. You feel me?" he explains with a sternness I actually listen to this time.

I cross my arms as my eyes travel away from him in response, despite the fact that he can't see my attitude anyway.

"Kylah, I'm not gonna let you blame me for all of this. If you would take a second for once in your life to think outside of yourself, you might understand that the situation is way bigger than me just leaving."

"That's the problem, Jarell. *You won't tell me the situation.* So these are excuses. It's crazy because even Daddy seemed like he cared and wanted to have a connection with me, but you caused a lot of trouble with him, too. Just because you didn't have your dad anywhere in your life didn't mean you needed to come and fuck up the chance I had with mine."

Jarell's face completely relaxes for a moment, like he's speechless. The more the seconds go by, and he realizes exactly what I said, his eyes expand before he squints and balls his fists.

"What did you just say?" he asks with a raspy voice.

"You heard me."

"Kylah, if I wasn't saved, I'd punch you through that wall right behind you!" Jarell yells at me so loud, my nightstands rattle on the wood floor as I cringe to protect my ears. Even worse, he grabs me by the shirt, and shakes me back and forth so violently that I scream. All my organs inside turn to ice. He's never done anything like this, nor has he ever looked so full of rage. Now I'm scared he'll hurt me, so I cover my face to avoid a slap or punch.

"How do you even feel good about yourself to say that to someone?" he whispers and lets me go. Immediately, an energy of regret escapes him, and it's all over his face. After giving a long glare in my direction with wrinkled brows, he steps back, taking several deep breaths. Surprisingly, Jarell breaks.

The tears start falling for him, too, and he doesn't even attempt to hide it.

Oh man.

I try to regulate my breathing as best as I can to keep from melting down again, but all that comes out is a quiver I know he can hear. Jarell continues to shake his head harder and harder as if trying to get a thought out of his head, or to stop himself from getting any more elevated than he is. He continues to speak with a deep, teary voice.

"You don't have any idea how much I've sacrificed to make you happy, Kylah. Ma and I shielded you from all kinds of heartache about our family because we love and care about you. We wanted you to have a better life than we lived. So I'm sorry you were put in a position to watch Ma suffer and you had no one to turn to. I wish I could've been there to protect you, and I let you down. For that, I'm sorry. But because things were so hard for us, that's why I continue to pour into your goals and dreams the way that I have because you deserve so much better. You've always deserved better than I had ever gotten. And that's the shit you say to me, Kylah? You *hate* me? After everything I've done..."

I don't say anything, but a boatload of guilt tanks my stomach.

"I'm outta here. Before I do or say something I can't take back," he says.

With that, Jarell quickly exits my room, dragging his slippers across the wood. Once he's gone, an uneven breath tickles my throat before it releases into the air, and I sob uncontrollably until I get up and head outside to sit out on the back patio for some fresh, cool air. Putting my knees up to my chin, I wrap my arms around them and rock back and forth on the concrete as my soul releases an infinite river of sorrow for this whole situation.

Damn.

I didn't mean to crush Jarell like this. I really didn't. And I know I don't have all the details about everything. But he just doesn't understand how much his silence and this game of "keep away" is cutting me deep, and I just don't know any other way to show it. I'm so frustrated with myself because Dr. Anderson keeps telling me the ways I can show it in healthier ways, but in practice, I can never seem to get it right.

And for that, I cry. Until the sky turns from black to a dark blue – at dawn. Two hours before the first pitch of my next softball game.

Chapter Sixteen

AN HOUR OF sleep is nowhere near enough rest, but my alarm wakes me up anyway. And by alarm, I mean the loud ass neighbors upstairs stomping all around like they're on a drill team. I check my Chromebook, and it's seven o'clock, and our game is at eight. I'm so damn tired that I can barely even hold my head up, but I get up anyway and haphazardly throw everything I need into my bag, including my sketchbook and Mama's journal that still rests on my dresser.

For the first time ever, I don't even want to play today.

I can't keep that whole exchange between me and Jarell and that dream about Mama out of my head. She really should be here. She should be taking me to my game right now. The muscles in my face and around my eyes tense up, and I sniff. The room becomes blurry all over again, but I continue getting ready.

Pulling my bedroom door open, I walk to the bathroom to wash my face and brush my teeth. I don't even care about showering. Don't care about my hair, either. On my way there, Brooklyn's sitting next to Jarell on the couch, and they're talking about who knows what. I don't see Jarell and can only hear him, but I unfortunately manage to make very brief eye contact with Brooklyn. The smile in her eyes disappears the second she sees what I look like, but I don't give her a chance to make a comment. I'm already in the bathroom and doing what I need to do.

Once I'm done, I don't utter a peep to either of them. I walk right out of the door and, this time, opt to ride my bike to the diamond. They'll probably go to church instead of my game anyway since it's Sunday.

I'm late when I arrive. The team is already huddled up, preparing with Coach, and getting pep talks from the assistant. When I walk up, everyone freezes, looking me up and down all weird. Tina's eyes hold a load of worry, and Alaysia grills me with her lip turned up. I scoff and turn away from her.

"Kylah, what's wrong with you? Are you alright?" Coach asks.

"I'm fine," I say.

He shakes his head. "Nah. You look crazy. What did you do last night?"

"I said I'm fine, Coach," I insist.

"Alright, well you better be fine out there, too. Game starts in five minutes. Let's go!"

As the captain, I go out there and do the coin toss to see who's up to bat and who's out in the field first. We lose the toss and end up fielding first. I take a deep breath and head to the circle.

Come on, Kylah. What's a little lack of sleep? You got this. Trust your ability, I pep talk myself.

When I get on the pitcher's plate, the first batter's up. She's a lefty like me, which makes it easier. The catcher flashes a signal between her legs for which pitch for me to throw. I nod, swirling the ball against my hip. Just as I'm about to throw it, right behind the batter in the stands, a flash of Mama smiling and watching me like she used to years ago materializes right before my eyes.

What the hell?!

I get so startled that I blink several times, throw the ball, and it's the wrong pitch. And a wild one. The ball barrels right toward the batter. She immediately sees it's about to hit her, so she turns her back and allows the ball to strike her in the back of the thigh. She throws the bat and heads to first base.

"Fuck," I whisper, putting a hand on my forehead. Not a good start to the game for my very first pitch to hit the batter and permit an automatic walk.

I take a slow inhale in, and a slow exhale out. *Mental toughness, Ky. You know what that is. Use it. Shake it off.* I talk myself up again. My teammates in the dugout encourage me, and so does Brooklyn in the audience. But Jarell isn't there.

For some reason, him not being here gets to me. I don't know why Brooklyn decided to come, but it means a lot to me today more than any of our other games.

I gather myself and prepare for the next batter. I manage to strike her out, but the walk on steals second base. Whatever. Okay. Whew. I think I'm in a good place. The next batter comes, and she gets a ground hit to first base. One out, runners on first and third.

Next person comes, and I got her on a one-two count, an advantage for me. Catcher flashes a signal for a screwball. Cool. I get ready to throw the pitch, but a distinct and familiar cheer from the audience cuts through my team's chant for the batter to strike out.

"Let's go, baby girl! You got this! Strike her out, baby!"

It's Mama's voice! It echoes in my ear over and over to the point where my eyes squeeze shut.

Inside, my stomach bubbles, and my chest constricts as it becomes impossible to breathe. I throw the pitch just to get it out of my hands at this point. It doesn't spin the way it's supposed to, and it goes down the middle of the zone. The sweet spot for any batter. Oh shit...

CRACK!

The batter sends the ball right down center field and out of the park. Oh God... that's three to zip. I knew that was coming as soon as it left my hand.

"Come on, Kylah!!" Coach screams at me.

As the hitter runs the bases and the crowd goes wild for her, Tina jogs over to me from her shortstop position. When she reaches the circle, she searches for any injuries before she investigates my eyes with hers.

"Hey, are you okay? Giving up runs like this isn't like you. You look really, really tired," she says. "What happened when you got home last night?"

It's taking every inch of me not to cry. I think she can tell.

"I'm okay, T. I just gotta shake it off," I lie.

"Okay... if you're fine, then come on! Do better!"

She runs back to her position. The top of this inning finally ends once we get an out on defense, and we go to bat. We don't score, so we're back on defense. The pitching for me gets no better. On out two, I give up another homerun. Once again, as the hitter runs the bases, I get another visitor. This time, it's Coach. He shakes his head before speaking.

"Kylah," Coach whispers, giving me an unemotional glare. "I think it's time for you to let the other team see something different. It's possible for us to get back into this game, but not with you in the circle right now. Go have a seat."

With the tears dropping from my lashes, I pull my mitt off

and walk to the dugout. Alaysia grabs her mitt and takes my spot in the circle. This is so embarrassing, but these ... I don't know... hallucinations are driving me crazy! I sit on the bleachers and drop my head into my hands, trying to reset my brain, and stay that way until we ultimately lose the game. I don't even take my at bats.

The second game goes the same way, except I don't even get a chance to pitch. I'm so out of it that Coach benches me. I'm in a little bit of a better place to watch, but we're playing so terribly that I'd much rather have my head in my hands, so that's what I do.

The wild cheers from the crowd, the chants from the other team, and the feet rumbling the bleachers, excited for us to lose, since we were the favorites to win, are just all white noise to me right now as Brooklyn sits next to me on the end of the bench, rubbing my back. Words can't even describe how thankful I am for her right now. At the same time, I feel so awful that I've had such negative feelings toward her just because she's with Jarell. She's really been there for me lately.

Our team is on their last at bat, and as soon as one of my teammates strikes out on the last out of the game, the opposing team rushes out to the diamond to celebrate this upset, jumping up and down while our team trudges to the dug out with their heads hung low to gather. I rise from the bench as Brooklyn's hand slides down my back and meet the team in the huddle.

As soon as Coach arrives with skin as red as an apple, he slams his clipboard down on the wooden bench and his hat goes with it. Half of the team flinches at his move.

"What the hell was that today!? How did we go from cruising and blowing out our opponents yesterday to just flat out falling apart today? Huh?! This was embarrassing! You all just let two sorry ass teams upset us!"

Some of us rub our arms and look at the ground, some scratch our heads without giving him eye contact, and some of us are strong enough to look him in the eye. The vein in his neck twitches as he glares at each and every one of us in disbelief. I'm his first individual target.

"Kylah, I don't know what your deal is, but you need to get your shit together. This is not a good start to the season for you to be the starting pitcher for the Senior Leagues in July!"

Everyone's eyes shift to me, but I keep mine on Coach as he starts to get more and more distorted in front of the wetness in my eyes.

"And I don't know why everyone's looking at Kylah! This ain't all her fault. You can't win a game without her?! Because that's how ya played. You act like you can't play defense, some of you act like you've never touched a bat in your life, and some of you made stupid plays that you knew weren't going to happen. Why would you try to throw a double play when the girl already touched the base? We had so many opportunities to win both games today, and we choked. See, what your problem is, is that you're so used to Kylah pitching shutouts that you've become complacent on D. So, for that, I'm drilling the hell out of you at the next practice. There will be no batting. Straight fielding. If we play like this again, we'll be out of the first round in the Senior Leagues. You understand?" he yells.

No one says anything, but everyone's silence say we agree.

"Get out of here. I'll see you all at practice on Tuesday. Four o'clock sharp. Any lates will be running sprints."

We all break from the huddle. I won't go back to Brooklyn. I just gather my things and walk to my bike. Once I have everything secured that needs to be on it and walk it toward the street, Alaysia and her parents are in a triangle in the parking lot. Everyone's body language is tense except for Alaysia, whose shoulders are sunk, and her face is sullen. I walk close enough to not be noticed but can hear. It's easy to gather every word too since they're so loud.

"What the hell was that today, Alaysia? You were horrible! The one time you get an opportunity to pitch because Kylah's out, you screw it up like that?! I can't believe you. You had multiple opportunities to win this tournament, and you didn't," her dad rips her.

Alaysia opens her mouth to defend herself with her arms out, but her mom swoops right in and shuts it down, tagging in for her husband.

"Don't you dare say a word. We spend so much money on your training and development, and you say you really want this, but putting up that kinda performance when you're on this elite of a team is unacceptable. And you wanna know what the real issue is? You rippin' and runnin' with your little fast friends is more important to you. We told you that we'd throw you a birthday party, but you needed to also stay focused on the tournament, too. And you didn't."

Fast? Ha. They should see her at school. By this point, Alaysia doesn't even try to interject. Her head hangs to the floor as her dad picks up at the end of her mom's last sentence.

"She's right, Lay. Your problem is that you don't wanna work hard, and you like the idea of the results more than the process of getting there. You gave up four homeruns in two games. You say you want to be the star pitcher, but your actions don't prove it. Keep on acting like this. Your future with softball is screwed, and you can kiss that dream high school goodbye. You're an embarrassment!"

Yikes. I don't even wanna hear anymore, but someone had to tell her. I'm glad it's her parents because everyone else just seems to worship the ground she walks on. Including Coach sometimes.

With that, I erase her from my mind and ride to another destination as I let my mind go wild, thinking of any and everything. Coach is right. Losing that tournament to a garbage team is embarrassing, and most of it was my fault. Plus, I refuse to go home. I've got a good feeling Brooklyn will try to have Jarell and I talk this out, and I'm just not ready. I just feel like I'm way too all over the place for that.

When I find my favorite little tree at a park hardly anyone knows about, I sink into the dirt about the absolute pile up going on right now. I don't have my phone back, and I'm not in the mood to draw, so instead, I pull out the small journal that's supposedly Mama's.

With her voice being in my head all morning, will the only thing that settles it to be reading her work and her thoughts? As much as hearing her voice echo in my ear gave me anxiety today, especially on the softball field, I guess reading whatever she has to say is the closest thing to her being alive.

I miss her so much.

Days like this, I just want to lay my head on her lap as she brushes her soft fingers through my curls like she used to on the days she seemed sober. She'd always do that when I'd have a bad day at school, had a bad game, or had a friendship issue.

I wonder if she wrote about those days in her journal.

Did she write about me at all? What did she prioritize thinking about? Who did she think about? Did she write about missing Dad? There're so many things she could write about, but it's not like her journal is that thick.

Unclipping the band around it, I let the pages flip with ease. The first maybe twenty or so pages are filled with writing, but the rest are empty. Hmm. What's her very last entry?

Mixed with feelings of dread, curiosity, and fear, I flip to the last time she wrote in the book.

#24

I seem to be doing a much better job the second time around. This whole mom thing, that is. Even with all the mistakes I've made as a mom, my baby girl just seems so happy, full of life, and full of energy. There's nothing more beautiful than her big smile. She literally smiles at everything, despite all the craziness that had happened with her dad. I really thought with her pulling that trigger on him, it would ruin her forever because for a while, she was in such a funk. But lately, it seems like she's bounced back to her lively old self again. It's only been a year and some change since everything took place, but watching her cry and cry about it at first, after a while I felt so guilty. I just don't want to ruin her like I did my baby boy. I'm so hurt that he's decided to move away and cut me completely off. But what can I really say? I suppose I deserve his silence after everything I've done. I just wish I didn't assume my baby girl would feel the same way about me that he does. Otherwise I would've never taken these pills to make the guilt go away.

Wow. She appreciated me more than I ever knew. But yet... based on what I'm reading, *Jarell is the reason Mama started taking pills.* She felt horrible about him leaving just like I did, and he never showed up or even cared.

I knew it. I don't even want to read it anymore. Who cares what mistakes Mama made – him leaving the family caused her to take pills. This is all I needed to confirm what I've started to think. I slam her journal closed and seethe to myself. I'm never going back to live with Jarell ever again. No wonder why he never wants to tell me anything...

For a while, I sit underneath the tree with my knees up, arms wrapped around them, trying to contain the rage rising in me. I'm already tired, so I work myself up to complete exhaustion, but I know I can't sleep at the park. So instead, I ride my bike to the batting cages and work on my swing to keep me awake and to allow me to think about where I'm going to go other than back home.

Jarell and Brooklyn are probably worried about me, now that it's late at night, but I don't care. They might as well consider me a runaway because I'm never going back. I will figure it out. Somehow.

When the batting cages close, around eight at night, I bike ride around the city until I can't even keep my head straight. I really need to find a place to go right now – only having an hour or so of sleep isn't safe. I'm about ready to pass out. It's really inconvenient to not have my phone, either.

I decide to ride to Prez's house because I don't really have any other option. I barely even know where I am right now, and I don't have GPS. So I'm gonna have to rely on my memory to go back home, and then go to Prez's house from there. And that's what I do.

By the time I arrive, it's around ten-thirty at night. It really sucks that it's a school night. I can't knock on their door without Prez's parents being worried and wondering why I'm out so late, but what choice do I have? They have a two-story home, so it's not like I can sneak through a window to Prez's room. And I haven't been far enough in the house to know which room is his to throw a rock and get his attention. Besides. It would likely scare him.

So... I settle for the doorbell. I notice they have a camera, so at least they'll know who it is.

After a few seconds, the door swings open, and Miss Juanita already gives me a bewildered look.

"Oh my goodness, mija, what's the matter? Are you alright? Why are you here so late?" She instinctively grabs my shoulders and scans me from head to toe, trying to find some injury or other physical reason for me being here.

It's a kind of look Mama would've given me, too, and it gut punches me. Now, I can't even speak without crying.

"Preston! Ven! Preston, ven aquí, ahora!" she yells.

All I hear is the floor pounding upstairs before Prez rushes down the steps. The moment we lock eyes, he balks, almost falling backward on the stairs. Damn, I must look like a complete wreck.

"LaLa? Yo... are you okay? What are you doing here this late? What's wrong? What happened, Mamí?" Prez questions as his attention ping pongs between his mom and me.

"No sé. Cuando abrí la puerta, estaba llorando," she replies, motioning tears on her eyes with her fingers.

"Gracias. Hablaré con ella."

"Bueno. Espero su familia conoce donde está ella."

Miss Juanita nods before giving me one last worried look before walking away and heading upstairs.

"Come on, LaLa. Let's go to the living room."

Once I'm in, he pulls me into his chest. I melt in his arms, weeping until I feel like I can't anymore. But Prez just stands strong, holding me up like the pillar I need. I separate from his body the moment I feel like I can stand independently.

"You know I don't like seeing you like this. What happened?" he whispers to me and motions Kleenex my way. I gratefully take it before the snot starts to embarrass me.

While I clean up my face, Prez shifts to sit on the couch in front of me, giving me a look like he's ready for me to start talking.

"So many things happened over the last day, Prez."

"Like what?"

"The first is that me and my brother got in a fight," I confess and blow my nose into the tissue again.

His eyes expand. "A fist fight?"

I shake my head. He sighs in relief with a hand on his chest.

"Oh. Okay. So, just an argument."

"Yeah, but it was really bad," I cry.

"Well, what happened?"

This time, I don't hold back and confess everything. The "everything" Prez has been hoping I'd spill for the last year. I start with my mom's death and how I found her, my dad's death without telling him the cause, Jarell's disappearance from my life with his unwelcome return and his secrets, and then the argument, including all the excuses Jarell had. At some points, I couldn't even get through talking without flat out sobbing. Prez watches me the whole time, but he doesn't say a word. He simply positions himself as a listener, and I couldn't be more thankful.

"After we argued, he just walked away and said he needed to leave before he said something he can't take back. But, that's the thing, Prez. I want him to say it. I don't want him to take anything back. I'm tired of his secrets. I'm not going back there. He's the reason why my mama started taking drugs. He left and never talked to her again, and it really hurt her to the point of her taking drugs to feel better. I swear, there are just so many times where I feel like I *hate* him." I finish, squeezing my fists, shaking, and trying to regulate my breathing.

Prez lowers and shakes his head before looking back at me with sympathy. He takes a deep breath as a small, but sad smile spreads.

"Thank you for telling me all this after so long when I've been trying to figure out what's been going on. I'm glad you finally opened up, but sad that it took all of this for it to happen."

I nod, pressing my lips together.

"Like dang, LaLa. I can see why you've got this chip on your shoulder. I can't imagine going through what you did. I'm sorry you lost your parents that way. That's rough. I wouldn't know what to do if I didn't have Mamí and Pop in my life. But here's where I'ma be honest with you. The way I've seen you treat your brother, I know you're leaving out the part about how *you* handled the argument."

"Seriously, Prez? After everything I just shared, that's what you have to say?" I shout.

"Come on, LaLa. I'm not trying to dismiss that. I just said how tough going through all of that must've been for you. But you know me good enough by now that I gotta understand both sides. You know we're like this with each other. You call me out on stuff all the time, so let me do it for you, too."

I smack my lips and roll my eyes. I don't want accountability! I want someone to just listen!

"What did you say to him that got him mad? Don't lie to me, man..."

I take a deep breath and a long pause. I'm not telling him. Ain't no way I'm gonna have a repeat of Prez's silent treatment after I reamed Jarell the last time in front of him. Instead, I just give him a long, teary look. His shoulders relax in disappointment, reading my body language like a book.

"You said something mad disrespectful, didn't you?" he utters. "Just like you did last time."

I squeeze my eyes shut as the tears pop off my face and nod in honesty.

"See." He shakes his head. "This is what I'm talking about, LaLa. The anger you got. Your brother is the only fuckin' family you have. And now you're playing softball on the big stage, you go to a good school, and you have a normal life now. Can you maybe figure out why he left? Or maybe you can go to therapy or something."

"I already go to therapy, but it don't really work for me."

"Yeah, I see that."

"Whatever, Prez." I look away, wiping more of my tears with the Kleenex. "I don't wanna talk about this anymore if you're just gonna lecture me. It seems like you're downplaying everything I've been through just to defend someone you don't even know. You're supposed to be there for me! I just told you he's the reason my mama started taking drugs, and you're just going to disregard that?"

He shakes his head, looking at me as if I'm stupid. "Listen to yourself LaLa. Were you planning on always living with your mom? Don't you realize he would've left anyway?"

I turn my head and cross my arms, pouting.

"I think you're just trying to find any reason to hate him and that shit sucks, LaLa. I've only met him once, and he seems like a nice person."

"Being a nice person doesn't change the fact that he's keeping secrets from me. And the whole time, he's just watching me struggle because I keep having to guess why things happened the way they did. And he refuses to care about this part of it. He *has* to take some fault in that, Prez. Because I think he's scared to tell me that everything actually is his fault. Why else would he be so quiet?"

He stands and puts his hands in his shorts pockets as if he's preventing himself from going off or to regulate himself. "Or, maybe it's not that at all. Instead of planning to run away, you should go back and fix this because you've been an asshole. You're really gonna sit in my face and say that you hate your brother after knowing what happened to mine? After knowing what I said to him right before he drowned? I said I hated him. I would give anything to have my little brother back and take back what I said, and yet, you're ungrateful for yours!" Prez yells.

"Don't make this about you, Prez. I'm literally pouring everything out to you. I just need you, for once, to take my side and not try to reason with me! I need my feelings to be heard. Let me be frustrated! Let me vent, damn!"

"I'm not letting you do shit!" he screams over me to the point where it echoes.

I gasp and stare at him with wide eyes hoping his parents don't come into the room. I know one hundred percent for a fact they heard that. My heart starts to race.

"Like damn, LaLa. I love you for real, but you don't realize what you have." Prez frowns. "You gotta go fix it with him before it's too late. Seriously. What would you do if he died tomorrow?"

"Prez, I promise you, you never take my side about anything..."

"That's not true, LaLa," he counters. "That's not true. I really do hold you down, but when you're wrong, you're wrong. You gotta own it, man. At least when you call me out, I own it! At least most of the time."

My eyes sink to the floor, knowing damn well he's right. I can't even argue or dispute that without looking completely ridiculous.

"Get out of here and go make it right, Kylah. And don't come back here until you do," he firmly demands, pointing toward the door. Oooh shit. I know he's dead serious if he calls me by my real name. "And if you think about coming back here, all I'ma do is ask you about it, so if you ain't got details on how you made things right, then you can turn right back around."

I fall silent, giving him a look like he's gotta be kidding. But his light brown eyes glower right back at me with an intensity that nearly makes me shrivel up in shame.

"Bye. I'll be waiting for updates," he says, snatching the Kleenex away from me and swiftly walks to the front door. He opens it, and motions for me to head out.

I sit there for a second, stunned, staring at him, and waiting for him to take what he said back. But he's persistent and jerks his head toward the door, signaling for me to leave.

"Prez, I can't go back there tonight." I shake my head. "I've only had an hour of sleep, and if I try to ride home, I'm gonna pass out. Please. Just let me stay the night with you. I can talk to your mom and convince her, but I promise, I will head home in the morning. Please..."

He gives me a long glare, still not showing an ounce of sympathy before he finally releases a huge huff and shakes his head in surrender.

"Fine. You're sleeping on the floor then. Let's go."

With that, Prez turns on his heels and heads upstairs, leaving me behind. I quickly rush to follow him because I'm unfamiliar with that part of the house and refuse to get lost like an idiot. As I catch up, he's already grabbing an extra blanket from their linen closet and moves to his room. I, again, follow. I don't even pay attention to what his room looks like. I just watch him snatch an extra pillow from his bed and throw it to the floor along with the blanket.

"Thank you, Prez," I whisper.

"I'ma go let my ma know," he says and walks out. When he comes back, he barely has an expression on his face, letting me know that everything seems to be okay.

Without another word, Prez gets in his bed and turns his back to me, shutting his lamp off, signaling the end of our night and the end of this discussion.

I close my eyes and sigh, hoping I can get rest. Even if it's just a little.

Chapter Seventeen

NO MATTER HOW hard I try to sleep as peacefully as Prez does, I can't. I'm still awake, it's three a.m. Since I've been here, I've been grappling. Ruminating. Struggling. Bargaining with myself. What needs to be done to make things right?

What is wrong with me? What is seriously *wrong* with me?

I'm such a bad person. A bad sister. A bad friend. A bad human.

This is the second time I've made Prez royally upset, and this is the first time Jarell completely lost it, in tears, in front of me. The two most calm and even-tempered people I've ever met. And it's all because of me and my stupid mouth.

For some reason, Dr. Anderson keeps coming to my mind. I keep thinking about our conversation together about impact and intent. About how we intend to do something with a specific goal in mind, but our impact can be so damaging.

But Dr. Anderson never talked to me about how to fix the damage. That's the hardest part. That's where I'm stuck. But I guess the best place to start is saying the S word that I'm learning to not dread so much with Dr. Anderson.

Sorry.

The thing is, I'm sorry about certain things, but I'm not sorry for others. I'm sorry for the way I'm acting and making other people feel, but I'm not sorry about how I feel about everything, and I don't know how to break that down without being a complete jerk. I just can't win with this, but there's gotta be a starting point. Somewhere, somehow. But the bottom line is...

I can't keep going through my life like this. Everyone, eventually, will hate me, and I won't have anyone in my life I can turn to.

I continue contemplating until it's right before the crack of dawn, and now, I've gotta go. Prez is still sleeping, but I sneak out his room, down the stairs, and out of the door to ride my bike back home.

Once I'm there, I sluggishly head inside the main doors to Jarell's apartment and lean my ear up against the door to see if he's awake. I don't hear him at all, but Brooklyn's voice floats through to the outside.

"Heavenly Father, we ask that you protect your child from any danger on the streets, wherever she is, God. I pray that she has a safe place to lay her head. Father, I also ask that you touch her soul. She has clearly been through things that are not in your will, God, that she has yet to overcome, so please reveal your love, mercy, and kindness to her, Jesus. God, I ask that you intervene in this sibling feud and help them to restore their relationship. Whatever it is, God, that they need to do to get over this hump, I pray that you are in the center as they move forward. God, I pray that she's safe. I pray she returns home before we have to call the police, Lord. We need your mercy right now. Lord, please..." Brooklyn prays with such emotion and a tinge of mourning that I nearly start crying. I've never heard someone pray for me this hard. The tears fall when Jarell jumps in.

"Lord, I pray for many things over my baby sister. Safety, well-being, protection, and her mental health, Jesus. At this point, only you know the cure she needs to overcome the darkness she's experiencing right now. You were so gracious to me in helping me find that kind of light and joy in my life when I thought I had no hope, and I pray that you have that kind of grace and mercy for her, God. Lord, I pray for the spirit of forgiveness. Not just for Kylah, but myself. I aspire to love like you love people, God, and I want to have those qualities for my sister."

I can't take hearing anymore. I turn the knob and barge inside. Both of their heads whip toward the door, and Brooklyn's eyes nearly explode.

"Kylah!" she exclaims. She barrels toward me like loose soda cans after ripping the cardboard box open. Her arms stretch out to pull me in, but I step back and put my hand up to guard myself, stopping her right in her tracks. The whole time, I'm looking at Jarell, and he's looking in our direction with a myriad of emotions.

"My bad," Brooklyn whispers and puts her hands in her yoga pants pockets, blushing. "I'm happy you're safe."

I don't acknowledge her. I take slow, measured steps to Jarell whose eyes travel to my feet because he hears them. The closer I come, the more he struggles not to blink and display any more emotion than he's already trying to keep in check. I stop right in front of him, and he looks up, since he's still sitting down.

"Jarell, I'm sorry." The second I open my mouth, the tears well, but they don't fall. "I'm so sorry."

Jarell turns his head, breaking any contact I have with his eyes.

"Uh, maybe I should go and let you guys talk this out. Once again, I'm so happy you're safe, Kylah," Brooklyn speaks.

She grabs her things quickly and leaves the apartment in haste. The air becomes still once the door closes, leaving us to deal with the massive elephant in the room on our own.

"Jarell... I'm so sorry," I whisper again.

He sits still for a minute, keeping his gaze averted. I stand there, hoping deeply for him to say it's okay and move on. Instead, he closes his eyes as his chest expands with air, and he huffs it back out before standing up. We're nearly nose to nose. His eyes droop with exhaustion, but he keeps his chin up with a kind of resolve that makes me swallow. My hands tremble at my sides.

"You know I forgive you, but that ain't enough. If you're not already cleaned up, go get dressed. Let's take a walk down at the boardwalk so we can work all of this out," he says. "I'll excuse you from school today, and I'll call in for a sub."

I nod. "Okay."

By the time we get to the beach, the sun has risen, shining over the blue ocean water and giving it a starry look. It's a little windy today, but I don't mind as my thick hair blows like a cape behind me while Luna's walk pitter pats the wood we grace, leading Jarell down the path. Wow. What a beautiful morning. I guess there truly is a kind of beauty to San Diego that I never gave a chance.

"Kylah," Jarell starts after being in this deep, pensive state. "Thanks for coming out here with me. I know I didn't say anything at the apartment, but I'm glad you came home. I was almost a hundred percent positive that you'd run away for good and never come back."

Jarell's voice trembles when he speaks, the worry, sorrow, yet relief evident in his voice. Guilt rises in my stomach as Jarell continues.

"I'll be honest and say that I don't know where to really start because there's so much to talk about. But the most important thing for me to do is apologize to you, too. I'm sorry I've made you feel like you can't trust me at all because of my silence about everything. I never wanted that to happen, but it did. So I want to own that."

My gaze remains on our feet walking slowly down the wooden boards as the waves crash against the sand and Luna treads shortly ahead of Jarell. A deep part of me wants to say that I forgive him, but my ego suppresses the words from forming. I had done the hardest thing by apologizing first, and my body won't let me be any more vulnerable than that.

"I've been praying a lot to God for patience, clarity, and understanding of where your head is as a teenager. And I, of all people, should know how you feel and should be the last person to argue with you because I've been there and felt what you feel. At your age, I was very angry, too. Angry about my life. Angry about the things that had happened to me. But I just showed it differently by not expressing any emotion at all and let it destroy me from within until it boiled over. You're the complete opposite because you wear your heart on your sleeve, and you never hide how you feel. I haven't built the skills to deal with that, yet."

I never look up at him. I don't know what it would take for me to gain the kind of humility Jarell has. It would probably kill me. It's almost uncanny, and the remorse rising in my belly is now in my throat.

"Thanks for hearing me out," he says. "I'm sorry, Kylah."

"You don't have to apologize, Jarell," I whisper. I pause for a while before I continue speaking. "You've been trying to make things work with me, and I keep being a jerk. But you're right... I guess I really am angry. Prez told me I am, too. Obviously Dr. Anderson knows how mad I am. There are so many things unanswered for me. Things I'm in the dark about and don't know why they are."

"I know..." Jarell admits.

"Jarell, I'ma be real with you and say one of the biggest reasons why I've been acting this way toward you is because you moved away and left me without answers. What I said to you about that is real. I don't know why you did, but I ... I felt so lost without you being around."

Jarell looks my way, now his turn to feel guilt.

"Why did you leave?" I ask.

His eyes shift around, searching for the words to explain before he tilts his chin toward the ground.

"I don't want to get too deep into this. But because my life and past with Ma was so traumatic, I needed to move away to have a hard reset and establish a happy life on my own. I was so mad at her for all the things she allowed to happen to me that I couldn't stand to be around her anymore and be reminded of what we'd been through."

"But what about me, Jarell? I was the most hurt by you leaving..."

He closes his eyes and breathes in. "Leaving you was the only thing I regretted back then and still do now because I loved you so much. But I knew if you were around or if you were still in my life, Ma would be around, and it wouldn't achieve the goal I was seeking. So, I chose myself because you were Mom's responsibility. Not mine. So... I ultimately was willing to sacrifice our relationship to have a better life."

I nod slowly. Damn. What did she do? I guess I can kinda relate because of the situation she found herself in with raising me, so I can't imagine what she potentially did to him.

"What made you so upset with her?"

He shakes his head immediately. "And that's where I stop sharing. It's not anything that I want to resurface, and I don't want her actions to tarnish your image of her. I'm just being open and honest about why, so let's just leave it at that."

"Well, at least I got something. But I still need more answers about it," I reply.

"You're never going to get them from my mouth," he asserts.

"Okay, well can you at least tell me this? How did you know where we lived? And why did you come home when she was already dead when you had never come home before? Don't you see how that would've made me feel? For you to show up too late when she's already gone?"

"Well, first of all, I always knew where she lived, in case of emergencies. She always knew where I lived here in San Diego too, just in case. But the night before she died, she sent me some text messages outta left field. Like, paragraphs. At that point, I hadn't heard from her in about four years, so I was shocked. She was saying that she'd lost herself, wished she never had kids because she ruined them, and that she's found other things to be dependent on to bring peace. I had started to gather that to be either alcohol or drugs, but then, when I was in the middle of listening to the text, she called me. Crying. She just said I should look after you, and that she doesn't want to ruin your life the way she ruined mine. She and I started arguing about her responsibilities as a reliable parent, and then she said that she doesn't think she's going to make it. It scared me, so I had some friends from church drive me to LA. And then... When I got there, she was passed out on the bed. Trust me, I wasn't trying to come shake things up. I just wanted to do a wellness check and ..."

"So, she committed suicide?" I hoarsely ask.

"No, I think before I got there, her suppliers came to give her the drugs they normally do, based on the way the house smelled. She just overdosed."

I shake my head. Man, I wish there was more that I could've done for Mama. Maybe I should've talked to her more. Should've talked to someone at school for help. Talked to my old coach. Maybe she could've gone to rehab, and I'd still be in LA the way I want to be. I just didn't do enough. I was too scared, and now Mama is gone. But most of all, I feel incredibly shitty for even thinking Jarell had a hand in her demise. Man, I wish I could read that text she sent him. I know he still has it, but I already know he won't share it.

Why did she turn to drugs in the first place? What happened to her when Jarell was little? And my dad... what was his deal?

"I have so many questions, Jarell. Tell me about the man who helped me kill my dad," I plead. "I need to know, and I need to know why it had to be me to do it. Why were you guys fighting to where I had to pull the trigger? Tell me..."

"No," he flat out replies. "I'm not doing that."

"Come on, Jarell. I can't be left in the dark about who I am and the people I come from. And why things happened the way they did. This shit is really killing me inside."

"I hear you, but no," he insists. "Besides, you should take the time to figure out how you're going to address your resentment toward me. The only reason why I told you what I've told you is because we need to repair our relationship for us to coexist. At least until you're eighteen. It'd be even better if we were more than just coexisting and had a real bond the way we used to. You're not gonna be able to repair anything with your parents no matter what I tell you or how you feel," he explains.

"So, you're really gonna leave me in the dark? That's not cool at all. I keep having these nightmares, and they're literally becoming too much. How am I supposed to have closure when you won't tell me?"

His brows wrinkle. "You think having information about your parents will stop your nightmares?"

"Yes! I need closure, Jarell."

He shakes his head. "Trust me, it won't stop them. I know you want closure, and it's a normal feeling to have when things don't make sense. I've been where you are, frustrated with other people and their choices and frustrated with the circumstances you didn't create. But there is a huge difference between knowing and closure. Knowing is having the information you seek to questions and situations you don't understand, but closure requires a different level of maturity that you're not ready to tap into yet."

"What do you mean I'm not ready? There's nothing wrong with trying to get closure. Having answers to what's tugging at you brings peace so that you're not always wondering," I say.

"I want you to be honest about your intentions. Would knowing *really* bring you peace? You can know or find out something and still be angry at the person or the situation. It may even make you more upset, depressed, or resentful, and to me, that's not closure. That's a kind of struggle only maturity can address. If you want closure, you've gotta be mature enough to take some heavy information and turn it into something that you accept so that you can heal and not let it tear your soul apart."

Mmm. I let all of that sink in. Damn. That was some deep shit, and a gut punch of reality. I hang on to his every word and attempt to process it.

"So, with that said, you need to think long and hard about your intentions for wanting to understand our family history because there's little that is positive about it. Until you truly feel like you're in a space where you believe you can heal, serve others, give others wisdom, or use what you know as a learning experience, then I won't be saying much else about our family dynamic or your dad."

"But," I try to interrupt, but he puts a hand up.

"I'm not saying that you have to be fully mature because no one is, and no matter what, knowing the information will bring you some scars. But you have to approach this with a genuine heart of forgiveness and acceptance. That's real closure. And I know you're not ready yet. To help you get ready, I suggest you start to build a personal relationship with God and take therapy seriously, which you're not willing to do either right now. Yet, I'ma tell you, I believe they're the keys to your healing. You'll know when you're ready. Only then will I open my heart up to you about it. So there. There's a lesson for you that took me almost fifteen years to learn, and I'm trying to save you the heartache by teaching it to you now."

He and I continue to walk the beach with nothing but the trees whooshing and the waves thundering to shore as his words bask into my brain. I'm trying to figure out how to counter them to get what I want, but I can't. He's just too smart. And says things in ways I understand that my therapist is unable to do. She treats me too much like a baby.

"You know? I'll admit," I start, cutting into the comfortable stillness between us, "you've always taught me the best lessons. Even when I was in kindergarten. I still remember the one about me being beautiful and how much I matter. I guess this is just another one I'll have to take."

"Good." He nods, the left side of his mouth curling upward. He stops walking, turns, and looks toward my direction, not quite meeting my eyes, but close enough. "I need you to know that I love you so much, Kay Kay. You are part of what I believe God has called me to do to fulfill my purpose in life. I will do anything, and I mean anything, I can to help you live a life that you can look back on and say that you're proud of. You deserve that. You just have to trust me, okay?"

I nod, but he can't see.

"Jarell, you know... I don't hate you. I do still love you. I never stopped. I was just so mad and didn't know how to deal with everything. Lowkey, I still don't, but Dr. Anderson said I've been handling it all wrong."

"Forgiveness is easy for me, Kylah. I know it's hard for you, but starting over is all I've ever wanted. Be honest. Don't you want to?"

I know he can't see me stand in agreement with nodding, so this time, I step to him and pull him in for a hug, now wrapping my arms around his belly instead of his legs the way I used to and rest my nose on his shoulder. His body completely freezes at my move. I'm surprised at my move too because no one could tell me four hours ago I'd be even touching him, much less walking next to him in public.

But he just doesn't know how much I *need* this hug. I refuse to lie to myself anymore.

"Yes. I wanna start over."

Once Jarell comes to terms with being stunned, he returns the love and completely swallows me whole with his embrace.

Man. Maybe Brooklyn was right. Maybe Mom and Dad passing on was the very thing I needed to have another shot at this thing called life with someone who honestly has always been my true father figure.

We let each other go and proceed to walk down the boardwalk in a mix between awkward silence and relief. Jarell breaks the tension in the best way he knows how. By asking me questions about softball.

"So are you ready for your tournament in LA?" he asks.

"More than ready."

"Good. Well, since we're starting fresh and we're about to travel soon, here's your phone back. I haven't gotten a call from school in a while, and your teachers are telling me you've been improving, so I figure you've earned it."

Taking my phone from his pocket, he motions it toward me. Looking at the phone and then back at him, I frown, waiting for the joke to end. He motions it toward me again, waiting for me to take it. I accept it this time without hesitation.

"So, um... the second thing. I've been thinking a lot about something. I just thought maybe since we're visiting LA that... maybe we can go visit Ma together. It may bring you some peace after what happened this week. Us some peace."

I nearly stumble at his suggestion.

"Visit Mama?"

"Yeah. I know things haven't been great between us at all. But I think it would be a great healing activity."

"But Jarell..."

"You don't have to answer right now. Just think about it. Have you been reading her journal?"

I gulp. I had only read her last entry, which was the fuel to my fiery anger at Jarell. Had Prez not set me straight, we probably wouldn't be walking together right now.

"Yeah, just one page, though."

"Okay. Well, I encourage you to keep reading it. Maybe that'll help you get prepared. But anyway. I, again, appreciate you coming out here with me, Kylah. As rough as this has been, everything happens for a reason. This is a breakthrough for us, and I pray we get back to where we used to be. I know it'll take time, and things don't just turn around overnight, but I'm hopeful we will get there."

I nod my head.

"I hope so, too."

We continued to walk in comfort, and I take this opportunity to send Prez a text, now that I have my phone, in hopes it starts the forgiveness process. There's nothing worse than him being mad at me, especially if my intentions have shifted since our argument.

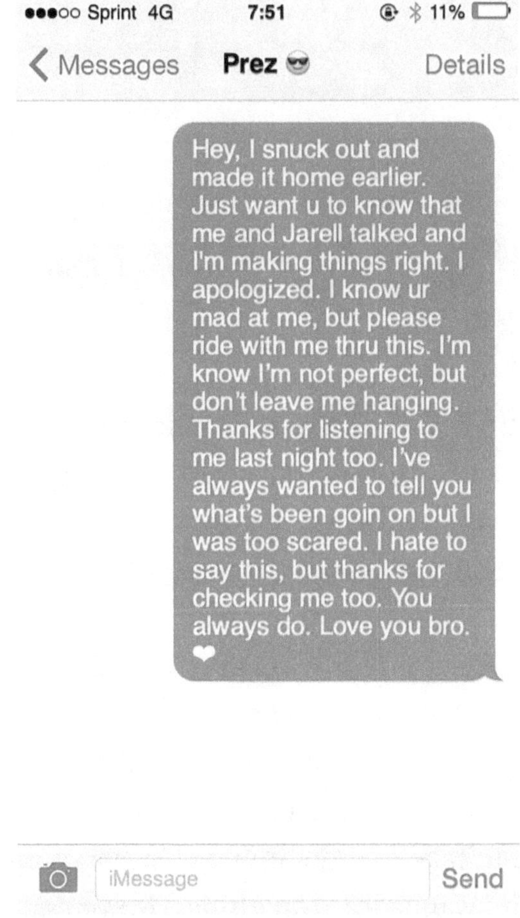

I can only beg the sincerity of this message comes through. A fresh start with both men in my life, despite all my shortfalls, is all I can hope for.

Chapter Eighteen

AFTER THESE CRAZY few days, it's back to reality at school. This week in Social Studies, we have a group project due for the American Civil War, and I really don't wanna engage with it. Last week, the teacher picked groups of three, and I'm the only one not in a group because I refuse to be the reason why the group gets a failing grade because I won't pull my weight. So, while everyone's in their groups and doing research, I sit at my desk right in the middle of the classroom with Mama's journal sitting closed right in front of me.

After the conversation Jarell and I had at the boardwalk, I know I'm gonna have to take matters in my own hands and read Mama's journal myself if I wanna learn anything. He even said it himself that he wanted to read it together, but at this point, I think doing this on my own is the route to go.

Unhooking the latch that binds the pages closed, I flip to the very first page instead of at the end. Mama's handwriting is beautiful. She had always written in this lovely cursive that made me so mad I couldn't read until she taught me during my fourth and fifth grade years how to both write and read it. Now, I'm super grateful she did.

#1

I've never been the type to journal, but I come to this blank page heartbroken. I hope writing will help me through the hell I'm in. I've been stuck in this house for almost a year now with my baby boy. And with a man I truly thought would be the love of my life... only for me to be so caught up in this trap of abuse I can't find or fight my way out of.

Why did he change so much on me? When I first met him with my homegirl, he was so charming. The way he took care of me and Lynn, buying us drinks, learning more about who we were, listening to our stories of loss with us having to be evicted from our apartments. But, for some reason, he took more of an interest in me, looking at me with such a desire I've never felt before. He loved me with his eyes. I fell in love with those eyes, too. It felt like I was floating on my back on the waves when I looked at him because they're so blue. I've never been interested in white guys before, and at the time, barely had seen them in my life unless they were on TV. But he was different. When did things go so wrong? What had I done to make him flip the switch?

I wish he was still the man I met two years ago to start the family I thought we could've had. Maybe one day he will change. I guess it's all I can pray or hope for. Because there is no other way out.

"Kylah," Ms. Harris, my case manager, calls out, interrupting my reading.

"Yep," I respond, annoyed.

"Are you going to at least attempt to do this project? If you don't, you are going to fail the semester."

"Nope."

"Seriously?"

"Yup."

She smacks her lips. "How about an alternative project?"

"What's the alternative?"

"How about you draw something in your sketchbook relating

to the American Civil War? Write a couple of paragraphs explaining your drawing, and then we will call that your project."

"I'm not writing the sentences, but I'll draw something."

"Fine. That's a start. I'll convince you to do the sentences later because I know you can do it. Let's start building healthy habits for high school. You're too smart to be throwing an entire project away."

I sigh. My head is not in a space to think about any schoolwork right now. After a weekend like I just had – losing the first tournament of the season as an elite pitcher, nearly running away from home, and getting into another heated exchange with both Prez and Jarell – school is at the bottom of my priorities. I know even just thinking about this project will crush my lungs to the point of having an anxiety attack in front of everybody just like I did at the mall.

I guess I'll do the alternative because I need at least a C on my progress report to remain on the softball team. But I will be returning to reading this journal later. Because what I just read has me shook. I can't imagine my dad... the one who seemed so loving and caring, would be abusive to Mama. But that ain't something I'm gonna think about here. It's just gonna ruin my day, and the last thing I need is another crappy day. This requires a more private setting.

Ms. Harris leaves me to begin working on my drawing. There are so many ways I can go with this. Despite what everyone may think about what I do and don't do in class, I can say with certainty that I listen to what the teacher is saying when she's instructing, especially when I'm drawing.

With the American Civil War, it was all about the Confederacy and the Union. The southern US states and northern US states. The confederacy wanted slavery to sustain their economy and spread it west while the union wanted the abolishment of slavery to allow the full industrial era to happen in the country (not because they truly wanted Blacks to be free, but some did). A kind of unjustness and inner turmoil in the country that never really got resolved since Jim Crow came shortly after. And... well... to me, the civil war really didn't end because the country still is racist, period. It just looks different. I don't care what anyone says.

For some reason, I feel like my life is just that.

Turmoil and unjust.

I had never felt it to be truer than when I held the weight of a gun in my hands. The gun that would end one life in order for the other to live. Jarell, or my dad. That's what the civil war boiled down to. Something had to end for the other one to thrive.

With my pencil, I start outlining the gun as the central symbol for my drawing. The gun as I remembered it until its shape fully takes form. It's symbolic in my life, and it's symbolic for war. Once the shape is outlined, I shade in the details. The ridges and grooves of the metal, some places shiny, and other places full of shadows.

The bell rings signaling the end of class. Damn, I got so sucked into this drawing that I lost track of time. Closing my sketchbook and gathering all my things, I leave Social Studies to meet up with Prez since our next class is science together. I haven't heard from him since my text yesterday, so my heart is in my throat in anticipation of our first interaction since leaving his house in the wee hours of the morning.

When I get near the class he just left from, Prez walks out with Andre by his side, and I smile at them both. Prez gives me a knowing grin in return, which I consider to be a reply to the text he didn't respond to. That makes me laugh as my heart blooms with comfort. Nothing feels better than to know I can make mistakes with him, and everything gets to still be alright. Even after he checks the shit outta me. A real friend.

Andre acknowledges my presence with a wave and nod, and we walk as an unspoken collective to a spot to quickly hang out before we have to be in our next class. Every one of Prez's friends and some of my other friends are in a circle talking. The three of us stick our heads in to see what the conversation is about, and the second bowling alley comes out of one of their mouths, I immediately realize they're talking about Alaysia's birthday party this past Saturday.

Ugh.

I step away from the group but lean on a wall nearby. Without much expression or a word, surprisingly, Andre joins me in a space on the wall. My heart rate spikes, and I hug my sketchbook to try and get it to slow down.

Prez stays in the other group to talk. This just reminds me that I have a bone to pick with him about what I saw on Alaysia's live. With everything going on this past weekend, I forgot all about getting on his case about entertaining that broad who had her tits all over him. I'll wait until he's done.

Andre and I are both quiet for a while until I'm the one to break it again while he scrolls through his phone, seeming to be bored.

"Did you go to the party?" I ask.

"What party?"

"Alaysia's…"

He shakes his head. "Oh. Nah."

"Oh." I shrug and look away. "I'm surprised."

"Why is that surprising?" he asks with genuine curiosity and puts his phone in his pocket before giving me direct eye contact.

I hold my breath and stare right back to show him that I'm strong.

But damn, I'm kinda weak in the knees. His eyes are so beautiful and intense that they literally clam me up.

"Because. Prez went, so I'm surprised you didn't go, too."

He lightly chuckles. "Just because P is the homie doesn't mean I do everything he does. You don't do everything he does, right?"

"True. Why didn't you go?"

He leans his head against the wall to relax a bit more.

"Ain't my kinda circle."

"Really? Basically, all your friends went. What you mean that ain't your circle?"

"I don't mean *my* circle. I meant *her* circle ain't my kinda circle."

I make an O with my mouth and nod big. "Why? Everyone likes Alaysia. Especially the boys."

He shakes his head before clearing his throat. "She's a bit too much for me."

My eyes balloon. What's with him being full of surprises today? I wish I could just bum rush him with a hug. I like him infinitely more now. Didn't know he could be any more attractive.

"I feel that. I don't really rock with her either," I say.

His eyebrows flex, and then he gives me another direct gaze before he emphatically replies, "I know."

I take a moment to try and figure out why he said it like that, but it's interrupted by none other than Alaysia herself, strolling up to the group who's talking about her party.

At least I thought that's what she was gonna do.

Instead, she walks past everyone and heads straight to Prez. Everyone kinda makes room for her to do so, too, moving out of the way as if they're going to bow down or something. I scoff and roll my eyes. I'm so tired of everyone kissing her ass.

"What does she want from him?" I mumble, thinking it's only me who hears what I say, but Andre does.

"I don't know," he says, watching it all unfold. "Wondering the same thing."

"Hey Preston," Alaysia greets him in that same ass, corny ass flirty voice that continues to make me sick.

"Sup, Alaysia." Prez looks her up and down, ogling her outfit. This time, she's got on a button up shirt in which the top three are loose with a skirt that would definitely flash her ass if she bent over. But his eyes don't suggest the kind of lust most other boys give her. His gaze is pretty neutral, but I'd pay to know what he's thinking. She's gotta be changing clothes when she gets to school because there's no way her parents would let her out of the house like this.

"Thanks for coming to my party. That shit was lit, so thank you for bringing your people to join us."

"Aww, no problem. Besides, we pretty much all came to your party. You shouldn't be thanking just me."

"No... I mean, I'm especially glad that *you* came," she emphasizes, and then kind of cuts a look at me with a side eye. Like she needs to see if I'm watching.

I almost lose it. What a clueless ass bitch. I think Andre sees what she's tryna do too because he makes a small little laughing sound in his throat.

"Why am I so special?" Prez asks her.

"Oh, I don't know," she says wistfully and steps to him.

She wraps both of her arms around his shoulders and latches them around his neck. They're so close that they, lowkey, might kiss. I gasp inside.

What?! Hell no! What the fuck, Prez?! What are you doing? Code red, get away!

I look up at Andre, and his eyes expand as well, but it's way more subtle than mine. Either way, I wish I had her confidence, I'm not gonna lie. If I even had half of it, I would've been all over Andre months ago. I won't dare show how impressed I am and watch Prez's expression. He looks at her arms, and then back at her with creased brows.

"I'll be honest Preston and say that it kinda seems like you're feeling me. So, I'm just tryna see what's up."

"What makes you think I'm feeling you?"

"I just felt like we had a connection at the party when we talked. I don't know. I guess I'm just getting that vibe."

"What vibe?"

"You know exactly the kinda vibe I'm talking about, Preston."

"There ain't no vibe. I told you I have a girlfriend. So, you need to put your arms down."

Oof. Yikes. Not him checkin' her in front of everyone... not the girl who thinks she's hot shit and that all the boys want to "smash"! I cover my mouth to stifle the loud laugh rumbling at my lips. I'm not the only one either. Multiple people turn their heads away with secondhand embarrassment, and others cover their mouths, too.

"I don't know what idea you're getting from me, but we're cool. I'm not feeling you that way."

Prez then takes her arms off him when she refuses and steps away, looking at her like she's nuts. At this point, I can't help myself and laugh to break the silence no one else dares to out of fear. That's what her thirsty ass gets.

"Bitch, what the fuck you laughing at? The one who couldn't stop crying at our game this weekend and made us lose? You shouldn't be laughing at anything or anybody with all that weird shit you be drawing, so don't make me put your stupid ass on blast," Alaysia reams me with eyes ablaze.

I instantly stop laughing and step away from the wall with a frown so deep, my forehead hurts. My skin cools as my fists clench.

"What? Say it again," I test her.

"Don't play dumb, bitch. Don't think nobody saw you drawing a gun in class today. I should tell the principal on your psycho ass, and then we'll see who has the last laugh. I hope you get arrested, too."

I blackout. Rage sparks a fire so quickly in my chest that my strong body charges at her with full speed as my fingers yank her by the shirt with two fists and slam her against the locker with a very loud bang that echoes down the hall. She screams right along with the bang. I keep my grip on her shirt and raise her up to meet my eye level, which forces her to the tip of her toes and pin her there. Everyone steps out of the way, and from my peripheral, a couple people pull out their phones to record.

"Stop always recording shit you snitch ass pendejos!" Prez yells to everyone. If they put it away or not, I don't know. Either way, I can always count on Prez to have my back so that I can keep my attention on this low life.

"Alaysia, I swear to God if you weren't my teammate, I would've been rocked your shit. You gon' fuck around and find out just how psycho I am," I threaten to only where she can hear. "I saw the kinda pressure your parents put on you after the games, and I feel bad for you, but that ain't no excuse. You better start figuring out how to be friends with me before I beat the games you play outta you or accept that you will *always* come second to me. You choose."

I've instilled some substantial fear in her because her eyes say so. She tries to play it off by blinking it away, but the way I have her hemmed up, blinking makes it worse.

Let me stop. I don't want to, but I need to. I'm the real bully here and will mop the floor with her ass. She should already know, considering how I deal with everyone else who tries their number with me, but she's lucky I've got a whole lot of restraint that I don't always choose to use. I let her go to breathe so I don't hurt her.

"I dare you to hit me," she says with a shaky voice once she's free. *Hmph.* She just won't learn. "Hit me. So, everyone can send the video to Coach, and then your ass is off my team for good. That'll be worth so much more than fighting you back."

"LaLa, let's go," Prez says softly to me. "It's a lost cause dealing with her." Once he does, Andre steps in with a silent agreement and pulls me away from Alaysia and gently toward Prez. I oblige without resistance and the three of us walk away with Prez to my left and Andre to my right.

"Oh, and I got you Preston! You'll regret tryna call yourself embarrassing me. Just watch!" she screams after us, but we all ignore her and keep it pushing.

I don't know where the teachers are for this passing time, but thankfully they weren't out supervising because I'd be in some major trouble right now for getting aggressive. I'm sure someone will snitch by day's end though, and I'll be in the office explaining to Ms. Evans what I did this time. Once again. The thing is? What I just did was essentially *nothing* compared to all the other things I've done to get in trouble, so I don't anticipate getting suspended. At least I hope not.

We continue walking away to a space away from everybody. I close my eyes and take a few deep breaths to calm down. Once I'm regulated enough, and we're near the science class that we have together, I cut a long look at Prez that could send him six feet deep.

"Prez, this is what happens when you entertain a snake bitch. She's been doing all of this to get me upset because she thinks I'm feeling you. Don't you see that she's tryna get me to fight? If she gets me to the point of doing that, I'ma get kicked off the team. You know that!" I scream.

"I know!" he bellows at me. He sighs, realizing his tone and dips his head, breaking eye contact. "I know. Lo siento, LaLa." He taps his chest with a small smile. "That was my fault, and I should've listened to you. I won't entertain her again. I promise."

I stare at him for a while, searching in his eyes for anything disingenuous, but I don't find it.

"You better not," I say, poking out my lip. "And what is 'lo siento'?"

Prez grins. "It just means that I'm sorry."

I frown. "Why didn't you just say that?"

His smile spreads wider. "I did... in Spanish."

I'm about to say something slick to him for thinking this shit is a joke and trying to use humor to get me to calm down, but Andre's voice cuts in between us. Like he's trying to save him.

"Aye, I'ma catch y'all after class, a'ight?"

"Alright, man," Prez says, and they dap each other up. Andre politely waves to me and heads to his class.

Man. For some reason, I don't feel mortified by Andre seeing all of that. I guess it just hits different to know that he doesn't like her either. Honestly, knowing that is what's going to make the rest of this day lovely, no matter what happens. I just hope I don't get in trouble.

~ ~ ~

There's nothing more peaceful than a tree, beautiful weather, a park, and my sketchbook. When everything feels so crazy, a reset in a place like this is always welcome for me. Especially since I have practice in a couple of hours, which has its own set of drama, so tapping into calmness before the storm feels right. I'll pick up on reading Mama's journal later. Gotta keep the rain from pouring.

So, I don't go to the usual neighborhood park that Prez and I sneak to at night to play on the diamond and where our team practices usually are. Too many people know I frequent that park, and Jarell knows I'm there a lot too. I can't take any chances of him showing up to grill me about the incident with Alaysia if the principal ended up calling him.

Much to my demise, people who were there when I hemmed Alaysia up and watched it all go down wouldn't shut the hell up about it, trying to egg us on to fight at recess. It got back to the teachers, who then told my case manager by the end of the day. Ms. Harris asked me about what happened, but I kinda shrugged it off and kept it moving. I hadn't heard from anyone else since, so I'm assuming I'm in the clear.

Staring at my current work in progress, a portrait, I smile to myself, satisfied with the start of the favorite face I love to look at.

Andre.

I think more about the interaction between him and I more than me pinning Alaysia up against the lockers. I can't help but nearly squeal, replaying how he just followed me and stood by my side during that whole incident and talked with me like we'd been friends for years. He was so... *comfortable*. Yet, the whole time, my stomach was doing a whole Simone Biles routine.

I continue to shade in the sides of his wide nose, leaving highlights down the bridge like he has in real life. But it's his eyes for me. They're dark, but they look like they hold a million stories that I can't wait to hear one day. I don't know why they're so captivating; all I know is that they put me in a trance every time we make eye contact.

I begin to perfect the outline of his eye shape and lids, which are hooded and deep set, the culprit of their intensity, before I draw his corneas and pupils. When I'm done, I stare at the finished product. Woah. I snapped with this. It's like he's looking into my soul.

"Aye, yo! That's me!"

A deep voice above me and to my left rattles me to the point where I wheeze hard enough to hit the back of my head on the tree bark.

"Ouch," I hiss and hold my head.

"Oh, my bad!" the voice says again, and he kneels to me. "My fault, I didn't mean to scare you."

Looking up after rubbing the pain, I'm staring into those mesmerizing dark eyes again. *The real ones*. It's like I'm in cardiac arrest for a moment and get trapped into his gaze before I even realize what just happened. Gasping, I slam my sketchbook closed as my cheeks ignite.

"Andre, what are you doing here?" I yell.

He's smiling like I didn't basically just tell him to get lost. "I should be asking you that. I never see you around here. I live right over there," he says and points to his two-story townhome that connects with another home. "My mom made me take my little brother and sister out to play."

Wow, I hadn't even realized that he lived so close to me and Prez. I should've known, though. We all do go to the same school...

"I thought I'd come and say wassup since I saw you against the tree, but I didn't expect to see my face as a drawing in your book."

Hugging my sketchbook tight to my chest, my face relentlessly roasts. I probably have already turned three or four shades of red. Even worse, he starts laughing before taking a seat next to me. Good thing I don't detect it to be a mocking laugh to send me running home like a humiliated girl running off stage in a talent show.

"Hey, don't be like that," he says. "I think it's really cool. I'm not thinking too deep into it, I promise."

I snap my head to him to see if he's lying. He just glares back with a soft look. It doesn't change how I feel though. I'm longing for the ability to absorb into the grass at this point.

"Can I see it again?"

I press the book even tighter to my breasts and shake my head.

"What's with you not speaking all of a sudden? What's wrong? You can't show me?"

"I-I've never shared my drawings with anyone before," I whisper, dropping my head low.

"Why not?"

"It's just... that... they're my personal way of expressing myself. I guess it's kinda like my diary or whatever."

The right corner of his mouth lifts. "Really? How should I feel about me being in your diary?"

My brows wrinkle and I quickly turn my head away from him as my face burns again, just as I thought it was about to start cooling down. This time when Andre laughs, I know he's laughing at me.

"Yo, this is like a whole new side of you that I don't ever see at school. You're usually super hard with a wall up, but now it's like ... you're just different, I guess."

"You're catching me off guard, that's all," I mumble. "Besides. I act like that at school because I hate it."

"You gotta like it enough to keep coming back."

I shrug and keep my gaze on my lap, still hugging onto my book and sitting pretzel style.

"Aye, so what was that whole thing Alaysia was talking about? Something about you drawing a gun. Is that in there?"

I huff and roll my eyes.

"Seriously? You even think she's too much, so you're gonna listen to her?"

"Well, is it true?"

"Yeah, because it's for our Social Studies project. Here, let me show you," I say and flip it to the gun I've started. I lay it flat on the ground so that we can both see. He marvels at every detail that I've drawn so far, scanning the photo from left to right, then up and down.

"It isn't finished because I have to draw something that represents the union group and confederate group, but I drew the gun first because it's a symbol of war. This gun was the deciding factor of whether slavery ended or stayed. That's why I drew it. Not because I'm crazy. Alaysia blew this outta proportion like she does with everything else."

He nods, still contemplating on what I've shared for a while before he speaks. "I really like the explanation. It makes a lot of sense with the concept of war, and it's super deep. So, you do like school and listen in class." He smiles.

I shrug. "No, I like making meaning of things with drawings."

"Mmm hmm. You wanna know what else?"

"What?"

"You showed me a drawing in your book. You said you never show anyone."

My mouth slightly falls open, but I catch myself and swallow, giving him a look like he busted my ass. The smile he was already displaying spreads wider before he and I both break into a laugh.

"I promise I wasn't lying when I said that. I really don't show other people," I say.

"Then why'd you show it to me?"

"Because I was trying to prove that I wasn't drawing it as a plan to shoot up the school or something," I say with a small chuckle afterward.

"Well, now that you've already got it open, show me some more drawings," he coaxes.

"Come on, Andre..."

"Please? I've never seen anything like this in my life. How you drew me was so..." He frowns, trying to come up with the word to describe it. "I don't know. *Real*. You're crazy talented, Kylah."

My face softens and cools. "You think so?"

"Yeah! Now show me what else you got!"

Blinking, I set the book back down and turn to the portrait I drew of Prez and his little brother with Prez's arm wrapped around his shoulder. Just like the one I saw in the photo on his parents' wooden end table.

"Woah." Andre marvels, his eyes perusing, once again, over every single detail of the sketch for longer than the last one. But this time, his smile disappears, and the humor vanishes from his eyes. After a while, and to my surprise, they become moist.

"Andre?" I call out in concern. "You good?"

He blinks several times before shooting a split second mortified look my way. Then, his gaze settles back on to the drawing. "Sorry. It's just that... Rico... he was like a little brother to me, too. How are you able to do that? Make it look so ... *real* like this? It's like he's back on

Earth with us. Have you ever met him?"

"No. Only saw him in a photo, but Prez told me all about what happened."

"Wow. Has Preston seen this?"

I shake my head.

"How can you draw something so perfect like this, only having seen him in a picture?" He smiles.

"I don't know." I shrug.

"Such a dope picture. You know you're talented if you can make me damn near cry like that. You should show Preston one day. He'd keep it forever."

"Maybe..."

"Now, can I see my picture again?" he presses.

"Nooo," I whine. "It's so embarrassing. I swear, I hate that you saw it."

"No, it ain't," he counters. "And why are you being so negative about it?"

"Because! Don't you get it? I'm not embarrassed at how it looks. It's that you caught me drawing you in the first place."

He shrugs and gives me a low gaze, saying what seems like a million different things to me, but I'm not quite sure how to interpret it. Like he's flirting, but he's trying to tell me to get over myself, while also confused at why I'm acting out of what he sees as my ordinary. Those are just my best guesses. I shouldn't even consider that he's flirting, especially since that isn't the vibe he's given since he's been here. It would be mad stupid of me to get my hopes up. I don't want to pull an Alaysia.

"I'm not trippin' about it, Kylah. I genuinely think it's dope. To be real, it's not super surprising for you to draw me, anyway. P is our best friend. I could see if we never interacted before. Then, I'd think something's up, for real."

"That's true..." I mumble.

"Sooo..." he eggs me on.

"Okay, look. How about this? Can I show it to you when I'm done?"

He tilts his head to the left and right a few times before he nods. "Alright, deal. I can do that. But I'ma hold you to it."

"Cool..."

"A'ight, well, I gotta pop by the house to see if dinner's ready with my lil' brother and sister. You wanna come?"

My eyes widened. Um, hell no, I do not want to meet his family yet! I don't even consider myself worthy of that opportunity.

"I'll pass," I try to say politely as possible. "Thanks for offering though. What y'all eating?"

"Jollof rice with fried bread dough."

"I've never heard of that in my life," I say.

"That's 'cause you ain't Nigerian."

"You're Nigerian?"

"Yeah. My mom is full Nigerian, and my dad is half Nigerian, half Black American. We came back to the states when I was a baby, so we have dual citizenship."

"Oh wow. I didn't know that. Would've never guessed since your last name is Carter."

"Yeah, that's because of my Dad, and he carries his father's name, who is from the states. My mom's maiden name is Adebayo. Anyway. I gotta run. You want me to bring you a plate or something?" he questions.

I shake my head and rise from the ground. "Nah, I'm cool," I reply.

"I got practice in a few, so I gotta head over to the other park. I just came here for some peace and quiet because I know it would've been interrupted over there. Thanks for offering, though."

"No problem. I'll see you around, alright?" he says, giving me a toothless grin and that same low gaze he dished before.

What's up with that?

"Cool, see you around."

With a light jog, Andre catches up with his siblings before taking them by the hands and walking them toward the house. I take a deep breath and wipe the beads of sweat from my forehead away. Whew, I was not expecting that to happen.

Picking up my sketchbook and pencils, I pack up and head over to the softball diamond at the other park.

Man. After that kind of peace, and that kind of good and bad anxiety, the last person I wanna deal with right now is Alaysia. The school getting a hold of what I did to her and calling Jarell to tell on me is one thing. It's a whole 'nother if Coach has already found out about it.

It makes me not even wanna go.

But I do anyway.

Chapter Nineteen

A FEW WEEKS pass by, and softball practices have been brutal. Coach has been hard on us. Relentless. I get it; we lost an easy ass tournament we shouldn't have, but at this point, I feel like this is punishment and not actual practice to get better. Anyone who drops a flyball, drops any catch, or lets the ball go between their legs on ground ball drills, we have to stop what we're doing and sprint the bases in less than thirty seconds. Everyone has to make it otherwise we all have to start over.

Usually, I don't have a problem with the workouts, but lately, I've been doubled over with cramps in my side because the running is so intense, and the rest of the team are either on their knees or doubled over too. And now, our team just fights with anyone who makes mistakes... which is essentially everyone. People got annoyed with me too for overthrowing the ball to second base to catch a steal, and we had to do sprints. So, I'm more than thankful that what I did to Alaysia a few weeks ago didn't get to the Coach because practice is a problem in and of itself. Alaysia and I don't have time to be mean to each other.

Maybe Coach is putting us through a test. Making us build community and teamwork through this. Who knows. I just hope the torture is over now that we're heading to the City of Angels for our first traveling tournament of the season.

It feels bittersweet to come back home. Deep down, I've been longing just to smell the smoggy air of LA, but another part of me tries to forget all the loss I've experienced and what I've left behind. Since I promised Jarell to go back to therapy again, in my last couple of sessions with Dr. Anderson, we talked about preparing to "be" in the city and how it would make me feel. She gave me good advice. Home will always be home, regardless of the good and bad.

At first, I was going to ride to the tournament with one of my teammates and her parents, but Brooklyn finalized her commitment to tag along with us and offered to take the two-hour drive with Jarell and me. She's particularly excited because she's never been to Los Angeles and felt it would be fun to experience the city with two knowledgeable people. I'm kind of glad I'm not going with my teammates this time. I just wanna be in my own head and focus. This is a big tournament especially having lost the first one, so being locked in is important, and I know Jarell and Brook are gonna be so into each other on this car ride that they'll leave me alone.

I take a few moments during the drive to text back and forth with Prez before settling in. He's so proud of me that I made up with Jarell that you'd think he's my granddaddy or something, waiting to give me the golden sticker of accomplishment. He's got a tournament this weekend too, except in Phoenix, so we talk baseball and sports as I wish him luck.

I wrap up my conversation with him and pull out Mama's journal again to kill more time as Jarell and Brooklyn sing worship songs in the front. I open it up to the second page, hoping to learn more about her dynamic with Dad. I just pray this entry won't put me in a shitty mood.

#2

I have the best son a mother could ask for. If there's anyone who loves me unconditionally no matter what, it's my baby boy.

But I don't know how he feels about me anymore. Every time we lock gazes, the light in his eyes dies. I can't even look at him without feeling so much guilt. Before we ended up here, Jarell and I were so happy, even though we had so little. Living in the hood was a blessing and a curse. Blessing in the sense of the community it brought. Curse in not having no money. But none of the bad of the hood beats living here with Nathan. Words can't explain how hurt I feel about dragging my son here. I just didn't think things would end up this way. My baby deserves a father... I thought Nathan would've been such a great one. The way he elevated our lives at first, pulling us out of homelessness after six months, giving us a hotel, buying my baby clothes, showering me with gifts, and promising to take care of us... I just knew he was the one. I've never felt like someone would protect me the way I felt like Nathan would've, except for Jarell's daddy, Johvantae.

I wish Joh wouldn't have gotten killed. We would've made an amazing family. I think I'll write more about him in my next entry. Either way... I believed so deeply in what I thought Nathan could've brought to the table. When I was dealing with a guy who tried to take advantage of me after we had gotten evicted, Nathan was there to get me out of it all. I was so desperate to keep Jarell safe, but also genuinely felt like allowing Nathan to take us was the best thing to do. And now, it seems like I've miscalculated this whole situation, and now I can't make up for any of it.

I just didn't mean for all of this to happen...

Whoa. This journal is getting really weird, confusing, and heavy.

Jarell and Mama were homeless? Which Dad had pulled them out of? How did they lose their house?

What did Daddy do so wrong? Why would Mama regret letting him take care of her and Jarell?

I've got so many questions. No wonder why Jarell got mad at me when I said I'd rather be homeless than to stay with him… I close the journal and put it back in my bag once we're about ten minutes from our destination to the community center and park we're playing at and continue to ruminate on Mama's writings. How did Mama and Jarell survive not having a place to stay before Daddy saved them?

Man… that must've been hard.

It's been generally quiet until Brooklyn turns down the worship music. I look up to see why she would, and I catch her gazing at me in her rearview mirror.

"So, Kylah. You gotta tell me. Since we're here for the next few days, what's the best spot to eat at?"

"Roscoe's Chicken and Waffles," I immediately reply.

"Yeah, you know, I've actually heard of them before, but never had them. What makes them so good?"

"The soul," I say. "Something San Diego ain't got."

"Hmm. Okay. Babe, you down for Roscoe's after the games tonight?" Brooklyn questions.

"You know I'm not picky. I'll eat wherever we go, so I'll leave that up to you two."

"So, Roscoe's, Kylah?"

"I'm all the way down." I nod with a smile.

We proceed to drive in silence until we reach the diamond. This place is packed, and Brooklyn doesn't hesitate to make her displeasure about it known. Literally, packed from the street parking to the parking lot. Good thing Jarell has a handicapped car sign that we can hang up because anyone else would literally be walking for miles just to get to where they need to be. Scouting is about to be heavy and in full force this weekend with such a massive crowd.

When we get out of the car and walk toward the fields past the community center, I start to understand why it's so packed. The outdoor stadiums are pretty widespread, allowing for multiple tournaments and events to take place. There are a lot of girls walking with their bat bags and cleats who are in my tournament, but I also see smaller children who are probably there for their first tournament. They're so cute! I can't really remember my first tournament days; I wish I had pictures.

Jarell, Brooklyn, and I try to find the diamonds we're going to be playing on for the next few days until Brooklyn abruptly stops.

"Hey, y'all, I tried to keep going, but I gotta stop and use the bathroom. Can y'all wait for me by the restrooms?" Brooklyn asks.

"Yeah, of course," Jarell says, Luna's leash wrapped multiple times around his wrist. "It was a long drive, so thank you for driving, baby. I appreciate you."

"Not a problem. I don't mind at all." She smiles, giving Jarell combination looks of gratitude and being flirty. I roll my eyes. "I think the bathrooms might be in this building. I hope so because I ain't tryna use no port-a-potty."

We follow Brooklyn to the pavilion, and she goes on her way to the restroom.

"Luna, find the water fountain... good girl." Jarell encourages her after she finds it for him, and he takes a slurp of water from the fountain.

Once he stands up and we're leaning against the wall to wait, a woman with long black hair, who kinda looks familiar, walks up to us. Well, I should say, she makes a beeline for Jarell. She's got a skeptical frown on her face, but the closer she gets, her wide smile dominates it.

"Jarell?" she calls out once she's standing directly in front of him. Jarell blinks with confusion.

"Yeah, who's asking?"

"Oh my God! I can't believe this. Jarell, it's me! Jade!" She beams.

My eyes should be rolling on the floor at this point with the way they shoot out of their sockets. Jade?! Wait... isn't that Jarell's ex-girlfriend? My mouth silently falls open, but I cover it with my hand.

"Jade?!" Jarell exclaims, his face lighting up like a Christmas tree. "Yo... I..."

Immediately, with no other words, she jumps into him for an embrace, and he wraps her up in return. Passionately. They rock back and forth for a long time with her nose buried in his neck and his face in her hair. Oooooh...

This ain't just any hug.

The way she has her arms enclosed around his neck, and the way his arms hold her waist... Let's just say I hope Brooklyn's in there taking a dump.

I ain't gone lie. I, of course, don't remember specific details about Jade because it's been so long since I've last seen her, but today? Right here and right now? She is fly. Like, FLY. She's got the kinda body anyone would trip over themselves to get. Perfect amount of chest, flat tummy with a six pack like mine, thick legs, and a nice, round backside. She's got on an all-black workout fit (a bra and capris), and ooooh her shoe game! She's got on the red and black Retro Eleven Breds! Her hair flows down her back effortlessly, and she doesn't need makeup. Her skin is so clear, like she hasn't had anything other than water for the last five years.

"Oh my goodness, look at you!" She squeals at Jarell as they finally pull away from each other. She scans him from head to toe, taking in every inch of his body. "I can't believe what I'm seeing. You smell great and look great!"

"I feel great." He nods. "Yo... this is crazy. How have you been? This is the last place I thought we'd run into each other. Your voice definitely matured. What are you doing here?" Jarell asks with a huge smile.

"Well, I come here to the community center on Friday mornings to hold a free beginner's exercise class in dance to serve low-income communities, and I was just leaving early because of all the events happening here today. I stopped to use the bathroom, came out, and saw you at the water fountain. You looked so familiar but so different, and I was like, that can't be him. But when I stepped closer, I had to say something. I should be asking you what you're doing here! How long has it been... about eight or nine years?"

"Yeah!" Jarell nods emphatically. "Nine years. We last talked when I was nineteen, and I just turned twenty-eight, so yeah. Nine years."

Damn. He even remembers the last time they talked...

"Wow." She shakes her head in awe. "It's crazy what time does. You look amazing, fresh, and happy." Jarell blushes and turns his head. Aww! I've never seen him blush like this! "No, seriously, Jarell. First, I'm gonna ask about your eyes. That's what made you look unfamiliar. They're brown... are you able to see?"

Jarell shakes his head.

"Prescribed colored contacts to cover the damage if I don't decide to wear sunglasses..."

"Makes sense. So your beard grew in, you got a fresh taper, you're wearing a different color other than black or white, you've got your ear pierced... I just... I can't. You've always been handsome, but... you look *good*. Healing looks really good on you." She shakes her head with a smile. Jarell continues full on blushing. "And you've got a guide dog! It's adorable. That's so amazing. So, yeah! Why are you here?"

"Well, look to your right. I'm here for her softball tournament with her traveling team."

Jade slightly frowns and looks at me before her eyes swell.

"Wait a minute. *Kylah*?!" she whispers.

I nod.

She screams like a fangirl and pulls me into a humongous embrace, rocking me back and forth where I can hardly breathe. I don't mind it. Her scent is enough to comfort me for the next month. I hug her back, pressing her into my chest. Her arms secure around my tummy like a tight belt. We stay that way for what seems like forever. A forever I don't want to end.

"You've gotten so tall! Shit, you're taller than me! How tall are you?"

"Five ten."

"Wow. And look at those big, beautiful gray eyes. My goodness, girl. Hell, y'all both should model; you both look a lot alike and like your mom! Your skin got so dark, and so did your hair. Beautiful. Must be all that time in the sun."

"I ain't all that," I say through an uncomfortable laugh.

"Girl. Stop. If someone ain't telling you how beautiful you are, then I will make up for all the opportunities everybody missed. How are you? Do you remember me? How old are you now?"

"I'm good. I do remember you. And I'm fourteen," I reply to the interrogation with a slight smirk.

Bewildered, she gazes at me. "Fourteen?! How? How did that happen?"

I shrug. "I dunno. Time went by."

"Dang! You're a whole teenager! It's really been almost a whole decade since I've seen you! Are you still hyper and a ball of energy?" She cuts her eyes at me with a laugh.

I look away while rubbing my arm and elbow. "I mean… everyone else seems to think so."

"What's that supposed to mean? Why the long face?" She questions with a blink. Her entire body language shifts for a second, but when my eyes meet hers again, her eyes harden with curiosity.

"It means nothing."

There's no way I'm gonna let her in on the reputation I have for being a wild child. I don't want to tarnish any positive image that very few, if any, have of me.

"Jarell, this is insane. Kylah's a teenager, now?" Jade questions, shaking her head.

"Yup." He nods. "Every bit of one. She'll be in high school in the fall. Kylah, you remember Jade, right? You were little, but she used to come by the house all the time? Get you presents for Christmas and stuff?"

"Yeah, I already said I remember her, and I definitely remembered the presents." I reply. "She always wanted to play Barbies with me, too. You were so nice."

"That's right. Man. Incredible how time flies." She awes again.

"So, what are you doing these days?" Jarell asks.

"Well, I run my own dance studio now in Baldwin Hills with several different classes a week like Monday pole dancing, Tuesday youth dance, and Wednesday hip-hop dance. I'm also still dancing for artists at concerts and events. I tend to stay in Cali for the summers because a lot of the award shows are here, so I get to hold these kinds of community-based exercise classes when I'm able. I travel the country a lot throughout the year. I'm gearing up to dance with Kehlani at the BET Awards here in LA next month."

My mouth drops again. BET Awards?! Kehlani? R&B Singer Kehlani? Bad bitch Kehlani? Wait, how? Was Jade famous this whole time? And she's just walking around here like she ain't known? At a park's community center?

Jarell smiles in inspiration. "That doesn't surprise me at all. I knew you'd become this."

"Yeah, but you know me. It's always been my dream, and I think I got there. Do you still dance? I'd love to have you at my studio some time. You're still one of the best I've ever seen after all these years."

Wait, Jarell dances? Since when? Before Jarell can respond, Brooklyn comes walking up past Jade, stopping at Jarell's side.

"Hey, babe, you and Kylah ready to go?" she asks Jarell, not giving a single ounce of attention to Jade.

The pocket of silence that lingers after her question is as loud as fireworks. Jarell smiles awkwardly before wrapping an arm around Brooklyn's waist from behind, and that's when Brooklyn stares at Jade.

"Y-yeah, I'm ready, but I wanna introduce y'all first. Jade, this is my girlfriend Brooklyn, but I call her Brook. Brook, this is Jade. We met in high school," he says.

Jade's eyebrows quickly raise as she blinks but suppresses that stunned look off her face so fast, I nearly wonder if she had it to begin with. Brooklyn sticks her hand out first, leaning against Jarell with her arm on his shoulder. She sizes Jade up and down in a non-threatening way while at the same time, sends a very clear message about who she is to Jarell.

"It's nice to meet you, *Jane*," Brooklyn responds without affect. "It's Brooklyn to you."

"Likewise..." Jade shakes her hand with an unoffended nod and toothless smile but gives Brooklyn a strong unwavering gaze in return as if she's not fazed at all.

Yikes.

"Well, it was good to run into you after all these years, *Jade*. We gotta get going, but take care, okay?" Jarell says.

"Sounds good," Jade replies with her arms crossed and a smile. "You take care as well."

"You ready, Kylah?" Jarell asks me.

"I'ma stay back and talk to Jade. Since it's been a while. Our game isn't for another forty-five minutes," I say.

"Okay cool. Well Brook and I will find the diamond and be in the stands, okay? Good luck, today," Jarell says as Brooklyn pulls him away by the hand without acknowledging what I said, and Luna follows suit. Well damn.

When they're long gone, Jade and I give each other our attention.

"So, beautiful, how are you? Tell me more about your tournament."

"Well, this is our first traveling tournament of the season. Our team is one of the state's top teams. I'm the lead pitcher. They say I'm supposedly the best in the country, so I'm gonna be playing for the Senior League World Series on ESPN real soon. You should check it out when you get the chance. First game of the brackets is July 21ˢᵗ."

"World Series? You, mean, you're playing people from all over the world?"

"That's the plan," I confirm.

"Yo! That's so cool! I'm so proud of you, Kylah. And you guys travel the state? Since when did you become a girl with a ball and not a Barbie? There's just so much I want to ask you. We need to catch up!" Jade says with a beam.

"Yup, we travel the state and sometimes beyond. Some of the teams we may play this weekend are the LA Lady Runners, the LA Hard Hitters, the Compton Catchers, and the San Francisco Stylers. If we win today, we play more on Saturday, and then the championship is on Sunday. I'm super happy I get to come back home."

"What do you mean 'come back home?' What's your team's name?"

"The San Diego Sluggers."

"San Diego? You guys moved away from LA?" she asks with wrinkled brows.

"Yeah, we moved years ago. Well, Jarell moved out there years ago, and then I moved in with him my sixth-grade year."

"Oh, wow."

My eyes move away. "Yeah. It's a long story."

"How's your mom doing?" she questions.

"That's a long story, too." I shrug.

"Hmm." She ponders. "Okay."

"Well, I gotta go, though. I see my team is about to start warming up. I wish we could talk more. Besides, I didn't know you danced or worked with celebrities! That's so cool. Let's keep in contact though. Can you give me your number?"

"Absolutely. I wouldn't let you leave without it," she responds, pulling out her phone. I take it from her, enter my number in it, and then send myself a text so that I have hers.

"Thanks. I'll see you around, Jade." I smile and wave.

"Good luck, Kylah! Take care, and congratulations on everything."

Without another word, I haul my batting bag over my shoulder and pick up my cleats I dropped to the ground with my other hand and move toward the empty diamond to my team.

Chapter Twenty

THE FIRST TWO games are a breeze – we take the wins. For some reason, these two games seemed way easier than the games in our first tournament. Guess all that working out Coach put us through paid off because I barely broke a sweat and I'm definitely not ready to turn in since we're still early in the afternoon, around four o'clock. Now that I've got my phone back, I've set up some time with my old friends from back in fifth grade to hang out with later around seven. I can't wait to finally see them in person and not on social media.

We finally check into the hotel, which gives me a few moments to hop in the shower and dive into a cozy bed before I prepare for the evening. When we walk inside, the room is beautiful. I wish it would've been a suite where Brooklyn and Jarell have their room and I have mine, but I'll settle for the two queen beds with this huge flat screen TV, nice pull out couch, and an amazing window view.

I'm not sure if Jarell or Brooklyn paid for this, but it's really dope.

Once everyone sets their bags down, Jarell claims their bed and lays flat on his back with a loud yawn.

"I'll be right back," Brooklyn says and barely allows either of us to respond. She just walks out of the room swiftly and nearly slams the door in the process.

Hmm...

Jarell doesn't pay it that much mind and lays there with his hands behind his head, "staring" at the ceiling. I take this time to get in the shower and wash my hair. When I get out and I'm starting to lotion myself, Jarell's pulling things out of his duffle bag and organizing his belongings in the dresser area. As he does that, the hotel door swings open and Brooklyn abruptly walks back inside, heading straight for the bed without even looking or saying a word to me or anyone. I start to grab my towel to cover up since I only have a sports bra and boy shorts on, but she moves so quickly and doesn't even give me an ounce of attention that I don't even bother. I just shrug and opt not to rush, then.

Once I'm finished getting dressed, Jarell makes his way to a shower, too. Brooklyn just lays back and scrolls through her phone in silence. I guess this is a good time to pull out Mama's journal and read a little bit more before I finalize some of the plans I started with my old friends here in LA.

I hope with this entry, I learn about what happens between Mama, Jarell, and Dad, but Mama's writings are so... mysterious and written in a way that's not very direct, and it makes me have to put dots together in my head.

#3

Johvantae would've never done what Nathan is doing. Each day I've been in this hell hole, I think of Joh. His dark skin. His moody eyes. His strength. His whole demeanor. He was the epitome of the fine ass hood nigga every girl on the block wanted, even as young as eighteen. We were two years apart, but he wanted me out of all the girls throwing themselves at him. And he showed he loved and wanted me every chance he got. Joh and I grew up in the same foster home.

Luckily for him, he didn't move around as much as I did and had stayed in his home for many years before I moved in when I was thirteen. Not long after, we hit it off.

I just don't know why life has to be this way. Jarell was weeks from being born, and some hater just had to kill him. He would've protected Jarell the way he always emphasized protecting me. He always talked to me about being the father he never had. He and Jarell would've been the best of friends. It's just so hard because Jarell reminds me so much of his dad even though he looks like me.

Nathan does everything but protect. He causes the damage. Today, Nathan broke my baby's skin open with the leather of his belt. I watched, through my two black eyes, the moment his skin broke open, too. Hearing my baby's desperate cries suffocates me. I just want Joh's spirit to come and save us somehow.

I slam Mama's journal closed. There was a lot of that entry left, but I don't wanna read it. Two black eyes? Mama has already suffered enough with drug addiction that I've watched with my own eyes. I can't take any more of her suffering. It's just going to make me throw up.

I sigh as my head falls back.

So Dad was abusing Mama *and* Jarell? How awful. Why? Is this what Jarell meant when he said he had a hard life? That he sacrificed so much? I'm so confused. Things must've turned around for the better if Mama and Dad decided to have me together... right? Mama wouldn't just have kids with someone who constantly hurt her...

As I ponder this, Jarell comes out of the bathroom fully dressed as if he never took a shower, but his skin glistens from the steam to prove it. When he walks out, he realizes Brooklyn's return due to her shuffling on the bed.

"Hey, you're back. Where'd you go?" Jarell questions in innocence.

"Nowhere worth sharing," she responds flatly.

This time, Jarell detects her energy.

"B, you okay?" Jarell asks.

"I'm cool. Just don't feel well," she says and sits upright on their bed to take off her shoes.

"You sure? You were in a way better mood when we first got to the city."

"Yes, Jarell. Like I said, I'm not really feeling well right now. Maybe... maybe it's just the sun and the fact that it's so hot today."

"Aww, baby. Here, let me give you a backrub," Jarell offers, walking over to her, but she puts a hand up to stop him, and his belly runs into it.

"No. I'm just gonna lay down," she rejects. "If you could turn the air to a lower temp, that'd be great."

Jarell pauses with a baffled look as his hands plop back down to his sides.

"Uh... okay, I guess. Do you want to be alone or something?" he asks.

"That would be amazing, actually," she replies.

"Oh... alright. Well, I'll just take Kylah out then. Kylah, you wanna go visit Ma? Or are you trying to spend some time here at the hotel with your teammates or something?"

Oof. Right. He had asked me about visiting Mama before. My stomach turns at the possibility. But at the same time, I want to see if I can push myself. I haven't talked to Dr. Anderson about actually visiting her, and wish I would've before coming here. Especially going with Jarell, since we've been extremely rocky; we are by no means in the best place yet. I don't know. I guess this could be a start.

"I'll go with you," I force myself to say with a shaky voice. "I spend enough time with my teammates as it is." I put on my athletic slides, giving Brooklyn a side eye as she lays in the bed with her back toward us.

I shake my head. She really didn't need to do all the lying she just did, but whatever. Maybe it's because I'm in here that she won't keep it a buck, but no one really gets moody about the sun being out. Or about it being hot, since... well, it's southern Cal. It's always hot. And it's already freezing in this room. Turning it down any more than it already is, would create an ice box.

"Okay. Let's give Brook some space," he says, grabbing Luna's leash as she leads us out of the door. Neither of us turn down the air conditioner, an unspoken agreement between us about the temperature of the room.

Jarell, Luna, and I walk to the elevator and wait until one opens for us. Thankfully, we're the only ones to get on.

"What's wrong with her?" I ask Jarell as we descend.

"I don't know. It was like she was fine during your first game, but then the second game came around, and she was just... I don't know... standoffish. She didn't want to talk to me or to anyone. Maybe she's just tired. The drive here was kind of long with all that traffic."

I nod. I don't want to call out the elephant in the room, so I just keep my mouth shut and let Jarell figure it out on his own. He can't be that dense or oblivious to his girl's feelings and why she feels the way she does but... I don't know. Maybe that's just a guy thing – they don't have the skills to detect why and how another person might be feeling the way that us girls can.

We leave the elevator and head outside to get in the Uber that Jarell ordered through voiceover on his phone.

"Jarell, I'm scared," I whisper as we settle inside the backseats.

"What do you mean?"

"I've never visited Mama before... other than the funeral..."

That day was so chaotic. I barely remember a thing. I only remember how my body felt. How tight my stomach was, how raw my throat was and how I had a massive headache because of the screaming and crying. And a consistent hand on my back when I was on my knees, which was Jarell's.

I really don't recall him having much emotion. I think that was the actual start of me being incredibly upset with him. It just seemed and felt like he hadn't cared that she died. I guess I'm just gonna conclude that she's put him through so much that he feels numb about her being gone. Or maybe he's staying strong for me. I don't know.

"It's okay to feel that way," he responds.

"I don't want to feel this way, though."

"It's a part of grieving, Kylah. Allow yourself to feel whatever your body feels," he says as the driver heads to the cemetery.

"I don't know how I'm gonna take this..."

"You'll be fine. I'm here with you. I think it'll be healing for you. For the both of us."

"Okay. I'll try." I tremble.

We get to the graveyard, and our Uber drives away.

"Alright, now I have to remember where she is. I put the directions in my phone a while ago..." Jarell mumbles. "Hey, can you look in my notes and find the title that says Mom's Resting Place?" he asks me, motioning the phone my way.

"Yep."

I take his phone and find the note he's looking for. They're pretty concise, straightforward directions, so I lead him and Luna there. Slowly. I don't want to walk too fast because I need to get my own emotions together.

We wind the path to the left, one way to the right, and make another left.

"I think we're here," I whisper once there are no more directions.

Jarell doesn't say anything. His face is as blank as an empty canvas, waiting for something to bring it to life. But he nods. He walks over to the nearby tree, caressing the tree bark with his fingers.

"Yeah. We're here..." he mindlessly says.

Oh God. I remember this tree... It was the tree in which, after I was finished wailing at them lowering Mama's body in the ground, I cried and cried silently against it until I felt a little better.

I take deliberate footsteps toward Mama's headstone. Jarell follows me. As soon as I read:

In loving memory of Radiya Marie Hendricks...

My chest closes up. I claw at my neck to try and breathe, but the air is lodged in my throat. My fists clench, body shakes...

I lose it.

When I'm finally able to break out of my freeze, a teary gasp escapes my lips. My knees buckle and they're about to strike the ground hard, but Jarell catches me by one strong arm like he knew I was going down and lifts me back to my feet, allowing his body to be the support to keep me standing.

"Mama please... please come back," I weep against the side of him.

Jarell caresses my shoulder as he pulls me to him, quickly becoming my pillar of strength. This lasts for a while, about ten minutes, until I stop crying. Once I'm done, I stand up straight, no longer needing the support. When I look up at him, my heart tanks.

A huge puddle of tears pool at the bottom of both his eyes, but they don't fall. He, literally, is holding on by a thread.

"Jarell?" I call out.

"I just wish I had more time, Kay Kay. I wish I didn't take so much time away from her. It was my plan to let her know that I had forgiven her for the things that have happened in our lives, but I kept pushing it off and pushing it off, so I never got the chance," he whispers the last part, and that's when his tears escape, rolling down his cheeks.

"It took me years to get to that point of true forgiveness, and I couldn't tell her how much I've healed. It probably would've been a fresh start to a new relationship that I had always wanted. I loved Ma, Kylah. I really did. She made choices that were harmful, but she did the best she could. It really hurts that she went out the way she did."

Damn.

This is how he really feels. Behind the unemotional wall he always puts up. You'd think he was made of stone sometimes. I wrap my arm around his belly and hug him from the side, leaning my head against his chest. He hugs me back and wipes his tears with the other hand.

"Any good memories with Mama?" I ask. "I don't want this visit just to be sad."

"Of course! I have many, many great memories with Ma when we lived in Chicago," he replies.

"Y'all lived in Chicago?! All the way up north?" I turn to look Jarell upside the head.

"Yep. That's where I was born and pretty much raised. We didn't come out here to Cali until I was about eleven or twelve. We didn't move to LA until I was around fourteen or fifteen."

"Wow. Whole time, I thought LA was home... where our family was from..."

"Nope. We've got that Chicago blood. Those winters were cold." He quivers.

"That's crazy. Tell me a story about Mama when y'all lived there."

His eyes smile.

"She took me everywhere. I was her right-hand man. Her ride or die ace. Oh! Here's a story or memory. Whatever you wanna call it. I remember her taking me to Six Flags Great America one day, north of Chicago. I was maybe nine or ten, and we went with my best friend Alex and his mom Lynette. Ma was really into rollercoasters, so she was tryna force us on. The rest of us were scared because it was our first introduction to rollercoasters. She made me sit in the very front row with her on the Raging Bull, which is the most intense rollercoaster in the park, and our friends were behind us in the second row. The drop on it is crazy steep, so when we were on the incline going up and Alex and his mom saw how high we were going, they literally screamed like they were dying or being maimed. Had all of the passengers rollin.' The ride was wild, I ain't gon' lie, but Alex and his mom took it to the next level. When we got off, Alex peed on himself, and his mom's wig had fell off during the ride. Me and mom laughed so hard at them that she peed on herself too, but she took off to the bathroom before it got too bad. You had to be there. You know Ma's laugh is crazy, so it just made it all the better." Jarell chuckles.

I smile at the memory, hearing Mama's laugh in my head. She had such an obnoxious cackle that you couldn't help but join her because it was too contagious. I shake my end and end up giggling in reminiscence.

"What about you? Any good memories?" Jarell asks.

"Yeah. I don't have a funny one like yours that I can remember off top, but each and every game she watched me play softball are my favorite memories. Always the loudest one cheering for me, always the one who made sure we all got snacks after the game if other parents couldn't get them. She was the team's favorite mom," I say, trying not to tear up. "That's why I don't mind when Brooklyn's out there cheering loud for me. It kinda feels more normal than not."

"Those moments are priceless," Jarell whispers wistfully.

"I know, right? Ones that you can never forget. I also remember her hugs, too. How warm they felt."

Jarell's eyes get big. "Yo! You ain't lying at all. Ma had the best hugs."

I start crying again, feeling that deep, deep void in my stomach again.

"Oh Kay Kay..." Jarell sighs and pulls me into his chest, rocking me with an embrace.

"I miss Mama so much, Relly," I weep.

"I know..."

I bawl into his body, longing for her to just rise from the dead and kick it with us again. I don't care what anyone says, but before Jarell left and we were together as a family, I don't really remember anything feeling better. Obviously, I would've been too little to understand any drama behind the scenes but... everything felt so much happier.

"Thanks for coming out here," Jarell states. "This was healing for me. I hope it has been for you and that this didn't make things worse. I'm sorry if it did."

I wipe my eyes with my shirt. "It didn't make things worse. I'm happy we got to share some happy memories."

Jarell nods, giving me a fond and sympathetic look.

"Well, I don't want this to weigh down your day. You got other plans tonight with your team?" Jarell asks.

"Actually, I'm planning to link up with some friends I went to elementary school with before I moved. They're super excited to see me, and one of their moms is picking me up from the hotel. We're going bowling."

"Oh, dope!"

"I'm surprised you don't have friends here that you can link up with from high school," I say, pondering.

"Nah. I don't have friends at all here, but that's a different story," Jarell replies.

I so badly want to mention Jade, but I don't wanna go there and make him uncomfortable.

"Alright, well let's head back to the hotel then so you can eat and be on your way. Remember what I tell you when you hang out with friends. I don't know these people the way I know your teammates and now... what's his name? Prez?"

I laugh in my throat. "It's Preston, but my nickname for him is Prez."

"Yeah, I don't know your LA friends like I know Preston and your teammates. And I barely know Preston. So here are my rules, Kylah. No drinking, no smoking, no drugs in general. No sex, no stealing cars or from stores, and no fighting. Understood?"

"I got it." I nod. "I'll stay out of trouble."

"Good. Text me when you make it there and send me your location so that I know you've made it safely," he says. "Send me your location every thirty minutes. And I'll need the number of at least one adult who is transporting you."

"Damn, Jarell!" I growl.

"I'm serious. I don't trust anyone. Do what I tell you, please."

"Okay. I'll do all of the above."

"Cool. I'm probably gonna spend some time in the hot tub area at the hotel with Luna for the night."

"What about Brooklyn?" I ask.

"She'll probably come to the pool with me if she's up to it."

"Okay, bet. Let's get outta here," I say.

With that, I kiss Mama's headstone and tell her I love her. Jarell smiles small, yet I can tell he had been longing for this moment with me.

I'm glad we had it.

Chapter Twenty-One

THERE'S NOTHING I want more than my bed at this point. I had an amazing time at home in Los Angeles, but there's something about my bed that's unmatched by anything else. Me, Luna, Jarell, and Brooklyn don't arrive back in San Diego until about ten-thirty at night. We unload the car of my softball gear and our overnight bags to head inside. Jarell and Brooklyn have to do multiple trips because they helped me with my stuff first before grabbing theirs.

I go straight to my room and into the blankets, pulling out my phone to call Prez. How'd he do with his tournament? I haven't heard from him since Friday, so it must be because of traveling. I call and he doesn't answer. Welp, I guess it's time for me to turn in.

But I kinda wanna finish up Andre's portrait, too. I'm not ready to go to sleep yet.

I pull out my sketchbook and turn to his almost finished drawing. But I yawn the biggest yawn, and my limbs flop like Jello. Yeah. It's not best to draw like this... don't wanna mess what I have up by being sleepily reckless.

Just as I'm contemplating whether I should draw or sleep, my phone vibrates. It's Prez.

"Bout time!" I answer the phone. "I ain't heard from you all weekend."

"My fault. Just got out the shower. We just got home about thirty minutes ago from the airport."

"Yeah, we just got in from LA, too."

"How was the tournament? Did y'all win?" Prez asks.

"Yeah, we did." I smirk. "Got the first place medal."

"How many strike outs did you get in the championship?"

"I think twelve," I reply.

"Damn. That's a crazy good percentage."

"How about y'all? How was Phoenix? Hit any home runs?"

"It was smooth. We got second place. I didn't hit any homeruns, but I did get a triple and a single after striking out once in the championship," he says. "Thanks for always practicing with me."

"No problem. Let me know if you wanna go to the diamond to practice batting tonight. It sounds like you're getting better," I say.

"Nah, not tonight. Jet lag's got me tired as fuck." He yawns.

"That's real. Aye, this ain't about baseball, but I just realized the eighth-grade dance is coming up in a couple weeks," I say. "We graduate in less than a month. That's wild. Going to high school doesn't even seem real."

"Yeah, I know. What you finna wear?" he asks.

"I don't know if I wanna go femme or masculine yet. I've been eyeing this turquoise, sparkly two-piece set that's a high crop top and long skirt at the mall. I think it'll really show my shape. But then there's this really dope red and white suit that'll go real nice with some Jordan's, a chain, and a watch. I don't know."

"Seriously, LaLa? You already dress like me majority of the time. You gon' wear a suit to the dance? Do you wanna be a dude or something?"

"No! I'm attracted to dudes; I don't wanna be one. I just like the style of how y'all dress because I'm not curvy enough to wear all the cute girl stuff. And I'm too tall."

"Since you're going with me, wear the two-piece, please. Trust me, you're feminine enough to make that look good."

"Who said I'm going with you?" My brows raise. "You have a girlfriend."

"Yeah, at a different school whose dance is the week after ours. Since our dance is on a Thursday, her parents won't let her go out on a school night. Plus, it's just a dance. Who else you gonna go with?"

"It's not good to make assumptions, Prez. What if I got someone else in mind that I wanna go with?" I ask half-jokingly.

"Who?"

My stomach flutters. Should I say it? I kinda think it's time to. I can't keep hiding these feelings I have. I've got to address it, and Prez, being my best friend and all, is the start. He's gonna end up realizing it one day anyway.

"Andre," I confess.

"Andre?!" he exclaims.

"Yeah, Andre, and I'm kinda ready to make a move to ask. This might be the perfect time to."

"You're not serious, are you?"

"Yeah, I'm dead ass. It's bigger than the dance, though. You should hook me up," I say with a smile.

"Wait a minute... hook you up?"

"Yeah, like... hook us up so we can be boyfriend and girlfriend."

"Woah, you're feeling the homie, *Andre*? Since when? Why?" he asks again in disbelief.

"Prez don't be like that. You're literally embarrassing me. You heard what I said."

"You know how weird it's gonna be for both of my best friends to date each other? And you're asking *me* to hook y'all up? I don't wanna be in the middle of that. Why can't you shoot your shot yourself?" he interrogates.

"One question at a time, please! It's not weird, yes, I'm asking you, and finally, I'm too shy!"

"You're not shy about anything else, LaLa."

"Prez, please. I've lowkey been feelin' him for a while now, but he seems so... out of my league. I don't know. I'm too scared to talk to him because I don't know how to bring it up without being awkward. Does he have a girlfriend? Does he like someone else?" I ask.

"Come on LaLa..."

"Prez... please. Is he a nice guy? Is he like... worth dating?"

"I don't know!"

"Just answer this. Does he like me? Does he ever say anything about me?" I question.

"Man, look. Here's what I'll tell you. Andre is definitely a good dude. He has a great family; he stays out of trouble, gets good grades, and everything. He wouldn't be my best friend if he didn't. I just don't know if he'll be able to handle a hot head like you, though."

"Prez! Really?"

"I'm just bein' honest!"

"I'm different when it comes to dating... I promise," I say with a laugh.

"Yeah, nah. I don't know about all that. I can handle you before he does."

The tone in which he said that last sentence throws me completely off. I blink and jerk my head back.

"Um, what's that supposed to mean?"

"It means what I said," he replies matter-of-factly.

"Are you calling yourself trying to shoot your shot with me? Because Gina can continue to have you," I assert with another giggle.

"Why you say it like that?" he says, his voice sounding like he'd been afflicted.

"What, you tired of Gina, so you want me, now?"

He goes quiet for a while, but then he clears his throat and says, "I ain't say that..."

"So then, what are you saying?"

Prez pauses for a moment before he starts talking to answer me, but voices in the distance conflict with whatever he's saying to the point where they eventually drown him out. Now I can't hear what he's saying at all. I put my phone to my chest and frown to tune in to the noise outside of my room.

"Jarell, I don't know if I can do this!"

"What do you mean that you can't do this?" he snaps back in offense.

"You're literally hiding things from me! I've told you about my past, my past relationships, my family, and everything, and you haven't said a whole lot about yours! I've been patient and kept faith that you'd share more with me about who you are. I shouldn't have to find out like this!"

"Brook, it's not that easy..."

"What do you mean it's not easy? You couldn't be honest and tell me at least a little bit of your history? We've been together for two years. That's not a short amount of time. You and I have both been praying about what God wants for us long term, and it seems like He's showing me signs that maybe you're not so honest."

"Hello? LaLa, are you even listening to me?" Prez yells after a frustrated growl.

"Oh shit, my fault. Hold on, Prez. I think my brother and his girlfriend are arguing..."

"Man for real? So, you heard nothing I said?"

"Yes, I'm for real. They're getting heated, too. Let me call you back," I say and hang up before he can say anything. Rising from my bed, I go to my door and plant my ear up against it.

"I'm not sure why you're trying to pit me as dishonest," Jarell says. "I care a lot about you, B. I've done nothing to show you that I'm dishonest or that I'm doing you wrong."

"Jarell, you have a whole 'nother job I had no clue about. A whole 'nother income that you're just now admitting to me all because I found your ID you dropped in the parking lot trying to unpack the car. It says 'Sexual Assault Support Group Lead Facilitator' at the National Human Trafficking Resource Center with your picture on it! Were you trafficking people or something in your past? And now, with a guilty conscience, you support the survivors?"

"What? No!" he exclaims.

"So then, what it is? What is it that you would keep a whole job from me? Is this why you won't tell me anything about your past? This is what I mean by not being honest."

"Brook, I'm sorry that you found out this way, but it's not what you think..." he tries to explain, but she keeps talking.

"And then, that girl you saw at Kylah's tournament. Jane, or whatever her name is. I saw the whole thing, Jarell. I just haven't said anything because I don't want to believe that you're into someone else."

"See what? What are you talking about? I didn't do anything with her!" Jarell shouts.

"Oh, come on. I saw the look all over your face when she hugged you. It's certainly not a look that someone who's just friends give. It's more than apparent that y'all had some kind of romantic relationship, so don't lie to me!"

Jarell falls silent for what seems like a really long time. Damn. He really didn't do anything, but this silence feels a whole lot like guilt.

"So this is why you were acting so distant in LA?" he asked.

"Don't you dare deflect. Who is she, Jarell?" Brooklyn asks, her voice cracking. "Tell the truth."

"An old friend from high school that I haven't seen since I was nineteen."

She scoffs. "Don't play me for some fool. Be honest with me."

Jarell, once again, pauses for a while before he speaks.

"Well..." He clears his throat. "Yeah. She's my ex-girlfriend. We dated for about a week or so during our senior year of high school before she called it quits with me, and we were friends after that. That's the truth. That's why I said she's an old friend. We weren't even dating that long."

"See... I knew it. Your ex-girlfriend, Jarell? And you got her hugging you as if I wouldn't come out of the bathroom?!" she cries. "How disrespectful can you be?"

"It's not that deep. It's been years since I've been in contact with her, and it was just an impulse reaction. I'm telling you, we only dated for about a wee—"

"Forget how long you were dating! You might not have dated long, but it doesn't mean your connection didn't last longer than that! Some little fling you had for a week wouldn't have the kind of reaction she gave to your sister, and your sister wouldn't have remembered her enough to stay back and talk to her. You clearly had a deeper connection than you're letting on, you clearly still have feelings for her, and you clearly haven't let go. By the looks of it, she hasn't either!"

"Brook, it's not like that. It's been nine years since I've last seen her... I don't even have the woman's number. We don't even live in the same city."

"It doesn't matter. Moving on, now that the cat is out of that bag. Why do you work at the Human Trafficking Center? Huh?"

Another long pause ensues before he sighs and confesses.

"I lead a support group of male victims and survivors of sexual trauma or those who have survived human trafficking."

"Why?"

"Why not?" he shoots back.

"Jarell do not play with me with that smart aleck reply. What happened that would land you there? This is something I should have known, especially if it's another form of income."

"That's not something to be pressuring someone to share," he declares pointedly.

Now, it's Brooklyn's turn to go silent. It lasts for a while before she lets out a sarcastic chuckle.

"Wow. You know what? Fine. Maybe we should call this relationship quits until you're ready to open up and share with the person you claim you wanna have a future with. Or decide who you really want. Me, or that Jane bitch or whatever her name is."

"Wait, so you're really gonna break up with me? Over something like this?" Jarell asks, shocked.

"Wasn't I clear? Until you decide you want to reciprocate necessary communication about yourself, I can't do this. I should know who I am dealing with in and out before we think about engagement and marriage, and I've gone far too long putting up with you not doing so. Being a nice guy isn't enough. I don't know a thing about your history, your family, your sister, and you think we're supposed to survive with this relationship being one sided like that? You're making it sound like none of what you did is a big deal!" she screams.

"... it ain't," Jarell responds with patience as if he's completely unbothered.

Woah, shit. This is the first time I've ever heard Jarell be somewhat of an asshole. No clue he even had that in him. It almost takes my breath away.

"Oh really? It ain't, huh? Finding your ID in the parking lot of another undisclosed form of income after two years of us dating is a huge deal. Hugging up on your ex-girlfriend when I'm in the vicinity and then lying about who she is when I ask you about it is a huge deal. I love and care about you, but I have to protect me, too. The ball is in your court, Jarell. When you decide what to do with it, call me."

Not much else gets said after that. Only noise I hear is the front door opening and slamming shut.

Wow. That was the fastest break up I've ever heard. It's like she didn't fight for him, and he didn't fight for her. Makes me wonder how real the relationship was to begin with. Or maybe, they just need some time to process because they're not the type to beg. But I don't really see either of them having that kind of pride to not want to beg for something they care about keeping, though. Who knows? I shake my head. Damn, I was really starting to like Brooklyn.

But I love the idea of him and Jade, too. Just like the old days.

I let a few more moments go by with me standing at my room door. Should I call Prez back and continue the conversation that was starting to get serious? Or should I check on Jarell?

Nothing feels worse than a breakup. Even I have enough of a heart to acknowledge that. I'm kinda in the same boat as Brooklyn though. Like, why did he keep so much about himself from her? The same way he keeps so much from me?

Hell, I didn't even know he worked as a sexual trauma support group leader either. I thought his only job was teaching kids how to read and write Braille. He must've been going to that group when he says he's elsewhere. No wonder why he comes home late sometimes...

With a deep breath, I turn the doorknob slowly, hoping Jarell doesn't hear it. I tip toe out to him sitting on the arm of the couch, staring toward the ground. I amble as quietly as I can, hoping not to intrude on what seems to be some deep thinking.

"Rell... are you okay?" I ask just above whisper.

He turns his head slightly toward me, startled. With his hearing being super keen, I'm surprised he didn't detect me earlier.

"Uh... yeah. I'm fine," he says and gets up from the couch without giving me even a millisecond of his eyes.

He doesn't say anything else. He just moves to the kitchen, leaving me standing there. He turns on the kitchen faucet and it runs for a while. Everything and everywhere else is dead silent. Closing my eyes and taking a gulp, I follow him. He's rinsing off dirty dishes that were previously stacked on the counter. I join in a space right next to him to help, adding more dishes that were on the stove top and into the sink.

Whew. The air here is heavy. There's just so many things unspoken, lingering above us that I feel a pressing urge to discover after that whole conversation. But there's something else throwing me for a loop. This weird, intense feeling of sadness in my stomach. I don't know why. It's not like I'm the person who got dumped. To break some of the tension between us, I clear my throat to speak.

"I didn't know you worked at the Center for Human Trafficking," I say. "You probably don't think I know what that is, but I do. How long have you worked there?"

He doesn't say anything. He just continues to rinse the dishes and now, the ones I've added. At this point, the feelings of sadness are so intense, I can barely look at him.

"D-Did you..." I stumble. My eyes are glued to the sink as my eyes water up. Both of us stand very still – side by side. Close enough that I could hug him. "Did something ... happen to you? I heard y'all arguing about it..."

Water hisses from the kitchen faucet again for a short while to fill up the sink to prepare for a deep washing, and when Jarell turns it off, only the buzz of the air conditioner loiters. His shoulders drop a little bit, but his eyes never look up from the baking pan he begins to scrub. I look away from him and grab the wet pan that he motions my way. I accept and dry it with a large towel in a circular motion, the same way my brain spins to try and figure out what to say next. Once I do, I swallow. By this time, Jarell has already washed another dish.

"Maybe I... maybe I should be more clear. Were you ... did someone... you know..." I swallow again to stop stuttering my way through. "Sorry. Let me start over. I overheard you and Brook. The... sexual trauma group thing she was talking about ...are you supporting someone you know who went through it? Did you hurt someone? Or... did it happen to you?"

Brooklyn has this idea that he may be the aggressor, but I *know* my brother. He doesn't have that kind of heart. But his lips are sealed. He just methodically grabs another dish to wash and motions for me to dry. The longer he's mute, the more I think I get my answer. Knots in my stomach multiply until I can hardly breathe.

We work like a machine on the dishes as the tension between us grows again. He washes and rinses, and I dry and put away. His eyes and whatever he sees through them never leave the water. Whole time, I've been trying to come up with the words to express my sympathy.

I can't picture Jarell going through that kind of pain. Not that I wanna picture it. He's too strong and too protective for that...

But then I think of the blow up he and I had. I quietly heave as an awful, awful thought comes to my mind. One I hope isn't true, but somehow, I feel the urge to ask anyway. The little things Mama's saying in her journal is starting to plant seeds around what his life with my parents may have been like. A way of life I probably wouldn't have survived. But the unspoken truth from my last question encourages me to reluctantly probe further.

"I don't want to ask this but..."

My mouth suddenly goes dry. I lick my lips to try and moisten it.

"Was it... was it... was it my dad that assaulted you?"

Jarell's body goes immobile. The plate he's washing slips from his wet fingers and drops into the dishwasher with a *thunk* and splash. Tilting his head back, he calmly inhales without letting it out and leaves the kitchen, abandoning me in solitude. After a few long seconds, he lets out the breath he held onto that I'm sure he hoped I wouldn't hear because it's not just any breath.

My stomach twists, and I lose it, slamming my fist on the counter as my tears quickly add to the dishwater.

Fuck.

FUCK.

I just happened to put two and two together, but I do not want that to be true. Please don't let that be true.

I can't even imagine. How do I even make sense of this?

No wonder why he wouldn't ever say a single word about our family... I slap my forehead several times until I know it turns red. This whole time, Jarell took custody of me, *his abuser's daughter*, and never once complained about it.

Now I get it.

I get his silence.

I get his hurt about the way I've treated him.

I get why he cried when I told him I hated him.

He absolutely could have said "fuck you" to me years ago. But he loved me from the moment I could remember being alive like I was *his* daughter and not his sister. And here I am, having been such a complete dick because of his lack of answers... How can I even be okay with myself?

Fuck...

But why? Not only physical assault like Mama wrote in her journal, but... *sexual assault? Why would Dad abuse my brother like that?* What did Jarell do to deserve it? Why would he do something so vile and ...gross? Did Mama know about this? The way Jarell talks about being so mad at her, I'm sure she knew... she had to.

God.

Jarell must've been so torn up inside ... and if Mama really did know, I'd likely hate her too if I were him. Now, I have even more questions. On the surface, it seemed like Jarell was the common issue in all of these problems.

But with this new information and Mama's writings in her journal ... it's all starting to make sense. Everything that ever happened to me and Jarell is our mama and my dad's fault. Yet, Jarell still didn't want me to see either of them as bad people.

That's a level of selflessness I can't even begin to comprehend.

My silence breaks as I let out audible cries in sorrow and guilt. Now, I'm wondering how I even got here. Actually, I don't even wanna know. I carry my dad's DNA. His blood flows through my veins, and there's nothing I can do about it. I cover my mouth to stop the cries from escaping when I hear Jarell's voice in my ear of what he said to me on the boardwalk the other day.

"You've gotta be mature enough to take some heavy information and turn it into something that you genuinely accept so that you can heal and not let it tear your soul apart. No matter what, knowing the information will bring you some scars. But you have to approach this with a heart of forgiveness and acceptance. That's real closure."

I kneel to the floor but remain on my toes, quietly weeping. I don't know if he's truly accepted what happened or not, but from what I've seen and how he lives his life, it's clear he's come to terms with the situation in his own way. He seems way too mentally and emotionally free. Maybe he's just upset that I figured it out. I don't know.

The real person I'm pissed at right now is Brooklyn. He needs her more than ever. Not for her to leave him hanging and breaking up with him just because he didn't tell her about some side gig.

My blood boils at the thought.

He needs her *right now*.

But then, Jade, and the fact that Brook saw them at the diamond. That's a whole 'nother layer to their breakup. I can't lie – I'd be mad too if I were Brook, seeing my man hug up on someone else. And it wasn't just that. When their bodies collided, it was like sparks literally ignited between them.

Rising from the ground after wiping my tears and leaving the dishes right where they are for me to take care of later, I go to my room and cuddle with my teddy bear in bed. The rest of the house remains numb and silent. Good. It allows me to think of the million and one ways I can, and should, apologize to Jarell. For *everything*.

Chapter Twenty-Two

I DIDN'T SLEEP very well last night.

I had another nightmare about my dad, but this time, it was some weird dream of me sprinting, trying to escape the city. I don't even know why I was trying to escape, but all I remember was being chased by wolves and my dad had them on a leash, running after me.

My heart raced in the dream the same way my heart raced when I held that gun in my hands. At least the dream wasn't debilitating, though. Especially after everything that happened last night and the things I learned from Jarell. I still can't even fathom...

This whole situation is just so sad. I don't want to know an ounce else of information about Mama or Daddy. I've never wanted to admit how right Jarell is. That I'm not ready.

Because I'm not.

So, I'm not going to finish her journal right now. I think I'll sit on it for a while. Maybe a few years because I still haven't even processed what happened last night. I've gotta talk to Dr. Anderson about this one.

I'm tired, but I'm actually glad to go to school to occupy my mind with other things. By the time I'm dressed and ready for school, Jarell hasn't even come out of his room yet, and it's seven thirty.

This never happens.

Usually, he's awake by five o'clock in the morning taking Luna out for a walk, doing pushups in the living room while listening to music that wakes me up, or he's eating some freakishly healthy breakfast like sweet potatoes, arugula, and plain eggs or a green fruit smoothie.

With rare footsteps in this direction of the apartment, I head to his room and knock on the door.

"You good in there? You're usually up by now," I ask.

"Yeah. Just overslept."

Damn. Sounds like he's got a frog in his throat.

"You going to work or nah?"

"Already called in sick."

Hmm. Is he lying? But he does sound awful. I don't know if he even slept last night. Either way, it ain't good. He needs a little intervention. Someone who can come over and get him out of his funk, sickness, or whatever he's really got going on. Take care of him and cheer him up a little bit.

I kinda wanna go in there and hug him myself, but... I'm not sure if that's a good idea. What would I even say? How will Jarell react if I bring it up? What would he think if I went to hug him, considering how I've been acting over the last couple years? A part of me feels like he'd say, "Don't be tryna act all sorry now," even though that's not really in his nature. I don't know. I don't want to make him upset. I wish I had the words to let him know how much I *want* to hug him, though.

To let him know I'm thinking of him and this whole situation, I text him a broken heart emoji with a regular heart next to it. It's the best I can do at this moment, but it's from my heart. Hope he can detect that. I just gotta find the right time for the words he deserves when I can come up with them.

I check myself in the mirror, happy with my khaki cargo joggers, plain yellow tank, lip gloss, and all white Air Force One's with my hair down before I leave the house with all my bags and walk to the bus stop. On my way there, I pull out my phone and scroll to Brooklyn's name to text her. She needs to come back here and make up for what she did. It was a stupid reason to break up with someone, but of course, I ain't gon' say all that. So I take a different approach and play the dumb card.

> Hey Brooklyn. This is Kylah. Jarell's really down at home and he's sick. Are you able to help him out today?

Send. I get on the bus and ride to school, stomach tumbling, hoping I get a response back. I don't get it, at least for as long as my bus ride lasts.

When I arrive, Prez is just getting here too, and we literally exit our respective bus doors at the same time. I jog straight for him, and he throws a dark look my way. I give him a teasing smile in return, and he can't keep up the mad front for too long. His face breaks into an exasperated grin when I jump on his back, and he catches me, giving me a five second piggyback ride with a laugh before he lets go of me and keeps strolling toward the school.

"I'm sorry about last night, Prez," I say, walking alongside him. "My brother and his girlfriend broke up."

"Oh, dang. That sucks. Isn't she the one who's always at your games?" Prez asks.

"Yeah, she is. It's kinda sad because I was just starting to like her," I reply. "I hope she keeps her word. She said that she wanted to develop a relationship with me no matter what happens between her and Jarell. So, we'll see if she's a real one."

"Yeah," he says as his thumbs move a million miles an hour on his phone screen and not paying attention to where he's walking.

He's so into it that he doesn't even see me take a small peek at his hand. He's texting Gina, looking like he's responding to a big, long white paragraph. I shake my head. *What could she possibly be whining about to send him that essay?*

"Hey, you wanna stop and finish what we were talking about last night?" I question.

"Hold on, gimme a second..." He stops, but he's still glued to his phone, not even giving me his attention.

I pause and wait impatiently with my arms crossed and weight shifted to one leg. When he's done, he looks up and puts the phone in his back pocket.

"My bad. Yeah, let's go sit."

He and I walk to the front courtyard and sit on a bench. We've got about fifteen minutes before class starts, which is plenty of time to catch up and chop it up.

"Alright, so back to what we were talking about..." I start.

"Yeah. I'm not hooking you up with Andre, LaLa," he says, shaking his head.

"Why not?" My hands shoot out.

"Because! I told you it would be weird. And... I was tryna tell you this yesterday but..." He falters and looks toward the sky.

"What?" My phone dings as I ask. I look at it, but it isn't a text.

"I'll just put it out there. I'd be a little jealous if y'all end up together."

My head snaps to him so fast that I nearly break my neck. He refuses to give me his gaze.

"Jealous? Why would you be jealous when you have a whole girlfr—"

"I know!" he yells, and that's when he looks at me. "I know I have a girlfriend. I care about her, too. But I ain't gon' lie. I get to spend more time with you than I do with her sometimes. She's not into what I like the way you are. She doesn't care about baseball, video games, none of that. She's super girly. All she cares about is hair, makeup, and nails. But you get me, you like all the things I like, and we vibe. I can yell at you and you'll listen, and you can do the same to me. We don't stay mad at each other for long because we want each other to be better. And... you're pretty. It's your eyes for me. So, I mean, yeah, I'll admit I kinda like you more than just being my best friend."

"Prez..." I start, but he puts a hand up.

"Let me finish. I also know getting together will ruin the good things we have. It won't feel like how it does now if we start going out. I have this feeling that it won't," he says.

"I agree," I nod emphatically.

"I guess ... I guess I want a girl that's just like you. But not you." He laughs. So do I. When the laughter between us ceases, he gives me a tender look. "I'm not gonna try and get with you, LaLa. I just wanted to say how I felt."

"Thanks for being honest." I smile. He gives me a glance of gratitude in return. "You already know how I feel about you, so I don't need to repeat it much, but you know me and you being together is not a good idea."

"Yeah. I know. It ain't gonna be all awkward between us now, will it?" he questions.

"Nah. I'm glad you were straight up. I like that. I just wanna know why you'd be jealous of your best friend if he and I hooked up."

"I don't know. I just feel like Andre is such a good dude, and I'm scared that if me and Gina don't work out that I'll never have a chance, ever, with you because he ain't the type of dude any girl would wanna leave."

My eyes get big. Wow. Prez feelin' me like *that*? And he's got a load of respect for Andre. Even though I'm not feelin' Prez in that way, he really is a dope guy. He deserves so much better than clingy ass Gina.

"Prez, you should be happy that your best friend, me, is with a good guy, your other best friend," I reply.

He lowers his head. "I know. I'm just being selfish."

"Mmm hmm," I nod.

"Yeah. Guess I need to get over myself."

"So... you gone hook me up with him or nah?" I ask, cutting him a side eye with a grin.

"Arrghh!" he rumbles with his head peeled back.

"Come on, Prez! At least can you see if he'd go to the dance with me?"

"Well, yeah, that's dead." He shrugs.

"What you mean it's dead?"

"He already asked someone to go with him."

"Who?!"

"Destiny. Destiny Melada."

I roll my eyes. Of course, he asked a pretty girl. I don't even talk to her; we're not even acquaintances, but if the boys aren't talking about Alaysia, then they're talking about Destiny.

"Are you lying?"

"You wanna see the texts?" Prez raises an eyebrow.

"No, I'm good."

"So, you and I are going together." He laughs. "Right?"

"Yes, of course I'll go with you, Prez. Under one condition."

"What now?"

"You have to help me plan how to ask him to be my boyfriend. Since you won't hook me up. That's the least you can do."

"Come on, Kylah, man," he whines.

My phone buzzes against my pocket. I pull it out and see Brooklyn's name pop up. Oooh! She responded!

"Yup. But I gotta dip. We'll talk more about the dance and this plan later," I say and rise from the bench we're sitting on.

"Bet."

He and I walk into the school building and go our separate ways to our homeroom class. I walk and read Brooklyn's text in response to my initial message this morning at the same time.

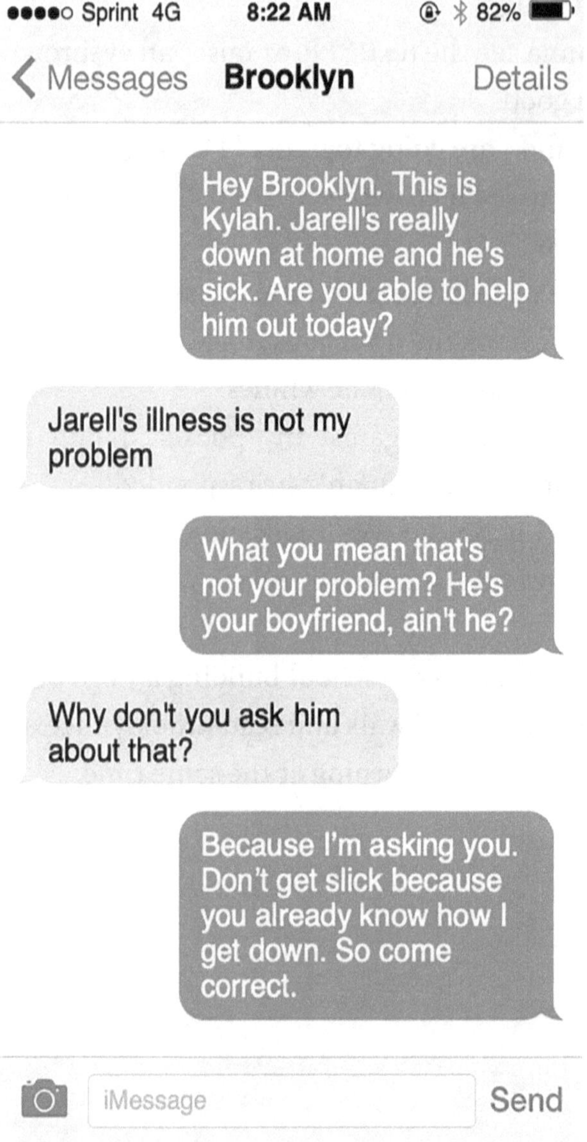

When I don't see the pending text response signal, I shake my head. That was super brash and rude of her, but she already knows not to argue with me. Because I got time.

I'm just about to put my phone away as I'm walking to class, but it's like I run into a brick wall, slamming right in the middle of someone's chest. My phone tumbles from my hands, the drawstring bag with my sketchbook goes flying, and I fall straight down to my ass, my hands hitting the ground with a big fat SPLAT. Multiple people laugh at me who watch it all go down, pointing at me.

"Yo, what the f— ...Andre?" I stop myself the moment I look up and we lock eyes. His mouth drops as he gives me a wildly mortified look.

"Aye... I am so sorry, Kylah," he says and bends down immediately to pick up my phone and bag. "I was coming around the corner way too fast, trying not to be tardy."

I close my eyes and sigh. "It's okay. I wasn't watching where I was walking, anyway. I probably could've avoided you," I respond and slowly get up from the ground, dusting my shirt and pants off. He motions my belongings toward me, and I take them.

He stuffs his hands in his jean pockets, standing awkwardly like he doesn't know what else to do to rectify what happened. He doesn't really need to do anything. Just being as fine as he is fixes it all.

"Well... I guess I'll see you around," I mumble, ducking my head and trying to walk away, but his arm reaches out to stop me.

"Hey. Did you finish that picture of me, yet?" he asks. "It's been a few weeks..."

I pause for a second. Oooh, how should I handle this? I'm definitely just about finished with it, but I also feel like right here and right now ain't the time to show or give it to him. Wait. I got a better idea...

"Yeah, it's close to being done." I smirk. "I'll give it to you at the dance." I look him up and down with bold, flirty eyes and walk away, not wanting to see his reaction and not wanting him to catch on to what I just did.

My heart is literally pounding in my throat, and it feels like I'm gonna die of a heatstroke! Who knows what he's gonna tell Prez about that, but I'm likely to hear from him about it. Maybe. If Andre even detected what I did for him to say something.

~ ~ ~

School flies by today faster than it normally does. I don't stay and hang out for a few minutes with Prez before we get on the bus. Instead, I ride straight home to make sure everything's good with Jarell. When I walk inside though, Luna's curled up in the living room chewing on her bone toy, and Jarell's keys remain on the kitchen counter. But he's nowhere to be found in the common areas.

"Jarell?" I call out.

I don't get an answer. My heart starts pounding the same way it did when I called out for Mama, and she wouldn't answer me... only for her to turn up dead a few minutes later. My mind starts playing flashbacks, but I slap my head a few times to get myself out of it. I pick up the pace, my throat clamming up as I head to Jarell's room.

His door is never open, but it is now, which makes me feel worse.

I peek my head around the corner inside. He's lying in his big king bed with a blanket over the top half of his body, and it looks like he hadn't even washed himself up today. But thankfully, his chest slowly rises and falls, indicating his presence here on Earth.

My shoulders completely relax, and I release the breath I'd been holding onto.

His hair is unkempt, his beard is scruffy, and his contacts are out, showing the full extent of his blind eyes. His forearm drapes across his forehead while he "stares" at the ceiling, but who knows what he's really seeing or thinking. I've never seen him look so ... exhausted.

"Jarell, are you okay?" I ask genuinely and take a step inside.

I look around his room, too. The small, flat screen TV plays in the background, but again, he has such a guy's room. Grays, blacks, and whites with no real color nor decorations. If Brooklyn wasn't being such a jerk, I'd phone her up right now so we can shop and do a room makeover.

"No," he answers. His voice cracks as if he'd been coughing all day.

"That's crazy. You were just fine yesterday before y'all's breakup. Are you really sick? Or is it because you feel bad about what happened last night?"

"Both," he says. "I'm sick for real. I got some sort of sinus infection or something because I have a fever."

I glare at him for a while, but he doesn't budge. He simply lays there, not having moved a muscle. The more I watch him, the more I realize that he's definitely ill, for real. His eyes droop, and his mouth is open as if he's stuffed up.

"Alright, well what do you need me to do? Need any medicine? Need me to get anything from the store?" I question. "Need me to warm you up some soup?"

"Nah, you good." He sniffles. "I took some medicine already. I'm not hungry either. Already threw up this morning."

"Okay..."

Damn. I don't like this. I don't think I've ever seen Jarell sick since I've moved here, since he's a health nut and all, so this is strange. Regardless, I think someone's gotta come take care of him. He can't be sick and heartbroken. That sucks.

I close his door, go into the living room to sit down, and chill on the couch and turn on the TV to binge watch an old school TV show, Degrassi: The Next Generation. I pull out my phone and see if Brooklyn texted me back yet, and she hasn't. But she read it, and the receipt says that she read it hours ago. I roll my eyes.

Well, since she wants to be petty, I know who to reach out to next. Opening up my contacts list again, I scroll down the middle and find Jade's number. I click a new, fresh textbox open and fix my fingers to type, but I pause for a second to think. What should I say? It needs to be something that isn't unnatural and cringy. And something that doesn't mention Jarell. It would be a dead giveaway if I do.

I hold my breath, hit send, and put my phone down so that I'm not tempted to watch and wait in anticipation. I get real deep into this show, occasionally laughing at the young Drake known as Jimmy in this series when my phone vibrates against the couch. I pick it up to see who it is, and Jade's name pops up.

"Oooh!" I whisper to myself and pause the show.

●●●○○ Sprint 4G   4:08 PM   @ 39% ◼▭

‹ Messages   **Jade**   Details

Hi Jade, this is Kylah. It was really nice to see you this past weekend.

Hey, Kylah! It was so nice to see you too. I can't believe you grew up the way you did. Makes my heart happy to see you doing well. I miss you guys so much. I've thought of you and your brother often throughout the years.

I wish we would've had more time to talk. Maybe you can come to San Diego. Can you come tomorrow some time in the evening?

iMessage

●●●○○ Sprint 4G   4:09 PM   @ 38% ▮▭

❮ Messages   **Jade**   Details

Well, I live in LA, and that's a two hour drive. I would need more of an advance notice to come there.

What you think about having lunch on Saturday? I don't have any games this week. Are you busy?

I do have rehearsal for the BET Awards from 1pm to 4pm, and it's a two-hour drive to San Diego. I can do dinner around 6:30.

Dinner's cool too.

 iMessage 

●●●○○ Sprint 4G   4:09 PM   @ 38%

< Messages   Jade   Details

Is your mom okay with that? You need to get permission first.

Remember, I don't live with her anymore. I live with Jarell. I'll tell you more about that when we meet. Can Jarell come?

Well… only if he's ok with it. He's got a girlfriend, though. I don't know if that'll be a good look

Mmm, you're right. Let's just go as the two of us.

That sounds like a much better plan.

iMessage

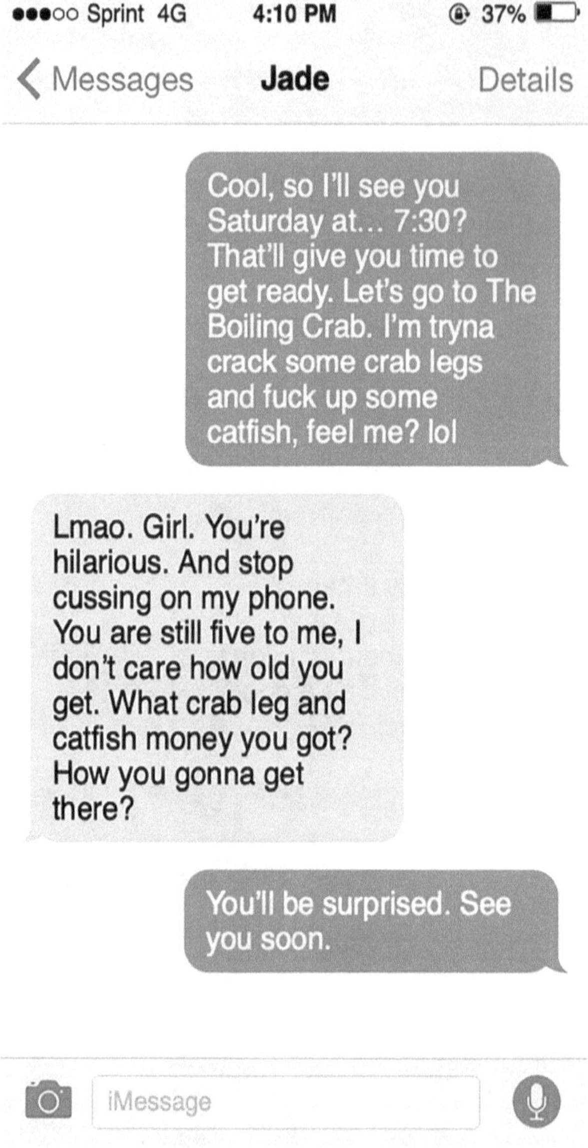

I squeal quietly to myself with excitement. I'ma need this week to hurry up and be over with. I have so many things to look forward to now. The dance, Jade, the Senior League Tournament… and it'll keep my mind off the news I found out about Jarell and our family.

Chapter Twenty-Three

SATURDAY IS HERE in no time, and it's nice to not have a tournament to play in after that long one in LA. That doesn't stop me from going to the diamond, though. Prez and I take some time super early in the morning, six a.m., to practice pitching. He's not the pitcher on his team, but he likes to practice them just in case he'd like to be one day.

The bulk of the time was me practicing my pitches, doing change ups, fast balls, rise balls, curveballs, and screwballs while he plays the role of my catcher. I pitch about a hundred of them before I call it quits, and he and I do ground ball drills, then we run a mile in the park's trail. Last, he and I practice batting in the batting cages that Miss Juanita takes us to. All that takes about six hours, and now it's noon.

Prez says he's gotta head out so he can take Gina to the movies and go out to lunch, so Miss Juanita drops me back off at home when we're finished. I spend the next few hours doing yard work and mowing lawns, babysitting little ones while their parents run quick errands, and getting groceries for our neighbors in the complex for some pocket change before I shower and get ready for dinner with Jade. I purposely don't eat lunch today to work up a beasty appetite, and boy is it beasty! And I made about two hundred dollars today, so I'm ready to give up these coins for this fish!

By the time I'm out of the shower and ready, Jarell comes in the door with Luna, super sweaty to the point where his entire shirt is drenched.

"Where were you at all sweaty like this?" I ask, looking him up and down. "You must be feeling better? Because you were in bed earlier today, too."

"Yeah, I'm feeling a lot better. Fever finally broke last night. But I was jogging on the beach in the sand along the shoreline. Definitely an intense workout. You should join me one day," Jarell huffs.

With his shirt wet like this, I notice how sculpted his abs are in ways that I never knew! I thought I was the one with a defined pack... he's on a whole 'nother level!

"Dang Jarell, I didn't know you were that cut! That's not even a six pack. That's like an eight pack!" I awe.

"What you mean? Oh, my abs?" he asks, rubbing his belly.

"Yeah!"

He unfastens Luna's harness and hangs up the leash on the hook next to the door. "Aww, yeah. I try to take care of my body as much as possible. You only get one," he says and takes a swig of water.

"Yeah, I know you eat super healthy and all, but I didn't know you had it like that. I'm pissed. Now I gotta get mine a little better so I can compete!"

He laughs. "You don't need to compete with me. You're only fourteen. You'll get more defined when you're an adult. And it's all genetics. The fact that we both have abs probably speaks to our mom and her genes," he replies.

"True. Anyway, I'm going out to dinner tonight," I say.

"Are you telling me? Or are you asking? Because telling me ain't gonna cut it," Jarell replies with his arms crossed.

I smack my lips. "Fine. Can I go out to eat tonight?"

"That's much better. Yes, you can go, but you've been out all day. Don't you want to rest for a little while?"

"Not really. You know I have limited weekends because of the season, so any time we don't have a tournament, I wanna take advantage of it to hang out."

"Well, okay. I understand. Do you need money?" he asks.

"No, but I'll take it if you tryna give it." I chuckle with a hand sticking out that I wish he could see. I'll save that two hundred for something else.

He smacks his lips. "Wow." He pulls his wallet out from his pocket and gives me five twenties. "Here. Don't spend it all at this restaurant, Kylah. This should last you for the rest of the week."

"Thanks. I won't spend it all."

"Who are you going with and who's taking you? Where y'all going?"

"Tina. Her mom's picking me up. And we're going to The Boiling Crab."

"Alright. Be careful," he says, heading to his room. "Send me your location when you get there."

"I will."

~ ~ ~

I don't ride with Tina. Obviously. When I get off the bus, I send Jarell my location and walk just a short distance to the restaurant. Jade is already here, leaning up against the wall next to the front door. Her head is down in her phone, not even realizing that I've walked up.

She is seriously drop dead gorgeous. Her hair isn't straight as she had it when we saw her at the community center in Los Angeles. This time, they're loose curls and waves held back by a thick headband. Her boyfriend jeans, for whatever reason, fit her shape in some areas and lay baggy in others, giving her this Aaliyah vibe with her form fitting tank.

After I stare at her long enough, I shout out to her loud enough to get her attention, but not too loud to startle her. Her eyes shoot up at me.

"Oh, hey! Glad you made it safely. Does Jarell know where you are?" She smiles and opens her arms for a hug.

"Yeah. Duh."

I easily accept it, and we hug very briefly and go inside the restaurant, getting a table for us.

"You been here before?" I ask.

"Yep, a couple times. They're pretty good. I like their shrimp basket," she says.

"You've never had their crab legs?" I ask.

"Yep, but I just like the shrimp. Sometimes, the crab legs can be too much."

"Oh, well that's what I'm finna order. And the catfish."

We do all the formalities with all restaurants, like order drinks, get asked about appetizers, and get told about the menu. We do away with all the extra stuff and order our drinks and entrées right away. I got exactly what I said I was gonna get. King crab legs and the catfish dinner.

"Girl, you ordered all that? How you gonna pay for it?" Jade asks.

"I work for my money." I shrug. "You know I'm old enough to

have a job, right?"

"I guess you are..." she admits. "And you're gonna spend it all on food. Man, to be young again..."

"I don't have an actual job, but I do services for other people around the neighborhood on the weekends when I can," I say. "Cut a few lawns, babysit a few kids, get groceries for the elderly in the apartment complex, and boom. You can get up to two hundred dollars in a day."

"That makes sense. I'm surprised people would have you do that kinda stuff anymore, since we've got DoorDash now."

"Because I'm cheaper than DoorDash." I laugh.

"True." She nods. "So, you're gonna eat all of what you just ordered?"

"Just watch and see," I say.

The waiter comes back shortly with our drinks. That's when Jade speaks, feeling comfortable to not be interrupted for a while.

"I'm really glad you invited me out here to catch up. I didn't think you'd even care or be interested enough to wanna do something like this. It's been so long since we've last seen each other. You were nearly a toddler."

"It's 'cause I remember how much you made me happy," I confess and sip my drink. "I don't forget people like that. I'm interested in any one from my past who made my life feel good. I loved when you came around."

"Awww!" She blushes. "That's really sweet of you. I'm glad you remembered me, even if it was short lived."

I shrug as my face warms.

"Yeah, but we spent a lot of time together whenever you did come around. You used to play Barbies with me for hours." I laugh.

"Yesss. I remember that. You used to have some of the best little Barbie scenarios and scenes. It was so fun to act them out with you because you were hilarious, Kylah," she reminisces.

"Yeah, I don't play with them anymore. I'm for real a tomboy now. I mostly stay away from anything super girly. Except my stuffed animals. I still sleep with those."

"I can tell just by the way you dress. Well, I guess you have a pretty solid balance of masculine and femininity. You grew up to be really beautiful, Kylah."

I sheepishly smile in return.

"So, how is school going? What's been going on all this time? You're graduating from eighth-grade soon, aren't you?"

My lip curls and my eyes roll.

"Yes, and I can't wait. School's not my favorite." I shake my head. "I'm definitely not at this dinner to talk about school. I wanna know about you and the BET Awards you said you're performing at. How'd you get to do that? What are you performing?"

"Well, I'm a choreographer and celebrity dancer," Jade says. "I dance with many of the artists you probably listen to and have been doing this for years."

"Yeah, you said you're performing with Kehlani, right? I love her! I literally get my style tips from her. That's so dope! I wanna go! Who else have you performed with?"

"Girl, I've danced with some of everyone at this point. Usher in Vegas, Cardi, Mario, Ty Dolla Sign, Chris Brown, SZA, Chloe, and yes… even Beyoncé," she says.

"Beyoncé!?"

"Yep. About two years ago when she went on tour, I toured with her."

My jaw drops. "No way. So… you're a famous person? Like, I should be getting an autograph right now?"

Jade laughs.

"It depends on what you consider famous…"

"Jade, you went on *tour* and danced with Beyoncé. You're famous. Show me a video or something!" I squeal.

With a smile, Jade pulls up her IG account, @jadewilliamsdance. Woah. She's got 1.3 million followers! I take my phone out and follow her. She follows me back, and I feel all the pride in the world that I'm one of the few 126 people she's following. Jade scrolls down her feed and pulls up a video of the live Beehive concert. And there Jade is, dancing behind Bey with another set of dancers. Our food is served as we're watching the video, which is fine because then we don't have to answer the waiter about what else we need. The more I watch, the more I'm shook.

Jade looks incredible. Flexible, sharp, and brings all the energy. She doesn't miss a step. Miss a beat. All done in the thinnest heels. I can't even…

She and the rest of the dancers definitely understood the assignment.

"Wow, Jade. This is sooo wild. I had no idea!"

"Yeah, that's my life," she says with a satisfied sigh and puts her phone away. "Aye, this food looks amazing!"

"Yeah, it does," I agree. "I'm 'bout to max it out, too."

Both of us pause our discussion about Jade's celebrity status and take a few first bites. Both of us melt in our chairs at how good everything is.

"Good choice to come here," she says.

"Thanks! So, back to the conversation. When we were in LA

last week, you mentioned something about Jarell dancing and him coming to your studio. He's a dancer? I've never, ever seen him move a muscle for a dance move in my life." I actually laugh at the thought. There's no way...

"Girrllll!" Jade emphasizes with a humongous smile in her eyes since her mouth is loaded with food. After she swallows, she continues. "Jarell may not have shown you, but that man is one of the best dancers I've *ever* seen. I've been doing this for years now and still haven't seen anything like it."

I shake my head. Visualizing Jarell dancing is like hearing him sing. Tragic. I laugh this time out loud.

"I don't believe you," I say.

"You don't have to. I caught him dancing in our school parking lot when we were in high school one day, and that's when he and I started to get close. Through dance."

"I don't think he dances anymore, Jade." I still shake my head in disbelief. "I have literally never seen him bust a move."

"If not, that's really too bad. But I kinda believe it. He only really danced as a coping mechanism."

"Whatever that means," I mumble.

"His story to tell, dear," Jade replies.

I don't reply and simply accept her response to my curiosity. A lull in the conversation settles between us as the topic of Jarell dancing fades with the silence, opening the door for a shift in the subject.

"Can I come to one of the award shows you have coming up? Not the BET Awards this year, but other awards. Maybe next year? I'd love to meet some artists!"

"I'll consider that. But you should be gearing up and preparing to be a celebrity yourself rather than trying to meet some," she says, dipping some of my crab leg I let her try in butter. "I guarantee you that the celebrities you wanna meet are gonna be trying to meet you first."

"What do you mean?" I frown.

"Kylah, you're about to play in the Little League Softball World Series on ESPN."

"You mean Senior League..."

"Yeah, it's the Senior League, but it's a part of the Little League program. I looked it up. You're probably living a very normal life and you may feel like a regular girl right now. But that's because this tournament hasn't started yet. It's all about to change. Look at what they did with Mo'ne Davis when she played on the baseball team. She's an icon now."

"Jade, what are you talking about?" I ask.

"It's a really big deal that you could be the first Black American female softball pitcher to win the World Series in a White dominant sport. And you're the favorite to win it all. This is going to come with some serious social media attention, and it'll start with the Black community noticing first. Your followers are probably gonna skyrocket. And because folks are always in tune with Black entertainment and success stories, your success is gonna come with interviews from news channels, blogs, and other media outlets. You're gonna be so excited. It'll seem amazing at first, like the world loves you. But then the racists will come out of the woodworks to tear you down, negative comments will start coming on social media at any blemish on your face or any mistake you make and cyberbullies will be out to attack."

"You mean like The Shaderoom?" I question.

She ponders for a second. "Maybe. Actually, yeah. One minute those people love you, and the next, they rip your soul out. People are very fickle, Kylah. But it depends on how your story is framed because you and Jarell have compelling stories that people would eat up. Either way, you have to be very strong, secure in yourself, and have a deep love for yourself."

"So, what am I supposed to do?"

"Well, I'd be happy to help you navigate how to manage your social media accounts and work on your media personality. I understand what it means to be in the spotlight because I have a million followers on my Instagram and Tik Tok myself with a lot of exposure to the entertainment business. You need someone like me to help you handle the stress that comes with such a following because Jarell ain't gonna know how. He's extremely reserved and not a spotlight person at all."

"I don't know if all of what you're saying is gonna happen, but I'm definitely down for you to help me out," I say. "You probably know way more than me about these blogs."

We go silent again for a couple of moments, focused on tearing up our food. For Jade to be super in shape, she's throwing down like it ain't no thing. I guess she could say the same about me.

"So, do you have a boyfriend? A husband? You're wayyyy too pretty to be single," I ask, shoving a huge piece of hot sauce filled catfish in my mouth.

"Nope. I'm single and mingling," Jade says. "I travel too much and got too many things on my plate to have a partner right now. I tried it a couple years back, but things didn't work out. My entire life revolves around dance."

"You think you'll ever settle down?" I question.

"Well... maybe. I guess it depends on if I find the right person, and if I do, I'll take a hiatus because I do need a little break. I've been going hard at this dance thing since I was your age, and now I'm twenty-seven."

"What happened with you and Jarell? Why ain't y'all just stay together?"

Jade shrugs with a twisted smile. "It just wasn't the right time. I was extremely ambitious with a lot of goals back during my senior year of high school. Around the time we were together, he was working on himself in therapy and my career was starting to take off, so we had to focus on ourselves. I ended up breaking up with him and... we just kinda left it there."

"Do you still love my brother?"

She frowns and raises one brow before releasing an uncomfortable chuckle. "Girl, why you asking all these questions? What's your end game here?"

"Nothing! I'm just asking. It's just a conversation. I've always kinda wondered what happened, so... yeah."

"Jarell will always have a special place in my heart because we've been through a lot together. But he's got a girlfriend. She's stunning, too. Like, *stunning*. I'm not in the business of messing that up."

"No, he doesn't," I say.

Her brows crease. "He doesn't what?"

"He doesn't have a girlfriend. They broke up last Sunday."

She blinks several times in disbelief.

"What? Kylah, don't play around with me. They were just together last Friday."

"And they broke up two days later. I'm telling the truth. Long story short, he didn't tell her about a side job that he has. She found out about it because he dropped his ID in the parking lot next to her car after we got back from LA. She found it on the ground and asked him about it. She felt like he should've told her that he had another form of income, especially after dating for two years."

Jade freezes with skepticism. Her eyes remain on me, though. "Seriously? That's it?" she asks.

"Yep. Well, that's not it, but... it was one of the reasons."

She finally looks away from me, crunching on another piece of shrimp, her eyebrows raising up and down quickly. She tries hard not to show any of what she's thinking with her expression. I glare her down like a hawk to see if I can gather anything, but I can't. "Oh wow."

We sit and brood for a while as we slow down on stuffing our faces. Some of these people are gonna have to roll us outta here.

"Whew, I'm stuffed. You ready to go?" Jade asks, rubbing her belly. "I'd be glad to give you a ride home. I don't want you riding the bus this late. I didn't even want you taking the bus here."

"Jade, it's the city bus. There's nothing wrong with me riding the bus by myself. I'll literally be fifteen on September second."

"I'm sorry." She wipes a hand down her face. "I'm not used to you being older and independent. What happened with your mom? Why can't she pick you up?"

"I keep telling you I don't live with her anymore." I roll my eyes to my drink and sigh. "She passed away two and a half years ago. Overdosed on opioids."

Jade's eyes widen and her mouth slowly drops. It's like the air from her lungs get sucked away.

"Oh my God. I am so sorry," she whispers. "Not Miss Rachel..."

"You mean Radiya?"

"Yeah, but she also went by Rachel. You've gotta be kidding me..."

Rachel? At this point, I guess it really doesn't matter. She's not here for it to matter 'cause it ain't like I can ask her about it. And I know Jarell won't tell me either. I shrug and keep my eyes away.

"Jesus Christ, your family has been through so much. How are you holding up about it?" she asks.

"Not good."

She shakes her head. "Wow. That's news I did not wanna hear..."

"Yeah, and I don't wanna really talk about it."

"Okay. I won't ask about it anymore. Let me give you a ride home, honeybun."

"Thanks. Will you come inside when we get there?" I question.

"Ehhh." Jade tilts her head from side to side, squinting her eyes, but I plead with mine. "I don't know about all of that."

"Come on, Jade. Please? At least you can say hi to Jarell. He'd be glad to see you."

"Uhhh," she groans, but I keep begging. "If he's going through a breakup, I wanna give him space."

"Please!!"

She huffs. "Fine. Come on, let's pay the bill so we can go."

Chapter Twenty-Four

AFTER GIVING SEVERAL directions to Jade to make it safely to Jarell's apartment in her sharp white and black Jeep Sahara, we park, get out, and walk toward the main doors.

"This is a really nice area! You guys live close to the beach, too. You gotta be making some decent money to live around here!" Jade marvels, spinning around in a circle and checking out the neighborhood. She pirouettes like such a dancer. Her long hair swings around too, ending over her shoulder.

Man, her hair reminds me so much of Mama's.

"Yeah, it's a nice area, but the apartment is so bland. You'll see," I complain.

"Well, Jarell is a guy and can't see. I don't imagine it would be a place that's aesthetically decked out," Jade retorts.

"True," I say and let us both inside the main doors and then the apartment.

After Jade and I move past the dark kitchen and follow the light to the living area, Jarell is sitting on the couch with Luna curled up next to him, her chin on his lap, just chillin'. His AirPods are in, and the worship music blasts to where we can both hear it. Jade and I chuckle at it. He's got something in his hand that he's trying to manipulate, and once I realize what it is, I smack my lips and check the floor to see the damage. Thankfully, no papers are scattered everywhere.

"I see you still do origami, huh?" Jade says.

He doesn't even look up to acknowledge her comment. He's still trying to fold the paper in his hands, not even aware that we're home because his music is too loud.

I turn the lights on and off several times because, for whatever reason, Jarell can detect changes in light. Don't know the science behind the why for blind folks, but he just can. It gets his attention, and he pulls an AirPod from his ears with a frown.

"Kylah why are you flicking the lights on and off like that?"

I don't respond. I just smirk.

"Some things never change, do they?" Jade teases him. "Always got a paper in your hands."

"Jade?!" He drops his origami immediately and sits up straight, scowling. "What are you doing here? How'd you even know where I live?"

"Kylah and I went to dinner, and I'm dropping her off. I thought you knew that already," Jade says with a frown.

"She went to dinner with you? How? When? When did you get into town? I didn't know anything about that." Jarell's brows wrinkle even more.

Jade's eyes expand. "Wait a minute, she didn't tell you who she was with tonight?"

"Yeah, but she told me she was going to dinner with her teammate Tina," Jarell clarifies.

Jade slowly turns to me, giving me a glare like she could punch me right now. I bite my lip awkwardly and smile. Jarell throws a disappointed glare my direction, too.

"Ha. Uh, yeah." I laugh nervously. "I thought I'd just ... ask for forgiveness later."

"You're definitely a teenager now because you act and make stupid choices like one. This is not okay, Kylah. For several reasons. You're putting me in a situation that I shouldn't be in."

"I'm sorry!" I say with a grin, and her glare gets even more dark at me.

"You'd better wipe that little smirk off your face because I'm not joking. I shouldn't be in someone's home that I'm not invited to, nor did he have any idea that I was even around. And you shouldn't lie about who you're with. What if something happened to you? Then what?" she lectures.

My smirk grows wider. "But did I die, though?"

I can tell Jade is about to say something real slick because her lips tighten, but Jarell interjects.

"Kylah! Cut the crap. You may be able to get away with acting like that with me, but that won't fly with other people. Go to your room. *Now*," he orders.

"Okay. Fine. You ain't gotta yell," I mumble and saunter to my room, shutting the door.

But I sit near it and put my ear up against the door to listen in to anything I can. Good thing these doors are hollow, and the walls seem paper thin, just like I heard everything go down with him and Brook last week.

"Jarell, I am sooo sorry. Kylah texted me earlier this week saying she wanted to catch up and go out to dinner since she was excited to see me at the park. I was excited too and thought that I'd catch up to see how you guys are doing after all these years. I thought you knew because she asked if you could come, but we ultimately decided for it to be a girl's thing. I didn't think she'd lie to you about it."

"Jade, no need to go into a long explanation," Jarell replies.

"Why? So, you're not upset?"

"Upset with who? You or her?"

"Her!"

"Yeah, I am! Of course, I am, but that don't mean I need to express it right now. She already knows I'm coming for her butt later," he says.

I roll my eyes at that. Now that I know he's upset, whatever he's about to nag about is just gonna go through one ear and out the other.

"I guess..."

"Well, since you're here, make yourself comfortable," Jarell says, his voice inviting and genuine. "Take a seat."

Jade pauses before speaking. "Jarell... I don't know about this. This is awkward. It's been damn near a decade since we've seen each other. I feel like I'm imposing, since I really wasn't invited or expected to be here. Shit is embarrassing."

Jarell laughs. "Yo, it's really not that deep. Since when did you become uptight? Here, come sit down. We have way too much history for you to be embarrassed about anything around me. You know better."

Some shuffling and moving around takes place in the distance, but they don't exchange words for a little while. I keep my ear pressed to the door.

"I see you still do origami," Jade breaks the silence.

"Yeah, not as often though. I ran out of ideas of new things to make, so I stopped doing it after a while. I'm trying a lion now. I don't know why I've never tried to make one of these before," he replies.

"Wow, that's crazy. You know, I still have the one you made me. I'll never forget it because... well two reasons. We were trapped in a trunk, and it was the only thing I could see. But the new one you recreated… it was the day I had broken up with you."

What the heck does she mean by "trapped in a trunk?" Why would they be in a trunk together? *Weird.* Jarell chuckles in his throat.

"Those were not happy days," he says.

"I hated seeing the look in your eyes when I did," she confesses.

"Mmm. I can only imagine."

"Speaking of breakups, Kylah told me at dinner that you're going through a breakup right now. You good?" Jade questions.

Jarell smacks his lips. "Of course, she did," he grumbles. "I'm… coping though. I really care about her but … I mean, I messed up. Wasn't very forthcoming with her about a lot of things she deserved to know."

"Well, are you gonna try and make it up to her?"

"I don't know anymore. I tried calling her multiple times and tried to stop by her house, but she's avoiding me. We've been texting back and forth, though, and I just get cussed out any time I say something. She's not happy with me at all."

"You think Kylah's doing all this to try and hook us up again? Since you've broken up with your girl?" Jade asks.

Jarell laughs again. "I really don't know why she'd be invested, but I wouldn't put it past her. I know you knew and remember a smaller and sweeter version of her, but Kylah's a handful now, Jade. She's bad as hell and does a whole lot of things to get herself in big trouble, but I think she's trying to turn a new leaf. I'll give her credit for that. At least I hope she's genuinely trying to."

Ugh, now see? Why does he have to be all negative about me? I scrunch my face. I should go out there and punch him.

"Well, she's supposed to be naughty, Jarell. She's a teen," Jade counters. "You remember how we used to act. I'm sure we were way worse than what she's doing."

"I guess."

"She also told me you guys lost your mom to an overdose, so you know that impacts her behavior. I still can't believe that. It's got to be devastating for you both."

"Dang, what didn't she tell you? It's true, though. I'm happy she's no longer in a place of suffering. She's spent pretty much her entire life going through hell. I feel more comfort with her resting than her being here to still struggle, you know? I just wish I had been able to spend more time with her as an adult."

She sighs. "Yeah, I understand. I don't want to bog down the conversation with this, so what are you doing these days? What happened in nine years for you?" she questions.

Jarell laughs.

"That's a loaded question. You and I are gonna have to spend way more time together to understand nine years, but for the major things? I've gotten saved, baptized, gotten right with God, and developed a strong relationship with Him. I'm abstinent until I get married for many reasons. I went through some real intense therapy back in LA and continued it here in San Diego. It was one of the best things I've ever done for myself, so thank you for being the one to push me there all those years ago.

"I got my GED about... I think six years ago now. Then right after that, I enrolled in an online program and got my associate degree in community and non-profit leadership. So now, I teach young kids how to read and write Braille. I also work at the Human Trafficking Center to support survivors. I'm working on getting my bachelor's degree in business management and maybe one day, get an MBA. I'm enrolling for classes this fall for the bachelor's now that Kylah's going to high school. I took a break for a little while to adjust to raising her, but I have two more semesters left before I graduate."

"Are you serious? Jarell that's amazing! Getting a college degree after being a high school dropout on top of everything else is such a flex. What do you want to do with those degrees?"

"I've been thinking a lot about what God has called me to do in the larger community context. It'll either be starting my own business with those who are visually impaired, something with hands on art, or something to combat human trafficking. I haven't fully fleshed out my thoughts around all of this yet."

"Wow. Just so inspiring and selfless. I am so proud of you, Jarell. Just looking at you, I can tell you've come a long way and have had a deep sense of restoration. It's just your energy. You have a kind of light in your eyes that I don't ever remember seeing. You seem way more relaxed and generally happy. After everything you've been through, it's incredible to see. It kinda makes me wanna cry," Jade says. "I'm excited to get to know the real you."

"Hmm." Jarell chuckles in his throat again. "You stay hyping somebody up."

"You know I'm the ultimate hype man." Jade giggles. "Real talk, Jarell. I'm beyond proud of you."

"I appreciate that. How's your mom doing?" Jarell asks.

"After everything she's done to you, I'm surprised you're asking. We don't talk. At all," she says.

Damn. What happened with her and her mom? That's pretty intense for someone to not have an ounce of a relationship with their mother. Now I guess I can kinda see how Prez feels when he was on me about how I treated Jarell. She doesn't know what she has, with her mom being alive and all.

"Really? After all these years?" Jarell questions.

"Yep. She's doing her thing in the fashion industry, but... honestly Jarell, I haven't talked to my mom since the day we last spoke. Nine years ago."

"Hmm. Let's talk more about that later. Are you planning to drive home tonight?" Jarell asks.

"Oh shit. I didn't even realize it's ten."

"Why don't you stay here? You can always leave in the morning."

"Jarell, no. Like I said, I'm already here uninvited. I'm not going to intrude to spend the night here. That's out."

"Jade, it's late. I don't want you driving home this late on your own. It's a pretty long drive," he argues.

"I'ma say it again and repeat myself, Jarell, I'm already here without you anticipating me. I'm not going to take up your space. Besides I didn't even bring clothes."

"I've got clothes!" I blurt out and immediately cover my mouth once I realize what I've done.

Shit! I was not supposed to blow my eavesdropping cover like that.

"Oh my God, somebody needs to get this girl," Jarell whines.

Footsteps come thumping toward me at a relatively quick pace. I rise from the floor immediately and dive to my bed like a swimmer and pick up a book, pretending like I'm reading it. The bed is just about done bouncing when my room door busts open, and Jade is glaring at me with a blank expression. She steps inside and walks toward me, squinting.

"Don't try and act like you weren't listening to our conversation this whole time. Look at you, the book you're even reading is upside down. Busted," Jade says, and tries so hard to refrain from smiling, but it breaks the second I start giggling.

Her eyes glisten with humor as she rushes my bedside and starts tickling me all over. I scream, throwing my book in the air, laughing, and trying to hide under the covers. Jade laughs and sits down next to me on the bed.

"Ugh, I want to be so mad at you so bad, but I can't," Jade growls, shaking her head.

"I'm sorry for real. And by the way, no, I'm not trying to hook you and my brother up. He had a really hard day last week, was really sick, and he's been kinda down at home, so... I just thought an old friend coming over would be a good idea to cheer him up, that's all. Looks like my plan worked."

"Mmm. I'll believe you this time. What clothes do you have? I think we're kinda the same size. You're just taller."

"Uh, no. You've got way more boobs and butt," I challenge.

"Yeah, but I'm not that much larger. What do you have?"

"I can give you some leggings and a t-shirt." I get up and start to search for them. "Does that work?"

"Works for me," Jade says.

Jarell stops by the room and leans against the door jamb with a white t-shirt and gray sweats on and bed sheets in his hands. Jade's eyes scan him up and down, mostly lingering at his abs. I scrunch up my face in disgust.

"Hey, sorry to interrupt y'all. So Jade, if you're planning to stay the night and leave in the morning, I usually wake up around four thirty or five o'clock in the morning to go for a walk and then make breakfast before going to church. I don't know how early you wake up, but... would you like to come? Kylah, you too?"

"I'll pass on that walk. It's too early for me," I say.

"Jarell, I'd love to go on the walk with you. I wake up pretty much around the time you do, too. Except I go for runs, so if you'd like a challenge, I'm down for jogging," Jade replies.

"Dope. Let's jog on the shoreline down at the boardwalk, then." Jarell smiles.

"Sounds like a plan. I've gotta be back in LA by nine for my classes, though."

"Okay, sounds good. Well, I'm gonna go get the sheets set up on the couch for you. I've got an extra toothbrush, bath towels for a shower, and anything else you may need. You can come out whenever you're ready."

"Thank you, Jarell."

Jarell gives Jade an affectionate look and a half, toothless smile in her direction before he walks away. Jade stands up from my bed and takes a huge breath in through her nose, and out through her mouth.

"Good Lord, this man done got sexy as *fuck*. Someone please help me..." Jade whispers to herself, planting a hand on her chest.

With a huge smile, I watch her before she continues out of my room. I laugh when she's gone. Man, there's just no doubt about it at all.

Jarell's got Jade's heart.

And, somewhere deep inside, Jade's got to have his, too.

Even after this tough break up with Brooklyn.

I just feel so bad because I like them both. A lot.

Chapter Twenty-Five

"**MAMACITA! YOU LOOK** so beautiful!" Prez's mom squeals after finishing the final touches on my hair. She styled it in a fish braid with some of my natural curls hanging in the front and on the sides. Then she slicked my edges down with edge control to complete the look. "Now, you're ready for tonight and for graduation tomorrow."

I grin with a satisfied smile in the mirror. She really did an amazing job. It's regal, but not too much for it to be an eighth-grade dance. This seems like it's gonna be a lot of fun. And then, tomorrow, I get to kiss middle school goodbye. Finally! June came quickly. It feels like we just got back from the tournament in LA in early May.

"Thanks, Ms. Juanita." I stand and give her a hug. She squeezes me tight.

"Anytime, my dear."

I appreciate her so much for filling the abyss that is supposed to be me and Mama having a bonding moment together during times like this. Although a part of me is sad about it, I mostly feel a sense of gratitude. It makes me feel better that I am actually going with Prez to the dance instead of Andre. Andre's parents don't know me at all, so I would've been left to try and style my hair on my own.

"Oh, to be fourteen again. I remember I had abs like yours." She sighs after eyeing my outfit.

Instead of the masculine suit which I actually preferred to wear tonight, just to please Prez, I went ahead with the two-piece sparkling turquoise set with the crop top and skirt. I will say, I kinda remind myself of a biracial, gray-eyed version of Jasmine from Aladdin with this outfit, from my hair to my belly ring.

"Now, can I do your makeup?" Miss Juanita asks.

"Nooo, I don't want to do make up. I'm good with this eye liner, mascara, and lip gloss I've got on."

"Oh, alright, alright. I'll wait for prom to do your makeup." She laughs.

"Am I all set then? Do I look good?"

"Sí, mija, you look gorgeous. Preston is gonna have a hard time choosing between you and his current novia with you looking like this. I'm just saying. Muy linda."

"Thanks, Miss Juanita."

I give her a hug again and slip on my clear sandals. Ugh. This is like the first and only time anyone would ever catch me in shoes that ain't sneakers. I hate girly shoes and heels, too. I am way too tall to be wearing heels, and I'm self-conscious about my feet being too big in sandals. I hope I'm done growing because being any taller than five foot ten would make me feel too Amazonian. I know I get my height from my dad, but I'm hoping Mama's genes kick in to keep me where I am. Because she's extremely short.

Once everything is on, including my gold accessories, and an important item in my small purse that I also hate carrying, I walk down the stairs, and Miss Juanita follows me. Prez and Jarell are sitting on the couch talking to one another until our arrival ends their conversation.

"Goddamn…" Prez whispers the moment he lays eyes on me but catches himself. "I mean… dang, LaLa! You look amazing!" Prez says with a huge smile, looking me up and down. My lip curls in a slightly smug grin.

"Preston, your language…" Miss Juanita warns, hitting him upside the head with her flip flop. He winces and holds his head.

Jarell takes off his sunglasses and cuts a grim look toward Prez, basically telling him to watch himself and how he talks about me. I giggle.

"Sorry, Ma. My bad, Jarell," Prez says, noticing the look. "I don't mean any disrespect. It's just that Kylah dresses like me most often, and I'm not used to seeing her like this."

"Mmm hmm," Jarell nods, without expression, but it's so funny to me because I already know he's just being overprotective.

"Alright, hijos. Let's take some pictures! ¿Dondé está mi esposo?" Miss Juanita asks.

"Oh, Dad's just outside cleaning out the car so that he can take us," Prez replies.

"Rob! Get in here so we can take pictures!" she yells toward the back door.

"Coming!"

Prez stands up, giving me the opportunity to check out his fit. He doesn't look half bad himself with his crisp white button up shirt that's slightly open at the chest to show his silver chain, unique blue dress pants, and white and gray Retro One's.

"I like the fit, Prez. Let me borrow those shoes later, though," I say.

"No. Buy your own," he says with a smile.

I huff. "Whatever."

"Your sister is beautiful, is it... Jarell, right?" Miss Juanita asks.

"Yes, that's right." He nods.

"You're gonna have to keep close tabs. I can tell a lot of boys are gonna come for her at the high school," she says.

"Don't speak it into existence," Jarell replies with a groan.

As he says that, Mr. Rob comes in, clapping with excitement.

"Alright! I'm here. Let's take these pictures!"

We all take several photos with me and Prez together, Prez and his family, me and Jarell together with Luna, and then, on a selfie stick, all of us together. When Miss Juanita shows me the pictures, I nearly tear up. I'm so glad we were able to capture moments like this.

"Okay, kids, y'all ready to go?" Mr. Rob asks.

"Yeah, I'm ready," Prez says. "LaLa, you good?"

"Yep. Let's go."

"Alright. Hop on in the car. Jarell you can come, too. I'll drop you off at home after," Mr. Rob says.

"Nah, I'm okay. You guys aren't that far from home. I gotta take Luna for a walk anyway," Jarell politely declines. "Besides, I'm sure Kylah would be embarrassed for me to be in the backseat when you drop her off at the dance."

I smile because he's not lying...

"Alright, understood. It's really nice to meet you. You've raised a nice young lady here. Congratulations," Mr. Rob replies.

"Still got a long way to go," Jarell says with a light grin and tells Luna to find the exit to the front door. She guides him there. "Y'all have fun tonight, okay? Stay out of trouble. Kylah, your curfew is ten tonight, okay?"

"Alright..."

"Thanks, Jarell," Prez says. "See you soon."

~ ~ ~

When we arrive, everyone else does, too. Everyone's getting out of their parents' cars making a beeline for their groups of friends near the front entrance. Phones immediately come out to take pictures and videos to post on SnapChat. I follow suit, pulling out my phone to take a selfie with Prez. I'm not really a SnapChat kinda girl; I'd much prefer Instagram or TikTok.

"Prez, look up," I say, still holding the phone up with the front camera on.

He looks up and smiles bright as his deep dimples poke through. Man, he's so cute! But because he's got a girl, out of respect for her, I'll keep this picture in my phone for memories. I actually might draw a portrait of us like this, too.

"Aww! I really like this picture of us, Prez!" I say when I review it.

"Yeah, that's dope. Send it to me."

I nod and go to my share button in an attempt to air drop it, but it's not cooperating. As he and I are trying to figure it out, we get an unexpected guest. An annoying little fly that just needs to be smacked one good time with a newspaper. Except this fly is dressed like she's going to the fuckin' prom and not an eighth-grade dance. Her gown is long with her entire back out and low cut in the front, as she usually wears all her shirts. I don't understand why the staff at school never code her for dress. I hope she gets kicked out of the dance this time because of it.

"I see that you have no problem taking Kylah to the dance, but you supposedly have a girlfriend. Yet, you dissed me in front of everyone, using the whole girlfriend thing as some excuse. I don't get it..." Alaysia says to Prez.

"Alaysia, that ain't for you to understand. Mind your business," he responds calmly. I look her up and down with a haughty smile. She gives me a sinister look in return.

"I don't care what is or isn't for me to understand. This shit is wack that you're playing in my face like this Preston, but I got something for both of y'all. Don't even trip." She nods and walks away to meet up with some of her girls, who apparently, are her date.

Prez and I look at each other and laugh. What a joke. She needs to get over herself.

Prez and I walk into the gymnasium where the latest hip-hop music blasts. Oh yeah, and we got a lit DJ tonight? It's about to go up!

Many of our classmates are already starting to dance, some of them, inappropriately. But there are a lot of staff chaperones around with their flashlights and whistles, blowing them any time they see or think a female butt would meet the front male pants. I laugh every single time someone gets caught. On the other hand, Prez and I just chill up against the wall, vibing to the music, not quite comfortable to go out there and dance yet. The night is still extremely young, and I feel like the DJ hasn't put on his best, yet.

"So Prez," I say out loud so that he can hear me over the bass of the speakers.

"Sup?"

"I need you to help me tonight with Andre. Help me get his attention without seeming too obvious that you're helping."

"Come on, LaLa," he whines, and his head peeled back. "I thought you forgot about this."

"Now, Prez. I'm serious about hooking up with him. Help me!"

"Okay, damn. What do you need me to do?"

I scan the dark gym that's only lit by colorful strobe lights to search for where he is. I didn't see him arrive in the parking lot when we did.

"Is he even here?" I ask.

"Yeah, he's right there." Prez points, and I find him near the middle of the dance floor, holding his date Destiny by the waist and stepping side to side to the clean version of Paint the Town Red by Doja Cat. I laugh and so does Prez.

"Man." He shakes his head. "My bro gotta do better than that."

"Right! I was gonna say to use some sort of song to get him away from Destiny, and maybe you dance with Destiny instead or something but let's go show them how to vibe because that weak ass two step to this kinda song ain't it," I say and pull Prez to the dance floor.

"Agree!"

Prez and I go over by Andre and Destiny and start dancing near them. I smile at Prez as I'm bouncing to the music. He's so smooth and vibey with his moves, sunglasses, and outfit. Coolest kid here. Prez moves closer to Andre, still dancing and slightly elbows him, giving him a look like he should stop with the lame moves. Andre gives him a look back with some humor in his eyes, but also tells Prez to leave him alone. He doesn't give him any more attention than that and keeps dancing with Destiny. Prez shrugs and comes next to me again, grabbing my arm and pulls me in front of him. Our bodies aren't touching, but we dance in similar moves, in sync with one another.

"Ayeee!" Our classmates come around to watch us dance together because we truly do got a whole vibe going. Nothing but positive energy and fun. It's to the point where Destiny and Andre stop dancing too to watch us. And then... I Just Wanna Rock comes on.

Everyone starts jumping up and down, gettin' hype and screaming every lyric. Some people can actually do that fast Tik Tok dance that I can't even dream to do.

Prez and I take a quick step away and to the side walls to take a break.

"Whew, it got hot in there. Glad we stepped out," I say.

"So what's the plan to get Andre's attention, now?" Prez asks. "Because what we just did ain't work."

"I think there's gotta be a song where you can take Destiny, and I take Andre."

"What song would that be?"

I put a finger on my chin and think for a second.

"I don't know. Maybe we need to come up with a different plan."

We stand in silence for a moment, contemplating.

"I got an idea. I'll ask the DJ if he can play a song so that we can bachata," Prez says.

"Huh? What is bachata? And how will that get Andre's attention?"

"You'll see. Let me take it from here. Just stand where you can see me, alright?"

"...Okay," I agree with hesitation.

Prez walks over to the DJ and exchanges a few words with him. Shortly after, a slow kind of song comes on with a Latin beat. All the Latina girls squeal and grab each other by the hand or by the hand of their dates, and they start doing this dance they all seem to know the footwork to. Even all the Latino boys seem to be in it with each other or their date.

Hmm. Prez might be onto something...

Prez motions me over to him, and I follow. We both go near Andre and Destiny again. Andre's standing kinda lost because he doesn't have any clue what this dance is. But Destiny, who is Latina, is so pumped about the song that at this point, she doesn't care who she dances with.

"You wanna dance, Preston?!" Destiny asks Prez. "I know you gotta know how to bachata... you're Puerto Rican! Andre doesn't know how."

"You guessed right. Aye bro, can I just dance with her for this one song? Kylah doesn't know how to dance to this, either." Prez asks.

"Go for it," he says, shrugging.

"Cool."

Prez takes Destiny by the hand, and they bachata or whatever. Prez gives me eyes like this is my chance and I need to do it now. Dang. This really is my dawg for life. Can't say enough about him, and I'ma need to figure out how to show my thanks one of these days.

"Well, I guess it's our time to sit this one out," I say to Andre, and he looks down at me with eyes in agreement. "You wanna go out to the hallway?" I ask. "I need to talk to you privately about something anyway."

"Yeah, that's cool. Let's go."

Andre and I go out in the hallway together in a secluded area of the school. Thankfully, the chaperones and supervisors didn't catch us coming back here.

"So... I have something for you," I say with a nervous edge once we become stationary.

"What is it?"

"I'ma give it to you in a second. But I... I guess I'll just put it out there. I don't know if you really notice but... I get a little shy around you Andre. Actually, it ain't even a little. It's a lot. And it's because I... kinda like you. Okay, not kinda. I've been feeling like this for a while…"

"Really?" Andre says, blinking in surprise and disbelief. "You *like* me?"

"I know I have a weird way of showing it," I admit, rubbing the back of my elbow. "But yeah. I really started feeling it in sixth-grade."

Silence swells between us. He really does look taken aback, still blinking several times to comprehend what I've just revealed. I hold my breath.

"Wow. I would've never guessed. You really didn't talk to me. I thought you liked Preston."

"I don't like Prez like that. If I did, we would've started dating a long time ago. We're friends, and I started to like you a lot because I thought you were super chill, nice, and really cute, but I was scared to talk to you," I say. "So, with that… I have what you've been asking for."

From my small purse, I pull out a folded paper and open it up. It's his portrait. His eyes light up the second he sees the finished product and my signature, stamping my artistry in the corner. A warm, perfect smile slowly spreads across his lips the more and more he stares at it.

"Read the back, too," I say.

He turns it over and reads my print handwriting.

Will you be my boyfriend?

I cover my face with my hands but leave a little open between my fingers so I can see. He has a cute grin on his face before he looks up at me from the portrait and laughs.

"Yo, well first of all, this portrait of me is insane. I've never seen artwork this realistic and amazing in my life. I wish you would bring out that side of you more so that people know how talented you are. I can't wait to show my mom," he marvels as his gaze returns back to my work. I watch his eyes move back and forth all over the image, taking in the beauty that is him.

"No. Don't show anyone yet. That's for your eyes only," I say, still covering my face.

Andre gently pulls them away from my face. His eyes pierce mine with care before he smiles.

"Hey. You ain't gotta hide. Thank you for giving this to me. I'm excited to frame it or something."

I nod. "Thanks, Dre. Can I call you Dre?"

"You and your nicknames for everyone. Yeah, that's cool since people call me that anyway. Now, the whole boyfriend thing..."

I groan and put my hands back up over my face. He chuckles and takes them away again.

"This isn't bad. I'll be honest and say that I don't know you like that to say yes right now. We rarely talk. I think we should get to know each other more. Then I think we'll know if this is what we want," Andre says. "I do think you're really pretty though, no doubt about that."

My heart dances. I take a deep breath, feeling more relieved than sad. I'm so glad I finally got everything off my chest! And I don't get flat out rejected like I thought I would.

"I think that's fair." I nod.

"Cool. Summer's coming up, so that'll be an excuse to hang out more," he says.

"Right. So... should we get each other's numbers or something?"

"Of course."

The both of us share each other's number. I lock him in on my phone, and he does the same.

"For starters," I say, "I have a tournament at Eastman's Park starting tomorrow after our promotion ceremony. You and Prez should come through and check our team out," I offer.

"Oh, cool. Yeah, I'll ask my mom and see if I can come through. I'm planning to come."

"Perfect." I huff again in relief. "We should go back to the gym. I think the song everyone started dancing to is over."

"Right. I don't want my date getting mad at me," Andre shares, and we both leave the hallway and enter the gym again. The DJ has turned on the Cha Cha slide, and everyone's already dancing as a collective.

Andre and I hop into the line next to Prez and Destiny, picking up right where they are. Prez doesn't even ask what happened; I'm sure he doesn't care, but he nudges me a little as we dance, glad that I've rejoined him because it's all in his eyes. Destiny barely realizes that Andre's back as we all dance the night away together as one, big happy eighth-grade family.

Chapter Twenty-Six

WE HAVE TO win this tournament. We just have to, otherwise it'll ruin the entire vibe of the weekend. I just promoted from eighth-grade this morning, and Jarell agreed to throw me a graduation pool party on Sunday after I begged him to. I can't head into my graduation party with an L. That would be crazy.

Jade's in town to come to my party too since I invited her. I'm lucky that I'm able to get her this weekend because the BET Awards are literally in two weeks, and her dance rehearsals have ramped up. I think she'll be here tonight, will travel back to LA on Saturday for business, and come back on Sunday for the party. She promised to come to one of my games to check me out, so she chose tonight. I'm excited to show her what I'm made of, and I'm excited that we're playing at our neighborhood park that we always go to and practice in.

That means Prez will likely be here today. I love when he comes to watch us play because then, later on, he gives me feedback on things for our team to work on. So, I'm looking forward to it. I hope he brings Andre this time, too, since he was already planning to come watch me. That would make my day! Especially after everything last night at the dance.

Man, it was such a dream. So many memories were made. Hopefully Miss Juanita can send me all the pictures we took before the dance. We can start to hang some up in Jarell's drab apartment to start capturing all the good, positive times we have moving forward.

Our game starts in just a half an hour at five tonight with two more games on Saturday. It's a small tournament, but still important for us to secure our spot in the Senior Leagues. My team is here early, which isn't surprising since this is home turf. We all stretch and warm up, the talk of the day being our respective dances at our schools.

Some people thought theirs was lame, all the teammates who go to the same school as me thought it was really cool, and others just didn't bother to go. I'm glad I'm on the squad of people who actually enjoyed theirs. One person I expect to be running her mouth about the dance is Alaysia, but she's actually pretty quiet today.

It ain't like her to be mute about something like the dance, whether it's complaining about the DJ and music, someone else's outfit, or bragging on herself about how she had the best fit. I don't pay it too much mind, though. It's actually best that she's quiet for once.

Now we have about fifteen minutes before we're set to hit the field, and we're in our pre-game ritual huddle to give each other pep talks. Tina, who leads the ritual, starts our chant, but stands up straight with unease as her eyes fixate on someone or something that isn't us.

Most of our team notices, too, and stand to give their attention to whatever she's looking at.

"Hey, are you looking for someone?" Tina asks. "What's up?"

Two girls around our age come charging at us with a frown, glaring at our team as if searching for a fight. Ultimately, after their eyes scan the whole team, they land on me, and the light in their gaze changes from disoriented to an air of familiarity.

"Are you Kylah?" one of the girls asks me directly.

"Yeah, why? Who wants to know?"

My eyes shift back and forth between them. Both are fair skinned and look to be a mix between Asian and Latina, but one looks slightly older, is taller, and is heavier set. The other is shorter and skinny. Either way, they've got to be siblings. The resemblance is way too strong for it not to be the case.

"Me, bitch," the younger looking one growls. "I'm Gina, Preston's girlfriend. Why are you trying to be a homewrecker? Going to the dance last night with you as his date when he told me he was just going with a friend? Are you the girl who he's so-called playing baseball with at night when he claims he's by himself?"

I raise a brow. Homewrecker? What home do they have? She's too much, like I had already anticipated her to be for our first face to face encounter. I smack my lips and take a step back to separate myself from the conflict and put my hands up in surrender.

"Look, I don't have time for this. I'm trying to get ready with my team for this ga—"

"Does it look like I care about your little stupid baseball game? I want to know why you're in my boyfriend's face when you know he's dating me. Answer that. Because it's not like you're that fucking cute to be messing around with. Pimple face bitch."

Alaysia makes a satisfied sound in her throat, and I turn and give her a look I wish could send her to the next lifetime. She just gives me a mean grill back, daring me to say something smart. For once, I wish Alaysia would be a good teammate. If this was her, I'd definitely try to stop what's going on. You're supposed to have your teammate's back, no matter what. I could really rat Alaysia out for being the real one to flirt with Prez just to make me jealous, and I'd have a whole lot of people who could vouch.

I shake my head and give my attention back to the little monster at hand in front of me. I don't even care about her insult regarding the acne that I've always been self-conscious about, which has gotten way better over the years. I'm not even sure what acne she even sees right now.

"Gina, I don't want Prez, alright? He's my friend. I know he's dating you, and I've known that for a while. He makes it very clear. Trust me, I don't want any trouble with you, or to ruin your relationship with him," I try to explain, but she won't let it go.

"If that's the case, then why are you going to a dance with him as his date if you already knew? That's even worse!"

"Because we're friends, and he asked me. He's still going with you to your dance next weekend!" I exclaim.

"Stop lying! He didn't ask your ugly ass!" she screams and steps closer to my face. I take another step back. "And stop fuckin' calling him Prez. His name is Preston."

"I'm not lying, Gina. Actually, I think he might be here. Why don't you ask him instead of approaching me? If you think he's cheating, then you should be mad at him. But I'm telling you right now that there's nothing going on between us. I'm actually into somebody else. Out of respect for *Prez*, I'm not going to fight you so stop walking up on me."

"And why would he be here? To watch you?" she interrogates, looking me up and down.

I shrug. "Probably. We've been watching each other play for the last two years because *we're friends*. That doesn't mean I want him or that he wants me."

"So, explain this then," the other girl who came with Gina chimes in. She shoves her phone toward my face to force me to watch a Snap. It's of Prez and I, dancing together at the dance to Doja Cat's song.

"Who posted that?" I frown. Who would be trying to take a video of just me in a sea of my classmates doing the same exact thing with their dates? Why was I the only person singled out?

"Don't fuckin' worry about it. You both were dancing real close for you to be 'just' friends," the older girl retorts.

"It was one dance, y'all. I danced like that with other people, too. Everyone was doing the same thing," I say. "You can see that in the video."

"You have a whole lot of excuses and trying to downplay what you're doing. Here's the deal. From this day forward, whatever you and Preston's got going on ends today. You need to stop talking to my boyfriend," Gina demands.

My head jerks back with my lip curled.

"Uh, no. I'm not losing my friendship with Prez because you're insecure. Deal with that on your own. That ain't got nothing to do with me," I challenge.

"I'm gonna tell you this one last time and hear me loud and clear. Stop talking to my boyfriend, or else I'm going to beat your ass in front of this whole park. Your choice," Gina says, waving her pointer finger back and forth.

I shake my head. "Girl, I ain't scared of you! You're gonna have to try and intimidate someone else 'cus I ain't the one. Go work on your insecurities somewhere else and leave me out of it. Or better yet, go to talk to Prez since he's the real one you have a problem with."

I turn away from them and give my attention back to our huddle with my teammates who look scared to death like they don't know what to do. I almost forgot they've been watching this whole thing go down. The tension in the air is thick, but to give them credit, they all try to move on and focus on our pre-game ritual.

Suddenly, my hair gets yanked from behind. My neck and head snap back, and I stumble toward the force like my world has been tilted upside down. Next thing I know, I'm absorbing two hard punches to the face: one in cheek and one in the nose. I try and twist to gain control, but several blows start to come from multiple directions while my hair is still held. Wait. *Am I getting jumped?*

It's fight or flight at this point, so I grab on to the nearest person's clothes and throw punches as hard as I can. I don't know where or who I'm punching because my hair is all over the place and my head is down. I wish I would've either kept the fish braid Miss Juanita did or put my usual game time ponytail in much earlier. All I can comprehend is that my punches are connecting to a body while someone's pounding me in the back of the head trying to knock me unconscious. I can't keep up much longer with them both coming hard at all angles, so I eventually fall to my knees. Now, I'm getting dragged back and forth by my hair on the concrete, causing whiplash while being kicked and punched hard in the back several times by the other. This seems to go on forever until I hear, "Gina! Gina, stop!! Let go of her hair!"

It's a familiar voice, and I think it's Prez, but the vise grip on my scalp remains.

"I said, let her go, Gina! Why won't you listen to me?!" Prez yells.

Eventually, the hold on my hair releases and the force that is Gina disappears. I slowly stand to catch my breath and recover from the pain, but the larger girl lunges at me full speed with her fist cocked back, ready to pummel my face. Adrenaline kicks in. When she reaches me and swings, I slap her fist away mid swing, grasp her by the shirt, and body slam her to the ground right on her back.

"Ooooh!" I hear multiple people scream.

When she's down, once again, my hair is pulled as she tries to bring me down with her. I fall to my knees again, but I punch her several times to try and get her off me.

"Kylah! Kylah stop and get off her!" some adult voice yells.

"I'm trying! She has my hair!" I cry out. I don't know who's telling me to get off her, but I'd be glad to. "Let go of my hair!"

I stop punching and try to pry the girl's fingers away, but she's got it so tight in her fist that her nail digs into my finger. It isn't until grown man strength lifts me up and back that my curls become free again.

Once my feet are on solid ground, I pull my hair swiftly into a high bun before someone else tries to yank it. I huff, puff, and take a moment to regroup and gauge my surroundings. At a short distance, Prez is holding Gina back and attempting to push her away as far as he can as she's screaming profanities at me, calling me all types of bitches and yelling to the world that she whooped my ass. The other big girl is writhing and threatening me, trying to break free, but is held in a tight grip by *Andre*.

Once again, my stomach plunges to the floor.

We stare at each other for what feels like eternity. His brows are furrowed like he's angry, but those deep brown, almost black, eyes hold a significant level of concern for me that catches me off guard because they minutely toggle back and forth all over my face. Breaking the silence between us, he asks, only loud enough for me to hear, "Are you okay?"

I'm so shocked that I can't even answer. A burning sensation overwhelms the entire left side of my face. I reach up to feel it, and my hand is drenched in blood, dripping on my uniform or the ground. I melt into sobs. I really just got jumped! Beat up off a cheap shot sucker punch! For no reason!

"Kylah!" a voice calls out. A disappointed voice at that.

I turn my head and Coach Harper is standing right behind me.

I sigh and give him a pained look. His face is tight and strained. Especially his lips. His wrinkles normally aren't noticeable, but those lines are carved deep around his brows today. I swallow.

"Coach..." I say before trying to explain, but he cuts me off.

"Kylah, I need you to go home. Right now. You are done playing for me for the summer," he professes with closed eyes.

I blink a few times to make sure I heard what I think I heard. "Wait a minute, what?!" I bellow. "Done for summer?! What do you mean I'm done for the summer?"

"You heard what I said. Done for the summer, meaning your season for softball ends right here, right now. I can't keep putting up with the attitude, the drama you're bringing, and the failure of meeting my expectations of staying out of trouble. You need to take some time to improve your behavior before I will allow you back on my team."

"But Coach, I didn't start this! They approached me! What was I supposed to do?" I shout with my arms out.

"I don't care, Kylah. I'm sure you had several opportunities to walk away from the situation and tell an adult, but you chose to fight and embarrass not only me, but your team, our organization, your family, and most of all, yourself. You will not be representing California on the international stage at the Senior Leagues this year.

Not after this. I'm sorry Kylah, you're a great player and all, but you have way too much baggage."

"Coach, that's not fair!"

I barely register everything he says. It's like my soul splits apart. I've worked so hard for this opportunity, and now all my dreams are down the drain. All because of that stupid ass bitch Gina and her jealousy!

"I swear to God, I would never start a fight to embarrass our team like that. I would never do that before a game. You can even ask the team! I tried to get them to leave me alone, and then they jumped me!"

"Have your brother come and get you. I'm done talking to you," Coach says with an even tone, but I can tell he's steaming hot as a couple of other parents try to move the coach away from me and calm him down.

"Her brother's here with someone. They're heading over right now," one of my teammate's mom whispers to Coach.

"Good," he mumbles and turns away from me.

Clutching my forehead, I let out a raw, ear shattering scream and rush to a nearby tree. I sink to the grass as my tears soak my jersey. FUCK! I was having such a good day, too! Not long after, footsteps come charging toward me, along with the familiar clinking of a dog's tag. With blurry eyes, I see Jade and Jarell stand over me with worry all over their faces. Especially Jarell.

Goddamn it! Jade came all the way from LA to see me play, and now she can't. I *hate* for her to see me like this!

Jade gasps. "Oh my God. Jarell, the whole left side of her face is bloody and bruised... she may need to go to the hospital." She pulls out several Wet Ones antibacterial wipes from her purse and puts it to my face. I hiss as the moisture burns the wound.

"Kylah, what happened? Are you okay?" Jarell bends down and asks with a hand on my thigh. His voice is so calm, which I'm grateful for because anything more would spike my anger more than it is.

Jarell's now on both knees and pulls me to him. I'm too exhausted to even fight it, and when he wraps me up tightly and my forehead meets his chest, I lose it and wail into him in agony. My cries don't travel out; his chest absorbs everything. His embrace is the best thing I've ever felt. For the first time in a very long time, I truly feel wanted, cared for, and protected.

Jarell rocks me back and forth and says a few unintelligible soothing things into my hair until I stop crying and hiccup until I find some air in my lungs to speak.

"Jarell, I've tried so hard to stay out of trouble. You know I have! Prez's girlfriend and her sister jumped me just because they think I'm messing around with him. But you know Prez is my best friend, and I don't even like him like that. I tried to walk away, but they grabbed my hair from behind and started punching me in the face. I fought back, trying to defend myself, and now Coach said I'm done for the season. I can't play in the Senior League World Series anymore. He's kicking me off the team because of this fight. It's like whatever I do is never good enough for him!" I break down and weep into his chest again.

"Wait, what?!" Jade exclaims. "Are you serious? He's putting YOU off the team when you're the one who got hurt?"

I nod. This time, Jarell's body tenses up against mine before he takes a deep breath.

"I need you to go to talk to him real quick, Jade," he whispers. "I know you haven't met him, but I'm sure he's got their team colors on.

I'm gonna stay here with her, and I'll be over there in a minute. This decision is not okay. She got attacked. That's not her fault. Just hold him up for me."

"Oh, you know that ain't gon' be a problem. Kicking you off the team... what the fuck is he thinking?!" Jade shrieks as she storms over to Coach, her hair flying behind her.

Jarell doesn't say anything else. He just pulls me back into his embrace again as I weep some more.

In the distance, Jade's loud voice splits the air as she firmly tells Coach what's on her mind. I can't hear all of it, but the few phrases I do hear are "don't know me," "pathetic," "didn't see if she was okay," "no good reason," "care if the game starts in five minutes," and "dreams because of someone else's choice."

I don't know where this fuzzy feeling comes from during all this chaos and bad news, but damn. I have a family who's got my back right now. In a major way. Nothing feels better than that.

"You good baby sis?" Jarell asks in my hair.

"I don't know."

"You okay enough to come with me to talk to Coach Harper?"

"I don't want to talk to him," I whine.

"Well, I want you to still come with me. I'll do the talking, but I need you to hear everything we're going to talk about," he says with resolve.

"Okay."

With his help, I stand from the ground, and hold his strong arm. Jarell grabs Luna's leash and motions her forward. I give him directions so that we get there safely.

"Harper!" Jarell calls out firmly with a level of bass in his voice I even get startled at, ending the back and forth Coach and Jade are doing in a snap.

Both freeze and give their attention to him.

"You kicked my sister off the team for the rest of the season?" Jarell bellows. "For what?"

"I sure did, so you better watch your tone with me. She can't be out here fighting and misrepresenting our brand as a team and embarrassing me as a coach. It's not a good look. You need to invest more in her behavior and mental health. She's got to get her act together before high school or else she won't be on any team at all."

Jarell's eyes squint, and his jaw clenches. Uh oh.

"Aye first off, from a man to a man, check yourself. I ain't your kid, so I ain't watching my tone for no one. Second, don't tell me how to raise my sister. You already know firsthand I've got many different supports in place for her as her guardian, so don't stand here in my face and try to gaslight me. I came to you with my full trust to help hold her accountable and support her. You need to hold up your end of the deal instead of throwing her away like trash. You didn't even see if she was okay when she was the one who got attacked and hurt. So why is she being punished for it?"

"She could've walked away and told someone instead of engaging in the argument," Coach says. "She sucked herself right into that conflict, and I'm fed up with giving her chances. She was even going to fight Alaysia during practice earlier this season. Enough is enough."

Jarell scoffs. "Come on, Harper, that's ridiculous, and you know it. I usually keep quiet, and I usually side with the adults because Kylah does have her issues and she's made many mistakes, but this ain't cool. You didn't even try to help her when you know she got hurt by those girls, and they initiated it, so what you're saying makes no sense. What, she's not supposed to defend herself?"

"Call it what you want, Jarell. She will not be playing in the Senior League Tournament this year. She's got three other years of eligibility, but I have standards and a reputation to uphold, and I don't tolerate bad behavior that impacts the image of our organization. We're going to the international tournament, and we don't need any negative press."

Jarell's frown deepens, and I can tell he's about to raise his voice, so Jade steps in.

"So, you're saying that you care more about yourself than your role in developing a high-quality young athlete?" Jade questions. "These girls are fourteen years old. Of course, they aren't going to be perfect so what 'standard' are you talking about? Who cares about the press?"

"Right. If anything, because of Kylah's performances on the field, she's been the one to elevate your brand and your ego, so let's be real here," Jarell tag teams in agreement. "You wouldn't be traveling to the World Series let alone the favorites to win this year without her. You also know she has a severe PTSD with emotional dysregulation diagnosis, so your expectation of perfection was never going to happen."

Coach shakes his head and shrugs. "It doesn't matter. I'm not in the business of arguing with either of you, and I can call the shots however I want for this group. This is my team, and she's done for the season. I got a game to prepare for, so will you excuse me?"

The way he just blatantly disregards not only me, but Jade and Jarell make me sick to my stomach. I don't know if he's doing that because Jarell is blind, but I've never seen him talk to any other dad the way he's talking to Jarell right now. Jarell's doing a pretty good job of staying composed though because he could be much hotter than he is. I know the kind of anger he's capable of, and what I've experienced is likely just a snippet, and even that snippet was unbearable.

"You know what?" Jarell licks his lips and nods. "You're a sorry excuse for a coach. You don't have her back at all. Best of luck to you and your team, Harper. Let's go y'all."

Jarell puts his hand on the small of Jade's back and motions her away when Jade bites her fist to prevent from saying more. When we turn our backs to Coach Harper, Jarell holds his hand out for me to take, and with a small smile, I hold on to it, and we walk away as a unit toward Jade's car. On the way there, we pass by Prez and Gina, but from a distance.

"Gina, that was wrong, and you know it! I don't give a fuck about you what you call being territorial, whatever that means. It's not cool when you go seeking out fights. Especially with my best friend. We're not even together! She did nothing to you!"

"Why are you taking up for her? You should be on my side! Unless you got something else you wanna share with me. And it better be the truth!" she screeches.

"I'll tell you what's going on alright. You and me? This shit between us is over. That's what's going on. I can't believe you and your sister jumped her like that! For what?!"

"Really Preston? You're breaking up with me?!"

I don't hear anything else beyond that point. During that exchange that Jarell and Jade likely heard too, they both acknowledge me in some kind of way. Jarell squeezes my hand with reassurance, and Jade wraps her arm around my shoulder and hugs me tightly toward her side.

Right before we reach Jade's car, loud footsteps behind us come running in our direction. I hear them before I see them, and I turn around in defense mode in case it's Gina or her sister, but it's Andre.

"Kylah, wait up!" he shouts, out of breath.

"Hold on, y'all," I say to Jarell and Jade. They stop walking and turn toward Andre as well.

Once he reaches us, he bends over to grab his knees. Jarell and Jade step back a little bit to give us some space and privacy.

"Sorry." He huffs and puffs. "Ran pretty far to catch up, so I gotta catch my breath."

"What's up?" I ask, my head lowered to the ground. After all of that, I barely even wanna look at him.

"What happened was real messed up. You didn't deserve that," he says softly. "I know how hard you've been trying to keep your cool with Alaysia, and the fact that she's the one that set this off got me heated."

"What do you mean she set this off?"

"She posted the Snap video of you dancing."

"How'd you know it was her?" I ask.

"Because I saw the Snap right after she posted because I was scrolling through my feed. I screen recorded it, too. It had her username and everything."

"Oh..." I clench my fists. If I wasn't already hurt and defeated, I'd run over to the diamond to beat the daylights out of Alaysia. I can't believe her... no wonder why she was so quiet today!

"I know you didn't really ask for advice, but as her teammate, you shouldn't let this be swept under the rug. Everyone's looking at Gina and her sister as the main ones, but Alaysia's the one that needs to be addressed since she instigated this whole thing."

"It doesn't matter whether I address her or not, Dre. I just got kicked off the team."

His eyes inflate. "Wait a second, what?!"

"Mhm. Coach kicked me off the team. Said I got too much baggage and that I need to work on getting myself together because I make the team and the brand look bad. That means I can't play in the Senior Leagues this year."

He jerks his head back with a frown and turns his lip before shaking his head.

"Nah, you can't just give up that easy. Preston and I won't let you!"

"There's nothing I can do about it, Dre!" I shout and start to cry all over again. "Besides. I do make the brand look bad. I've been so mean to Jarell, mean to everyone at school, and getting in trouble the whole time I was in middle school and ... still all of y'all are coming to my defense. And I don't know why. Maybe I deserve what's happening to me right now." I dip my head.

"Kylah..." Andre says.

"Andre, just leave it alone. It is what it is. I'll have other years to play in the tournament."

Jarell and Jade start to step in, but Andre puts a polite hand up to stop them.

"Hold on, let me just talk to her for a second. Please."

Exchanging worried looks, they continue to keep their distance.

"Kylah. You're really gonna let Alaysia win? And cause you to not play on the biggest stage of your career in the World Series and have three years of eligibility? Come on man, I've seen you have way more grit about way less important crap at school. You gotta fight for this. You know she did that on purpose, and she succeeded. You can't just walk away from this," he reasons.

"By doing what? What is there left to do, Dre?"

"I got an idea. Let's link up tonight at eight at the park by my house. I'ma have Preston come through, and I'll work on getting some of your teammates there, too. The ones who don't ride Alaysia's butt."

"What are you planning?" I ask.

"You'll see. Just meet me at the park at eight, a'ight?"

Taking a deep breath, I'm a little weary, but I ultimately agree.

"Cool. I'll see you then."

He gives a farewell nod to Jarell and Jade before sprinting off in Prez's direction, who is still arguing and fighting with Gina. She's swinging on him and cussing him out, but he ducks or blocks her punches. But one swing connects as she slaps him across the face. Hard. I keep watching from yonder in disbelief as Andre gets in the middle of them and pulls him from the situation. Prez's face has gone from mild red to tomato red. I've seen him mad at me, but this is a whole 'nother level of angry. He is *enraged*.

I turn toward Jarell and Jade again, and Jade is looking directly at me with a sympathetic smile, and Jarell's gaze still holds concern.

"Looks like you got a good friend there, Kay Kay," Jade whispers to me and runs her fingers through my hair, motherly, to detangle it.

I nod. "Yeah. Two good friends."

"I see. Come on, sweetie. Let's go home and relax for a little while. Do you need to go to the clinic?"

I shake my head.

Jarell gives me a small smile before turning to face me squarely. He reaches out to touch me, and I grab his hand so that he knows I'm with him. Once my smaller hand is covered comfortably, he squeezes it.

"Hey. I know you just told your friend that you deserve what's happening to you right now, but you don't," Jarell starts. "You've had a rough transition to San Diego. You've made a lot of mistakes, but ever since the day you threw that chair at your teacher... I've noticed how hard you've worked to be better even though some parts have been rough. Your resentment toward me was the hardest. But I realize all of the trouble you caused came from a deep place of hurt. A kind of hurt I know well. So yeah. Feel remorse. I want you to feel that. But don't ever feel like you deserve this outcome after you've worked so hard to turn things around. Hell, old you would be going over there to fight Alaysia and that girl Gina as we speak."

I laugh. Man is he right. Three months ago? I'd be getting my licks back, no matter if I won or got beat up.

"Thank you, Jarell," I whisper as more tears drop to the grass.

"No doubt."

Jarell gives me a firm but loving nod, and walks away toward the passenger seat. We load up the car, and I get Luna settled in. After I put on my seatbelt, my head slams back on the headrest.

Wow.

I got jumped.

Got kicked off the team.

Can't participate in the Senior Leagues.

But I also gained a ton of respect for Jarell and Jade. As well as Andre and Prez.

I guess that matters more than a game and my dreams, even if it feels like my world is falling apart. I have a family and dope friends. And they have my back in a major way.

Chapter Twenty-Seven

EIGHT O'CLOCK ARRIVES, and me, Prez, and Andre are already at the park near where Dre lives. We sit under a pavilion, waiting for my teammates to arrive. For the most part, we sit in silence, regrouping and recovering. Andre's scrolling on his phone, Prez is leaning back against the picnic table, staring out into the playground and field, and I'm laying my head down on the table to control the raging headache that has taken over me. After a while, I sit up, accepting that it's not going to go away unless I take some meds. So, I move over to Prez. He snaps out of his daze and gives me his attention with a smile in his eyes.

"Prez, are you okay? Gina slapped you hard when y'all were arguing, and you also broke up with her. I know you care about her, but she's wild for all of this, man," I say, shaking my head. "Only reason why I didn't fight her was out of respect for you and my team."

"Yeah, I'm cool. I can't believe she showed up with her sister just to fight you over something so stupid. She really is crazy for that."

I give Prez a knowing glare, as if telling him that he should've listened to me from the beginning about her.

He squirms. "I know, I know. You don't have to chew me out. I'll own it," he mumbles and rolls his eyes, shifting his eyes away from me.

"I don't know what it is with you and these messy females, but if they're gonna keep coming for me and trying to mess with my life, Prez, we gon' have a problem. So the next girlfriend you have, can you at least tell them you're friends with me or something? So that it ain't an issue? And in the future, please don't be getting all chummy with my enemies. Please and thanks."

"Yeah. I'm really sorry, LaLa. All of this wasn't on purpose, trust me. I can get what you mean about Alaysia, but I honestly didn't see that coming with Gina."

"Bro, I told you since you got with her that she be doin' too much. The minute she started calling you every minute about where you are when you're not with her, that's a red flag," I say. "Girls like that are the type to bust tires when you get older."

"Yeah. I should've peeped it. My bad. It's over though. I can't be with someone who can't respect my friends," he replies.

"I feel that."

"Are you good, though? The whole left side of your face is red, and it looks like bruises are coming in," he says, moving his head to examine me.

"Yeah, I'll be alright. I just have a really bad headache."

"Yeah, I'm not surprised. That hair pulling was vicious," Prez says and smacks his lips.

Andre puts his phone away and slides closer to us to join the conversation.

"Are your parents gonna press charges? Those are your parents, the ones who took you home, right? They look so young," Andre innocently asks with worry in his eyes at my face too.

"Andre, those can't be my parents. I'm mixed. Plus, my parents are no longer living. That was my brother and his ex-girlfriend," I reply.

"Oh. I'm sorry about your parents. I didn't mean—"

"Don't worry about it. It was an innocent question. But to answer you, we talked about the whole pressing charges thing in the car on our way home. Jarell and Jade want to, but I don't think I wanna do that. I'll just take the L. They said as long as we have a plan to resolve the issue, they'll leave it alone, but if they come at me again, then they'll step in and call the police or take it up with their parents."

"That sounds fair. I'm glad they're backing off a little bit, even though what happened was really serious," Dre responds.

As we converse, five of my teammates, Keisha, Katie, Tina, Libby, and Sarah, which is almost half the team, come walking up toward us with clothes that aren't their uniforms. Good. Now we can get this meeting started so I can hear what Dre's got up his sleeve. He doesn't take too much time with formalities and gets right to business since it's already late.

"Alright, y'all. Thanks for coming and gathering here tonight after what happened earlier today. We need to talk to y'all about how we're gonna move forward. Coach Harper kicked Kylah off the team today, and now she's not gonna be able to play in the World Series," Dre starts.

"Yeah, and you know she's the best pitcher in this country at her grade level right now, so we need to stage an intervention," Prez jumps in.

"Wait, Coach kicked Kylah off the team?" Tina emphasizes.

"Yes."

"That's such bullshit!" she screams, standing up simultaneously.

"I know, and that's the exact kinda energy we need to stop him,"

Andre asserts.

Keisha smacks her lips and crosses her arms. "Yeah, it is bullshit, and I ain't happy with that decision either, but talking to Coach is like talking to a brick wall. It's always his way or the highway, so if he said she's gone, then she's gone."

Prez scoffs. "So? That doesn't need to stop us from letting our voices be heard. And you can't go into this with that attitude. She's not gone."

"How are we gonna do that? Make our voices heard?" Sarah asks.

"We're gonna crash the next softball game y'all have tomorrow morning," Andre reveals.

"Crash the softball game?!" All of my teammates yell.

"Yeah. Crash it. No one plays until this gets addressed. Kylah's the one who got jumped. Weren't y'all there? She didn't start that fight, right?" Prez asks.

"Yeah, they came out of nowhere," Libby says. "It was scary."

"And do you know that Alaysia's the one that started it? She posted a video of me dancing with Kylah at our eighth-grade dance and tagged my girlfriend in it. My ex-girlfriend I should say. Kylah and I ain't even together, and Alaysia don't even know the reason why we were dancing anyway. She was the one to start this."

"Are you serious?" Katie exclaims.

"You wanna see what she posted?" Andre asks.

All of our team agrees to see the video, including me even though I've kinda seen it, but not in detail. Andre pulls it up, and all of our heads come together to watch. It, indeed, is Prez and I dancing close, but our bodies aren't touching. The caption says: *When someone's got a girlfriend, but they're dancing on someone else... @ginanguyenmontes*

My jaws clench, and so do my fists.

"Wow..." Katie says.

"So, we need to crash the game to allow Kylah to tell the team the truth about why your teammate just sabotaged her. And your coach needs to realize that Kylah isn't the problem. Alaysia is. She's been trying to get Kylah kicked off the team since the beginning of the season," Prez explains.

"She's so damn annoying! Ugh, I could just kick her butt myself if I had the guts," Tina utters.

"That's the thing, I'm really not trying to see nobody's ass get kicked," I finally speak. "And if y'all really wanted to kick some ass, y'all would've jumped in to help me when I was getting jumped, but that's a different story. We're supposed to be a team, and teammates have each other's backs, no matter how much they annoy us. That's the only reason why I haven't charged Alaysia up. She's a cancer on this team y'all, and she's all about herself. She needs to learn how to be a good teammate, and Coach has to know the truth."

"I don't know if she's ever going to see that, Kylah," Sarah says.

"That's her problem, but your whole team's gotta know the truth," Andre says.

"Facts," says Prez.

"Alright, so how we gon' do this?" Keisha asks.

"First of all, we all need to agree to keep this whole plan off social media. Don't put this on Snap, Tik Tok, IG, or any of that. As soon as this plan gets leaked, it won't work. Can we do that?" Prez questions. "And don't start recording when we get there either. This is team business; this ain't for the public or for likes."

The team agrees.

"A'ight, cool. Let's talk about how this is gonna look."

We all huddle up, coming up with our plan and assigning

everyone their duties, losing track of time and getting lost in the planning for justice.

~ ~ ~

Bright and early – six thirty in the morning early – I leave Jarell's apartment to head to the softball diamond while he and Jade are knocked out. Both are snoring on the couch. Loudly. I'm surprised they aren't up by now, being the early birds they are, but from first glance at them on my way out, they truly looked exhausted with Jarell sleeping sitting up, and Jade's head resting on his lap.

Jarell wouldn't be caught for a single second sleeping with his mouth all open like that with Brooklyn. Hmm. Very interesting... this dynamic between these two. I shake my head and laugh at their whole situation.

I get to the diamond, and just as I'm walking up, so is Prez on the other side of the field, coming from the direction of his house. We meet in the middle of the field, giving each other dap, and shortly after, the rest of our crew arrives, including Andre. Tina's got an ancient bullhorn announcer thingy in her hand, and I smile. She's not messing around.

"Alright, this is it, y'all. Everyone got their duties and assignments?" Prez asks everyone.

"Yup," Katie says.

"Cool. For the people in the dugout, make sure you're the first ones there so you can keep track of who's coming and going. Tina, you've got the PSA, and me and Andre will hide behind the bushes with Kylah, and we'll come once you've got the team, the coaches, and the parents all together," he directs.

"That sounds perfect," Tina says.

"Bet. Let's get in position," Prez says, and everyone breaks and moves to their assigned areas of the field.

Prez, Dre, and I find a bush nearby and sit down behind it, waiting for everyone to come, which is a smart move. If I'm visible, Coach would likely be more focused on getting rid of me than listening to Tina and the rest of the team since he's so adamant about my season being over.

Around seven o'clock is when our other teammates start to arrive at the diamond. Keisha, Katie, Libby, and Sarah sit in the dugout, wearing normal clothes and cross their arms like they won't move a single muscle to get up and get ready. From where I can see, I watch a few of them interact with our other teammates, shrugging their shoulders like they don't care. Our other teammates just walk away, getting ready on their own.

Around seven thirty is when most of the parents arrive and sit in the bleachers behind the fence that separates the crowd and the field, and Alaysia arrives with her parents. She splits from them and heads to the dugout. Jarell and Jade also walk up around this time, too, except they don't sit down. They lean up on the fence, making their quiet but strong presence known that they aren't giving up on my membership on this team either.

Good. Got all my people here.

"This is gonna be good," Dre says. "We got a nice turnout already, and it ain't even close to eight."

"Yeah, but we gotta get this started. If they're still gonna play today instead of postponing, and they're supposed to start playing at eight, then the PSA gotta start now," Prez says.

"True," Dre agrees.

The three of us keep watching out for Tina as Coach and his assistants arrive at the park. Coach Harper, like he normally does, stands outside of the dugout, reading his clipboard to prepare for the team huddle. He's largely oblivious to half of his team not even dressed in uniform or the fact that Jade and Jarell stand nearby. However, the assistants are in for a rude awakening when they see the four of them not dressed.

I can't hear the words the coaches say to our crew, but our crew's body language goes from defiant to angry. The angriest of them all is Keisha. It gets to a point where a shouting match ensues, with the coaches starting it and Keisha pretty much finishing. Libby, Sarah, and Katie are super indifferent about their raised voices, but Keisha on the other hand ain't come to play.

"You can get up out of my face with all that yelling, Coach. We're not playing today unless this shit gets addressed," Keisha says. "We got team business to take care of first. Ain't no way we just gonna move on without talking about what happened yesterday."

Yes! Go awf, Keisha! Now, I'm just waiting for Tina to come with her bullhorn to get this officially started. And right on cue. She comes from the opposite side of the diamond and stands in front of the bleachers where our team parents sit.

"Good morning, everyone!" Tina announces. "Thanks for being here after the crazy day yesterday. I just want you to know that the ladies of the San Diego Sluggers will not be playing in today's game unless we address some important team issues. If we can figure things out in the next thirty minutes, we might be able to still play. This matter is very important for us to be successful at the Senior League World Series!"

All the parents, friends, and families in the stand look at each other, confused and whisper among themselves. Alaysia comes rushing at Tina with her hands out and a frown.

"What do you think you're doing? You don't speak for us. We're playing in this game and I'm pitching, so you can put that old school bullhorn up," Alaysia screams.

Tina turns to Alaysia and talks to her through the bullhorn right in her face. Alaysia cringes and covers her ears.

"Alaysia, as your teammate, I am holding you accountable and ordering you to the dugout. We are meeting largely because of your actions. Go sit down," she demands.

Alaysia's parents look at each other with a frown before standing up and stomping down the bleachers.

"Excuse me, Tina little girl, but what's your problem? This is not a way to solve or handle conflict with anyone, but I'm certainly not going to allow it with my daughter. You do not need to make a public service announcement to embarrass your teammate like this," Alaysia's mom rushes to her defense.

"Embarrass? Funny you mention embarrassment because your daughter wasn't thinking about how she embarrassed our teammate yesterday," Tina claps back.

"What are you talking about?"

"Why don't you come to the team meeting and find out? You'll be happy to know we're trying to problem solve in a healthy way once you realize what's really going on," Tina replies.

"Fine. Let's head on over, then. I wanna hear this."

"Good," Tina says in the bullhorn. "Any other parent can join us, too."

Tina, Alaysia, and the rest of the team all meet in the dugout. A lot of the parents follow, including Jarell and Jade.

"I think this is our time. Come on," Prez whispers to me, grabs me by the hand, and pulls me near the meeting. Dre follows us.

Once everyone is settled either in the dugout or just outside of it Tina stands in the middle of everyone and puts the horn back to her mouth.

"Thanks for meeting here this early in the morning. As you all know, one of our teammates, Kylah, was attacked by two girls when we were getting ready for our game yesterday. I'm not sure if you all know this but after being brutally attacked, Kylah was also kicked off the team by Coach Harper. We don't think this is fair. We want to meet as a team family so you have the real story as to why things happened the way they did, but to get Kylah back on the team."

"What the hell is going on?" Coach Harper yells as he enters the dugout.

"Coach, you need to stand back and listen. We are calling a team meeting, and we, as the players of this team, feel like what you did to Kylah was wrong. You gotta understand why it was so wrong."

Coach Harper tries to storm over to Tina, but her mom and dad step in front of him and wag their finger.

YES! I am *loving* this!

"Kylah is with us this morning, and I will give her the horn so she can explain her side of the story. What she had to say yesterday was ignored, and as the captain and the best player on this team, it's not right. Every member of the team should have a voice, not just the best, but the way Coach treated her isn't fair. So here, Kylah. It's all you, now."

I weave my way through the crowd as many of them move out of the way to let me in. I pull Tina in for a hug and express my gratitude before taking the horn.

I take a deep breath and look at everyone. Wow. There are a lot of people here. But I'm not really nervous. I'm used to the big stage, being in that pitcher circle every week. I clear my throat and begin.

"Thank you all for being here and listening to me. First, I just want to say to everyone that I'm sorry. I was involved in the fight and made us look bad. I wasn't planning to fight; I had no idea they would even show up to our game, and I didn't know anyone was even looking to fight me. But it happened anyway, so I'm sorry. I would never embarrass our team on purpose. I want to start there. Second, I want to express why it happened, and my two friends here can vouch for anything I'm about to say. So here we go."

I clear my throat again.

"Many of you on this team and folks who go to my school know Alaysia and I don't get along. We have this rivalry going on with the pitcher spot that I ain't finna get too deep into, but it's important for you to know because it relates to why yesterday happened the way it did. So to start, Thursday night, our school had our eighth-grade dance, and I went with my best friend Preston, who is right here."

Prez waves. I continue.

"Preston has a girlfriend, but her school's dance isn't until next week, and her parents wouldn't let her celebrate with him on a school night, so he and I went to the dance together. What does this have to do with Alaysia? Well, she knows I was getting in trouble at school a lot and that I'm on strict behavior watch by Coach. I've been working real hard to stay out of trouble, but Alaysia been trying different ways to get me to fight so I can get kicked off the team. She's been doing that so she can be the lead pitcher. It's been unsuccessful, so at the dance on Thursday, she took a video of me and Preston dancing together, uploaded it, and tagged Preston's girlfriend to the video on SnapChat. His girlfriend saw it and came to our game with her sister yesterday to confront me about it. One of them pulled my hair from behind after I tried to move away, and they started fighting me. The person who started this whole fight is Alaysia. For her to try and sabotage me ain't cool. We're supposed to be teammates. We ain't gotta like each other, but we do need to respect each other and not set each other up to fail."

Alaysia shifts uncomfortably, folding her arms and looking toward the ground while many people's gaze land on her.

"I got the screen recorded video too, if you want proof that she posted and tagged his girlfriend on Snap," Andre ad libs in the horn. After that, Prez takes it from him.

"I just wanna say that Kylah has worked mad hard to be where she is on this team. She moved here from LA and knew nobody, yet she *earned* her spot, not only on this team, but in the state and the country. Y'all are the favorite to win the World Series because of the hours she puts in, and as her best friend, I've seen how hard she works. She practices hundreds of pitches with me. It's her dream to win this tournament. If you're gonna kick your best pitcher and batter off the team because of something my ex did with Alaysia setting it up, then maybe y'all need to think about what it truly means to be a team. And that includes you too, Coach Harper," Prez challenges him.

The crowd is stunned.

Especially the coaches.

When the silence lingers too long, Tina takes the bullhorn from Prez.

"So what's it gonna be, Coach? Are you kicking Kylah off the team? Because if you are, I'm going with her," Tina says, and the other four ladies who were at our meeting chime in to agree.

Still, it remains pretty silent until bodies shift in the parent section, and Alaysia's mom emerges from the small crowd. She walks to Tina and requests the horn. Reluctantly, Tina gives it to her after her mom promises not to do or say anything crazy.

"First of all, I want to thank you ladies and the gentlemen over there for being brave and willing to address this important problem head on. Thank you for inviting us families to be a part of the discussion because you're right. We're a team and family. I just want to allow my daughter the opportunity to share her perspective and disprove or confirm the actions she's being accused of. That's only fair. Alaysia?" Her mom gives her a look. "You have anything to say? What's true, and what isn't?"

Now, Alaysia's in the hot seat. She gazes at several different people with a kind of dark tinge in her eyes, clearly irritated she's being publicly held liable for the chaos yesterday that she didn't think she'd be held to task for. But when her eyes land on me, I give her an expression of hope and anticipation. Just for her to do the right thing for once. We exchange stares for a while and I watch, with my own eyes, that look of defiance shift into a serious load of blame.

She blinks away, and her eyes well up with emotion.

"It's true," she confesses in a whisper with a sullen expression, like she's about to fall ill.

"What's true?" her mom follows up in the horn.

"All of it. I did all of it. You see that they have the proof, right?" She glowers at her mom. Her mom's eyes expand.

"Are you serious right now, Alaysia Denise? Don't stand over there looking all sad when you're the sole behind the scenes instigator. I am extremely disappointed." She points at me. "That is your teammate.

No matter what kind of rivalry or competition you've got with one another, your father and I have raised you to have integrity. Look at the side of her face. It is completely bruised. She got seriously hurt yesterday, and it could have been a lot worse. I am beyond upset with you right now, little lady. I want you to apologize to this team, but most importantly, I want you to apologize to that young man whose girlfriend got tagged, Kylah, and her family. Right this instant."

When Alaysia doesn't move, her mom's frown gets deeper. "Get yo' ass over here right now and straighten up your face before I choke you out in front of all these people."

Alaysia sluggishly mopes over to her mom and dad and takes the bullhorn from her hands. She turns to face everyone head on as the dead silent group gives their undivided attention to her.

"I'm sorry for what I did yesterday. I shouldn't have done it, and it obviously made us look bad and caused a lot of drama," she talks and trembles while doing so.

"Okay, and the apology to her and her family?" her mom coaxes.

"...can I just do that in private?" she asks.

Many of our families and teammates groan low in disapproval at that request. Jarell and Jade have been standing in the back listening this whole time, but one of the parents pull Jarell and Luna toward the front to stand next to me, leaving Jade in the back.

"Absolutely not. Do it now before you end up in more trouble than you're already in," Alaysia's mom demands.

She smacks her lips, rolls her eyes, and turns to face me, Prez, and Jarell.

"Preston, I'm sorry for recording you and Kylah and tagging your girlfriend," she mumbles. "And Kylah, I'm sorry for instigating the fight. And Jarell... whatever your name is, I'm sorry."

Alaysia's mom comes over and snatches the bullhorn away. "You know what? That's a weak ass apology, but that's okay. You, your father, and I will go home, and we will discuss and handle this matter further as a family. Brian, take your daughter to the car. She will not be playing for the rest of this tournament this weekend. I'll be there in just a minute." Alaysia's dad grips Alaysia by the arm and pulls her away as she cries. Her mom keeps talking in the horn. "Jarell, Kylah, and Preston, on behalf of our daughter, we sincerely and wholeheartedly apologize for her behavior and for what happened. This is completely unacceptable, and that is not how we've raised her. She will have a better apology later, so I'm sorry that the one she gave right now was insincere. As for Coach Harper..."

I forgot Coach was even here after he got stopped by Tina's parents. When he hears his name, he stands up straight and takes a few steps forward."

"You need to put Kylah back on the team. My daughter doesn't deserve a spot right now. She will be on punishment, so I will let you know when she's able to play again."

Tina takes the horn.

"So Coach, is she back on the team?" Tina asks.

Coach takes a huge breath in and huffs it all out. He walks over to Tina and takes the horn.

"Well. Looks like I've got a whole lot of apologizing to do, don't I?" Coach says. "I am very sorry to the whole team for this. This should not be something on your minds right now. You all are fourteen-year-old young ladies who should be having fun. Second, I apologize, Kylah and Jarell, for treating you the way I did yesterday. I have some reflecting to do. This was not your fault, and I should have gathered all my facts before I made assumptions. We can talk more off the record, but I wanted to give my public apology to you both. Yes, Kylah is back on the team."

"Yay!!" My teammates jump up and down and crowd around me, patting me on the head, shaking my shoulders, and one of them even dumps cold water on top of my head. I just smile and laugh through it all.

"Thank you, Coach," I say. I still don't like him for all of this mess, but I'll focus on my attitude with him later. I'm just glad I get to see my dreams through again.

"With that everyone, our meeting is over. Thanks for coming, and we will be set to play in ten minutes!" Tina announces, and the group scatters to where they all need to be. As the rest of my team prepares, I turn around and hug Andre. His long arms encase me, and he briefly presses me into his body before loosening his grip.

"Dre, this is really all because of you. Thank you for being here. This was your idea, and it wouldn't have happened if you didn't push me to fight for this," I express.

He gives me a small smile and warm eyes. "You're welcome. I'm really glad things ended the way it did. You did a good job holding your own up here."

I nod, and shift my attention to Prez, who has a huge grin on his face that turns into an excited laugh and strong embrace, squeezing the life out my stomach and lifts me up, causing me to yelp out. He puts me down and allows me to catch my breath while giggling. Man. What did I do to deserve such great friends?

"Thank you, Prez. You're truly a real one."

"You know I got you for life," he says, daps me up in our rare handshake that we created together, and taps Andre on the chest with the back of his hand. "Aye, man. If y'all get together, don't mess it up."

Andre cuts him a look that basically tells him to shut up. Prez chuckles.

"Chill out, bro," Andre says with a shy smile and puts an arm over Prez's shoulder, proceeding to walk away with him. "We'll be the stands to watch you play, Kylah."

"Cool, I'll see y'all after the game," I reply, waving to them.

When they're long gone, I turn around and Jarell's standing with Jade and Luna nearby, glaring proudly toward me. With a smirk, I walk slowly up to Jarell first and reach out to touch his arm so that he knows I'm in front of him. His features soften in return.

"Thank you for being here and always supporting me, Jarell. It really means a lot. Especially today," I say.

The deep appreciation he feels rises in his eyes before he reaches up to the top of my head and ruffles my hair the way he always used to do when I was little. I tear up a little bit and laugh as the memories of those days flood my mind.

"Proud of you, kid," he simply says. "I always will be."

With that, he takes the dog leash and moves toward the open field nearby to play fetch and other games with Luna. Once Jarell unclips her leash, Luna goes wild, running quickly across the field to grab the ball Jarell threw to bring it back to him.

When my attention leaves them, I finally end with Jade. I'm taken aback to see her full on crying. It doesn't look like she's sad, though, but she's shedding a lot of tears like she might be.

"What's wrong, Jade?" I ask.

"I'm just happy," she whispers.

"About?"

"Happy to see you have such good friends and a supportive environment. You kids are able to solve problems on your own and in ways that are healthy and accountable. It's so refreshing. I hope you cherish every bit of it, Kylah," Jade says, wiping her eyes.

"Yeah. My friends truly are the best." I nod in reflection.

"They really are. My friends when I was your age were terrible influences, and Jarell didn't have any friends at all. All four years of high school, he was severely bullied and constantly picked on with absolutely no support. I don't know if he ever told you this, and I'll apologize to him later if he wanted to tell you himself. But watching this today gives me so much hope and faith in people again."

I turn to look at Jarell once more. He's smiling, bending over to massage and scratch Luna's chin as she pants with her tongue out, happy to be bonding with her caretaker. Jarell just seems so open and free, and he's extremely kindhearted. I seriously can't even picture or imagine him living the kind of life Jade's alluding to, the life he experienced with my dad, or even some of the small comments he's made about how life was for him that I had been largely shielded from.

"He's raised you well, too, it appears," Jade speaks again.

I drop my head. "He's been trying. I haven't been good at all to him over the last couple years. We're getting on the right track though. Prez was the one to push me to do that."

"I'm glad you both are making that happen for yourselves. You need each other. I just pray that Jarell gains something from God… something that rewards him for every sacrifice he's made in his life that he's had to overcome. Your brother deserves that."

I nod, crossing my arms.

"I don't know all the details about his life or anything like that, but from what I do know, I hope he does, too."

Jade smiles, wrapping her arm around my shoulder and pulls me into her chest.

"I'm proud of you, Kylah. Do your thing on that field out there. I gotta get going and head back to LA, but I'll be here tomorrow morning to set up for your graduation party. Sounds good?"

"Sounds great. Thanks for supporting and being here, Jade. You really could've left last night and not come back until Sunday, so thanks for seeing this through."

Jade laughs. "Anything for my sweet honeybun." She squeezes my cheeks like she used to as well and taps my nose with her finger. I blush, feeling like I'm five all over again. "I'm gonna go say bye to your brother."

"Cool. See you, Jade."

She waves, walking away with her hair whooshing with the breeze. She heads toward Jarell, and when she reaches him, she jumps on top of his back. He tries to catch her, but because he was caught off guard, he stumbles to the ground, and she topples with him. Both of them laugh together in the grass as Luna comes up and licks Jarell all over his face. He hugs Luna in return as Jade strokes Luna's back.

Man...

I've never seen anything sweeter than that. Not even with Brooklyn and Jarell, and they've had some pretty romantic moments that I've watched.

I sigh, feeling so grateful as I walk back to the dugout to get ready for today's game.

A game I know we're gonna win.

Chapter Twenty-Eight

IT REALLY SUCKS to celebrate my graduation with a bruised face. After we won our games, and ultimately the tournament yesterday, I cried to Jarell last night, considering cancelling the pool party because the bruises are embarrassing. They've gotten so dark since the fight, and the scab from the cut on the side of my temple is starting to harden, making it incredibly noticeable. Sometimes, I hate having light skin and wish I had Jarell's mocha complexion. At first, Jarell tried to call me over dramatic and downplay how I feel about the injuries, which I understand and empathize because he can't see the damage, but it took me yelling at him for him to realize how serious this is to me. He managed to calm me down and give me a solution to the problem.

So now, I'm thankful that Jade, who's coming early to help set up the party anyway, will also be doing my makeup to cover any blemishes and make me look like a queen. The only bad part is that I won't get to swim. Which really sucks, but whatever. It's the compromise I'm willing to take in order for this party to still happen.

Just as Jarell had gotten home from his early morning walk with Luna and hops in the shower, our door buzzer sounds off. Knowing that it's Jade, I let her inside. She's got her hands full with makeup bags, groceries, and other items for the party. I give her a hand with anything that remains in her Jeep and bring it inside.

"Thanks for doing my makeup, Jade. I hate this kinda stuff, but I'ma do it anyway," I say to her once everything's inside the apartment and I give her a moment to settle in.

"Not a problem. I'll make you look good, and I promise I won't put too much on," she responds, leaning against the kitchen counter.

"Cool. Well, Jarell's in the bathroom, so let's go to my room to do this and knock it out."

"Sounds like a plan."

We head to my space, and Jade gets everything set up on my vanity table while I pick up some scattered dirty clothes off my floor so that my room isn't so humiliating. She doesn't even seem to mind, but I still clean up a little bit anyway before I sit on my bench for her to work her magic. She starts with my hair first, putting it up so that she doesn't get make up on it or my edges.

"Kylah, you have such beautiful hair," Jade says softly to me as she brushes it back and detangles it at the ends.

"Thanks. I think yours is, too. Your hair reminds me a lot of Mama's," I reply.

"That's such a great compliment." She smiles. "I appreciate that."

Jade pulls my hair into a high bun before walking around to the front of me to examine my face to see where to start to apply the makeup.

"So... tell me about your dreams for high school. What are you excited about? What are you nervous about?" she asks, massaging a bunch of some lotion-like product on my face. I wince a little when she gets to the bruised areas. She apologizes before treating that area a little softer.

"Hmm... I'm excited about the softball team," I start. "Happy that it'll be bigger, and I get to make more friends. I'm happy that Prez, Andre, and I will go to the same school. I'm not really nervous about anything, but I do hope I'm not in special ed anymore."

"Special ed?"

"Yeah. I have an IEP or whatever they call it, so they put me in special ed. Jarell and the doctors told me that I have what's called PTSD. Jarell said something to Coach the other day about emotions or something else that's attached to the PTSD. I still don't really understand what it all truly means. I understand some of it, but it's kinda confusing."

"Hmm, that doesn't seem surprising," she says with a nonchalant shrug and pats another sort of colored substance all over my face that matches the color of my skin.

I frown. "What's that supposed to mean?"

"I don't mean to offend you, sweetie. I'm sure Jarell had PTSD as well. It stands for post-traumatic stress disorder. It means that some really significant, traumatic things have happened in your life that affect your emotions. For example, with your mom being gone, that could absolutely trigger a PTSD diagnosis."

"Then why am I in special ed if it's that simple?" I ask. "There are many people who have lost loved ones, like Prez. He's not in special ed."

"Because traumatic events can significantly impact some people's mental health, behavior, sleep, and emotions more than others to the point where they may need extra support," Jade answers. "People process loss and other traumatic events differently."

"Oh..."

"Yeah, so it's not a negative thing that you're in special education, even though I know that it holds a kind of negative stigma."

"It does. I hate it."

"Or you can embrace it and show everyone that it doesn't have to be stigmatized. Look, you're about to be a kid in special education who wins a world championship. That's going to inspire so many kids your age who have mental health conditions," Jade says, looking down at me with a warm, fuzzy glare.

"I guess that's true. And some of the stuff they do does really help me, like the fidgets and bouncy seats, the breaks, and some of the other things in my plan because I get really bad night terrors that make me anxious the next day. A lot of schoolwork makes me anxious too, so I get extensions and stuff. But I don't want to be treated differently in high school."

"I totally understand that," Jade says, adding some pink stuff to my cheeks. "But don't look at it as being treated differently. See it as support to help you be the best you can be. Everyone, and I literally mean everyone, needs support with something."

I nod, taking her words in. She makes it sound so good, but then when it comes down to other people seeing it that way, it doesn't actually feel the way it sounds. I don't say much after that and allow her to work on my face. When she's done, she sprays some sort of smelly liquid on my face and fans me with her hand.

"Okay. Take a look, and let me know what you think," she says and lets me turn to look in the mirror.

Woah. I look amazing! It's like the bruises aren't even there! I scream and jump up to hug Jade. She laughs, holding on to me before she stumbles or falls.

"This looks so good! Thank you!" I exclaim.

"I'm glad you like it." She beams.

"What's going on here?"

My celebration is interrupted by none other than Jarell, standing in the doorjamb with a robe on, but his face and legs are wet.

"It's nothing, Jarell," Jade confirms. "Your sister is just excited about her makeup. That's all. Nothing to worry about."

"Okay, cool. I just heard screaming, so I had to come and check. It's good that she likes it. Looks like the party is on for this afternoon after she did all that begging to have it to begin with."

"Yeah, that's right, huh Kylah?"

"Yes. Party is on," I verify.

"Perfect. Now she can stop crying these crocodile tears to me about it," Jarell says with a slight smirk.

"Shut up, Jarell," I chide and cross my arms.

"Leave her alone. That's not funny. Those bruises are worse than you think," Jade defends me, giving Jarell a serious look like he's being insensitive. I could thank her forever for that, and even though he can't see it, I'm sure he detects that she's not joking in her voice.

He rolls his eyes. "Whatever. Anyway. Any help you need setting up in the pool out there in the courtyard?"

"Uh... nah I think I got it all. There aren't really any huge things that are needed to set up. I just need to grill the burgers, get the balloons out there, and get the cake set up. That's it. I'm not going to start that for another couple of hours. I gotta change out of these sweats and put some good clothes on. I brought things to shower in if that's okay with you."

"You know it's not a problem, Jade. Use the apartment however you'd like. Let this be the last time you ask for permission about anything," he says.

She puts her hands up in surrender. "Okay, okay. I'm sorry. I'm not used to you and I being adults in the same spaces together. You gotta bear with me."

"Mmm hmm," Jarell says and walks away to his room.

Jade sighs and looks at me. "Alright, girl. I'ma get ready. Make sure you hit up your friends and make sure they're coming. I gotta head back to LA around seven, okay? Then I probably won't see you and Jarell for a while until after the BET Awards. I'll try to make it down here a few times in July, but I've got a lot of dance stuff scheduled next month."

"Aww man." I pout. "So that means you can't make it to the World Series in Delaware at the end of July?"

"Yeah, probably not. I'm sorry, baby girl. But I want you to still call, text, or FaceTime me if you need to. Definitely FaceTime me when you get to the World Series."

"Okay. Thanks for everything, Jade," I say.

"You know it ain't no thing."

This party is such a vibe. The way I pictured it would be. A few of my friends from Los Angeles were able to make it here, which has got me so geeked because their parents really didn't have to take this drive, but they did anyway. As soon as they walked inside the pool gates, able to meet my San Diego friends, both groups seemed to hit it off pretty well, even exchanging info at times! It just feels so good to be surrounded by people who care about me, and I care just as much about them.

After all the craziness over the last few days, there's a kind of peace settling in my tummy. About a lot of things.

Everyone's vibing to some summertime Afrobeat and R&B playlist, comfortably lounging around in our swim gear near the pool in beach chairs, soaking up the sun, posting on Tik Tok and Snap.

One of my LA friends, Tiara, who I knew since third grade, has found her way to Prez to flirt and attempt to shoot her little shot. Prez plays along, as I knew he would because he can't help himself. If Tiara lived here, I'd love to see them together. She's so pretty with a sweet soul that Prez would eat up. *Hmm.* Maybe they could do long distance.

Jarell and Jade are near the patio and upper deck, starting up the grill to cook for us, and Jarell is setting up the plates and the waters, as well as stacking towels for each of us to use. They look like they're good and preoccupied with their jobs more than each other, so I turn my attention back to my crew.

"A'ight, so who's the first person to get in the pool?" Prez stands on a patio chair to announce.

Everyone looks at each other like it won't be them.

"Andre," I volunteer, cutting my eyes at him, and he gives me a wild frown and shakes his head.

"Noo..." he challenges.

"I think that's a great idea," Prez says under his breath with a sneaky, plotting smile at him.

"P, I swear to God if you try to push me in the pool, we finna box, real talk," Andre says through a laugh.

"You ain't gon' do shit." Prez waves him off, laughing along with him as we start cheering Andre's name to jump in the pool.

"Come on, we'll go in after you! Well, I won't because I got this makeup on, but everyone else will. Right everybody?" I ask.

Everyone looks at each other, hesitant like they do not want to agree to this at all.

"Come on, y'all. We gotta get the pool poppin'. We can't be the Black folks that go to a pool party and don't get in the pool," I whine. "Who cares about the hairstyles? Y'all will be alright."

"Yeah, nah see, that's that White in you," Tiara says. "You can get your hair wet and be fine."

"Aye, I ain't White, and I agree," Prez defends me.

"Thank you, Prez," I say. "So, y'all finna get in if Andre goes first?"

"I will," says Prez.

"Alright, Dre. Jump in."

Rolling his eyes and sighing, every one of us chant his name over and over until he finally gives in and takes a running start, cannonballing into the deep end of the pool. We all applaud, and Prez follows right behind, diving in.

"Come on, y'all! It feels good in here!" Prez encourages when he surfaces.

Acting shy and timid, the ladies of the party get in the pool all prissy and whatnot, acting like they have to remain cute for the boys. I grumble. Man, if I could, I would dive in that mug headfirst just to show them that they can let their guards down. Prez and Andre, the only guys here, aren't the judging types. They just want to have fun. They couldn't care less about who looks the best at the pool.

I smile and leave them be, heading over to the area with the food so that I don't get too jealous that I can't get in. Jade's going to work on the burgers something serious, and it smells amazing. Jarell disappeared from the upper deck and made his way to the pool area to rest in the beach chair with his sunglasses alone.

"These look good, Jade," I say, peaking my head over her shoulder.

"Thanks! I wouldn't say I'm the best cook, but I've learned to master a grill for whatever reason." She chuckles.

"Well, you got me hungry. I see the plates and the waters, but where's everything else? The cheese, buns, ketchup, all that good stuff?" I ask.

"Oh yeah, Jarell and I forgot them. Can you go inside and grab it? Plus the soda cans?"

"I can't carry all that! Can you help me?"

"Fine. Let me finish up the meat. They're almost done anyway."

Jade finishes cooking the burgers and puts them in Tupperware before we go inside to grab everything else.

"You grab the buns and condiments, and I'll grab the sodas and more water," she directs.

"Cool."

Jade and I start to gather everything we need together, and in the middle of it, the apartment buzzer sounds off, startling us both.

"Who's that?" Jade asks.

"Probably my friend Shanice from LA. She's super late though. I thought she wasn't coming," I reply and press the button to let her in. When the knock comes at the door, I don't even check the peephole. Jade's right behind me holding all her items as I pull the door open.

It's not Shanice.

Instead, I'm face to face with Brooklyn.

"Oh shit," I hiss and drop several condiments unintentionally on the floor. I leave them there because there's no way I'm going to be able to pick them up without everything else falling. So my eyes stay fixed on Brooklyn.

Her eyes ping pong between Jade and me as if trying to figure out who she should address first. Her tears build up as if she's having this battle, meanwhile, Jade and I simply watch her and wait for the decision. But it never comes. She just dips her head low when she realizes that she doesn't have the words to say.

"Brooklyn, what are you doing here?" I question.

Her attention remains on the floor for a few seconds before she blinks several times, and the tears escape down her cheeks.

"I-I just... I wanted to stop by to talk to Jarell about a few things, but... looks like I came at a really bad time," she whispers.

"You didn't text him to let him know you were coming?" I ask, my expression moving from anticipation to annoyed.

"I did, but I didn't get a response."

"That's because he's kickin' it at the community pool in our complex. I'm having a graduation party."

"Oh... I didn't know that you were throwing a party." She swallows and rubs her shoulder, shifting her eyes away from me.

"I would have invited you, but you and Jarell broke up. I heard why y'all broke up too, and that's y'all business or whatever. But I haven't heard from you since we got back from LA, even though you made a commitment that you would hit me up no matter what happened between y'all. When I did hit you up, you were rude. You know it's been about a month, right?"

Brooklyn swallows again as her brows curl with guilt. She refuses to even look Jade's direction and keeps her focus on me.

"I just came to talk to Jarell," she utters, not even acknowledging what I said. "We've been texting back and forth, and I just thought I'd come and at least try to leave things on a much better note than they are right now."

I scoff and roll my eyes.

"It's kinda too late for that now, don't you think?" I ask.

"I see now that it is," she replies with a serious attitude, and that's when she looks at Jade up and down. "I didn't think he'd move on so fast, but I guess it shows that he wasn't into me to begin with. What is it? Jana, right? Seems like his high school sweetheart is more of a priority than what we built together. Why else would she be here when they've supposedly only dated for a week and supposedly haven't seen each other in nine years?"

Jade raises a brow and jerks her head back.

"Uh, because I invited her to my party. It ain't his party," I say like she's dumb before Jade jumps in.

"And hold up Miss Brooklyn. First of all, it's Jade to you. That's the second time you did this, and I'ma need you to show a little respect." She hikes up the waters and other materials she's holding to get a better grip. "I think you're absolutely gorgeous, and ain't got a negative thing to say about you. I get you feel some type of way about how things ended between you and Jarell, but *you* broke up with him. That was *your* choice, so don't be looking at me crazy or playing these passive aggressive games. I don't do sneak disses either, so say what you mean directly to me or don't say shit. Second of all, Jarell and I are not dating, and he hasn't moved on from anything. If you really want him, care about what you say y'all built, and wanna make things work, go get him. Like Kylah said, he's sitting at the pool."

Brooklyn just stares at Jade, searching her eyes as if trying to find any insincerity, but Jade stares right back, doubling down on what she said. I give Jade a side eye. Why would she want Jarell and Brooklyn to get back together? I know and have seen how she feels about him, so why would she allow Brooklyn to walk through that nearly closed door to save that relationship?

When Brooklyn doesn't find what she's looking for, she blinks and takes a step back.

"I should go," she says in conclusion.

"Should I tell Jarell you stopped by?" Jade asks.

"Don't bother," she replies and walks away.

I step up to the door and shout after her.

"I hope what you said was true," I yell. "That you'd still keep your relationship with me even if y'all aren't together. I still actually care about you, Brooklyn!"

With teary eyes, Brooklyn looks at me with a load of hurt. It's a gut punch, I ain't gonna lie. I kinda feel bad for her.

"You're right, Kylah. I just don't think it's very realistic right now."

"Wow..." I shake my head in disbelief.

"I will keep my word. I just need a little time to heal, okay?" she says, the tears falling to the ground.

With that, Brooklyn leaves the complex. I shut the door and let out a huge exhale. Now that was crazy. I set what I have in my arms down and pick up the other condiments I dropped before picking everything back up and rearranging them so that they're comfortable to carry.

"Jade, you really meant that? That she should try and go and make things work with him?" I ask with wide eyes.

Jade laughs. "Girl, that's to see how deep she really cares about their relationship. If she really wants Jarell and loves him like she thinks she does, she'd fight for him. And if Jarell goes for her, then I'll know where I stand. At that point, I'll get outta their way forever. But it's obvious that she's given up on the spot here, which to me means she has weak resolve."

"How?" I question.

"She knows deep down inside that she can't compete with me. It was all in her eyes, Kylah. Anyone from anywhere can see that Jarell and I have way too much chemistry, even after all these years. I lowkey think Brooklyn saw that when we ran into each other in LA."

"She did," I confirm.

"See. There you go. Honestly, as much as it sucks for them, it would be extremely difficult for any woman to compete with me when it comes to Jarell. And it would be extremely difficult for any man to compete with him, for sure. He was my first true love, and I'm his first true love. You can't erase that, especially if we left each other on those exact terms."

"Really?" I ask.

"Yeah! Jarell's last words to me before we split was that he loves me. We may have matured, and we very well may be different people now, but we are who we are at the core. He and I were able to experience the raw, true core parts of each other that no one else had seen, witnessed, or knew about. So, I don't anticipate his truth about me has changed."

"I know it hasn't, Jade," I admit. "I've never seen Jarell smile so hard or be excited like that when he saw you. Even Brooklyn outright said his whole demeanor changed when you hugged him the day she broke up with him. He's real smooth and cool with Brooklyn but... I don't know... he seems different around you."

Jade shrugs like she told me so.

"Let's see if she's real. She may come back tomorrow," Jade says.

"You're so petty for asking her if you should tell him that she stopped by." I cackle. She does, too.

"I was dead serious. If she wants it, she gotta go get it. I'll even assist her." Jade shrugs, and she and I burst into collective laughs again, and we walk out of the door and back to the pool to join the party.

"Bout time! What was y'all in there doing? Come on, we're starving!" Prez whines.

"Okay, okay. Sorry. We were just talking," I say, getting the plates set up.

All the hungry maniacs swarm around the burgers to eat, crying about who cut in line and who deserves to eat first. I'm left to manage it all on my own when I look up and see Jade walking toward Jarell.

Jarell's in his own little world with a large t-shirt and swim trunks on, sitting at the edge of the shallow end of the pool and wading his feet in the water. I'm surprised he's not up to come and eat, too. I don't know what it is, but he's been extremely reserved and quiet today, allowing me and my friends to be the life of the party. But it's not a bad mood vibe at all. His energy feels like a great sense of peace while still showing a genuine, celebratory support for me, despite his stillness. It makes me really happy that Brooklyn opted not to come and ruin everything.

I guess it's only a matter of time before she does, but I'm just glad it's not today.

When Jade reaches him with a wine cooler in her hand, she says something inaudible to me, but it's something that makes him look up and blush with a smile. She laughs at his reaction and takes a seat next to him, puts her feet in the water too, and lays her head on his shoulder. As she closes her eyes with a big inhale, soaking in San Diego's summer breeze, Jarell wraps his arm around her and pulls her close before whispering something in her ear to make her giggle into his neck. He hugs her tighter after that.

Geez.

That damn chemistry...

It erupts like a volcano almost any time I see them near each other. I don't know how else to really describe it to myself, other than the fact that they seem deeply, deeply connected by their souls. It just seeps from their skins when they're together, and not even in this weird kinda puppy love, flirty way that I picked up from him and Brooklyn.

It's like the time Jade and Jarell spent away from one another clearly bothered them, and they couldn't wait for this moment to arrive. And now it's coming true, picking up right wherever they left off. Like the time they spent separated doesn't matter.

"What you looking at?" a familiar voice with a mouth full of food startles me as I lean on the pool gate. I look to my right and it's Prez, following my gaze across the way to watch them too with his burger in hand. "He's got a new girlfriend? Already? Dang. What's this new girl's name again?"

"Her name's Jade. And trust me, she ain't new. That's his ex-girlfriend," I say.

He laughs. "That's wild. He must've not loved that other girl that much."

"You know? At first, I thought the same thing. He cares about Brooklyn for sure. But I don't think Jarell ever left Jade in his heart, even when he was with Brooklyn. There's levels to this love thing. Jade and Jarell definitely have some kind of love for each other no one else can understand."

"Mm. That's pretty deep," Prez replies and turns to look at me. "This doesn't even sound like you. Since when are you an expert on love? Can't be the one who threw a chair at a teacher. Can't be the one who wanted someone else to hook her up with her best friend's best friend." He raises an eyebrow, his eyes ready to explode with an accompanying laugh.

I punch him in the arm, giving him a look like I could choke him, and he falls out, snickering at me like he's five years old. I can't help but to break into a slightly mortified grin.

"I'm LaLa, and oooh, I'm a love expert now that I see my brother so trapped in her looovvvee... she puts him in such a trance," Prez says, breathy and mocking me, switching his hips back and forth and flicking his wrist, walking away from me.

"Shut the fuck up, Prez," I say through a laugh and walk away with him to leave the two adults alone and mind my business to party with the best friends the world could have.

Chapter Twenty-Nine

"COME ON, LALA. You gotta get this down. No more wild pitches," Prez says as he throws the ball back to me from home plate.

I've been trying to practice a new strikeout pitch with Prez to prepare for the Senior Leagues, but I'm super inconsistent with it right now. I'm getting real frustrated, and usually when I get that way over pitching, it's time for me to walk away, but I'm too determined to try and get it close to perfection before we get on the airplane to head across the country. Plus, I wanna get it done because I know Prez ain't gonna be around since he will have camps and other stuff to go to throughout the summer. Plus tonight, Jarell and I are hanging out to watch the BET Awards since Jade is performing.

When Prez is ready at the plate to catch my pitch, I do my normal pitcher routine before throwing the ball. My arm whirls around and the ball leaves my hands, trying to get it to spin the way it's supposed to, but it ends up driving low and hits the ground before it can even make it to the plate.

"Alright, LaLa, give it a rest," Prez says, taking off his helmet, glove, and drops the ball at home base.

"Prez, no. Please? I gotta get this right," I beg.

"Nope. You're gonna burn yourself out. You gotta come back to it," he says.

"Okay, just ten more," I reason.

"No," he firmly dissents. "You've already pitched about fifty of the same pitch. You gotta let it rest for a while and come back later," he says, walking toward me, further signaling his end to being my catcher.

"You're no fun." I mope.

He shrugs. "You'll be a'ight. And you'll thank me later. Go hang out with the homie Dre or something. You know he's waiting for us to be done anyway." Prez points to his left.

I follow his finger, and Andre is sitting on a bench with a drum pad on his lap, practicing what I think is his snare. He's so deep into it that he likely doesn't care how long Prez and I practice.

"No! He came out here to hang with you for the day. I have plans tonight, but I'll catch up with him later."

"Oh, so now you don't wanna hang with him no more? After I did all that fuckin' work at the dance..." he says with a deadpan face.

"Whatever dawg," I mumble as I pull out my phone and check my texts, since I felt it vibrate throughout my time practicing.

My brows wrinkle at the unknown number that pops up with three different messages, but when I open them and briefly skim the texts, the name that pops up makes my whole face tense up. Alaysia? What does she want with me? Actually, the real question is... who the hell gave her my number?

"What's wrong? What's with the frown?" Prez asks.

"I think Alaysia's texting me..."

His face scrunches, too. "Why?"

"I don't know! I'm 'bout to find out..."

I bring my phone closer to my face, reading the messages carefully because I still can't believe I'm even getting a message from her.

> Hey. It's Alaysia. I know it's real awkward for me to text you or whatever. I hope it's not a bad time, but... can we meet at Eastmann's?

> At around... 3?

> I just want to talk real quick.

I check the time. It's 3:13. Why would she wanna meet with me? At this point, if I see her out in public with no other adults around, I'm just gonna wanna beat her ass. And I hope Prez will allow it, too, for her ruining his relationship with Gina as well.

"What did she say?" Prez questions.

"She wants to meet me here. Right now."

"For what?"

"She said she wants to talk."

"About what?"

"I don't know, Prez! Cut it with the questions."

"Sorry, I just don't trust her. Are you gonna link up?"

"Let me respond to her first," I say as my thumbs go to work on the screen, crafting a mean response to her. As soon as I send it, the read receipt comes. And then, the bubbles that show she's working on responding. Prez comes by my shoulder and peeks over it to watch it all go down.

●●●○○ Sprint 4G   3:15 PM   @ 72% 🔋

❮ Messages **+1(619) 555-0191** Details

Hey. It's Alaysia. I know it's real awkward for me to text you or whatever. I hope it's not a bad time but... can we meet at Eastmann's?

At around... 3?

I just want to talk real quick.

first of all, how did u get my number? second of all, why do u even wanna meet? i don't like u.

I got your number from a friend. I'm not tryna start anything. I just wanna talk

iMessage   Send

●●●○○ Sprint 4G   3:17 PM   @ 72% 🔋

< Messages **+1(619) 555-0191** Details

should i bring someone just in case? bcuz whatever u have to talk about can be talked about with someone around. i don't trust u, & having someone around is for ur own sake too.

Bringing someone isn't necessary. I'm not tryna fight, and I don't want you to fight me. But if you think that it's a must... do you. I just wanna talk, that's all.

ok. come thru. just understand that if u try anything sneaky, ur gonna get dragged. believe that.

iMessage   Send

"Yeah. I think I'ma stick around," Prez says after that conversation wraps up.

"Good. She needs to understand that I ain't playin' with her ass," I say.

Prez and I wait for her to show up, and when she does, she gets out of her parents' big white SUV and walks across the field. I eye her the whole way up. This time, she isn't dressed like she's ten years older, but with a simple t-shirt and athletic shorts. When she reaches Prez and me, she sticks her hands in her shorts pockets, kinda refusing to give us eye contact. Prez glares at her with a blank look, but his eyes hold the scorn, and I just mug her openly, not for one second hiding how I feel as we both wait for her to speak.

"Kylah, can you and I talk without Preston being here?" she asks after clearing her throat.

"Why should I let you do that?" I ask.

"Because this should be a one-on-one conversation..."

"You didn't think about all of that when I got jumped. That wasn't a one-on-one fight... but this right here can be. You and me. Right now," I threaten and walk up on her. She turns her head away, signaling that she's not trying to fight at all. In fact, she steps back as Prez steps in.

"LaLa, don't. Chill out. Just see what she has to say," Prez says and pushes me back.

I cross my arms. "Fine."

Prez steps just a few feet away and monitors us as I keep a healthy distance from her with my arms still locked against my chest. Alaysia takes a deep breath before opening her mouth to speak, but nothing comes out.

"Why are you here, Alaysia? Don't waste my fuckin' time. Were you forced to meet up with me after you got your ass whooped by your parents? Or what?" I ask.

"No, I'm doing this on my own," she counters. "Kylah, I really am sorry for everything."

I stand there, waiting for her to continue.

"I'll admit. My parents have been super hard on me because they do want me to go to a private high school because they're scared I'm going to go down the wrong path in high school with my friends."

"And? What that gotta do with me?"

"Well... I've just been trying to live up to what they want, and what I want, too. The school I'm looking at has a really good softball program there and everything, and because you're so... damn talented, it's hard to compete for the pitcher spot on our team for me to showcase what I can do to the coaches there."

I stare at her, still waiting for her to say something new that's worth me being here.

"It sucks that I don't get many chances to show my talent and who I really can be on the field, and when I do get opportunities, I get so nervous that I screw it up. But that's not your fault, and I really shouldn't be jealous of you. And I let my jealousy get in the way by trying to get rid of you the dirty way, and it went way too far. I didn't think you getting jumped would happen."

"But it did," I say.

"I know, and I'm sorry. I shouldn't have used Preston to try and get rid of you on the team just because I'm not as talented as you are. You put in the work, and I should be putting in the time and effort to be just as good. I don't know. I guess I can admit that I'll probably never be as good as you because you eat, sleep, and breathe this diamond. I don't."

"Glad you've gotten to the point of being honest with yourself," I say with sarcasm.

"Yeah. Well... that's the truth, Kylah. I guess all of this softball stuff and what we have on this team is bigger than me. Especially with us playing in the World Series. I can't keep being a bad teammate if we're gonna win this thing."

"Glad somebody's gotten that through your thick skull..." I mumble.

"Yeah. So... I'm genuinely sorry. We don't have to be friends or whatever..."

"We won't be," I interject.

"I figured. I just hope you accept my apology."

"I do. Just don't think for a second that we will ever be cool. You're sneaky, a backstabber, and you still need your ass beat. We will do what we need to do to get along for the team, but other than that, it's a wrap for any kind of friendship. Are we done here?" I question with a raised brow.

"We can be..."

"Bye," I say, and walk away from her, heading back over to Prez, who is now talking to Andre.

"How was it?" Dre asks.

I shrug. "It's whatever. She apologized, I accepted, and told her ass we will never be cool. That's the gist."

Dre and Prez look at each other and laugh.

"Yo, LaLa really is spicy, man. If she ain't getting jumped, you can count on her to wreck shit," Prez declares.

"Man. I wouldn't even dare to cross her. I'd be too scared." Dre shakes his head. "But she's got another side to her, though. Soft side. A side I can get with."

"Aye... that's real. I hope you fall in love with that side," Prez says.

"Why y'all talking about me like I ain't standing here?" I smile, blushing.

"Because we can," Prez says. "But a'ight, me and Dre finna head out. Bouta go play Call of Duty at the crib. You wanna come?"

"I told you I have plans with Jarell tonight. Y'all have fun," I say and walk toward the diamond to pack up all my gear and wave to them with my back turned.

"That's good news! I'm glad to hear y'all are starting to get along. But a'ight. Catch you later, LaLa."

~ ~ ~

After showering and putting on comfy clothes, I meet Jarell in the living room area for the time we planned together tonight for the BET Awards. He's so funny. He's got the couch pushed back with several blankets and pillows stacked on the floor for a comfy watch party, bowls of popcorn on the table, candy, and soda cans right next to the food. I laugh. Dude really is making this whole thing an event. It's actually super cute and thoughtful.

"Dang. Nice set up for someone who can't see," I say with a genuine smile. "No shade."

"No offense taken. I appreciate that. You like it? Is there anything missing?" he asks.

"Ummm..." I look around the living room. "Nah, I think you've covered it!"

"Dope," he says and lays down on one of the pillows, turning up the volume for the awards pre-show. I join him on the ground, taking a handful of popcorn from the bowl and shove it in my mouth.

He and I watch the pre-show and the beginning of the actual show with Ice Cube hosting this year, occasionally making our opinions known to one another about the things that some of the artists say while I specifically comment on the outfits on the red carpet that people have on.

So many outfits are absolutely trash.

Some wear obvious cheap material that looks like it'd rip at the ass once they bend to sit down. Others act like they don't know their own bodies because the clothes don't hang well on them, and others just look stupid for the purposes of getting attention. It's like they're all going to compete in the circus for who looks the most like a clown. I've described them in such detail to Jarell, and he laughs his butt off, almost to the point of tears, at my commentary. I honestly feel so much joy in my heart to hear his belly laugh. It's deep, hearty, and genuine. I've actually never ever heard him laugh this way, so it makes me laugh too until our tummies hurt.

We settle down once the first commercial comes on. I take a sip of my Pepsi and stuff more popcorn in my mouth.

"Yo, Kay Kay, I never realized how funny you are. If you ain't playing softball, you should do stand up, for real," Jarell says.

"Uh, no. Not my thing. I'm definitely a people person, but I'm not into comedy. I'm into honesty," I say.

"Okay, so other than drawing, and softball, what would you do?"

"Be a shoe collector," I reply.

He smacks his lips. "I should've known…"

"So… Jarell… can I ask you something?" I question, wrapping my arms around my knees and rocking back and forth.

"What is it?"

"You know Jade's up to perform in a minute, right?" I start.

"Yeah…"

"How do you feel about her? Do you still love her?"

Jarell freezes for a brief second before he gives me a side eye and a small smile.

"What kinda question is that?" he says.

"I'm just asking! I see how y'all interact... so what's up? Y'all gonna get back together?"

Instead of answering, Jarell just chuckles and makes sure to check the emotion on his face, barring me from gauging any non-verbal answers he might give.

"Soooo?"

"Kay Kay, that's none of your business," he replies.

"What?! Seriously? Okay, how do you feel about Brooklyn, then?"

"Kylah, my relationships with women are none of your concern. That's a man's job to tell a woman how he feels. Not his sister."

"It's just a conversation!" I exclaim.

"So? I'm not answering you on either of those questions."

"Wow... so I guess we can't be close, then. I'm never going to tell you about my crushes, any boy stuff, or anything about dating." I shrug.

"Wait a minute. That's different," Jarell counters loudly, but I put a hand up and interject with several no's as he tries to make his case, but I keep interrupting him with no's until we both fall out laughing.

"Come on, man," he groans after catching his breath.

"Jarell, just tell me. I would love to see you and Jade together," I say. "You both seem to really love each other. But Brooklyn's really sweet, too. I just don't like how things ended up."

"It's complicated..." he says.

"So you love them both?" I ask with my eyes growing wide.

"It's complicated..."

"Jarell, stop playing."

"I'm telling the truth," he says, looking toward me with a serious expression. "It truly is complicated. I care a lot about them both for different reasons."

"Hmm... okay. I'll leave it alone, then."

Welp... I'd hate to be him. Stuck in between two women. *Yikes.* I guess I'ma really sit this one out.

As we wrap up that conversation, the show comes back on, and Kehlani is on que to perform. Tiffany Haddish introduces her, and the performance starts. Kehlani sings with her angelic voice to start in the dark before the bright lights come on, and her dancers join her.

And there Jade is, dressed in baggy pants, tank tops, and heels like the rest of the dancers, dancing the choreography to her songs while Kehlani dances with them in the middle.

This is so surreal. Jade's so good. Man, I wish Jarell could see this!

The whole performance is energetic. They do some real hardcore hip-hop moves, thrusting their hips and shoulders to the beat, but they also find small pockets where they slow down, showing their sexier dances that Jade leads alongside Kehlani.

I can't believe how limber Jade is. Her back, knees, and body bends in ways that make my joints ache, and I'm only fourteen. Hell, I can barely stretch my legs and touch my toes with my fingers.

As she sensually dances on her feet and eventually on the ground, she whips her head back and forth, using her long hair as a symbol of sex, especially since "Toxic" is the song that they're dancing to. Throughout the entire set, Jade and her dancers keep the energy up, absolutely killing it. When Kehlani's done, she gets a standing ovation. I clap with the audience, too.

"Wow. Her music is definitely a vibe," Jarell says, nodding.

"Yeah, Jarell, I wish you could've seen the actual performance. She killed it, and so did Jade. She didn't miss a step. Everything was so perfect and flawless. That's just so crazy. I can't believe you dated a celebrity dancer, and now I just have her number like it's no big deal,"

I say in awe.

"She ain't no celebrity to me. She's just Jade," Jarell says and lays back onto the covers, stuffing popcorn in his mouth. I shake my head. Jarell always tries so hard to be unemotional. A super tough nut to crack. But whatever, I guess. I'm that way, too. That's just who we are.

"Yeah, and she told me you dance, too! She said that's how y'all became close. Is that true?"

Jarell pauses, but his blank face slowly but surely morphs into a smile.

"When did she tell you this?" he asks.

"That day I went to dinner with her instead of going with Tina like I told you I would."

He sighs, still, with a reminiscent expression. "Well... yeah. It's actually true."

"You dance, Jarell? Seriously? To the point where she'd want you to come to her studio? That's what she said she wanted you to do. She said you're one of the best she's ever seen."

"She's not lying." He shrugs.

"How come I never knew this! I've never in my life have seen you dance. Why not?"

"Because you hated me, remember? Why would you want to see me dance?"

I smack my lips, and he laughs, mocking me. *Ugh.* Slick ass remark. I shove his shoulder playfully, and he continues to snicker at me.

"Jarell... I don't even remember seeing you dance when I was little."

"Because I always danced alone. Still do."

"But you danced in front of Jade..."

"That's 'cause she caught me."

"Well, can you show me? Like, are you really good?"

"I'd like to think so," he responds. "It's what I keep hearing. It's what Ma said when she caught me, too."

"Okay! Where do you dance? Can I come one day to watch?"

"Sure. You can't judge me, though. I dance for peace. It's how I've gotten through the days of raising you."

I nod. "I promise I won't. I'll just watch."

"Cool. You can come with me after we finish the awards."

"Dang, I'm excited now!"

Jarell nods comfortably and lays back without another word. In the meantime, I send Jade a text, telling her how amazing she was. She just sends a heart back. That's just enough for me to feel acknowledged and appreciated as Jarell and I watch the rest of the show.

~ ~ ~

The awards show is over, and it's close to eleven o'clock at night. Jarell, with Luna, leads me to a place near the beach I've never been to before. It's really secluded, but a beautiful backdrop of the water with the moon shining above it. I have no idea how Jarell found this place without sight, but I really wish he could see the natural beauty of this place. I'm sure he can feel it because the breeze is so peaceful as we're surrounded by soft, tall grass swaying with the wind.

"So this is where you dance?" I ask Jarell.

But he doesn't answer. His large headphones are on with his eyes closed, nodding and vibing to the music. He's already let go of Luna's leash, so I coax her over to me to relax. She does without hesitation. I take a seat on the ground and just watch, massaging Luna's back. He already seems to be in the zone.

I don't know what he's listening to, but his first movements are a series of pop and locks that's already got me trippin'. The way some parts of his body stops and the ability to move the other parts so fluidly is incredible. But even more? When he's ready to move the locked parts, he's able to lock the other side without missing a beat. It almost seems supernatural.

The more time moves along, the more fascinated I get with Jarell gliding along the ground in moves that look like he's dancing on water. The level of concentration, peace, and at the same time, effortlessness that he displays while his moves look so difficult gives me a whole new respect for Jarell and his talent. How'd he learn all this stuff?

Jade is right.

Jarell needs to be in a studio or a stage somewhere. This is... unlike anything I've ever seen. Hell, he needs to be on the Jabbawockeez!

My eyes stay glued to Jarell the entire time he dances without ever getting bored, awed by every new move he makes. When he's all finished, I check my phone, and it's nearly midnight. Time really flew! Jarell's sweating, but his whole demeanor is relaxed.

"Yo... I'm speechless. For real," I say.

He chuckles in his throat. "That says a lot coming from you!" Jarell replies.

"I mean... so... you should be on a dance crew or something."

"Nah. I only dance for peace of mind. Just like drawing is your peace. You don't show anyone your drawings, right?"

Damn. He has a point. I surrender right away.

"You're right. Your dancing is so similar to my drawing that I won't even push you on it. Because I know I get annoyed if people want to see what I draw. Just wanna say that was amazing, Rell. I guess there's a lot more to learn about you, now that I'm older and we're on better terms," I say.

He smiles, reaching out to wrap his arm around my shoulder. I allow him to, and he pulls me to his side, kissing the top of my head.

"I agree. And I can't wait for us to build that connection more. I miss you being my partner-in-crime," Jarell says.

I nod.

"No cap, I miss it, too." A comfortable but long moment of silence settles between us. "You know, Jarell?"

"Hmm?"

What's on my mind now is something I would've never thought I'd surface at this moment. But it's been weighing on me the entire time Jarell danced. I suppose today is full of surprises.

"This will probably be random. But that night... when you and Brooklyn broke up and we were washing dishes together..."

He hesitates. "Yeah?"

"I've been thinking of ways to talk to you about it, and I really haven't found the words to express how I feel about that whole situation. So I'm gonna try. Is that okay?"

"Uh... where's this coming from?" Jarell shifts awkwardly.

I clear my throat and swallow my phlegm, grabbing onto a lock of my hair to stroke it. Regulating myself. "Just hear me out. When I put two and two together about your job at the Human Trafficking Center and my dad's role in–"

"Kylah," Jarell puts a hand up right away, shifting his eyes away from me. "Please... you don't have to mention any of this..."

"No, Jarell. Please let me finish. I know it's hard to think about, but it's really important for me to say this because I don't know if I'll ever be ready to say it again."

He contemplates, but ultimately surrenders with his arms crossed, refusing to look up. "Okay..."

I take a deep breath and start again. "I've read a few of Mama's journal pages. I know you said you wanted to read it together, but I wanted to learn about our family on my own. But after that day at the sink, I couldn't even pick it up again. Jarell... I'm so *sorry*. Not just for how I've been over the last few months and since I've been here. But for what you went through with my dad... for what you went through with Mama... I don't know everything. But I know enough now. I've been so mad at you and mistreated you so much that I didn't even realize ..." The end of my sentence goes shaky and hoarse... and this time, without shame, I start to cry.

Jarell's emotions rise, too, but he tries to turn his head to hide it. It doesn't work. His Adam's apple bobs up and down as he attempts as hard as he can to control himself as a vein in his neck becomes more pronounced. I'm close to just telling him to stop avoiding it and let it happen, but I guess he's gotta deal with this conversation in his own way, too. I continue speaking once I've caught my breath.

"I didn't realize how much you were put in the middle of everything when it came to our family. Mama said y'all were homeless. Mama said Daddy abused y'all. I didn't know. I'm sorry for what I've done... all the assumptions, the disrespect, the hate... and I'm sorry for what each and every one of us did to you. *I mean it.*"

Jarell doesn't say a word. He just holds both sides of his waist, dips his head, and suddenly sobs. Quietly. Any words that come to mind to comfort him disappear with the wind. I'm not used to seeing this side of him at all, but I have to keep remembering he's human, no matter how strong I think he is. So I walk up to embrace him. He easily accepts the love in a way I never thought he would.

And we hold each other and cry together near the ocean waters as if we have no one else in this world.

Because we don't. We're seriously all we've got.

Chapter Thirty

I CAN'T BELIEVE this is happening. That butterfly feeling of anticipation in my tummy intensifies by a thousand as I step foot, for the first time, on an airplane with Jarell and Luna right behind me. It's so tight in this cabin, making me feel a bit crushed, but I think I can handle six hours. At least, I hope. All I know is that my headphones, my music, and I are about to get real close in order for me to fall into a zone so I can dream of holding the world champion trophy.

We are officially on our way to Delaware for the Senior League Softball World Series.

Summer between June and July has been full of fun, but intense training when it comes to softball. But the hard work has paid off. I'm in the best shape I've ever been, both in body and health, and I've been locked in to prepare for this moment. With a final record of 22-2, our team, the San Diego Sluggers who are now known as "California," are ready to win this whole thing.

Since our team has been through all the ups and downs and highs and lows, we're now closer than we've ever been as a unit. All the incidents, losses, team drama, arguing, and weathering that storm was what we needed to finally mesh and come together. After playing the game for a while, I've learned how important team chemistry is to win this series.

More than anything, the pressure of rising to meet everyone's expectations in this series is real. As of yesterday, with the final rankings on ESPN, I've remained at the number one spot all summer long as the best pitcher in the nation and internationally to win it all. I just need to keep it cool, calm, and collected. We can bring this trophy home. I just know it.

The takeoff and landing are the only scary things about flying. For the most part, I slept, and so did Jarell with Luna on his lap as she had her own seat for herself. As we wait to exit the plane, I sigh a sad one.

I wish more of my people who support me were able to come out here, like Prez or Jade. Jade's got all this dance stuff, and Prez's parents couldn't afford to come out here this year and promised they'd try to come out in the years to come. I mean, it's cool just having Jarell and all, but I don't know. I guess the more, the merrier for me.

We get off the plane and do all the luggage pick up, shuttle van, checking in to the hotel, and all the travel stuff that kids like me don't care about. What I do care about is the fact that it's media day when the ESPN reporters and other sports reporters are here at the Little League hotel to interview all the teams.

Coach made us go and change into our uniforms for this event. Because we're the favorites to win the whole thing, we end up with the first slot to connect with the journalists. So Coach, our assistant coach, and all the parents/guardians come outside the conference room where we wait for the media to let us in. We all kind of sit around, exhausted because it's already five o'clock pm. I sit with my team this time as Jarell sits kind of away from everyone against a wall with Luna and his sunglasses on. The way his head unnaturally slumps over to the side, I can tell what kinda state he's in.

As we wait, Coach hasn't said much about how this day would go or what we should do for this media day, even though many of us have asked him. He simply says that this is just as new to him as it is for us.

Soon, a short lady with blond hair comes out of the conference room doors with this kinda cheesy smile on her face, glaring at each of us, scanning the group to find the right person to talk to. Once her eyes land on Coach, she seems assured that he's the leader.

"California, right?" She confirms with Coach. He nods. "Perfect! Come on in, ladies and parents!" she expresses with this unnecessary grandiose voice.

Our team seems to get a boost of energy and charge in with anticipation while our parents sluggishly follow behind us. Once we're in, a few cameras are up, and some journalists sit in chairs like they've been waiting for us to arrive. Everyone's inside now, so the lights and cameras turn on and focus on us.

I kinda feel like a superstar! I know the rest of them feel like this, too.

"Alright, girls! I'm happy you all have your uniforms on. You will take a team photo for the website and social media, and then each of you will have a fifteen-minute individual photo shoot with several of our photographers with any gear that you want. Your bat, helmet, gloves, you name it. These photos will be used on national television as you all progress through the tournament. If you all make it to the championship, we will have another media day with more interviews and photos. Are you guys excited?"

"Yeah!" We all chime in unison.

"Oh, I'm 'bout to kill this shoot! Periodt!" Alaysia brags and grabs the air with her hand. Everyone around her laughs except for me. I roll my eyes. This might be the only thing she's good at. Posing for the camera.

"Kylah, we would like to have an exclusive interview with you, as well, being the number one high school prospect in the country for softball and all. So after your team photo, come on over to the table, and we will have your interview," the ESPN spokesperson says.

My eyes blossom as my homies Tina, Katie, and Keisha squeal around me and shake my shoulders. "Really? Me? What questions will you ask? Can I know them ahead of time before y'all interview me?"

"Well, I can give you a general sense of what the questions will be. I can't guarantee that there won't be follow up questions. They're just questions about who you are, what you're most excited about for the tournament, and your inspirations."

I nod.

"Cool. Those sound like safe questions," I reply with relief.

"Awesome! Well, let's get this show started!"

Everyone scrunches together against the green screen for a team photo, and then we all break into our respective photo shoots. Well, my team does. The lady who's the spokesperson encourages me to come to the table. I give her a wait signal with my finger and stop by Jarell first. He's leaning up against the wall near the door, his body language exuding nothing but the fact that he's ready to leave and go to bed. I smile at it, because he's usually super composed and doesn't often show much emotion out in public with people he's not normally around.

"Hey Jarell, I'm not sure if you know at all," I start, "but ESPN wants to do an exclusive interview with me today."

"About what?" he asks.

"Just about the tournament. Are you okay with that?" I ask.

"I mean, I don't see why not. But they need to keep their questions to just about the tournament," he says.

"Okay. I'm kinda nervous, lowkey," I admit, biting my knuckle.

"About?"

"Just... all the attention. I know I'm the number one in the country but... I don't know if I'm ready for the spotlight this is all gonna bring."

Jarell laughs.

"Kay Kay. You've been waiting for this moment. And you ain't, by far, a shy person. You thrive in social situations and with people. What's the problem?"

"I don't know. I guess I'm just... I'm scared about anything going wrong," I whisper.

"I understand. This is a really big moment and tournament for you. I know you've also never been out of California in a new place, so I get it. You want me to come with you to the interview?" Jarell asks.

I nod. He motions his head like he's still waiting for me to answer. *Oops.* Damn, sometimes I forget that I must use my words with him, that he can't comprehend body language at all. Sometimes, it's really a disadvantage, especially when it's something that I don't want to openly express.

"Sorry. I was nodding. Yes, I want you to come," I confess.

"Okay. Take my arm and lead me there," Jarell replies, and I wrap my arm around his and walk him toward the interview table.

The spokesperson lady's still sitting there waiting for me, looking a bit impatient, and stands up to get the mics ready. Two journalists come forward to my table, ready to get their piece from me.

"And who is this fella joining you?" the spokesperson lady asks.

"My brother. And what's your name?" I ask her.

"My name is Lisa. Sorry, I forgot to introduce myself earlier. I appreciate that you brought your sibling with you, but where are your parents?" she asks. "Only parents can be in the media room."

"I am her parent," Jarell interjects. "Yes, I'm her brother, but I'm also her guardian."

She blinks. "Oh! I'm so sorry. Shame on me. I shouldn't make assumptions," she mumbles. "And your name is?"

"Jarell," he answers.

"Jarell, I see that you have a dog with you, so are you visually impaired?"

"Yes."

"Okay. I am going to lead you both to the chair where guardians can sit for the interview. Kylah, if you can sit at the interview table, that would be amazing."

Lisa leads Jarell and Luna to the chair she's referring to, and I go to the table in front of another green screen. In front of me, the camera men are stationary, adjusting their cameras in order to capture their best shots of me. One of the journalists comes up and sits next to me at the table.

"Okay, let's get this thing rollin'!" Lisa yells and signals for the interview to begin.

"Hello, Kylah! My name is Stephanie, and I am a reporter for ESPN prep sports, focusing on high school softball. How are you today?"

"I'm good."

"Perfect! Tell me more about you. Tell us your full name, where you are from, and how old you are."

"Hey everyone." I wave with a smile. "My name is Kylah Hendricks, I'm from Los Angeles, California, and I am fourteen years old."

"And is this your first year in the Senior League Tournament?"

"Yes."

"Wow, so I just bet you're excited for this experience, aren't you?"

"For sure." I nod and continue smiling. *Ugh.* I feel so cheesy doing this.

"Well, speaking of experience, Kylah you are the number one prospect in the country that is entering high school this year and entering this tournament. Did you know that? If so, how do you feel about that?"

"I did know, but I don't really feel a certain way about it. I think it's cool, but no matter if I'm labeled the best or not, I'm always perfecting and working on my craft," I respond.

"Wow! Such a mature answer. That's what's needed to gain the top spot. So what are you most excited about with the Senior League World Series?"

"Um... I'm mostly excited about the competition and to be challenged. I know there are a lot of great players out there, so I'm excited to compete and see what I'm up against."

"And what about the city?"

"Um... I don't know much about Delaware as a state, so I guess I'm just ready to explore it once we're in the right space to," I say.

"Thank you for your time! I'm going to pass it off to my colleague, Matt Stoner," Stephanie says and cues the other journalist in with her eyes.

"Thank you, Steph. Hi Kylah! As Stephanie shared, my name is Matt, and I am a reporter for CBS's MaxPrep sports. So what would you say inspires you to play softball?" he asks.

"Mmm..." I ponder. I don't know how vulnerable I should get with these people. I honestly just want to keep it real light and real simple. "Well I would say my family and best friend inspire me to play softball. I like to make them proud."

"Awesome. What's your favorite hobby outside of softball?" he questions.

"Mmm... drawing."

"And last question. Who's your favorite softball player?"

"Keilani Ricketts," I say. "She used to play for the Oklahoma Sooners. One of the best pitchers to ever do it."

"Good answer. Well that's it for today, Kylah. I appreciate you taking the time to speak with us this evening. Good luck at the tournament, and we hope to see you soon!" says Matt.

"Cool. Thanks!"

Whew. Glad that's over. I never realized how big of a deal people make such small interviews behind the scenes and the creation of it.

With an exhausted grin, I walk over to Jarell, who's got a "proud dad" look on his face. I roll my eyes.

"Done."

"See, that wasn't that bad, now was it?" he jokes.

"Nah, it wasn't. Thanks for coming, though."

"No problem. A'ight, you ready for your individual photo shoot so we can go? Because I'm literally about to pass out."

"Yes. I am, too. Let me get this over with."

After the media packs up and heads off to wherever they need to go, I link up with Keisha and Tina to chill in my hotel room since Jarell allowed me to have my own for privacy reasons, which I greatly appreciate. At first we say we're tired, but somehow, we get a third wind to still hang out for the night. Keisha is meddling with the remote to turn on Netflix while Tina and I scroll on our phones. I've probably watched about fifty TikTok videos before I close out of it and head to Instagram.

Woah, holy crap.

I have a crazy number of notifications, and most of them are follower notifications. I scroll through them, and the scrolling literally seems endless. My eyes widen when I go to my main page and see that my follower number has skyrocketed.

"Yo, Tina! Key! Come look at this!" I exclaim, staring at my phone in my hand with wide eyes and my mouth agape.

"What is it?" she asks, walking over to me.

"Look at my followers..."

Keisha doesn't say anything but comes over without question. They both look over my shoulder from behind me and at my phone.

"Holy moly!" Tina exclaims.

"Damn, girl," Keisha says.

I don't know what it is about Jade, but man, she called it. My follower count on Instagram started at only three hundred before being here. Now? They're at thirteen hundred. Literally, in a day. But wait... how? The first pitch in the tournament hasn't even left my hands yet.

"I don't even know how this happened," I say in shock.

"I think I know why! Look, they're already starting to post our pictures and bios on the Little League Instagram page," Tina says. "They've posted yours and a couple of other pitchers already. I don't think they've posted everyone else's yet."

I lean over the bed to look at her phone, and my photoshoot picture, along with my short bio video with my favorite hobbies outside of softball and all the other questions already has over a thousand likes. The caption reads: *Check out the best pitcher in the United States in the Senior Division, Kylah Hendricks, and what she has to say about her arrival to the Senior League Softball World Series!*

"That explains it." I nod. "Damn, I ain't think it was gonna go up that fast!"

"Well, you are the best in the country. Of course they're going to start with you first, sis!" Keisha says.

"I mean, yeah, but... it's just crazy..." I whisper.

"That's a good thing! Just... don't forget me when you get famous. Actually, can I have your first autograph?" Tina jokes.

"Girl. No," I say, shaking my head with a smile.

"Shiiit, I'm tryna get some money when you become famous. You know you're gonna get them NIL deals if you go to college!" Keisha declares, and Tina and I bust into laughs.

"Key, you crazy," I say and shake my head.

"Well, let's put our phones away and watch some Netflix! Scary movie?"

"Yes! Choose a good one, too!" Keisha exclaims.

"How about... *It*? Or ...*The Orphan*? Or... *Texas Chainsaw*?" Tina lists.

"*Texas Chainsaw!*" Keisha and I both agree.

"Alright, sounds good."

"Hey, while y'all pulling that up, I'ma go out in the hall to make a quick phone call, alright? I'll be right back," I say.

I step just outside the room and scroll through my phone to FaceTime Jade. She's got to know about this whole follower situation on my social media accounts. I'm just afraid that it's going to blow up so fast that I won't know how to handle it.

The FaceTime call rings and rings.

When FaceTime makes the noise that it makes when people answer, Jade appears, drenched with sweat and loud music playing in the background. She's not quite looking down at the phone yet as she walks over to wherever she's going, and the music stops.

"Hey, honeybun. How are you?" Jade answers with a tired smile.

"Hey, I'm sorry for interrupting your dancing. It's bedtime here, so I forgot there's a three-hour difference between here and home."

"No worries. I'm glad y'all landed safely, and from what I see, it looks like you're in the hotel, right?" I nod. "Good. I told you that you could FaceTime me whenever, so it's not a big deal. I was just individually dancing and rehearsing anyway. So what's up?"

"Jade, you were right," I say.

"What do you mean?" she asks, wiping the sweat from her forehead.

"My followers on Instagram went from three hundred to twelve hundred in a couple of hours."

"Really? Already? The tournament hasn't even started yet."

"I know! That's what I said! I think it's because the media is starting to post on their accounts to hype the tournament up. They've posted my bio video on Instagram already and said I was the best in the country," I reply.

"Oh, well there you go. I told you this was going to happen. And you're a Black girl. Black folks who follow the Little League tournaments will start to tell their people about you. It's going to spread, and watch. Next thing you know, you're gonna end up on some Black Excellence page or The Shaderoom or something, and you're going to go viral," Jade confirms.

"So what do I do? I know my followers are going to blow up more than this if it's already starting out this way," I say.

"Okay. Advice. Keep being you. Don't let any newfound fame get to your head or scare you. You have your people who love and support you already, and those are the people who will ride for you with or without fame. In interviews with the media or the press, keep it positive. Don't let anyone ask you about anything unrelated to softball unless it's positive. Don't talk about nobody else's team, and don't say anything that will throw your teammates under the bus if things go wrong. Don't post nothing unless it's softball related or positive. Also, don't respond to negative comments on social media. Please. They're going to come. Many of them will be racist, even if you're half White. Many of them will try to get you to argue with them. If you did something at school, somebody's gonna bring it up. Actually? I advise you to turn off your comment section when you post things. It's going to save you a lot of headache."

"But what if I only want my friends to comment?"

"Then make sure you limit your comments to only certain people. I think you can do that. At least on mine, I can, but I'm not sure if that's for a verified account."

"I'm kinda scared about all of this," I say.

"Yeah, I understand. If I were you, I would be, too. You just have to manage it in a safe way. If it makes you feel better, you can set all your accounts to private."

"Yeah, but I also don't want to shut myself off from the world. Especially when I have a chance to positively represent us," I reply.

"Okay, so then you just have to manage yourself. Make sure you learn your limits too when it comes to screen time. I'll talk to Jarell more about that so can he puts limits on it. It's only for your mental health, so don't get too bent out of shape about it," she says once she sees my face start to scrunch up.

"Can you manage my accounts?" I ask.

"Honeybun, I'm not in the business of actually running or managing accounts because I have to manage my own. But what I can do is help *you* manage your own and give you tips, advice, and insight on how to deal with certain social media woes. Especially dealing with viral content because I've got a lot of that with dance."

"Okay..." I say nervously.

"Just trust yourself. You know what feels right and what feels wrong. Keep me in the loop with everything regarding social media content, and I will help you navigate this new normal, okay?"

"Okay. Thank you, Jade."

"Other than that, how was the flight?"

"It was good. I mostly slept."

"Good. Are you ready for your game tomorrow?"

"Yup! My teammates and I are about to head to bed. First game is at ten o'clock in the morning. We'll be on ESPN+ for this game, but I think some of the others will be on ESPN 2 or something. I'll let you know so that you can tune in," I explain.

"Sounds like a plan. But thank you for calling me! I do have to wrap up here to prepare for my class that's coming in at seven thirty, so sleep tight, okay? Hug Jarell for me. Is he doing okay?"

"Yup, he's fine," I say.

"Good. Well, like I said, hug him for me. I'll see you soon."

"Okay. Thanks. Bye, Jade."

We hang up, and I head back to my hotel room, entering inside just to see Keisha and Tina knocked out in the bed, cuddling up innocently with each other. I smile and look at the TV, seeing that they've fallen asleep right in the middle of the film. I turn it off and climb into the other empty queen bed and turn the lights off, drifting off to sleep almost instantly, hopeful for everything this tournament will bring.

Chapter Thirty-One

FOR SOME REASON, I keep thinking of Ms. Turner. Maybe it's because today is the five-month mark that I threw the chair at her and turned up in her classroom. My mind keeps attempting to flash back to all the bad that happened that day.

It was my breaking point. And it was everyone else's, too. Jarell's. Dr. Anderson's. My teachers. A lot of people. I can even say the whole school, too. The school lost Ms. Turner as a staff member.

I think of what I did that night after I was sent home. I just sat around, hallucinating about my dad, having nightmares about Mama, and longing to run away from home.

But also, that was the very last day I had gotten in serious trouble at school.

I couldn't say that about the end of my seventh-grade year. Or my sixth-grade year when I moved to San Diego. I was getting suspended up until the last day of school. Both years, I had gotten into fights that caused me to miss out on the last day of school festivities. Just taking my anger out on any and everyone.

Jarell had no idea what he got himself into by taking on a project like me.

I've come a long way since then. Deep down, I hope Ms. Turner likes girls' softball enough to turn on the TV to tune into the World Series. A small part of me wants to, if we win the championship, to dedicate the win to her. But the biggest part of me knows it's kinda cheesy and cringe. I'll keep my dedication to myself, but I just hope she's already read my letter and finds it in her somewhere to forgive me for everything I've done.

Secretly, since the plane landed here in Delaware, I've continuously ruminated about the fact that I don't even deserve to be here. The way I've been acting for the majority of the school year at home and at school... why me? Why do I have the talent? How am I the person to make it this far? Why am I given this opportunity versus others who haven't nearly done as much damage as me?

I don't know. Deep inside, I truly believe the universe wants my family to win at something for once. And by family, I mean me and Jarell. All the hell thrown at us for the majority of our lives would've driven anyone to a mental breakdown. We have no family, we're young, and we're trying to navigate our lives together. We both have disabilities that impact our ability to get through each day. But somehow... some way, we're still here. Trying. Grinding. Jarell would absolutely say that that is the will of God, but me? I just don't know what it is and why we were chosen for this kinda path.

But here we are.

Lock in.

Lock in.

Lock in.

I say this over and over myself with my eyes closed as I sit on the very end of the dugout bench before it's showtime in ten minutes.

You've made it this far.

Lock in.

Lock in.

Lock in.

I also don't know how our softball team is at this moment. We've screwed up so many plays, dropped many balls, allowed many runs to come through home plate this entire tournament.

But somehow, just like Jarell and I, we're still standing. At the World Series championship game. Best out of three games, where we've lost and won one against Japan. And today decides it all.

This tournament has been the hardest of my life. From the heckling from the fans in the crowd, the distracting chants when we're at bat, to the insanely talented batters that aren't phased by my aggressive pitching, forcing our fielders to play defense in ways that we've never had to at the state level, this has been a true test of our mental toughness.

Never in my life have I ever struck out all four times of my at bats on some pretty deceiving pitches and unforgiving umpires. But that's exactly what happened last game when we lost one of our best out of three games and a chance at the world championship. And that was even after hitting two home runs the first game. It got to the point that they just simply walked me to avoid taking any chances of running up the score.

So this is our last opportunity to take the title home.

And not to mention, all of the outside influences adding to this pressure.

Social media is one thing. With the first night of my follower count ending at about thirteen hundred, I'm now close to three hundred thousand. I've contemplated shutting down my social media until the tournament is over, but I've also been posting some behind the scenes pictures into the tournament that I know many softball lovers would want to see. Such as the great times I'm having with my favorite teammates, the best ice cream in Delaware, the practice pitching, and the sightseeing that our team as a collective does when we're not playing to keep our minds fresh and off softball at times.

But the actual press is another thing. A couple of journalists have wanted their time with me to talk about my story of how I got here and how I became the first Black girl to be the best pitcher in the country in my age bracket. Many people and reporters have already caught wind of the fact that both of my parents have died, and that Jarell has taken me in, adding an extra layer to this whole blow up about me.

Even some underlying conversations I've heard from nonmedia people are assumptions that I'm queer, based on how I dress. But Jarell has stood by my side for every last request and declined interviews on my behalf and have also declined to do interviews for me, too. At first, I was frustrated with him and his lack of personality with strangers and the press. But when intimate questions started to come, like how I feel with my mom not being here to celebrate this awesome moment and all this other stuff that I know is an attempt to throw me off my game, I'm grateful for Jarell's cold disposition to everyone. Our team families have even tried to give him advice to try and loosen up a bit, but he's firm in his resolve not to let others bully us into answering questions that we don't want to answer.

"Kylah, you ready?" Coach Harper asks, interrupting my meditation.

I open my eyes and look up at him with a smile. I nod.

"Good. You got this. I'm so proud of your growth, Kylah. I truly can't say enough about how incredible of an athlete you are. I've been right, but I've also been wrong about you. Thank you for leading your team to this point," Coach says. "Thanks for leading me here."

"I appreciate it, Coach," I whisper.

"Alright. Let's huddle up everyone!" Coach yells to the team.

Everyone comes to the huddle, pumped and ready to go, jumping up and down, and loose. I, on the other hand, am extremely quiet. I don't know. I just have a lot of nervous energy that I pray will go away when I get into the circle. I can't fuck around and fold or choke. I gotta see this through.

"Okay, everybody. We gotta come right out the gate strong, okay? We need to set the tone right away for this game before they do. Aggressive, aggressive, aggressive! Pitch aggressively and defend aggressively. Don't be afraid to be aggressive on the plate, either. Don't swing at everything but use your judgment. Umpires are calling these games real interesting and calling pitches low in the zone strikes, so keep your eye on the ball. The pitcher likes to work the bottom of the zone, so be aware of that."

Everyone listens keenly to what Coach is saying.

"Also, don't force a double play if it isn't there. You have to be a hundred percent confident that you can make the play to avoid the scare of overthrowing. Go after every flyball and communicate out there. We got this. Let's bring the trophy home, girls! Let's play our game and set our pace!" Coach revs us up, putting his fist in the air so that everyone can put their fists in.

"Cali on three!" Tina screams. "One, two, three."

"CALI!"

Our huddle breaks and rushes out to the field because we're fielding first after losing the coin toss. The others who aren't fielding sit down. I make eye contact with Keisha because I'm the last one out of the dugout, when usually, I'm first.

"Hey. Missing something, aren't you?" Keisha asks and hands me my handkerchief I always wear in my back pocket to wipe my hands dry in order to pitch effectively.

That breaks my nerves just a little. I smile.

"Thanks, Key."

"Hey. I see in your eyes that you're nervous. Come on. You got this. You're the best in the world. You got this, sis. I believe in you. We all do," she encourages me, placing her hands on both of my shoulders.

I take a deep breath.

"I needed that," I say. "Thank you."

Key and I do our custom handshake, and then we run out on the field to our spots.

This game is an absolute rollercoaster. We start out blazing. Three to zero in the first three innings. But Japan strikes us back. Hard. After getting three ground hits and getting on the plate as our defense keeps them to singles, I've given up a homerun, putting them at four to three. At first, I'm kicking myself, but Coach doesn't let me. He immediately gives me a quick pep talk in the circle before letting me work through this challenge on my own.

And I do, and our team punches back. After one of my teammates hit a homerun, and two get on base after a couple innings, now, I'm at my third at bat after striking out and hitting a double.

You got this, Ky. Trust yourself, I say to myself.

The chants from the other team goes wild in hopes of me striking out. But by now, after two games of playing this team, I've tuned them out.

I watch the pitcher, waiting for her to throw some heat. And it's definitely some heat, alright. Her ball comes speeding toward me, very close to my torso. I jump back a little bit to avoid it striking me without swinging, but it seems to have curved right back to the middle of the zone because the umpire shouts, "Strike!"

Damn, this girl is a crazy good pitcher. I need to get tips from her!

Hitting my bat on home plate, I put my hand up to the umpire until I'm ready. Now, I'm back in batter stance. The opposing pitcher stares ahead, waiting for her catcher's signal. When she winds up and throws her pitch, again, it's very wide in the zone. But oooh, that spin is so familiar. It curves toward me, toward me, toward me...

CRACK!

I swing, and the end of my bat slams into the ball. The ball flies super high in the sky, and it's gone. I hit that thing so hard that it clears beyond the stadium; no happy people waiting for homeruns in the stands are able to catch it.

"YEAAHHH KY!!!" my team cheers for me.

I run the bases, and when I reach home plate, my team jumps up and down all around me after the two other folks on base run home, too. Okay. We're up six to four. We've got to keep this momentum.

But Japan is relentless.

When they're up to bat again, they score two more runs, and for the rest of the game, we go back and forth. Back and forth with the scoring. Now, we're in the tenth inning, and we're up by one. I'm so exhausted from pitching that I'm almost delirious.

And it shows. I've given up three ground hits to load the bases. And now, their home run slugger is up for at bat. I'm in real big trouble now, but Coach and my team encourage me as much as they possibly can over this loud crowd.

"My sweet baby girl. You've got this. You can do this," Mama *whispers to me in my ear.*

I gasp.

Oh no.

Not these voices from Mama again!

"Don't be scared, baby. It's just me with you," she says soothingly *in my ear.*

I breathe in and try so hard not to cry.

"I'm with you, sweetie. You're the best in the world. Show them that you are."

I can't let this throw me off like the last time I lacked the energy to see a game through. We ended up with two losses and a load of disappointment. I refuse to allow that again. I close my eyes and take a deep breath, working hard to ignore the aching in my shoulder and bicep, allowing Mama's voice to be the massage my muscles so desperately need. I can't believe I'm on my one hundred and thirtieth pitch of the night. My legs burn with fatigue as they start to give out on me. All the rumbling and roaring in the crowd that rattled me before has now disappeared. It's just me and the batter.

And now, Mama.

I open my eyes and do what I do best. The first two pitches are two strikes and a ball. One she swings at, and one she doesn't. *Whew.* One more. Just one more. I open my eyes, locking in on the catcher's signal for the final pitch to throw. Curveball and changeup. Okay.

I twirl the ball against my hip. Wind up. My arm whizzes in a circle and my wrist flicks as the ball shoots from my hand, spinning the exact way it's supposed to. It veers outward before spinning back inside the zone. The batter eyes it and swings. Her bat connects, but the ball flies out left field behind the runner line.

Foul ball.

Whew. That was close. She almost hit that one straight down the third base line. The count? Two-two. Two balls, two strikes.

"Good pitch, baby. Give her another one," Mama speaks to me.

I twirl the ball against my hip. Wind up. My arm whizzes in a circle and the ball leaves my fingertips. The ball heads lower than I want it to go, and the batter doesn't swing.

"Ball!" yells the umpire.

Holy shit, full count. The score is still nine to eight in the tenth inning. Bases loaded. Their best pitcher on the plate. This is, literally, the biggest pitch of my life. At this point, I want the dirt to swallow me whole. The world is lounging on my shoulders. The lights seem to have gotten brighter. I squint, trying to stop a headache from coming as I watch Katie give me a signal between her legs. I nod, understanding what she wants. I throw the pitch.

Once again, the batter's bat connects, but the ball flies high behind her and into the stands, fouling it off.

The batter does this for four consecutive pitches, and every single time her bat connects, my heart stops. My legs are so heavy like boulders hang on my calves. I'm sure I've pulled a muscle in my shoulder now because at this point, I can't even rotate it anymore without a searing pain. But I can't stop. I can't give up. Maybe it's not a pulled muscle, but just soreness.

"Okay, baby girl. This is the one right here. Throw her some real heat. You got this," Mama whispers.

I smile and nod. I have to dig deep. Somewhere deep inside. I'm one pitch away from the world championship. I cannot let this moment crush me. I've gotta meet it.

I close my eyes again, inhale as much air as I can through my nose and let it out through my mouth. I look at Katie, and she signals for a screwball.

Hell no. That's too common.

In my head, I know what I'm gonna do. I have that back pocket strikeout pitch that I haven't quite mastered yet. The fast rise ball. The one I've been working on with Prez a lot, but it's so iffy. Sometimes it's right on the money, and many times, it's a wild pitch. My normal go to strike out pitch is the screwball changeup, and most people have already scouted it. I've got a feeling she's waiting for me to throw it, too. I can't give her that one.

I've got to take a chance.

So rise ball, it is. If I ball it... they score. And then we'll go to another inning that I know I can't survive.

I twirl the ball against my hip. Wind up and use the little strength left in my legs and core to throw this pitch, since it's going to be a very fast one. My arm raises, whizzes in a circle, and my fingers flick as the ball blasts from my left hand. It barrels down the middle of the zone until it rises, rises, rises...

I hold my breath. The batter swings.

And she swings at nothing but air as Katie catches the ball, securing our win.

The audience erupts. And so do my teammates in the dugout as they rush out onto the field full speed. My legs leap from the ground in celebration as I jump up in triumph, a supernatural sensation of euphoria bursting in my belly.

My fists, tummy, and arms clench, and I bellow out the loudest scream I've ever screamed in victory. The tears rush to my eyes, flooding the pitcher's circle as I drop to my knees with my forehead in the dirt. But my teammates won't let me cry in joy on the ground like that for any longer than a few seconds. They collectively lift me up to my feet and jump up and down around me with cheers as I double over with my hands on my knees in disbelief.

We, the San Diego Sluggers, representing California, win the Senior League Softball World Series.

And I am the best pitcher, in my age bracket, in the world. *The world*. After all the odds stacked against me… After all the heartache, the trouble… Mama would be so proud of me.

I haven't even realized the big banner they bring to the field, announcing us as the winners. All I see is the other team on the sidelines, crying. Standing up straight, I walk over to them first and start to shake their hands, one by one. My teammates follow me to do the same. I've got so much respect for them. No one has made me work as hard as they did in this sport so far. They've made me a better pitcher. A more mentally tough pitcher. A more disciplined pitcher.

After our brief display of sportsmanship, we go back on the field to take pictures as the crowd continues to applaud for us. Once the photo op is over, our team parents rush to the field to love and hug their own kids in celebration. My tears shift from joy to sorrow as that void and envy in the deepest pit of my stomach strikes me again at my mother and father not being here to congratulate me like all my teammates' parents get to do.

But the sadness disappears when, in the midst of the chaos, my gaze lands on Jarell wearing sunglasses, standing at the margins of the field with Luna and no one else near him. Left out of the celebration. Despite him not being here for the party on the diamond, he still shows a positive patience, waiting his turn to celebrate because he can't rush the field like everyone else can.

This crushes me.

To watch him, in real time, be rendered invisible because of a championship win that consumes everyone's attention puts so many things in perspective for me. *Nobody* thought to allow him, someone with total blindness, to come on the field first to celebrate with his sister, the lead pitcher. Watching our team family do that to him is like looking in a mirror at myself. Because that's exactly how I've treated him in the past, too. And now, I can't be more grateful that he's the only one who showed up to this big moment for me. Not Jade. Not Prez. Not Andre. Not Brooklyn.

Just Jarell. And Luna.

I slowly limp to their direction, leaving everyone else to their own happiness with their families so I can celebrate with mine.

"Jarell," I say above a whisper when I reach him.

His toothless smile widens when he recognizes my voice, and he opens his arms. Immediately, I wrap mine around his body, and he, once again, swallows me whole. My eyes explode with emotion.

"I am so, so proud of you," his whisper cuts through the loud music into my hair as I cry on his shoulder.

"Thank you, Jarell." I weep, pulling away from him to speak directly. "I owe you everything. I owe you my whole life."

The more I talk, the more the weight of the reality that Jarell truly saved my life creates a sense of profound gratitude I've never felt before. In response to me, he grabs my face with his semi-rough hands and brushes my tears away with his thumbs.

"You owe me nothing, Kylah. I would give everything I gave to see this through over and over again," he says, his eyes glistening. "I swear, I'd do this all over again, Kay Kay. Believe that."

This makes me cry harder. I just can't understand him. He's so at *peace* in ways I hope to be one day. Seriously one of a kind human being. This is unconditional love without my stubbornness barring his ability to give it. I squeeze his belly tight, hoping he feels every inch of my appreciation.

We're holding each other for some time, and after a while, the weight of multiple hugs surrounds me. I look up, and our team enclose Jarell and I, hugging us, too.

I smile, unable to stop the tears from flowing. I just can't imagine. I can't imagine any other feeling better than this.

Aftermath

I NEVER THOUGHT I'd appreciate peace and quiet as much as I do now. With the tournament now being over, the hype that followed over the last few weeks has been unbearable.

The texts, the calls, the social media comments, the social media tags, the blogs, and all this other stuff loading my plate has been insane. I've tried to lean on Jade for more advice on how to handle everything, and she's helping me from afar as much as possible. But I need serious public relations help from someone who's actually in the city.

Another part of me feels like giving it another week to die down. I hope something bigger happens with someone else that will drive everyone's attention away from me and onto the next big, breaking story in sports. I never would've thought me, a tall, regular ol' biracial girl with a chippy attitude, would draw this much attention. But Jade was right.

I guess first Black girl anything, especially internationally, will garner attention from some place, somewhere, somehow. I guess it's made me think more about my identity in ways I've never truly focused on. I'm Black, but I'm also mixed, so it's kinda interesting how the media is approaching this whole situation. But it ain't like a whole lot of people know my real background, though. I can only beg that folks never find out.

Because the pressure is just so high to be perfect at this point. I'm scared if I make one little mistake or mishap, my whole softball legacy is all gonna come crashing down. No one really prepared me for this moment and what's ahead. I now understand why Coach and Dr. Anderson were so hard on me about making sure who I am inside and my character are solid. I've grown a new level of appreciation for them both because of how everything is playing out. This newfound fame is definitely gonna take some getting used to.

But the people who have been in my corner from day one like Jarell, my old friends from LA, Prez, and Andre (not a day one, but whatever), haven't switched up on me at all.

They roll with me how they rolled with me before. I'm forever appreciative that they're giving me some level of normalcy. Not only that, I'm also grateful Jarell took me to my chosen restaurant to eat dinner tonight at a joint where I know no one will recognize me. Because today, September second, is a special day, and I want peace and stillness for it.

I chose this hole-in-the-wall local burger joint that's a little rinky dink, but super family friendly, food is amazing, service is on point, and it's ducked off. Our food just got served, refills on our drinks have been taken care of for the second time already, and it's time to chow down. I ordered a mega burger, fries, and a shake, and Jarell got a chicken sandwich, fries, and a lemonade. Jarell already said our waiter is getting a nice tip for exemplary service. He's so funny. He's always looking for ways to show love to somebody.

"Happy fifteenth birthday, Kay Kay. Man. You're really growing up on me. Crazy." Jarell says after blessing the food the way he always does when we eat together. "Life has been a rollercoaster for you."

"Thank you. And thank you for taking me out to eat. I really appreciate it," I respond with a smile.

"You know it ain't no thing," he replies before stuffing his mouth with fries. I'm surprised he's even going to town on the unhealthy staple, considering how much he takes his eating habits seriously.

"No salad today?" I chuckle.

"Mmm… nah. I like to treat myself every once in a while," he says and takes his first large bite out of his buttermilk chicken sandwich.

"I bet you're gonna work out for the next few hours after this," I tease him.

"Nope. This the kinda meal that will put you to sleep."

"That's real."

He changes the subject. "How are you feeling about tomorrow? First day of high school…"

I nod with optimism. "I'm actually feeling pretty decent. I'm ready for a fresh start, to be honest. Middle school was terrible," I mumble.

Jarell makes a small little laughing sound in his throat. "I feel like middle school is like that for most people. Your body is changing, you're trying to figure out who you are… it's a tough time. But you made it."

"Barely."

"Do you think after everything with the tournament that your first day will be overwhelming? With people coming up to you, asking questions, trying to take pictures?" he questions.

I shift my head from side to side.

"Mmm, I don't think so. Most people don't really pay attention to softball; they're into the boys with football and basketball, so I don't think it'll be too crazy. It's football season now. You know how people feel about that."

Jarell nods. "Yeah, true. Well, I hope you have a good first day. Not just the first day, but a good high school experience in general. It can be a fun time, but it can be just as bad as middle school if you allow it," Jarell says, taking another bite from his sandwich.

"Yeah, I plan on it being much better than middle school. How was high school for you?"

He freezes.

"A nightmare." Jarell's eyes widen.

Oh yeah. I remember Jade telling me about his experience all four of his years. I don't want to rat Jade out to him for telling me, but I am still curious. Learning more about Jarell, lately, has been a tugging curiosity in my belly that I'm more excited to explore than to learn about Mama from her journal. I've decided to shelf Mama's journal anyway since my whole perspective has changed around wanting to know so much about our family's history so badly. I've had way too many wakeup calls that've humbled my ass real quick. I'm gonna come back to it... just not at this time. I'm not ready to connect to Mama in that way yet, since she's experienced so much pain. It seems like there's so much to Jarell that I don't really know or understand, and I feel like if I know more about who he is, Mama's journal will likely make more sense anyway.

"Why was it a nightmare?"

"Bullies. A lot like you, I had moved away from my friends in Chicago, so middle school was rough. I moved once more to LA from northern Cali, starting over again in high school. Crenshaw. I got bullied a lot because of my blindness and how I used to dress. It was awful. They used to call me a crack baby, a school shooter, dirty... all kinds of things." A sad glow rises in his expression. "They used to tell me to commit suicide, too. One day, I got so fed up that I actually attempted."

My eyes get big. "Really?"

"Yeah. But... Jade stopped me."

My shoulders sink. *Woah.* Again, that's not something I would've ever thought Jarell faced. *Man.* I really did see Jarell as this perfect figure in my life. One who would never go through hardship. He was seriously a superhero in my eyes back then.

"Damn, Jarell. I didn't know. I'm glad you never went through with it. It would've crushed my whole soul," I say.

"Yeah." He sighs. "We can talk more about that another time. I ain't tryna ruin your birthday with heaviness. I'm surprised you don't want to spend your birthday with Preston and Andre. What happened that you'd wanna come here? With me of all people?" Jarell asks with his mouth full.

"What's wrong with hanging out with you?" I ask with a smirk.

Jarell stops chewing and gives me a long, knowing glare in my direction. At that, I break into a giggle.

"You really wanna ask that question?"

This time, Jarell has a kind of tone like he knows something I don't. I wish he could see the weird look I give him in return because he better start spilling the beans if he does.

"Aht, aht. What you mean by that?" I press, jerking my head back.

"Don't think I don't know about your little feelings for him..." Jarell mumbles.

"Feelings for who?!" I almost shout.

"Andre, Kylah," Jarell responds.

I gasp. "Who the fuck told you that?!"

"First of all, stop cussing. You're not an adult. And second, I'm blind, and it's still obvious. You don't know how to hide things well. At all. Since we've been back in California, he's the only person you wanna be with," he explains, and I dip my head, biting my lip. "Every time you're going somewhere to hang out, you're telling me you're meeting up with him and Prez. Or just him. Prez, I can understand because he's been your friend for a while now. But Andre kinda came outta nowhere."

I shrug, not confirming or denying. Was I that detectable? He's right, though. Ever since Andre told me we should take advantage of the summer time to get to know each other, I took that to heart. To be honest, he and Prez both were, and still are, my means to escape everyone else and the world around me.

After the championship game, I've been avoiding the media and interview opportunities pretty hard. When we came back to San Diego, the city had a mini parade for our team like they do when the NBA, NFL, or NCAA wins championships. Much of that parade was all over social media, too, as my followers continued to go up. By the time the tournament and all the celebration was over, my follower count plateaued around close to half a million people. But the requests to have me on news channels and other national platforms never stopped.

It's overwhelming, but I feel worse for Jarell than I do for myself.

I didn't realize how reserved he truly is until the World Series and the extreme spotlight it came with, including some serious invasion of his privacy as well. So many people have become interested in his life story along with mine as he's raising a sibling who's a softball superstar while he's only twenty-eight and completely blind. He's always having to tell people to leave us alone via phone, in person, or email. He seems a bit miserable about this new reality, but knowing him, he would never say that out loud. For the most part, Jarell's tried his best to show he's really happy for me. That I know for sure is genuine despite his feelings about everyone else.

At the end of the day, I just wanna be a regular kid who's a beast at softball. Besides, the more I'm on national platforms and visible, the more my history with getting in trouble at school will get out to the masses, and potentially, all different kinds of things about our parents. People who I went to middle school with are already talking shit about why I shouldn't have even deserved to win, so I don't think either Jarell nor myself are ready for that kind of widespread scrutiny.

"You're real mute over there. So I'm guessing you won't talk to me about Andre, huh?" Jarell says, interrupting my deep thoughts and daze.

I take a bite out of my burger and take my time chewing before I answer.

"There's nothing to talk about. Andre's in Nigeria anyway."

"Really?"

"Yeah. I hope he comes back, though."

"Why?" Jarell says sarcastically, almost mocking, as if trying to pry something out of me.

"Cut it out, dude." I blush, and I'm so happy he can't see my face. But I'm sure my tone tells my exact expression.

"Cut what?"

"Jarell, stop. I know what you're tryna do. I won't tell you about Andre at all if you won't tell me about your feelings for Jade. Or Brooklyn. Take your pick. You share yours, and then I'll share mine," I bargain.

Jarell's head tilts all the way back and he fully laughs, showing all teeth. I can't help but join him. It's nearly as contagious as Mama's this time, but in such a different way. Can't really describe it. "Wow. Is this slight blackmail?" Jarell asks once he's caught his breath.

"It's whatever you wanna call it, sir."

He glares my way for a second with a twinkle in his eyes, shaking his head with a smirk.

"You know what?" He stuffs more fries in his mouth. "I'ma indulge in this request."

"Really?!" I exclaim, sitting up straighter and leaning over my drink, nearly knocking it over.

He almost chokes. "Dang calm down, young grasshopper. Don't jump over the table," he jokes and coolly leans back in the booth, sipping his lemonade.

"Okay, so... spill!"

"I'm only gonna tell you about one of them, so choose wisely," Jarell declares.

"Jade. I wanna know all about y'all's situation. It's too interesting. Top to bottom. Tell meeeee," I plead.

"Okay, let's put some parameters on this..." he says before a chuckle.

"No! Tell me everything!"

"I'm not telling you everything, Kylah. The parameters are that I will tell you how I feel about her, since you keep asking, and maybe a bonus addition to my first response. I'll go ahead and answer that one."

"Don't let it be no dumb ass answer, either. Talkin' bout some 'I like her,' or something basic like that. Like, you gotta have a comprehensive response."

"I got you," he says in confidence.

"Okay. Shoot."

"Alright." He takes a deep breath. "Jade. Well..." He pauses for a stretched moment.

"WELL?!"

"I've loved Jade since high school, Kylah," he starts. "It wasn't always that way. She bullied me with her friend group, too, but I don't think she really meant it, if you know what I mean. When she and I started to become friends, which took a while to get there by the way, I started to see her true character. All that stuff she was doing with her friends seemed like it was more for show. So when I got to know the deepest parts of her, she showed me things that no one else really got a chance to get to know and vice versa. And I fell in love with those parts of her," he explains.

"You know what's wild?" I interject.

"Hmm?"

"She said the exact same thing to me about you. But ... go on..."

"Well if she told you that, it's actually true. So, all that to say... I don't think I've ever stopped loving Jade. Nine years ago, we left on terms that suggested we'd link and pick things back up one day, but with life happening, it wasn't a realistic option. Honestly, I gave up on ever being with her again after the first five years of our separation. I had no plans to go back to Los Angeles, she didn't know where I lived, no longer had my number, I didn't have hers, and I don't have social media. I just felt like I was never gonna be around her again anyway, so I suppressed everything I felt and moved on. It's truly a divine intervention from God that reunited us."

"Awwww!" I squeal, grabbing my cheeks.

"Bonus answer. When we ran into each other at your softball tournament for the first time, every feeling I've ever felt for her when we were together... I don't know... just *surfaced*. Looking back, I feel terrible for Brooklyn because she really doesn't deserve that but... at that moment, nothing else mattered but Jade, Kylah."

Now, he looks serious. The twinkle previously lingering in his eyes is now replaced with longing and a level of solemn that makes me gulp. I stop smiling, too. Geez. He's not joking at all. I know when Jarell is dead ass serious, and this is one of those moments. *This is his truth.*

"So, what are you going to do?" I whisper.

He shoves a few more fries in his mouth and shrugs. "Don't know."

Hmm. I wish he would just go ahead and share his thoughts about Brooklyn because then, it would be easy for me to tell him what the obvious next step should be. But I already know he won't. Jarell said he was sharing one thing, and that's that. He means what he says. I'm lucky I even got the bonus.

"Jade still loves you, Jarell. It's all in her body language. She's never moved on," I blurt out. I couldn't hold it in. Plus, it may get him to divulge more.

"Yeah, but it doesn't change the fact that neither of us probably knows what to do about it at this point. It's been too long," Jarell counters as if he's not even fazed by my revelation. The twinkle returns to his gaze.

"Uh... get back together? Duh!" I shout. "Who cares how long it's been?"

"And things just aren't that simple," he replies with a calm grin and leans back in the booth once more with his arm laid across the back. There's a certain level of closedness in his eyes that tells me any further conversation about this topic is over.

I pout.

"Have you heard from her lately?"

"Nope, not since your graduation party."

I blink. Dang. She and I have been texting back and forth about social media, but nothing much else beyond that. I'm surprised they've gone this long without communicating. My graduation party was in June. Maybe I need to be the one to bring them back together again. I'm happy to take on that role.

"Well, I hope you guys figure things out. You deserve each other."

"Mmm hmm." He nods. "Now. Your turn."

"To do what?"

"Don't play me..." he warns.

"Ugh," I grumble. "Fine. I guess since you went above and beyond about Jade, I'll do what I need to do. Truth is... yes I was feelin' Andre. Heavy. He's really sweet, don't got beef with nobody, gets good grades... was the student council president... I don't know. I've always thought he was cute and just a chill laid back kinda guy that no other girls really check for like they do Prez and other boys at school."

"Mmm hmm..." Jarell says, giving me a low gaze and waiting for the climax of my story.

"So... the real reason I wanted to come to dinner with you is because I didn't wanna stay at home moping around. He texted me earlier today to wish me happy birthday, but then he also told me he's not in Nigeria for a vacation. He's there for a family emergency. He left a week and a half ago because something's going on with his grandmas on both sides of his family. I think they're both sick. He said they're going to stay there permanently."

"Oh wow..." Jarell mumbles. "I'm sorry, Kay Kay. I could tell how much you really liked being around him."

"Yeah... just as we were about to get to know each other..." I look away. I refuse to even give my eyes an inkling of an opportunity to water up. No way I'm crying on my fifteenth birthday.

"I'm sure Prez is excited to have you to himself. He likes you as more than a friend, too, but I ain't gonna push you to talk about that. You already shared enough about Andre. I know that must've crushed you. I'm glad I'm able to take you out to cheer you up, though," Jarell replies.

"I don't even wanna think about how Prez feels. I should check on him, though. Dre is his best friend, so he's probably more hurt than I am," I say.

"That's a good idea. Call and check on him tonight," Jarell offers.

I don't say anything else, signaling the end of my vulnerabilities, too. I just grab my phone and begin browsing on Instagram as Jarell now falls into his own daze, thinking about who knows what. As I'm swiping, I see a whole bunch of nothing with some semi-interesting reels about softball and sneakerhead stuff sprinkled in between. However, one post makes me slow my scroll.

A post of Jade.

I stop and squint to make sure I ain't trippin'. That I ain't seeing what I think I'm seeing.

As I take both of my fingers and zoom in on the photo she's in, and I scan every inch of the picture as my mouth drops in disbelief.

It's another guy.

A guy that ain't Jarell.

Holding Jade at her waist from behind with his face buried in her neck. As if he's kissing or sucking it. And her body language doesn't suggest she hates it either. In fact, she's closing her eyes and grinning as if it's... blissful.

WOAH.

This kinda looks like a paparazzi picture, but I'm not quite sure.

I check the date of the post. It was posted yesterday, and she was tagged in it. So the guy posted it, but she didn't. I shake my head and put the lock screen on to close out of the gram.

Damn.

Damn...

DAMN!

Jade told me she was single! But... that was also four or five months ago... but the last time she was here, she was so flirty with Jarell! But I guess flirting doesn't mean anything because Prez does that to me all the time, but we aren't together. Maybe Jade and that guy are just friends. Jade said her feelings for Jarell never left. Right? But her and that guy... they look waaaay too familiar with each other. Almost like they've... been together for a while. Why did she lie to me? What's the point of hiding that?

Ugh!

Too many conflicting thoughts.

Man that really sucks. There's no way, after everything Jarell just shared with me, I'm telling him what I saw. I can't imagine how he'd feel.

I refuse for us to both be heartbroken. Andre gone? And now Jade's got a new guy? I can't bring myself to mention it. I guess Jarell will have to find this one out on his own...

BOOK FOUR COMING SOON

Acknowledgements

I am the proudest of publishing this book out of all the books I've written in this series. I've gone through hell and back over the last couple of years. Through loss, grief, depression, isolation, anger... I persevered to publish what I feel is some of my best writing. I have to thank God for that first. Thank you for giving me the ability to tell a story and to have fun with it. Thank you for walking me through such an awful time of my life. I want to thank my mother. For always reading my work and giving me direct feedback. Thank you to my husband who is my ultimate beta reader, giving me tips and ideas. Thank you to my editor, who has spent so much time with me and this novel over the last six months. Thank you to my readers. Thank you to my tribe. I could not have gotten through this time without any of you. Thank you.

About the Author

Born and raised in Wisconsin, author and educator Janeé Thompson pens novels that capture the experiences of Black teens and Black new adults in ways that are raw, relatable, accessible, and unapologetic. These novels transcend the notion that leisure reading for Black people must be about navigating racial stereotypes, racial trauma, and overcoming pain caused by anti-black violence such as police brutality or slavery. The experiences of Black teens and new adults are multifaceted and dynamic. We deserve to read more of these diverse experiences absent of white supremacy, and Janeé is intentional about making these stories known.

Kylah
HENDRICKS

Age: 14
Race: Black & White
Height: 5'10"
Birthday: September 2
From: Los Angeles, CA

Softball superstar
Sneakerhead
Portrait Sketcher
Stuffed animal lover

Preston
SMITH-RODRIGUEZ

Kylah's Best Friend

Age: 14
Birthday: December 14th
Race: Latino & Black
Height: 5'8"
From: Puerto Rico

Peacemaker
Video Gamer
Baseball
    Player
Family
    Oriented

Alaysia
SIMMONS
Kylah's Rival
Age: 14
Birthday: April 25th
Race: Black
Height: 5'5"
From: San Diego
Softball pitcher
Rollerskating
Fashonista
Bowling

Jarell
HENDRICKS

Kylah's Brother

Age: 28
Birthday: April 9th
Race: Black
Height: 6'0"
From: Chicago, IL

Visually Impaired
Health Freak
Origami Lover
Lover of Jesus
Dancer

Brooklyn
WYLES

Age: 26
Race: Black
Birthday: Jan 27
Height: 5'6"
From: San Diego

Food Truck Owner
Technology Guru
Lover of Jesus
Foodie
Optimist

Jade WILLIAMS

Jarell's
Ex-Girlfriend

xoxo

Age: 27
Birthday: November 15th
Race: Black
Height: 5'8"
From: Los Angeles

Confident   Flashy

Dance studio
owner

Celebrity
choreographer

palette